The
HUMAN
SCALE

The
HUMAN
SCALE

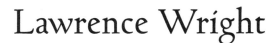

Lawrence Wright

ALFRED A. KNOPF
New York
2025

A BORZOI BOOK
FIRST HARDCOVER EDITION
PUBLISHED BY ALFRED A. KNOPF 2025

Published by Alfred A. Knopf, a division of Penguin Random House LLC,
1745 Broadway, New York, NY 10019.

Knopf, Borzoi Books, and the colophon are registered trademarks
of Penguin Random House LLC.

Library of Congress Cataloging-in-Publication Data
Names: Wright, Lawrence, [date] author.
Title: The human scale : a novel / Lawrence Wright.
Description: First edition. | New York : Alfred A. Knopf, 2025. |
Identifiers: LCCN 2024028525 | ISBN 9780593537831 (hardcover) |
ISBN 9780593686249 (trade paperback) | ISBN 9780593537848 (ebook)
Subjects: LCGFT: Thrillers (Fiction) | Crime fiction. | Novels.
Classification: LCC PS3573.R53685 H86 2025 | DDC 813/.54—dc23/eng/20240701
LC record available at https://lccn.loc.gov/2024028525

penguinrandomhouse.com | aaknopf.com

Printed in the United States of America

The authorized representative in the EU for product safety and compliance is
Penguin Random House Ireland, Morrison Chambers, 32 Nassau Street,
Dublin D02 YH68, Ireland, https://eu-contact.penguin.ie.

To Roberta
My darling

All fundamentalism is rooted in a profound fear of annihilation.

—KAREN ARMSTRONG

The
HUMAN
SCALE

1

Malik

Jordan, May 21, 2022

The bomb that didn't go off was aboard a United Airlines flight from Jordan's Queen Alia International Airport bound for JFK. It was another sweltering day in the hottest year on record, and the temperature inside the plane was insufferable. The pilot promised the restive passengers that the air-conditioning would kick in after takeoff, but a sandstorm suddenly swept out of the desert, pounding the windows like a desiccated hurricane and leaving the aircraft stranded at the end of the runway. The plane heaved. Passengers swooned. Eventually maintenance called the plane back to the gate and United scrambled to ready another aircraft, which would have to come from Cairo when the storm passed. Some of the passengers bailed out but most hung around the terminal, drinking cocktails in the bar, watching the sun surrender to a dust-choked sky.

It wasn't until the luggage was transferred to the new aircraft that a detection dog froze in front of a metal suitcase. Instead of barking or nosing the offending article, which would alert his handler to drugs, the dog sat and stared, as he had been trained to do in case of explosives. Any slight movement could set off the bomb. Within minutes, the airport was evacuated—because of a gas leak, passengers were told—so they stood in the parking lot shielding their faces against the stinging sand and cursing their luck. Nobody knew that they might all be dead now, their bodies shredded by the blast and scattered across the Mediterranean somewhere near the boot of Italy.

The bomb squad arrived an hour later with a portable X-ray machine, which revealed the commonality of modern improvised explosives: batteries and copper wiring, and what could be an altimeter, designed to trigger the bomb when the plane reached a specified altitude. The device was implanted in what looked, in the ghostly thermal image, like a stuffed animal. It was surrounded by powder-filled packets and nails tightly crammed in—a huge bomb, far larger than anything needed to bring down an airplane. The nails were a stylistic addition, useful only for killing crowds, not for knocking planes out of the sky.

The squad carefully loaded the suitcase into a globe-shaped containment vessel in an armored Humvee, which slowly made its way on the blocked-off Highway 45 to Zarqa. There, between the national police academy and the town dump, was a counterterrorism center run by Jordanian authorities in conjunction with the FBI. The Humvee passed through the gates of the dump and slowed to a near stop, navigating the potholes with fearful caution, then parking in front of a small cement-block building the color of a tangerine.

Inside the counterterrorism center a team of American and Jordanian intelligence watched on video as the bomb-disposal technician fitted up. The bomb suit, weighing nearly a hundred pounds, was made of Kevlar and flame-resistant Nomex with a ceramic plate to cover the torso. The polycarbonate helmet was equipped with amplifiers and a defogger, lit within so that the technician's face, known to everyone in the center, glowed eerily bright. He was Adnan, who was studying electrical engineering and coached a youth soccer team, but they did not refer to him by name. He was too deep in the death zone for anyone to save him, so they called him "the guy," as if using his name was bad luck. Not a single person watching in the center had the nerve to do what the guy was doing. It was like watching a man on a tightrope crossing a rocky abyss a thousand meters deep.

He took possession of the suitcase and carefully placed it on a Styrofoam table designed to avoid splintering into shards. He could receive radio transmissions but he did not communicate himself—the frequency might set off the bomb—so he worked alone, silently, with the team in his ear but frustratingly out of reach. They could observe what he was doing through a camera on his helmet with high-intensity lamps on either side. Despite the body armor every-where else on his body, his hands were uncovered. Dexterity was essential for sensing any hidden triggers or booby traps. If he missed the slightest trick of the bomb maker's craft, the suit might save his life but his hands would be sacrificed. An ambulance waited outside.

The technician dusted the suitcase for fingerprints, then pointed at the luggage tag and shook his head. An operator inside the coun-terterrorism center was able to zoom in on the luggage tag. It bore the name, in English block letters, Yahya Ayyash.

"Ayyash? Is this a joke?" An American FBI agent, Anthony Malik, abruptly stood. Everyone recognized the name of a notorious Hamas bomb maker, known as the Engineer. Back in the nineties, Ayyash killed nearly a hundred Israelis using suicide bombers. There were streets named after him all over Palestine. He was finally assassinated by Shin Bet, the Israeli internal security agency, twenty-six years ago. Now he was back, at least in tribute. "How did this get through air-port security?" Malik demanded. "It might as well have a sign on it saying, 'I am a bomb.' "

No one in the center responded. There was only one answer: someone on the inside had placed the bomb. Malik wasn't blam-ing anyone in the room. They all felt the same anger and anxiety; they were a team. But it was a colossal intelligence failure that might have led to hundreds of fatalities. Somebody had beaten the security and they were all more or less responsible. If some genius could slip through Jordanian controls, which were among the tightest in the region, where else might it happen? These things are contagious.

Malik, who was thirty-three, appeared a decade older with the severe lines that formed in his face, as if he had been mauled by age. His hair was dark and unruly, and his brows were black, but beneath them his eyes were green with flecks of brown—"hazel" is what it said on his driver's license. His long, down-pointing nose and jutting chin awarded him a distinct drama; he could have been a wary noble-man in an El Greco painting, not handsome but striking, impressive, the kind of face that assumed command. When he smiled, the lines in his cheeks widened like a drawn bow, but when he was angry, as he was now, his eyes narrowed and his brows knitted together in a fearsome scowl.

"It's got to be TATP," Malik continued, referring to the unstable, highly explosive formulation that Ayyash used. "It's way too volatile to be handled. There's a reason they call it the Mother of Satan. It blows up if you sneeze. We've got to get the guy out of there. Detonate it remotely."

"This guy is a pro," Husni Obeidat, the officer representing Jordanian intelligence, protested. He and Malik were close, they played tennis together at the American embassy. "There's valuable information to be gained," Husni continued. "We don't place people in danger for no reason—"

And that's when Malik's memories were blown out of his brain.

He had horrible dreams. At times he was aware of people in the room, but they vanished or turned into cartoonish monsters. He tried to flee but he couldn't move. When he awakened he discovered he was paralyzed. This happened several times. When he woke again to find a nurse at his bedside he didn't remember waking before. He tried to talk but couldn't.

He fell back asleep. He had a sense of being lifted out of some dark spot, as if he were deep in the ocean and was slowly floating toward the surface, away from the safety of unconsciousness. He was so cold. Blood raced through his capillaries and his body tingled. The gathering brightness was alarming but he didn't want to be in the dark anymore. He heard voices. Someone said, "There he is."

His eyes opened although he realized he could only see out of the right one. Three people stood around his bed wearing tactical scrubs.

"Mr. Malik, welcome back to the world," said a man with wavy white hair. His name tag said "KUMAR." The silver oak leaf on his sleeve marked him as a lieutenant colonel.

"Where . . . ?" was the only word Malik could utter. It came out in a croak.

"Landstuhl Medical Center in Ramstein, Germany," Dr. Kumar said. "Our records show you've been here before."

Malik nodded. The scar on his leg from a Taliban AK-47.

"I know you're confused and your throat is raw. We just pulled out the intubation tube and it will take a while before you're able to speak easily. Also, you're probably not going to remember much of what we say today, but Lieutenant Adkins here will be helping you."

He gestured toward a nurse with a medical bonnet and a few strands of blond hair spilling out. "Can you tell us if there's anything you need?" Adkins said. "Like are you hungry? You can just nod or blink."

"Cold," he muttered.

"That's something we can fix right away," she said, as an orderly manifested a blue blanket.

"You'll be stronger and more alert tomorrow," said Kumar. "We've handled thousands of TBIs—traumatic brain injuries—and it takes a while for your brain to relax and begin forming new memories. Don't get frustrated. I'll check on you again tomorrow."

Malik was asleep by the time the door closed.

The next thing he knew a doctor held a bright light in his left eye. "The dilation is less pronounced," the doctor said. His name plate said "KUMAR." Malik had no memory of ever seeing him before.

"What's wrong with me?" Malik said. His voice sounded like he was speaking underwater.

"Say that again," the doctor said, "slowly."

Malik repeated it several times before the doctor understood, but Malik couldn't remember the response. This would happen twice more before Malik recognized Adkins when she came to take his blood pressure and told him once again about the bomb.

He summoned a name from the basement of his memory. "Husni Obeidat?" He didn't know why or how that name came to mind.

Adkins took his hand. "All gone. Five of them. You can't imagine how lucky you are to be alive."

Malik nodded, then turned away. To his astonishment, he began to cry. Adkins gently rubbed his wrist. "Listen, it happens. These kind of injuries turn up a lot of emotions."

"How long?" he asked.

"How long have you been here? A little over two weeks. Most of that time you were in a coma. It takes time to fully wake up from that."

Dr. Kumar was examining him again. Apparently he had been

doing so for some time. This may have been a different day. "How is he sleeping?"

"Irregular," said Adkins. "He tends to sleep in two-hour segments."

"Headaches?"

Malik nodded vigorously but the nodding made the pain worse.

"We can't do a lot about that," said the doctor. "We worry about bleeding." He turned to Adkins. "Acetaminophen. Five thousand. Nausea?"

"No," said Malik.

"He vomited twice in the night," said Adkins.

Wouldn't he remember something like that?

"Seizures?"

"None in the last three days."

"Looks like our boy is getting better," said Kumar.

Was that true? The boy in question had no idea. His head was exploding. His ears were ringing. He couldn't process what happened to him. He was nauseous at night. Apparently he had been worse.

"My eye," Malik managed to say.

"We're trying to save it. Despite your amazing good fortune to be still with us, the bomb did extensive physical damage. The femur in your right leg is broken as is your left wrist and several fingers in that hand. Those wounds will heal, I promise you. You're very strong. You're young. But you suffered a severe head laceration that involves the left orbital bone. Your doctors in Jordan sewed you up nicely but the eye itself is in jeopardy. We'll know better in a few days. But the eye is not the main problem. Your challenge is the trauma of the explosion itself, which damaged your lungs and may impose cognitive difficulties. That's something we'll have to sort out. The main thing is to get you moving, and that's the project for tomorrow."

Dr. Kumar left, trailed by interns who had come to observe and hadn't said a word during the visit. Adkins remained. "It's a shock to hear all that, I'm sure," she said. She held his undamaged right hand. "Do you have any questions about what the doctor said?"

Malik thought a moment, then said, "Mirror?"

Adkins brought a compact case from the nurses' station. Malik's face was covered with angry red scratches. A jagged line of stitches like a lightning bolt ran down his forehead toward his left eye, which was buried under bandages. His nose was bruised and puffy. Malik turned away. *I am hideous*, he thought.

Adkins left a spiral-bound booklet with pictures of the hospital staff and information about the hospital. He could point to a menu of common demands—"I'm hungry," "I want to go home," "I need to go to the bathroom." She also brought in a calendar, the days indicated by squares that began to fill up with art therapy and speech lessons and classes in mastering skills once done so unthinkingly, like tying shoelaces. Reading was nearly impossible, so he watched CNN during periods of wakefulness, trying to understand what was going on in the world, a world he used to be so engaged in but now seemed like another planet beyond the tinted windows of the head-injury ward.

"Is there someone you want to phone?" Adkins asked. "We've had several calls but you were a little too out of it. I can help if you want to give it a try."

Malik shook his head. He didn't know what to say because he no longer knew who he was. Except for the bomb, he had fair recall of his life, but he felt like an imposter, pretending to be who he used to be.

He was always tired and his head always ached. He had outbursts and fought against being kept in bed. Doctor Kumar warned the nurses not to let him wander because he would get lost and confused, but Adkins refused to let him be restrained. His restlessness was helpful in getting him to move around, despite the need for crutches. He hobbled about adroitly, moving with a determination that impressed the staff, although it didn't take long for him to weaken on these excursions and need to return to his room. Despite his foggy mind he recognized the immense care that surrounded him. In turn, they saw him as a special case. They knew the odds he was facing.

Each morning an orderly took him to rehab. Five other patients were there during his time slot. It was shocking how debilitated his fellow patients were. They had trouble lifting their feet. One had a harness holding him up as he walked with toes barely touching the ground, like a ballerina. Another man, withered from confinement, had a bald spot in his scalp where a section of his skull had been removed to reduce swelling. A therapist helped a zombielike woman with a helmet navigate between parallel bars. Malik was clumsy but able to use the treadmill, an immense advance compared to the others. He realized how lucky he was, and yet he was still subject to long fits of weeping.

He finally called his girlfriend, Lucy Walker. She was home in New York and frantic to hear from him. They had been together for three years. Friends in the bureau had kept her informed of the situation, and as bad as it was her imagination colored in more awful possibilities. Malik refused to do a video call because he wasn't ready for her to see him. "I'm not the same person," he explained. "It's not just that I don't look the same."

"Honey, I know. They explained it to me. Don't worry, Tony, I can take it, whatever it is." She couldn't disguise the uncertainty in her voice. She offered to come be with him, and although he longed to see her, he also dreaded it. After that first look at himself in the mirror he was sure his romantic life was at an end.

"I'm trying to get my head right, baby," he said. "I'll let you know."

Afterward, he opened a Facebook account under a false identity. The bureau frowned on employees having a presence on social media, but Facebook was a powerful investigative tool, one that every agent had learned to exploit. Malik looked up old army buddies to see how they were doing. Many weren't doing so well. Then he examined Lucy's posts. He had missed her birthday and there were pictures at the River Café of their friends and some other people he didn't know, probably from work. She was thirty-two that day. A group photo probably taken by a waiter showed them all standing on the terrace overlooking the East River and Manhattan. Lucy was next to a man Malik didn't recognize. It was nothing, he told himself, but he saw the same man in another shot. It wasn't hard to find his name, Lucy had friended him. Brian Henry. A fund manager at AllianceBernstein, rich, well educated, and unmarried. Malik didn't need proof. He knew that months alone was a price Lucy wouldn't pay.

. . .

SIX MONTHS AFTER the bombing an official from FBI headquarters paid a visit to Malik. Tommy Cantemessa was a big, jolly man who had played football at Notre Dame. They were in the academy together and served on the same counterterrorism squad in New York. The bureau must have had a reason to send an old friend.

"Jeez, Malik, they really fucked you up," Tommy said by way of greeting. Malik had graduated to a black patch on his useless eye. The stitches were out from the slash across his forehead, but places where the staples had been remained inflamed, like a smoldering railroad track. The casts were off on his wrist and leg, although the muscles had atrophied and much work needed to be done. His speech was coming back but he stumbled over words and easily lost his train of thought. The two men took a table in the back of the common room, where long-term patients sat around playing cards or dominos and the television drowned out their conversation. Tommy wore a blue suit and carried a backpack. Malik figured that whatever was in the backpack would determine his future.

Tommy brought some welcome gossip about old colleagues, who was divorced, who got promoted or sacked, but he didn't spend long on the niceties. "You got some choices to make, bud," he said. "In a way they're good choices. You could qualify for full disability given the nature of your injuries. The eye thing gives you 30 percent right off the bat."

"Get out of here. My bones are healed. I've still got one good eye. I can do the job better than most."

"You don't have to convince me," Tommy said, although in fact his assessment would be critical. "They're not worried about you physically. It's the other stuff. Lot of guys got blown up in Iraq and Afghanistan, you know that. They put the body back together but the mind is still broken, right? Emotional issues, drugs, rage, all that stuff. Hard to do your job when you're fighting those demons. So you take the money, do the therapy—"

"And then what? Go fishing? Don't put me on the bench, Tommy. I've never been more—" he searched for the word—"motivated. You know I'm the top man on the squad. You need me."

"Everybody knows you're the best, buddy, but we got protocols to deal with, forms to fill out. You're in the bureaucratic quicksand, which is designed to pay you off and make you disappear. But I'll do what I can, okay? No guarantees. There's another thing. What do you remember about the bomb?"

"Just that the joker who built it modeled it on Yahya Ayyash. He was sending a message."

Tommy finally opened the backpack and took out a manila folder. "As long as you're on the payroll maybe you can be of use," he said. "This is what we got. I can't leave it with you, but you can read over it. I'll go flirt with the nurses and come back in an hour."

The folder contained intelligence about Hamas in Gaza. The flow of weapons from Iran had increased alarmingly. The US had stopped one massive shipment of heat-seeking missiles and Italian-designed antitank mines, but evidence from informants suggested that many such deliveries were made, possibly through a vastly expanded tunnel system. Hamas was devoting more energy to creating their own weapons, including drones and rockets with more powerful explosives, and yet the Israeli assessment continued to be that Hamas was more concerned with governing the Gaza Strip than renewing a war with Israel that they were bound to lose. True or not, the military wing of Hamas was increasing its training and recruitment. New leaders had taken control.

Malik didn't have enough space in his brain to remember everything. One name popped up, the man in charge of explosives and suicide bombers. A nephew of Yahya Ayyash. His name was Ehsan Zayyat.

"So he's the guy who did this to me," Malik said when Tommy returned.

"I thought you deserved to know."

"WOULD YOU LIKE to go outside?" Adkins asked as Malik emerged from rehab. He hadn't been outside since he arrived at the hospital seven months before. He was pale as vanilla ice cream.

"Very much."

Outside was far away, down several floors and a long corridor past the cafeteria to a set of glass doors opening onto a courtyard. Malik still moved slowly, but without a walker. It was mid-December, crisp but not true winter yet, a welcome change from the canned air of the hospital. They sat together on a bench in the rose garden. Malik's senses were hyperalert. The brightness was physical, like an unbearable noise, but a slight breeze stirred his hair. He felt the rough wood of the bench; sparrows splashed in a fountain beneath the towering plane trees. The intensity of life surprised and frightened him.

"We're about to set you free," Adkins said. She looked older in the sunlight, with crinkles at the corners of her eyes, but more attractive, more fully human. Malik had been confined to the indoor world for so long that people had begun to lose their materiality, seeming more televised than real. Now here was Lieutenant Adkins sharply lit under a cloudless sky. Malik thought he might be in love but he couldn't trust his perceptions or his feelings. He decided it didn't matter, he would simply enjoy sitting with this lovely, caring woman in the morning sun.

"How soon?" He had thought he couldn't wait to get back to New York, to his job, to Lucy, to ordinary life, but the prospect of being on his own, outside this well-ordered institution, struck him like an electrical shock. He could remember not being afraid of anything; now the whole world terrified him.

"A week or so. You're doing well. There's not a lot more we can do for you."

"I still can't focus well enough to read the paper. When I talk it's like I'm composing in a foreign language."

"Your speech is much improved. You should be encouraged."

"I can remember the names of my first-grade classmates but I still don't remember what happened after the bomb went off."

"You never will. Your brain didn't have time to code it into memory. Even now it's still working on short-term recall. All those neurons got a terrible shaking and they're still reorganizing themselves. It'll get better."

"How much better?"

Adkins paused and looked at him. "You were in a coma for two weeks. People who have been through that usually have moderate to severe disability. Many of them never return to work."

"Does anyone just go back to normal?"

"About 30 percent have what we call a good outcome, meaning they can function at a decent level, but it's not the same. Bear in mind I'm just talking about statistical averages. There are some outliers. Maybe you'll be one of them. Based on your progress the last couple weeks, I expect you to be in the upper end of recovery, but there's no guarantee. I wish I could offer you more cheerful information."

"I thought by now I'd feel—not well, exactly, but more like me, or how I used to be."

"There's not a single person on the ward that hasn't had that same reaction," Adkins said. "You're still you but you've got more work to do. Aspects of your personality are adjusting. Simple mechanical actions are harder, like putting on socks, I hear that all the time, patients sitting there with their socks in their hand wondering what they're supposed to do with them. You're exhausted because your brain is struggling to repair itself and that uses up so much energy. There are blank spaces where words used to be. These things will get better. You'll do whatever you can to put the pieces back together, that much I know."

"Am I going to live without memories?"

"No! You're forming memories all the time. You're able to keep up with your lessons. You remember the names of your caregivers. We talked about a news story you saw on TV the week before." Adkins suddenly laughed. "Now I've forgotten what the story was myself."

"An elephant in the Bronx Zoo."

"See! Everybody forgets. When you have trouble bringing an event or a word or a person's name to consciousness it's not necessarily because of the damage to your brain. Yes, it's harder, but you will continue to get better over the next year as your brain creates new neural pathways. Meantime there are strategies that will help. Make notes. Take pictures. Video is good because you'll remember the conversation. Keep a journal. There are many ways of recapturing your memories. Work on your speech exercises, force yourself to read every day. And don't despair. I've seen a lot of guys just give up. You'll have a new life. It won't be the one you had, but that doesn't mean it's not worth living. You've been spared. Maybe there's a reason for that."

These words reached him but he didn't know how to respond. All he could think about was that he was leaving, returning to his old life broken and changed.

"Will I remember you?"

Adkins smiled shyly. "I hope so." She looked at him. Malik seemed lost, like a balloon floating aimlessly into the sky. "Give me your phone," she said. She held it out for a selfie of the two of them, and just before she snapped the shot she kissed him on the cheek. "Something to remember me by," she said.

2

Lucy

Brooklyn, Dec. 22, 2022

The Uber ride was both familiar and new. Even the traffic was like an experience from a past life. The city was rainy and miserable, the Christmas decorations somehow adding to the gloom. Pedestrians fought to keep their umbrellas under control as the rain whipped about in the wind.

Malik stared out the window marveling at the sights: Jamaica Bay, Canarsie Park, the Haitian restaurants on Flatbush Avenue. He and Lucy lived on Newkirk Avenue, a few blocks from the apartment where Barbra Streisand grew up. Their apartment was too small, meant for him alone, but when Lucy moved in it became charming in a way he could never have imagined. Between the two of them they could afford more. He once thought about securing a mortgage for a condo in the Battery they peeked at during an open house. It had a view of the convergence of the Hudson and the East River, crisscrossed with maritime traffic that captivated Malik—he could watch it for hours. Something had held him back from making the commitment. He couldn't separate buying the condo from marrying Lucy. Their relationship in Flatbush was provisional, at least that's how he thought of it.

Malik was embarrassed to realize how much he had taken her for granted. She was a fine person and would be a great life partner. Physically, she was impressive, a gym rat and a martial artist, no question that she could keep up with him. She had a decent government job in the mayor's office, with excellent benefits and better pay than Malik, plus a wonderful sense of humor and a fine singing voice, which she sometimes put on display in the FBI karaoke parties. Their friends liked them as a couple. She was kind. Pleasant company. They would have been happy together, he thought as the Uber turned in to his street. Why hadn't he married her already? Before, he was hesitant. Now he was desperate and certain he would lose her. She would see immediately how damaged he was.

He had an unsettling thought that the key in his pocket was for the wrong apartment. The door seemed a little off, the color was a slightly different shade from what he expected, he hadn't noticed the scratches around the lock. Also, there was a welcome mat that he was sure hadn't been there before. He stuck the key in the lock, half expecting that it wouldn't fit. But it did.

"Is that you, Tony?" Lucy said as the door opened.

He expected her to be shocked by his disfigurement; instead, she put her hands on his shoulders and studied him carefully. "Yes," she said. "It's you."

"Or what's left," he said with a pretended lightness.

Lucy embraced him. He felt the warmth of her, her slender back, her long sleek arms around him. He was filled with gratitude and desire and an overwhelming feeling of regret. All these sensations arrived in a gush.

"Oh, honey," Lucy said.

"Don't look at me," he said quietly in her ear.

Lucy went into the kitchen. She was somewhat lame in her right leg, a result of a break as a teenager. Her mother was a devout Christian Scientist and had refused to have it set properly. Most people didn't notice her limp, she disguised it so well, but something about her minor disability had always called to Malik. She was wounded and he could save her; all he had to do was love her. That had been an unspoken dynamic in their relationship. Now he was the one who needed saving. Self-sacrifice wasn't a quality that came easily to Lucy.

"If you're hungry I've got some snacks. We can go to this new Thai restaurant next to the park. Of course, that's just me, we can go that steakhouse you like so much, what was it, Lowake's? Of course, it's nasty out there, so I can whip up something. We got loads of food." The words came out in a nervous burst. "You should open some wine. We can celebrate, right? Do you notice anything?"

Lucy had gone crazy on the decorations. The Christmas tree nearly scraped the ceiling and fake ivy covered the mantel. The expectation of festivity added to Malik's anxiety. She returned with a tray full of cheeses. She sat on his right side, with the good eye. Malik admired her grace, which he supposed was also mixed with pity.

"So what should we talk about?" she asked.

"You start."

Lucy put a slice of Brie on a cracker and handed it to Malik. "Well," she said. "Where should I begin. God, I had a root canal. Have you ever had one? I don't recommend it. But anyway. Don't let me go on like this. I'm dying to know if you're okay."

"Parts of me are. Others need some work."

"Start with your eye."

"They had to take it out, there was just too much damage. I'm thinking about an artificial eye. What do you think?"

"I don't know. That patch is kinda dashing."

"I can see fine. I mean, my depth of field is shot and I have to turn my head all the time. I'm still working on stuff."

"What stuff?"

"Emotional things. I swing from one mood to another. One minute I'm a regular crybaby and the next I'm enraged. I'm warning you, it's a roller coaster. I've got some pills but they just put me to sleep. Or else I lie awake for hours. It's like I'm in somebody else's body. Maybe I'll get better or maybe I'll just get used to it."

"Are you in pain, Tony?" she said, her voice cracking.

"Let's talk about something else."

THAT NIGHT WAS the disaster he feared. Lucy was sweet and available, but he was impotent and filled with shame. He sensed that she was disappointed but hiding it. Then around two a.m. he jerked awake to find Lucy's bedside light already on. She was staring at him, her mouth open in alarm. "What happened?" she asked.

"I don't know. A dream."

"You're soaking in sweat."

Malik took a quick shower. When he returned he found that Lucy had changed the sheets.

"I'm okay," he said.

"You were moaning."

"I thought I'd be over this by now, but sometimes I wake up in a panic and I don't know why. I remember fragments of dreams but there's not like a narrative. Just sensations. Sorry I scared you."

"Come back to bed and let's start over."

Malik's body was cool from the shower. He lay still in the dark as Lucy ran her hands over him, a feeling both sensual and exploratory, fingers lingering on the little shrapnel scars. Then she touched his legs. She felt the indentations where the metal plate had been screwed into his fibula. She might have had a similar scar if her broken leg had been attended.

Something stirred in him. The scar on his leg was sensitive and somehow arousing. He groaned.

"Am I hurting you?"

"No. The opposite."

She moved up his leg, patiently, lovingly, and his sex awakened. It had been months since he had an erection and he wondered if it would ever happen again, but now Lucy lay on top of him, brushing her breasts across his face. He was hungry for her. When he came he arrived at the place where ecstasy was a step away from death.

BEING HOME made him feel more alienated from himself. He knew how he typically behaved in various situations—watching television, going to a concert, the things Lucy liked to do—but he couldn't fit the person he was now into the person he had been. Eating in restaurants was a challenge. He was impatient and rude to waiters with the slightest provocation. He broke down in tears in the Thai restaurant. He yelled at a person on the street who didn't clean up after her dog. He was so angry that the woman fled, leaving the turds behind. Malik found some newspaper in a trash can and handled the droppings, cursing in a way that Lucy had never heard from him. People on the sidewalk made a wide berth. "You need help," she said under her breath. He did need help, but it was tricky with the bureau. He desperately wanted to get back to work but any hint of mental instability was a career killer. It was as if the bomb was inside him, blowing up at the smallest things.

They were both relieved when the holidays passed, after several parties where Malik felt like an animal on exhibit. The day after New Year's Lucy resumed her old schedule, out the door by eight in the morning and back by six or so. Sometimes she worked through dinner. In the past when he did the same they didn't bother to apologize. Now he had to fight down the tendency to complain. He was still earning an income because of his medical leave, but how long would that last?

He made a point of waking up with Lucy and making the coffee, then going back to bed as soon as the door closed. He busied himself when she came home. His life became a performance for an audience of one. There were medications and therapies available to him, but he believed if the bureau found out he was medicated he would never get back. Each day he became more convinced that his professional life was effectively over. He fought back by walking an hour a day and doing crossword puzzles. He thought about taking up a musical instrument. He had to do something to fill up the emptiness.

"This can't last," Lucy said. It was a Sunday morning. They had a ritual of grabbing bagels and loading up on actual printed newspapers, everything from the *Times* to the tabloids, which were scattered across the table. It used to be a companionable way to spend the morning, followed by a walk and brunch at one of three or four restaurants they favored. A leisurely round of lovemaking in the afternoon. Now they still had sex but never as explosively as that first night. As the gloom buried Malik he became less interested and less capable, to the point that he stopped making advances. Lucy began treating him like a roommate rather than a lover. He was in an emotional sinkhole where feelings of any sort required heroic effort.

"I'm making progress," Malik said. "I ran three miles yesterday."

"Physically you're coming back, but you're deeply depressed. And

I'm not sure if you're actually reading those papers or just looking at them for my benefit."

"It's a struggle but it's part of my recovery."

"Tony, you need to give up on the idea of going back to the bureau. It's stopping you from getting the help you need. You're so worried that if you go to a therapist or start taking Prozac or whatever they'll blackball you. So what? It's not the world's best job, you said so many times. There are other opportunities, lots of them. You need to get out in the world and start building a new life."

Something in her tone panicked him. Behind the loving words he heard a threat. *She's leaving me*, he thought. Her patience was running out.

The next morning when Lucy went to work Malik began his campaign to recapture his life. Until now he had been thinking weak. He had to think strong. They belonged to the YMCA in Flatbush that he hadn't been to since he returned. His gym bag was stuffed with dirty clothes from his last workout months ago. He put them in the wash and thought how he was making a clean start in every sense of the term. While he was waiting he went online and signed up for an advanced course in conversational Levantine Arabic. He had never become fluent and now he had the one thing he lacked in all the years he had studied that language off and on—time. Time wasn't going to be his oppressor anymore, it was just the interval between events.

At the Y he found a trainer who had just finished with a client. The client looked reasonably buff but the trainer was awesome, reminding Malik of William Perry, the defensive tackle for the Chicago Bears known as the Refrigerator. Malik got to see him near the end of his career when he played for the Philadelphia Eagles. The trainer's name was Jerry and he was available. The next hour was one of the most demanding physical experiences Malik had ever endured, and yet Jerry knew what he was doing; he was a physical therapist in the afternoons. Malik arranged twice-weekly sessions.

All that was accomplished in a single morning. After lunch he polished his shoes and put on a suit. He took a train into Lower Manhattan. It was September 11, the twenty-second anniversary of al-Qaeda's attack, once again a beautiful late-summer day, clear skies, mid-seventies. He walked to the Battery. The park was full of baby carriages, pensioners, and pigeons. He found a building still under construction near the one that he and Lucy had looked at before. A smartly dressed woman named Carla was in a sales office just off the lobby. "You'll love it," she said warmly as they took the elevator to the seventeenth floor. The condo was half-finished, the utilities hadn't been installed in the kitchen, the sheetrock was unpainted. "I know it looks like we're months away from finishing but this team moves really fast," Carla promised. "We've already got tenants on seven floors. Buyers are scooping them up before the paint is dry."

They make it so easy, Malik thought, as he wrote a check for two hundred thousand dollars in earnest money.

HE TEXTED LUCY to meet him at the restaurant Robert atop the Museum of Arts and Design on Columbus Circle. He got the same table by the window looking out on Central Park. It was here that he had invited her to move in with him. The first big step.

"Look at you!" she said. It had been months since he dressed up. Although his suit jacket hung a little slack on his shoulders he was more than presentable. Lucy gave him an appraising smile he hadn't seen in a long time.

He asked about her day, which was another thing he had failed to do until now. "Not much, really. Just crazy office stuff," she said.

"Crazy how?"

"You know about Francine, right?"

"Your manager."

"She got into it again with the deputy mayor." Encouraged by Malik's attention, Lucy went on to talk about herself and her job, clearly pleased to have a confidant for what had been a taxing day. They had cocktails and watched the lights come on in the city.

"What's this?" she asked. There was a compact camcorder on the table beside Malik.

"I needed a new toy."

"I didn't know you were interested in photography."

"Actually, they suggested at the hospital that pictures and video are great memory aids. So I thought tonight I'd test it out. If you don't mind. I was just reading the instructions."

He picked up the camera and pointed it at Lucy, who smiled engagingly. "Say something," Malik said.

"The rain in Spain stays mainly in the plain."

Malik laughed and set the camera aside. "There's something else I want to show you," Malik said. He reached into his breast pocket and put a brochure of the new condo building on the table.

"Oh, wow," Lucy said as she studied the plans. She paused. "So how did you get this?"

"I went to take a look. You won't believe how nice it is. Spacious. Amazing views. And a nice walk to our offices."

"Uh-huh. Just curious, right?"

"I bought one."

"You did what?"

"I bought unit 17B. It's two bedrooms. They've got a lap pool and a gym. I think a spa, too."

"Jesus, Tony." She looked out the window. "When you say 'bought,' what do you mean?"

"I put down a 10 percent deposit."

"You think you can afford this place?"

"I've done the math. We can do this. It's a smart investment. Yes, it's a big step, but we've earned it. The lady didn't bat an eye when I told her our incomes and savings. You said this was what you always wanted, a great apartment on the water. I was the guy who thought it was over our heads. Also I guess I was ambivalent about our relationship and whether it would last. Well, I was a fool. I want to make you happy. I don't want to live without you. I know all this now. Maybe we're not rich but we can afford nice things. I'm getting my life back together, and that means being with you."

Lucy dabbed a tear from her eye with her napkin just as the waiter brought their entrees. Malik waited for her response but she stared into her plate. "I wanted to say something to you as well this evening," she finally said. "I had a speech all prepared, but this makes it harder. I love you, Tony. But I also love myself, and I owe it to my future to make the right decision. I took care of you when you came back, and I wanted everything to be like it was, or different in a way that I could accept. But I can't, I can't do it, Tony. I don't want to live an unhappy life."

LUCY MOVED INTO a friend's apartment the next morning. Malik suspected the friend was actually the wealthy investment banker on her Facebook page. Probably she had been seeing him and preparing for this day for months; that would explain some of the evening events she claimed were for work. Malik didn't blame her. He wondered why it took so long. He thought about skipping his date with Jerry, but he realized with absolute clarity that he was at a juncture in his life. One road led to something like recovery. It was imperfect. He would never be who he was but there was a chance to be somebody different, somebody he could still respect. Maybe this somebody would be alone, but he would have a life. He would still be effective in the world.

The other road led into total darkness.

He would not be defeated.

And yet the question lingered that had first been posed when he awakened in the hospital: Who am I? His identity was like a ghost in a haunted house, a troubled spirit, intangible, there but not there. He longed for a family. He had no siblings and his parents had passed away. It felt abnormal to be nearing the midpoint of his life and being so totally unrelated, so solitary.

He met some friends for drinks in a pub he used to patronize. It was fun but it wasn't the same. They treated him like broken crockery. People stared at him, or at least he thought they did, so he avoided the glances that may or may not have been cast at him. Alcohol hit him like a hammer; he would have to be careful.

IT OCCURRED TO HIM to examine his roots. He signed up for Ancestry.com and developed an interest in genealogy. His mother, Ina Magee, was descended from the usual genetic mélange that history produces, but if you followed the paternal line she came from Scotch-Irish Presbyterians who fled to America during the potato famine in the mid-nineteenth century. Her great-great-grandfather settled in New Orleans, where the family remained until her father moved them to Little Rock, Arkansas, when Ina was ten. The Magees were a fertile people, as Malik discovered when he found a raft of cousins he barely knew or had never met.

His father's side was sparser and less documented. The census first found him in Philadelphia in 1970. Tariq Abdul Malik was eighteen years old. He had immigrated by himself, an act of faith in his future and rejection of his past. Tariq and Ina met at a bicentennial event at Independence Hall, where Ina was a docent (she taught history in junior high) and Tariq was one of a hundred immigrants selected to receive his citizenship in that hallowed building on July 4, 1976. He was immensely proud of being an American. He asked Ina a question about Benjamin Franklin, who he said was his hero. Ina adored Franklin. Somehow two shy people found the words that led to a date and then a relationship.

Tariq came from Hebron, a city in southern Palestine under Israeli occupation. Tariq rarely talked about his past, but when he did his stories seemed like fairy tales, or Bible stories, with places named Bethlehem and Jerusalem, and tribal rivalries that dated near to the beginning of civilization. Tariq's eyes were always bright when he told these tales, and it made little Tony wonder why his father ever left.

Malik always knew Tariq had an identical twin, Abdullah Abdul Malik. He wasn't on Instagram but Abdullah's daughter, Dina Abdul Malik, was. She looked like many conservative young Palestinian girls, with a headscarf and large brown eyes that seemed so innocent. In one of her posts she noted that she was engaged to be married in October 2023, just a month away.

IT WAS TIME. Malik bought a falafel from a cart on Water Street in Lower Manhattan and sat on a bench on the esplanade watching the ferries come and go. He liked the regular commerce of trains and airplanes and boats of all kinds. Traffic signified life and roused his spirit. He waited until two in the afternoon, when most people would be back from lunch, then walked to FBI headquarters at 26 Federal Plaza to see Tommy Cantemessa. He had not called for an appointment, but his badge still worked and he breezed right in. He stopped to see his old squad in the bullpen. Everyone gathered around, patting his shoulder or embracing him with a delicacy that suggested he was too fragile to handle. He had rehearsed acting normal, which meant ready smiles and an imperturbable façade, slapping backs and gripping arms as he shook hands. He noted that his cubicle had not yet been reassigned, his squash racquet was still tucked under the desk. Everyone said they couldn't wait for him to get back to the office, but their eyes said it was unlikely.

Tommy closed the door and they sat in his office. He had been promoted to chief of counterterrorism right after he saw Malik in the hospital, and the job fit him well. He had souvenirs and knickknacks from assignments all over the world, including a Yemeni dagger on the wall and a gold Colt .45 rumored to have belonged to Saddam Hussein—how it wound up in Tommy's hands was a matter of speculation. Tommy was one of the great ones.

"Things okay with Lucy?" he asked.

"Great! She's really glad to have me home. I think we'll go up to Montauk for a few days, we haven't had a lot of time together. Work stuff." He didn't like lying to Tommy. He might have heard the news anyway; the bureau is a cloistered world. But the last thing he needed was to appear pathetic and abandoned.

Tommy's eyes were troubled. "And you're occupying yourself how?"

"You know, taking it easy, like for the first time ever. But I'm ready to dive back in, as soon as you give me the all clear."

Tommy swiveled his chair a few degrees. From his window he could see the World Trade Center, like a gigantic tombstone. "I mentioned this back in Germany, buddy," Tommy said. "There are some tests you'll need to take. Same assessments they did when you came into the bureau, so you know what I'm talking about. I'm holding a spot but I can't for long, with all the cutbacks. So I'll need you to address this."

"What if I could use a little more time?"

"I'll have to fill it by next month or I'll lose the position. We're short as it is."

Malik remembered the personality assessment. It was challenging when he was younger and his brain was intact. The logic problems were beastly, but they tested the very skills that an investigator required. The truth was, there was no way that Malik would pass, at least not in his current state.

"There's another thing, Tommy. I've got to go back to the region."

"I thought you were going to Montauk."

"When I return."

"Um-hmm." Tommy drummed his fingers on his desk. "And what brings you back to that part of the world?"

"My cousin is getting married. In Hebron."

"You gotta be kidding. Hebron."

"That's where my dad was from."

"I really think that's a little too dangerous these days. Are you close to these people?"

"It's family, Tommy. I can take the tests as soon as I get back. I promise I won't hold you up."

"This is on your dime, you know. Uncle Sam isn't buying you any airline tickets."

"Totally understand."

"Look, Malik, I can't tell you what to do on your own time. But last trip out you nearly got blown to pieces. Everybody else did. And I know you. You won't let that be a part of your past. You'll go out and try to be the hero. You're not playing from a full deck. You'll get yourself killed."

"It's a wedding, Tommy."

"Right." Tommy put his fingertips together in front of his mouth, prayer position. "When are you going?"

"Next Tuesday. I'll stop in Jordan for a while to pay my respects to some of the family members of the victims. Look around a bit. Back in a couple of weeks."

"I shouldn't bring this up," Tommy said. "There is something you could do. It won't qualify as an assignment, more as a favor. In other words, it's not official and you won't even get your meals covered. I wouldn't ask except some cop in Hebron has reached out to our legat in Jerusalem. Wants to talk but won't say about what. Our guys think it's not worth their time but they put out the word. So this would be a busman's-holiday type of thing. Just drop in and take his temperature."

"Happy to be of service."

"Goddammit, Malik, you gotta promise to keep your head down, what's left of it. When you get back we'll talk about the future."

3

The Chief

Israel

Jacob Weingarten was a peace-loving man, kind, honest, liberal in spirit, although not as gullible as such qualities would lead one to believe; quite the opposite, he was aware of the world around him and the meanness that characterized so much of human behavior. His natural inclination to be joyful and to believe the best in people was balanced by the strife and hatred that dominated his existence. It was a miracle that he could keep his spirits up. He was a family man in a family riven by dissension between him and his formidable wife, Miriam, which spilled onto his children, so that home, instead of being a sanctuary, was an arena of quarrelsome debate. So was the community he lived in, a West Bank settlement in Hebron renowned for its fanaticism. Jacob was not of this camp. He nursed an image of Israel as an enlightened society, secular and pragmatic, like its founders, one that would always defend its right to exist while respecting the traditions of other peoples—romantic sentiments of the sort that the renowned Jewish folk singer Theodore Bikel expressed in his songs. Jacob had a passable singing voice himself, and he often entertained in schools or elder-care facilities, plunking the tunes on a Gibson guitar, his most cherished possession. Even children were astounded by his optimism.

As regards his disastrous marriage, it should have been obvious the moment they met, at the ages of twenty-seven (Jacob) and twenty-two (Miriam), that they were spiritual and political opposites. This was twenty years ago, at a performance by Bikel as Tevye in *Fid-*

dler on the Roof, his greatest role, at Tel Aviv's Cameri Theatre, which Bikel cofounded. The Second Intifada was raging, and with the ceaseless bus bombings and rocket attacks sitting in a crowded theater was a foolhardy act of defiance. Israel was at a turning point; the idealism that Jacob embodied so deeply was being tested; and Miriam, who had not given much thought to politics until then, was awakening to the threat that the rebellion posed to her homeland and even her life. Day after day disaster fell upon the nation, Jews died by the dozens while the government and the army were incapable of putting a stop to it.

But this first meeting was on a gentle night in early summer, with no breaking news of catastrophe. During intermission the audience spilled into the plaza. Jacob was standing in the bar queue when he overheard two women behind him talking excitedly about which songs they liked the best, "Sunrise, Sunset" or "If I Were a Rich Man." They were in high spirits, buoyed by the exuberance of the music. Jacob couldn't help himself. He knew everything about the songs and the Yiddish short stories of Sholem Aleichem, upon which the play was based. One of the women in line was Miriam Levinger. She was in a kind of intermission herself between youthful apathy and fierce nationalism.

Buried in that first moment of meeting was a fundamental misperception that would poison their future relationship. For Miriam, the message of the play was that Jews are a people apart, different from others and hated for their difference, beset by pogroms and eternally subject to the whims of the mob and by people in power. At the end of the play the czar of Russia expels the Jews from their village. *Fiddler on the Roof* poses a political question in which Israel was the only answer.

Jacob grew up in Tel Aviv, which embraced modernity and pleasure. Enchanted as he was by Jewish history and music, the straitjacket of tradition that the songs celebrated was a horror. It was the world of his grandfather, an impoverished peddler in a shtetl in the Ukraine, who emigrated to Israel in 1925 as a teenager, leaving his religion and traditions behind with no regrets. To see *Fiddler on the Roof* from the safe vantage of a vibrant secular society was to appreciate the distance that Jewish culture had traveled in the century that separated Jews like Jacob and Miriam from the people depicted in the play.

First impressions are difficult to overcome. Jacob was knowledgeable and handsome (in a way that middle age would mercilessly erase), but Miriam also assumed that he responded with the same radical identity as she did to the themes in the play. That Jacob was in his army uniform—he was a major in the Israel Defense Forces, recently called back to service because of the intifada—colored her view of him. He was fit—back then—and still had a head of curly black hair. If you had asked Miriam what she was looking for in a mate, she would have specified intelligence, charm, and an attribute that was difficult to express but had to do with youthful insouciance, signaled by the curly hair and the gap-tooth smile. In fact, those weren't the qualities she really valued at all, they were the qualities you saw in a movie that indicated this was the boy who was going to get the girl. What happened later wasn't part of the story.

Miriam was living with her parents in Jerusalem, at the other end of the spiritual universe from cosmopolitan Tel Aviv. The Levingers were Orthodox, but religion was not the defining feature of their lives; nationalism was. Their house had belonged to a wealthy Palestinian family that fled to Gaza in 1948, during the war of independence; it was awarded to Miriam's grandfather for his service in the Stern Gang, a Jewish terror organization during the British Mandate. Despite the radical background of the Levinger family, Miriam steered away from the strident views common among her relatives, but the Second Intifada undermined her confidence. She opened her ears to the furious talk that dominated family occasions. When she met Jacob, she was already formulating the dialectic that would make her such a belligerent partisan.

But the Miriam that Jacob saw at that first encounter was smart, wry, and voluptuous. It was hard to see past her sexual appeal to the gathering ferocity of her political views, so he avoided discussing current events and let his silences discreetly confirm the presumptions she naturally made. He paid court to her beauty so ardently Miriam assumed that whatever disagreements they might have in the beginning of their relationship she would easily tame.

Married life inevitably drew back the sheets on this ill-matched pair. Miriam's temperament was so much more forceful than Jacob's, dragging him along as she searched out her destiny. Because her family counted as royalty among the religious Zionists, Miriam insisted that she and Jacob move to Kiryat Arba, a fortresslike settlement built of red tiles and the creamy white limestone the region is famous for. The settlement was founded by Miriam's uncle, Moshe Levinger, in 1968, on a ridge above Hebron's Old City, the place Moshe believed was the birthplace of the Jewish people. Kiryat Arba was not the very first settlement, but it was foundational to the movement and a deliberate impediment to a two-state solution.

When Miriam and Jacob moved there, in 2012, Kiryat Arba was home to about seven thousand Jews, guarded by fifteen hundred Israeli soldiers, in a region of seven hundred thousand Arabs, the largest Palestinian district on the West Bank. The residents of Kiryat Arba were mostly Orthodox Jews and religious Zionists, recognizable by the knitted kippahs men wear. It wasn't entirely populated by radicals; there was a swath of Jews from many regions, including Russians, Ethiopians, and Iraqis, embodying varying degrees of faith, drawn to the settlement more by government housing subsidies than by the politics of the founder; but for the most part the moderates—or let's say semi-moderates, there were certainly no liberals—held their tongues. Moshe Levinger and his wife, Miriam (after whom Miriam Weingarten was named) passed away a few years after the Weingartens arrived, but Kiryat Arba remained the center of the expansionist settler movement. The goal—usually unspoken outside the confines of the settlement—was to rid Israel and the West Bank of all non-Jews.

Jacob was woefully out of place in Kiryat Arba. Had it been up to him, they would have lived in a kibbutz, picking oranges, cooking communal meals, singing folk songs around a campfire with the children. Miriam could not abide being bottled up in such a setting. With her family connections, she immediately felt at home in the settlement, but she had enough compassion to recognize the sacrifice Jacob made by following her into a life he would never have chosen for himself. Soon after they moved into Kiryat Arba, she quietly explored occupations available for a man with Jacob's attributes. Her life on the front lines of the Jewish conquest was filled with purpose. Surely Jacob could find his own heroic path in this sacred environment.

Because Miriam profoundly misunderstood who Jacob was, she searched for positions more suitable for her. She imagined Jacob in a position of authority, which would dignify him and make him more acceptable in her eyes. He should be an asset for her, socially useful in some way. Subconsciously she also wanted to see him in uniform again, but Jacob had made it clear he was done with military service. When he resigned from the army, he had been happily teaching math in an elementary school.

Friends conspired to find a position for him, but Jacob's lack of ambition made it difficult to settle on an appropriate spot. Then one day Miriam had a revelation. She was standing in the garden of their house in Kiryat Arba overlooking the Hebron Hills. Before her was the Old City, including the souk, which was a shadow of itself, nearly all the shops having been shut down in order to "sterilize" the area, to use the freighted language of the occupation. Beyond that was modern Hebron—Arab territory "yet to be conquered," as the settlers constantly reminded themselves. Watchtowers rose like minarets in the Old City. Checkpoints marked the crossings; sentries stood at the intersections; drones, balloons, and satellites stared ceaselessly at the sacred quarter. One should feel safe with so many eyes, human and mechanical, a vast attentive audience whose gaze never wandered. But to watch is not to see.

Miriam observed this vista every morning, but this time her eye fell on a modest building just below the ridge she stood upon, hovering above the Old City like a sentry: the police station. Standing between the Arab city and the Jewish settlement, it was a symbol, although little more than that, of Israeli control. The fact that Miriam hadn't given it any notice was a consequence of it not being at all important. The army and other police agencies really controlled the city. Kiryat Arba was not a part of the Hebron municipality; moreover it jealously decided internal settlement matters, which left the Israeli police with little to do—authority without any vital responsibilities, perfect for Jacob.

Because of Miriam's influence, Jacob Weingarten was offered the position of inspector. His army experience included a year in the military police, so he knew something about the job. It wasn't unusual for the police to recruit from the settlers, several other officers also lived in Kiryat Arba, but it proved to be a powerful asset for Jacob. He came at a fortunate moment, in that his predecessor and three other officers had washed out of the police corps because of sexual scandals. He rose to chief within three years of his appointment, engendering resentment on the part of some of his colleagues, especially his second-in-command, Yossi Ben-Gal, who had far more experience but none of the sway among the settlers that Miriam commanded.

Chief Weingarten was an unpopular figure in the station—not hated, just not respected. Some of the officers blamed him unfairly for the dismissal of the previous chief and his cohorts. They saw Weingarten as a political appointment with few qualifications for police work, kind and passive, ill-suited to the constant agitation between the settlers and the Arabs. Although real crimes were rare, terror was always near; but terror was a job for the army, the intelligence services, and the elite Border Police. That was fine with Weingarten. Despite the evidence before him, Weingarten maintained a naive belief in the goodness of humanity—perhaps the last person in Hebron to do so. His strength was community outreach—speeches at the schools, the local citizens' council—but in the station itself he was isolated and disregarded. Another character trait soon surfaced: he became suspicious of the motivations of people around him, sensing he was being undermined. Some of this was true but it was amplified by his paranoia. He came to believe that there was no one he could confide in because there was no one to trust.

On the first day of autumn, 2023, he awakened early, as he always did; he made eggs and herring for himself and Miriam, then caught up on personal emails in his home office. Before he left home he had a telephone call. He told Miriam that he had an appointment that morning and a full day ahead, so not to expect him for dinner. There was nothing unusual about the last morning of his life.

4

Yossi

West Bank, Sept. 25, 2023

A convoy of vehicles came down from Kiryat Arba. They bore yellow license plates, indicating that they were Israeli citizens (white plates were for Palestinians). They were escorted by two stone-battered Israeli police cruisers, looking as if they had endured a torrential hailstorm. The convoy turned north on Route 60, the main road through the West Bank. Traffic was light at this hour, so the convoy flew along in the morning gloom, no sirens, the red and blue flashers on the police vehicles lighting up the roadsides. They weren't going far.

They passed watchtowers and sentries and shuttered shops. The convoy turned off the highway onto a single asphalt lane, slowing as the road sloped upward. Pale fieldstones milked the light like a pond reflecting a starry night. On the hillsides the rocky strata described geologic eras; the terraced vineyards and groves that had been there for millennia reinforced the sense of eternal changelessness.

The convoy halted in front of a billboard of a smiling man with a long white beard, his arms spread in welcome. This was Immanuel Cohen, a rabbi known to his followers as the Rav, around whom a sense of destiny had accumulated. Like Moshe Levinger and a long train of charismatic rabbis reaching back into history, Cohen spoke to Jews who believed it was time to redeem the promise God made to the Jewish people of a vast homeland, far larger than the tiny nation of Israel, stretching from the Nile to the Euphrates. The Rav drew his teaching from Meir Kahane, an American rabbi, who advocated that all non-Jews be expelled from Israel, excepting those willing to become enslaved to Jews. Kahane's party, Kach, was outlawed after being declared a terrorist organization, but in the decades since Kahane was assassinated, in New York, in 1990, his influence persisted through his spiritual progeny, including Immanuel Cohen. His followers became known as Kahanists.

Behind the billboard, on a low rise, stood the Rav's yeshiva, a disheveled stone structure built centuries before and repurposed as a yeshiva for the young Jews who had come from many different countries to ally themselves with the Kahanists. Each of them had been summoned through some private revelation to surrender their previous identities—their relationships, the ambitions they might have had, their native languages—and prepare for the arrival of the Messiah to bring on the End of Days. The first order of business was to ethnically cleanse the West Bank, which they called Judea and Samaria. After that, many contemplated annexing territories in Egypt, Iraq, Lebanon, and Jordan.

The Rav himself was already present as the convoy and the police cruisers arrived. He had a formidable bearing, with his white beard and fierce black eyebrows, but there was a serenity about him, fortified by doubt-defying prophecy. He could have been the model for a Renaissance painting of a biblical patriarch, one of the stern ones. He stood beside a backhoe, hands on hips, impatiently rising on his toes as he stared at a blueprint an associate had unfurled, then he spoke quietly to several of his followers, gesturing toward the ancient olive grove in front of them and, beyond that, a large vineyard, which ascended in a series of stone terraces to an imposing hilltop surmounting the entire valley. Other, less defended places would be easier to access, but this hilltop grove had a 360-degree view of the entire Hebron uplift. Its prominence and beauty had caught the Rav's eye. Declaring it a holy spot, he chose it to be the site of an immense temple that would one day rival the structure in Jerusalem the Romans destroyed in AD 70.

Inspector Yossi Ben-Gal led a force of four officers to reroute traffic while the Rav's followers did their work. It was a pointless assignment. Yossi and his officers had no authority to halt the destruction of land and the theft of property. That was up to the IDF—the Israel

Defense Forces—so it was ultimately a political matter. And these days the politics was on the side of the settlers and the national-religious Jews. He watched as about thirty settlers prayed beside the fence, carrying shovels and sledgehammers and chainsaws. They also brought lunches and ice chests, so they were going to make a day of it.

Yossi approached the Rav with a deference he reserved for very few men. "Rav, we hope to keep this day peaceful. The region is already on fire." A month before, a soldier shot and killed a protestor in Hebron who was lying unconscious in the street. The soldier was arrested but then released after three days on the order of the minister of national security, who called him a hero. The inevitable reprisal was on everyone's mind.

"We come in peace, you know that, Yossi," Cohen responded.

"Yes, but your men are armed."

"You would deny us the means of protecting ourselves?"

Yossi shrugged. The right of settlers to carry arms was unquestioned. The minister of interior was handing out assault weapons to settlers, so what was the point.

The Rav fixed his vehement gaze on Yossi, a look that might have been trained on an audience of thousands but was concentrated with full force on a police officer who was here for traffic control. "We offered the sheikh a fair price, but he did not accept our generous offer, despite the fact that he is not a Jew and has no real claim to property," the Rav said. "In any case, we can't hold back the Messiah forever." He said this with a glint in his eye, as if he was sharing a joke with Yossi but also acknowledging the awe-inspiring nerve it took to represent himself as an agent of the End of Days. There was always about the Rav a doubleness, an air of kindness mixed with the threat of violence. "He has one foot in heaven and one somewhere we don't know," a follower observed. "We hope it's in a good place."

A few of the Kahanists started a song, and others threw up their hands and began to dance, their faces ecstatic. Then the music died as the chainsaws cranked up and the men knocked down the fence and moved into the olive grove. It was accomplished in minutes.

Cars were arriving from either direction, most of them Palestinians commuting into Hebron for work. Angry drivers yelled at a young police officer directing traffic. The cop had nothing to say other than to order the drivers to turn around. But by now nobody was turning around.

At the back of the line of vehicles was a white Toyota with yellow plates. The driver wore a red cap. He stepped out of the car and began to video the scene. An officer dashed toward him. "Get back in your car!" the cop cried in heavily accented Arabic.

"I have an appointment," the driver said. "When can I get through?"

The officer only repeated his demand and reached for his weapon. The driver shook his head in disbelief, then sat behind the wheel. It was a small incident in the tragedy that was about to unfold.

YOSSI BEN-GAL WAS FIFTY-FIVE, two years before early retirement would put an end to an undistinguished career, marked by the slow decay of ideals and ambition in a post no one envied. He was not a large man but his face was long and hard and his body still strong, despite the soft indifference of middle age. Years after he left the army he kept his hair short. It was gray now, along with a mustache the color of steel. His eyes, flat and dark, failed to reflect the emergency flashers that illuminated the countryside like a forest fire. His nose was immense, beakish, the nose of a man without ordinary vanity but with another kind of self-regard: that he was who he was, he would stand his ground, he would not be pushed aside.

The young olive trees were decapitated in a few minutes. Heavy with olives, they were days away from the harvest. The older trees posed a challenge, gnarled and twisted by age, with mammoth trunks as big around as a Volkswagen. The oldest among them were bearing fruit when the Crusaders arrived at the dawn of the twelfth century; one olive tree in Bethlehem has been carbon-dated to be five thousand years old. Over the centuries a single tree can sprout new saplings that become a grove in itself. Hollows form in the trunks, providing hiding places for children or a refuge from the sun or rain. Such trees command a particular majesty, and one could see on the faces of the Rav's followers expressions of distaste for a job they knew was cruel and unnatural, and for which they blamed the Palestinians, whose resistance made such unfortunate actions necessary. The trunks of the ancient trees were too vast for the chainsaws, so the men labored over the amputation of the muscular limbs, leaving their naked stubs pointing this way and that in postures of anguish, with their leafy olive-laden branches wreathed around them in heaps on the ground.

Yossi noticed movement in the shadows. Arabs were approaching from the vineyard, joining those who had abandoned their cars, each of them stopping to pick up stones. The land was lousy with stones, there was no end to them. They have been at hand since David destroyed Goliath. Stones are deadly, they have always been.

As the Kahanists realized they were being surrounded, their hands found the pistols in their belts or pockets, their movements slowed as if they were walking on an icy lake. A young man holding an assault rifle stepped forward to shield Cohen. Yossi recognized him as Benny Eleazar, Cohen's grandson, the leader of the radicalized youth drawn to the Rav's movement. He was eighteen, short and slender, quivering with excitement. He had a patchy adolescent beard and wore wire-rim glasses that gave him a studious look, but he carried his weapon like an avid gunslinger. This was a moment he longed for.

Yossi's second-in-command, Aharon Berger, was built like a scarecrow with pipestem limbs and a sunken chest, but he was tall and easy to spot in the back of the crowd. In part because of his popularity with the Rav's people, Berger was recently promoted to deputy inspector. Yossi saw him as a competitor, political and ambitious and incompetent. It was his fault that the police were here at all. A small show of force, Berger had advised Chief Weingarten; it would be appreciated by the Rav's people. But this was not a job for the police. The army should handle it, although they didn't have the authority to make arrests. *We're all just pawns in this game,* Yossi thought, *nothing good will come of any of it.* People were going to die so the settlers could continue to claim more of what they determined was their ancient homeland. They would push Arabs out of Hebron, and then out of the West Bank altogether. It was a fantasy, an Arab land without Arabs, just like Hamas dreaming of the Holy Land without Jews.

Yossi waved Berger over. "Who owns this property?" he asked.

"One of the Malik clan," said Berger.

"We haven't had problems from them for a long time. Why does the Rav want this particular spot?"

Berger shrugged. "It's all Jewish land according to them."

Yossi spoke into his radio and summoned ambulances. He knew where this was going.

In the tense quiet of the standoff, the stone throwers had the advantage of being spread out, able to take cover behind the olive trees. But the settlers had guns. Mindless of the danger, or simply ensnared by his reverie, the Rav nodded at the man in the cab of the backhoe. When the engine coughed to life the stones came in a storm. There was no place to hide, it was as if the air itself had petrified. Several men formed a protective shield around the Rav as they rushed back to their vehicles, firing randomly. A movement caught Yossi's eye: it was Benny, charging heedlessly into the grove, squeezing off shots deliberately, lethally, seemingly untouched by the stones, even as the settlers were calling on Benny to "come back, the Rav has to be taken to a place of safety!"

The settlers' cars quickly vanished. The cops who were there for traffic control emerged from behind trees or the Rav's billboard, their guns drawn but unfired. Yossi walked into the grove. Some of the Arabs were crying "Allahu Akbar!" because there were martyrs among the mutilated trees. Yossi saw seven people down, most of them teenagers. One had been shot in the throat and was bleeding out; he was about fourteen, Yossi figured. Two more were already dead. There was nothing glorious about martyrdom; they were just bodies whose blood darkened the earth. *Perhaps now they know the truth,* Yossi thought. Soon funeral parades would convulse the city. New radicals would arise, overnight. In the morning it would begin again.

5

A Guide to the Holy City

Hebron

T he story told in Genesis is that Abraham (called Ibrahim in Arabic), the father of nations, wandered into Hebron on his journey from Ur of the Chaldees to the land of Canaan—that is, from southern Iraq to present day Palestine—sometime during the Bronze Age. He was a stranger in the land when he sought a suitable gravesite for his wife, Sarah, who died at the age of 127. With four hundred silver shekels he purchased a cave complex called Machpelah from Ephron the Hittite. The Bible notes that, at the time, another name for Hebron was Kiryat Arba. When Abraham himself died, age 175, he passed the ownership of the cave to his son Isaac, who is buried there with his wife, Rebecca, as are Abraham's grandson Jacob and his wife, Leah. The bones of Adam and Eve are also said to rest there. Kiryat Arba means "City of Four"—presumably the four couples, Adam and Eve, Abraham and Sarah, Isaac and Rebecca, Jacob and Leah—but it might also mean "City of Arba," Arba being the father of a tribe of giants that roam through the Hebrew Bible, along with Samson and Goliath.

All this Malik got from a frayed guidebook he had picked up in a used-book store in Amman. It was published in 1966, before the entire region was radically reshaped by the Six-Day War. The shelves were empty of any modern accounts of Hebron except for a useful volume by a Brit, Edward Platt, called *The City of Abraham*. But it wasn't a guidebook. Apparently there weren't enough tourists to merit one.

It is likely that Hebron was perceived as sacred long before the mythic figure of Abraham was conjured. Caves, tombs, forest groves, and high places have always evoked feelings of sanctity, mystery, and an onrush of awe. The concept of holiness may be enlisted to explain such uncanny encounters with nature. Even certain rocks and trees command reverence and accumulate legends. The Bodhi Tree in India—one of the most popular pilgrimage sites in the world—is said to be on the spot where the Buddha realized enlightenment. Hebron also had a sacred tree, the Oak of Mamre, where the Bible says Abraham pitched his tent. God and three angels came to him there and announced that Abraham's wife, Sarah, then ninety years old, would become pregnant with her first child. A Russian Orthodox shrine was erected near the oak in the nineteenth century. The legend of the tree was that when it dies the Antichrist will appear. The tree died in 1996 but the trunk remained standing until it collapsed in 2019.

Throughout their existence Hebron and Jerusalem have competed for which is the holiest, with Bethlehem a distant Christian runner-up. David Ben-Gurion, Israel's founding prime minister, had said after the 1967 war that Hebron was "more Jewish even than Jerusalem." It was the only part of the conquered West Bank he thought Israel should annex. Hebron was where Judaism was born, when God promised Abraham a land for his progeny, who would become a great nation. According to the Bible, David was anointed king of Israel in Hebron and ruled there for seven years before moving the seat of Israelite government to Jerusalem. After that, Platt observes, Hebron lost its standing and acquired the reputation of being "a home to fanatics." Malik wondered if that was the reason his father fled.

Although Hebron held the purported graves of the ancestors, Jerusalem had the Temple Mount, the center of Jewish worship, where the Ark of the Covenant once reposed. There Abraham prepared to sacrifice his favorite son to placate the Lord (for Christians and Jews, that son was Isaac, the progenitor of the Jews; for Muslims, he was Ishmael, whose descendants became the Arabs).

But Hebron still had standing as the birthplace of Judaism. Herod the Great, the Jewish Roman ruler of Judea in the first century BCE, surrounded the Cave of the Patriarchs with a wall of massive stones, two meters thick, some as long as seven meters. It became a pilgrimage site for Christians, who also considered Abraham their original ancestor. After the Muslim conquest, the Hebron temple became a mosque, although Jews were again permitted to worship there. The Crusaders turned the structure into a church and banned Muslims and Jews. Perhaps to steer some of the pilgrimage trade to Hebron, the Crusaders built the cenotaphs on the ground floor of the Cave of the Patriarchs, above the actual cave where the remains of the patriarchs were said to repose.

Over the centuries the region has been ruled by Persians, Greeks, Mamluks, Ottomans, Britain, Jordan, and Israel, but during that span of time few people have descended beneath the sanctuary into the sacred caves of Machpelah, which were jealously guarded by whichever occupying power exercised control. In 1113, a portion of the cave collapsed, and a group of Crusaders entered. They claimed to have found the remains of Abraham, Isaac, and Jacob propped against a wall. Other pilgrims also visited the crypt. Maimonides, the great Jewish philosopher and scholar, wrote in 1166, "I left Jerusalem for Hebron to kiss the tombs of my ancestors in the cave. On that day, I stood in the cave and prayed, praise be to God, for everything." Other visitors noted sepulchers in the third and farthest chamber of the cave complex. Muslim clergy began making pilgrimages to the site during the Mamluk era, including Ibn Taymiyyah, whose fundamentalist screeds haunted Islam through the centuries, eventually finding expression in Osama bin Laden.

For seven hundred years Jews were forbidden entry into the cave, allowed only to stand on the seventh step outside the massive walls and drop prayers and petitions through an opening. That changed with the Six-Day War in 1967. Moshe Dayan was the minister of defense and the author of the lightning attack that reshaped the Middle East. It began as a defensive action but events unfolded so quickly that unimagined opportunities presented themselves. Dayan was at military headquarters when he learned that Israeli troops had surrounded Jenin, the gateway to the West Bank. He turned to the other officers and said, "I know exactly what you want—to take Jenin."

"Correct!"

"So, take it!"

In that instant, the decision to seize the West Bank was made. On the fourth day of the war, Hebron fell to Israeli troops.

Malik was particularly interested in Dayan. From the moment he arrived in Israel and drove into the occupied territories, he noticed people staring at him. That wasn't unusual; the eye patch caught their attention. But there was a focus and an intensity that he hadn't encountered in New York. Several times he overheard Dayan's name muttered as they passed by, as if they had seen a ghost.

Daring and charismatic, implacable in battle, Dayan wreaked terror upon Arab communities during the 1948 war for independence: for instance, massacring more than a hundred Palestinian civilians in the village of Lydda, where present-day Ben-Gurion Airport stands. As a young soldier Dayan had lost his left eye in skirmish with Syrian forces, and his black patch—like that of Malik—made him instantly recognizable. After the war it fell to him to administer the holy places, including the Temple Mount in Jerusalem and the Cave of the Patriarchs in Hebron.

Dayan proved to be a bold overseer. In Jerusalem, he opened all the roads and bridges and took down the sniper nests so that Arabs and Jews could pass freely from one side to the other. Israeli officials warned that his decision would lead to bloodshed, but instead Arabs wandered peacefully into Zion Square and Jews into the souks. Dayan convened Islamic religious leaders in Jerusalem and conceded their right to administer the holy places.

In Hebron, however, tens of thousands of Jewish pilgrims came to worship, creating a tense situation where members of two different religions were attempting to occupy the same sacred environment. Dayan turned to Yehuda Arbel, then head of Israeli intelligence in Jerusalem and the newly conquered territories, to help work out an agreement to divide the great citadel into a mosque and a synagogue with special accommodations for each religion on important holy days.

The accounts of the few visitors over the centuries into the cave below the citadel don't match up easily—whether there were skeletons or tombs or nothing but potsherds. Arbel was seized by an idea that might resolve the mystery. At midnight on October 10, 1968, while Hebron was under curfew, he smuggled his slender thirteen-year-old daughter, Michal, into the disputed religious site in order to explore the cave complex beneath the structure. The only entry was an opening eleven inches wide—just wide enough for Michal to be lowered by rope into the dark grotto. She carried a flashlight, along with matches and a candle to determine if there was sufficient oxygen to keep her from fainting. She was the first Jew to view the site in modern times. She found three tombstones. Farther into the cave, she discovered an opening into another chamber leading to a stone staircase that would have opened into the mosque, but it was blocked by a boulder she couldn't move. In 1981, a group of Jewish settlers chiseled the boulder from above and descended the stairwell. They recovered ancient pottery and claimed to have seen human bones among the shards.

MALIK WAS A CHILD when the Oslo Accords created a process, in the 1990s, for achieving peace between Israel and the Palestinian Liberation Organization, which was headed by Yasser Arafat. With his stubble beard and military tunic, along with a black-and-white kaffiyeh wrapped around his head and carefully folded in the shape of Palestine, Arafat made himself the symbol of Palestinian liberation. Malik was just awakening to the idea that he was a Palestinian and that somehow Arafat represented him.

Arafat's promise of a Palestinian state was shadowed by a deep and destructive cynicism. He called himself a freedom fighter, but his movement often expressed itself in acts of terror. Through the connivance of Israeli businessmen close to the intelligence community, hundreds of millions of Palestinian tax dollars and foreign aid were skimmed and deposited in secret accounts held by Arafat and his cronies, much of it in Bank Leumi in Tel Aviv. Everyone knew the leadership was corrupt, and that knowledge demoralized the Palestinian people, who had no one else to turn to.

In September 1993, following the signing of the first of the Oslo Accords, President Bill Clinton corralled Arafat and Israeli premier Yitzhak Rabin into a handshake on the White House lawn, a promise that peace was on the way. The central plank of the accords was the right of Palestinians to self-determination (the accords stopped short of calling for a Palestinian state). Arafat renounced terrorism and retreated from the stated goal of the PLO to take over all of historic Palestine, settling instead for the West Bank and Gaza. In return, Israel recognized the PLO as the legitimate representative of the Palestinian people. For this, Arafat and Rabin received the Nobel Peace Prize, along with former premier Shimon Peres.

A rule of thumb in the region is that whenever peace seems near, a spoiler will arise. Extremists on both sides were inflamed and intent on destroying any compromise. In 1994, a Brooklyn doctor, Baruch Goldstein, who lived in Kiryat Arba and was a devoted follower of Meir Kahane, put on his Israeli army uniform and went through the door from the synagogue into the mosque. He murdered 29 Muslims and wounded 125 before being beaten to death. Forty days later—the traditional period of mourning in Arab society—Hamas began its campaign of suicide bombing, which would kill more than a hundred Israelis in the next three years. In November 1995 a right-wing Israeli law student, Yigal Amir, inspired by Goldstein, assassinated Rabin at a rally in Tel Aviv to support the Oslo Accords. The following year, Benjamin Netanyahu was elected to his first term as Israel's premier.

This is the backdrop to a meeting that took place in January 1997 between Arafat and Netanyahu in the middle of the night at an IDF base near Gaza. Neither man was capable of creating real peace. They were navigators of the peace process, a circular route leading nowhere. In his decades as the Palestinian leader, Arafat had proved to be a survivor, despite innumerable attempts to kill him or sideline him or render him irrelevant. Netanyahu was new in the office but not new to politics, and he would prove to be as cynical and manipulative as his Palestinian counterpart. Each had been forced into this meeting by the Americans, whose goal was to carry out one of the fundamental steps outlined by the accords: the formal return of 80 percent of Hebron to Palestinian control. This was supposed to be the prelude to more Israeli withdrawals, which would lead to "final status" talks on settlements, Jerusalem, and borders.

The protocol they signed that night divided Hebron into administrative zones. Most of the city lies in Hebron-1. Nominally ruled by the Palestinian Authority, real control of H-1 resides with Israel. Hebron-2, the official Israeli sector, includes much of the Old City—the Arab market, the Cave of the Patriarchs—and forty thousand Arabs. Far from easing the conflict in Hebron, the protocol froze it into a permanent state of hostility, which increased year by year as the population of the settlements in the region swelled and grew more radical and more demanding.

The Hebron Malik arrived in was basically a military cantonment ruled by the Israel Defense Forces, but even the IDF was constrained in its ability to control the Palestinians, whose resistance ranged from insolence to murder. The hatred of the occupied was mirrored by that of the occupiers, especially the settlers, who were largely immune to any law that the police might attempt to enforce—for instance, the killings Yossi Ben-Gal observed that morning. Stones can be fatal, so by law the settlers were protecting themselves, but they were also provoking the incident by attempting to seize the Palestinian land. No settlers would be arrested. Nor did Yossi choose to arrest the stone throwers, who could face twenty years imprisonment for the crime.

The balance of power became more lopsided when the Kahanists got into the Israeli government. The Kahanists were no longer just hooligans in the street, on the fringe of Israeli politics; now they had real power to enact the goals that the Rav and his followers advocated: mainly, annexing the West Bank and expelling the Arab population. Yossi's police department had to report to the minister of national security, Itamar Ben-Gvir, a resident of Kiryat Arba who kept a photo of Baruch Goldstein in his living room until forced to take it down in order to join the cabinet. Teenagers such as Benny Eleazar dropped out of school to join the Hilltop Youth—a movement of squatters who encroached on Arab land hoping to establish a presence that the Israeli government would recognize as a protosettlement. One day a Palestinian farmer might look upon his fields and discover a dozen tents in the middle of his grove, or vineyards that had been cut down to make space for a so-called yeshiva. "Security fences" popped up, infringing on a neighbor's land, and if not forcibly contested the fences advanced, like a vise, a gradual but unceasing form of ethnic cleansing—the stated goal of the Kahanists.

The Israeli police in Hebron nominally controlled all of H-2, but in practice there was little for them to do. Another entity, the Border Police, was authorized to manage conflicts between settlers and Palestinians, but even when squatters were chased off Palestinian property they returned. Eventually the government would make what seemed like a small concession to build a house or two, but within a year there would be a village. H-2 served as a prototype for the encroachment of Israeli settlers throughout the West Bank.

Twenty cops were assigned to the Hebron police station. They usually resided outside of Hebron, commuting from Bethlehem or Beersheba or from one of the other settlements that was not so extreme. At the end of their shift they couldn't wait to get out of Hebron. Most of them were young, recently out of the academy with no say about where they were assigned, or else they were transferred from other postings because of disciplinary problems. Hebron was not a place people asked to go. It was where they were sent.

"Help Me, Yossi!"

Hebron, Sept. 25, 2023

What a shit show," Berger said when they got back to the station. "The little bastards could have killed the Rav. Can you imagine? He's a truly holy man."

Yossi kept his thoughts to himself. There was nothing to be gained by opening a rift in the department over religious politics. The settlers and the Arabs provoked each other, and Yossi had little sympathy for either. He knew Berger lived in Kiryat Arba and was involved in the Kahanist movement, but how deeply was unclear. One could guess what he really believed. In a staff meeting he once made the case for expelling Arabs. "If you believe the Torah, God gave the land to the Jews," he said. "Case closed." Such talk came directly from Cohen, and before that from Kahane. Even if Berger wasn't a fanatic, he believed the apocalypse was near, as did many settlers. Their sole mission was to repopulate the Holy Land with Jews and bring on the End of Days.

Yossi had often worked with fundamentalists, you couldn't avoid them in Hebron. He thought they suffered from some kind of mental illness. Religious mania was different from cause-oriented fanatics, like animal-rights or climate-change activists, nothing wrong with causes so long as they didn't take over your life. But religious literalism was untethered to any reality except the word of God. Jerusalem was a beacon for zealots—latter-day Jesuses walking through the tourists on Via Dolorosa, carrying crosses, the Christians were the most conspicuous—but there were plenty of Jewish and Muslim crackpots on the streets. Ordinary people, not strong believers, might arrive in the Holy Land and suddenly be gripped with conviction that they were Jesus or King David. Such things never happened in Hebron, Yossi supposed because the city was just too dangerous and already brimming with fanatics.

At the front desk, Golda Radidowicz was taking a report from an old woman, Mrs. Telushkin, who was complaining about a lost pet, which she said had been stolen by Arabs. Golda nodded. Golda had spiky blue hair and a diamond nose ring befitting her bohemian sideline as a theater actor in Jerusalem. She had been memorizing lines for *Noises Off* when Mrs. Telushkin appeared.

"What kind of dog?" Golda asked.

"A dachshund. Very valuable." She had last seen the dog in the night when she let him out into the yard. Now he was gone. Therefore the Arabs took him. This was the kind of work the Hebron police faced every day.

The office was beginning to fill for a lunchtime staff meeting. Avi Leberman, the newest recruit, was in charge of ordering food. He had been waiting for Yossi and Berger to return to take their order. "Chicken and rice," said Yossi, not bothering to look at the menu.

"I still haven't heard from the chief to get his order," said Avi.

"He's not on the radio," Golda said.

"To hell with him, if he's not here for his own meeting," Berger growled. "I'm hungry."

"So text him," Yossi told Avi. "Show some consideration. He probably got tied up in a phone call."

Avi wandered into the staff room to use the computer. He was still getting used to the office. He was young, clever, and ambitious, and he quickly decided that working for the Israel Police in Hebron was a dead end. He had grown up watching American cop dramas such as *NYPD Blue* and *The Wire*. He affected the toughness that he saw in those characters. Basically he had the feeling everybody in the office was playing in a soap opera but he wanted to be the hero in a thriller. He dutifully texted the menu to Chief Weingarten, then spent a few minutes playing *Call of Duty* while no one was watching. An image came up on the screen that seemed at first to be part of the game, but it was a video response from Weingarten. Avi watched in confusion, then he realized what he was seeing and screamed.

Yossi rushed into the room. He found Avi standing three meters away from the computer with his mouth agape.

"What?" said Yossi.

Avi couldn't speak. He pointed at the screen, which showed Arabic writing against a black background. "What is it?" Yossi asked again.

"Start it over," Avi said, making no effort to do it himself. By now other officers had come into the room.

Yossi opened the link. It was a TikTok video. There were images of Palestinians being assaulted by police, shot and beaten, the sort of thing that happens every week, as men's voices intoned a jihadi chant called a *nasheed*. Qassam missiles launched, followed by explosions and the faces of terrified Israelis. The narrative of this video was that the heartless oppression by the Jews will be answered. Yossi knew how effective these videos were. He spoke Arabic, so he understood the words of the chant-like song:

> *Strike your awaited blow*
> *And kill the infidels as you go*
> *Our martyrs offer only grief*
> *For the armies of unbelief.*

Young Palestinians watching these images were frequently stirred to action. Incitement was the goal. It was not just that the videos were slickly produced, they were passionate, smart, and impossible to defend against.

Abruptly the *nasheed* ended and Chief Weingarten's face appeared on the screen. His eyes were wide and full of horror. A slender man stood behind him, wearing a black balaclava and sunglasses, so there was nothing useful for identification. He wore blue latex gloves.

Weingarten started to speak but his voice was warped by pain. "Help," he gasped. "Help me, Yossi, they're killing me!"

Then he made a sudden twist, perhaps an attempt to break away, but the man with the blue latex gloves grabbed him around the neck and pulled him out of the frame. The chief cried out, then went silent, save for the green flag of Hamas on the wall. Then the masked man reappeared, holding the chief's severed head toward the camera. His eyes were crossed and his tongue hung out. The killer never uttered a word.

The screen went black and the Arabic writing came on the screen. "What does it say?" Golda asked. Her voice was shaky.

"It says, 'Pick up your garbage in the Arab cemetery.'"

YOSSI DROVE DOWN Shuhada Street, which marked the boundary between H-1 and H-2, taking Avi Leberman with him and leaving Aharon Berger in charge of the station. Avi was inexperienced, but he had graduated from the police academy with decent marks and spoke some Arabic, so he might prove useful.

The handful of tourists one could usually expect were lined up at the checkpoint. Arabs weren't permitted on Shuhada Street, except in the large Islamic cemetery that ran along one side of the street and formed the boundary of the Arab sector. Yossi had never actually been in the cemetery; it had always been an invisible presence behind a high wall. He found it was a typical Muslim burial ground, with flat horizontal tombs, each oriented with the head pointed toward Mecca. Some still bore marks of desecration by settlers from several years before, "Kill the Arabs" painted on broken stones. Nothing to be proud of, but in Yossi's opinion there was trouble enough protecting the living. Acacia trees and pomegranates grew among the graves. At first glance, everything seemed in order. It took a moment to notice the figure resting on a bench in the shade fifty meters away.

Without a head the body looked like a giant sack of potatoes. Yossi pitied the absence of dignity, but war and terror had that in common, they were theaters of humiliation. He signaled to Avi to keep his distance.

Weingarten didn't deserve this, Yossi thought. He was a weak man, poorly suited for police work, or leadership, or really anything that required decisiveness. He rose in rank in part because of his inoffensiveness, but he wasn't a sycophant, and he stayed away from controversy—a wise strategy in Hebron, where disagreements have mortal consequences. There was some wisdom in making him chief, Yossi had to admit. The police had largely huddled on the sidelines under Weingarten, hewing to the shadows of the army and the intelligence services. But look where that got him.

Yossi looked around the cemetery trying to read the story of what happened here. The video suggested that the murder took place indoors, so the killers would have had to lug Weingarten's cumbersome body up the steps of the cemetery and then drag it all the way to the bench in order to stage this grotesque scene. How many? At least four strong men, one to carry each limb to hoist the body up the stairs. The soil near the bench was sandy, so there would be footprints hidden by the sparse grass. Yossi would have to get a forensics team from Jerusalem. He took a pen from his pocket and turned over some acacia fronds that appeared to be freshly broken. The day was overcast, so Yossi shined his flashlight on Weingarten's boots. The heels should be dirty if he had been dragged such a distance. They were not. That explained the wheelbarrow propped against the stone fence some distance away.

What purpose? he wondered. Why not just kill him on the side of the road and leave his body in place? Why the effort to create a larger mystery instead of some random and otherwise unimaginative act of terror? *It's all for the sensation,* Yossi thought, designed to make it seem more astonishing than what must have been a very easy murder to commit, killing an unsuspecting police official who had probably never drawn his gun.

He heard Avi being sick. "Go get yourself some water," he said.

"I'm okay."

"Then check out that wheelbarrow and see if there's any blood." He added: "Don't touch anything," he said. "There might be a bomb."

He slipped Weingarten's badge out of the chief's breast pocket and put it in the evidence bag. He noticed that his right hand was tightly clutched in a fist. He tried to pry open the chief's fingers to see if there was anything inside but it was impossible to open his hand. That was odd; there was no evidence of rigor mortis elsewhere. The body still had some warmth. He couldn't have been dead more than a few hours, probably killed just in time to prepare this display. Yossi made a silent vow to Weingarten's body that he would make his killers pay extra for the indignity they imposed.

Yossi studied the ground around the bench. He had encountered booby traps in Gaza; they could be damnably sneaky. They depended on human curiosity. One of his soldiers had been killed by a bomb in a child's backpack, triggered by a simple motion device. A bomb could be placed under the clothing of a corpse. He had seen a bomb hidden inside a gaping abdominal wound. Weingarten's boot could be holding down a trigger mechanism on a land mine. So many possibilities, but they all depended on someone like Yossi making the assumption that just because he didn't see anything suspicious, death wasn't awaiting a careless move.

He looked at the scene as he imagined a bomber would, knowing that a throng of investigators would rush to the scene, competing for evidence. They would be bumping into each other. After they took pictures, an ambulance team would lift the corpse and set it on a gurney while the cops continued to search for footprints and the track of the wheelbarrow. In that moment, if the bomber was lucky and the timing was right, he could take out at least a dozen people, maybe more. The corpse was just bait in a mousetrap.

Yossi heard the sirens and worked quickly. Avi returned. "You're right, Yossi. There were bloodstains in the cart."

"Have you ever filed an official report?" Yossi asked.

"In the academy."

"Why don't you do this one."

"Me?" Avi couldn't hide his excitement. His name would be on the report as an official investigator, a report that would be read by police and intelligence agents all over the country. *His* name.

"Make a sketch of the location of the corpse. Measure the distance from the tree and the south wall. Note the wheelbarrow."

"What about photos?"

"I'll let you know when it's safe to get closer."

While Avi was sketching, Yossi gently ran his fingers over Weingarten's garments, looking for the slightest unexpected bulge. Everything depended on the bomber's daring and skill. He brushed the chief's trousers, then gently ran his hand inside the pants' cuffs. Just above the right ankle he felt the wire.

"Avi, step back," Yossi directed. "Get behind that tombstone."

Avi's eyes got wide and he quickly retreated.

"Detonator wire running down the right leg of the victim," Yossi said. "Did you get that?"

"Yes sir."

The wire must go from the bomb to the trigger. Would that be a timer? Yossi guessed it was a motion detector, but you had to be careful. It was just as likely the bomber was watching somewhere out of sight with a detonator in his hand, waiting for the audience to fill this theater of terror. It could be set off by a call from a smartphone. Maybe a remote camera in the trees was relaying Yossi's actions. Anything you could imagine could be done these days. These devices had taken an evolutionary leap since the Iraq war and the rise of ISIS.

The wire indicated that there was a circuit, but cutting the wire might set off the explosion. Yossi traced the wire as it ran down into Weingarten's boot. He suspected that the bomb was triggered by a motion-activated switch. It would be a nasty job trying to deactivate. Try getting that boot off without blowing yourself to pieces.

Yossi heard the clatter of the Border Police in their tactical gear storming into the cemetery. They marched right up to where Yossi was kneeling beside the body, trampling whatever evidence might be underfoot, adding six new sets of footprints in the sand. "Carmi, it's a crime scene," Yossi said irritably.

Carmi, the muscular commander, paid no attention. "It's a dumping ground, Yossi. They murdered him someplace else. You know that."

"There will be clues," Yossi said. "Keep your men outside the perimeter."

"What the fuck, Yossi. This is not a cat in a tree. Border Police have jurisdiction on terror, you know that."

"We haven't decided what kind of crime it is."

"I realize it's your chief, Yossi, but let's be real." Carmi looked around. "Did you find the head?"

Three Arab men came through the graveyard from another direction. Yossi recognized Mohammed Faroud, chief of the Palestinian police. According to the protocol derived from the Oslo Accords, they had jurisdiction over Palestinian residents but weren't allowed to carry weapons or even wear a uniform. "You need permission to be on our side of the line," Mohammed said pointlessly.

"Hello, Mohammed," said Yossi. "We don't have time for diplomacy."

"Sorry about your chief," Mohammed said.

"You got the video too?"

"I guess we all did." Mohammed spat on the ground. "Why do they do such things? It was bad enough before."

"You tell me, Mohammed. They are your people not ours."

"We don't agree to cutting heads, Yossi. This is not the work of Hamas."

Yossi thought that was possibly true. Someone went to a lot of work to make this crime distinctive. Even the kids in Lions' Den were more respectful murderers. This was a signature killing. So far mysteriously without demands or anyone claiming credit. Probably ISIS copycats.

"Keep your people off the streets," Carmi warned Mohammed. "It's going to get ugly."

Yossi saw the soldiers enter the cemetery, trailing a solitary female figure, a civilian, recognizable even at a distance, tall, shoulders back, her face used to command, impossible to surprise or impress. Her hair was cut at a rude angle, long on the left side and short on the right, at once harsh and stylish. Yossi admired Tamar Levin in the way he might appreciate the qualities of a lioness, tough and impassive. She was no house cat, that was for sure. "We're taking charge," she said, meaning Shin Bet, the domestic intelligence force, informally known as Shabak. It was a simple statement of fact.

Carmi and Mohammed instantly deferred to her.

"Tamar, we'll sweep the city, pick up the hotheads, see what we can shake out," Carmi said.

Tamar nodded; this went without saying. "Sorry for your loss, Yossi," she said. "Did you find the head?"

"Not yet."

A group of Orthodox Jews wearing high-visibility yellow vests and carrying nylon body bags arrived. They were ZAKA. Their mission was to pick up every bit of human tissue and each drop of blood so that Jewish bodies could be buried—if not intact, at least as close to being whole as possible. They were invaluable during the suicide bombings, where they sorted out body fragments according to DNA, but they were also a menace to a proper police investigation.

"Tamar, we think the body should go to Abu Kabir," said Yossi, mentioning the forensic institute in Tel Aviv.

"To determine the cause of death?" Tamar said dryly. "I don't think we need an autopsy for that. But under the circumstances you can take charge of the corpse. I'm happy to let you deal with the widow. Especially this one." She paused and looked at him curiously. "This isn't a *crime*, Yossi. It's not like Agatha Christie. It's terror. You know it. Other rules apply." It was true that no one treated terrorist incidents as crimes; they fell more into the category of warfare.

"Just to understand the details, Tamar. To study their technique, their habits."

"Leave such matters to the professionals," she said brusquely. "You are more likely to get in the way than to help. We need a clear field of play." Then she turned and addressed the whole group. "The prime minister will be calling as soon as he hears the news. I can tell you what he'll say. He will want an arrest instantly, before the crazies get out of hand. Don't be too nice about it. Everything comes to me, is that understood? You too, Mohammed. If there's a new group in town, somebody looking to get on television, let me know at once. I want names and coordinates. Major Shihab will coordinate the raids with Carmi." Shihab was a member of the Druze sect, which was trusted by the Israeli security establishment. "This begins now. I want a massive presence in the city. Make it quick and clean. Get their phones before they can wipe them. If you don't find who you're looking for, take his family. I don't want the arrests to be the story, so *no incidents*. And somebody better find the head. This is going to be an issue."

Yossi noticed that Tamar's eyes were clouded by worry, but as soon as he saw it, the expression was replaced by her usual stern visage. She looked accusingly at Yossi, as if she had caught him peeking in her window.

"Confiscate the corpses of those killed in the olive grove this morning," she told him. "We may need to make a trade. Anyway, we don't want to see them parading their bodies through the streets. Everybody needs to cool off. Okay, we'll take it from here."

"Tamar, one thing," said Yossi.

"What, Yossi?" Like she was granting him a favor.

"Be careful of the bomb."

Everyone froze for an instant and then tentatively backed away.

"How do you know?" Tamar asked distrustfully.

"It's wired down his leg."

"Shit." Tamar motioned to the soldiers to move farther back, then she turned again to Yossi. "Do you know where the package is?"

"Likely it's under his boot."

Tamar's mouth made a sideways adjustment as she looked to the dark clouds.

7

"I Want Them to Suffer"

Kiryat Arba, Sept. 25, 2023

Miriam Weingarten was attired in black, posing theatrically on the stairway when Yossi arrived, as if any more drama were needed to underscore her rage. The immediate target of her anger was her dead husband.

"Why? Why, Yossi?" she demanded. "He trusted those people and look at what they did to him."

"You know what they are," said Yossi. "Animals."

"He was a fool and he left me alone." This despite the five children who followed her as she descended the stairs and ushered Yossi into the living room.

She was still an imposingly beautiful woman, Yossi thought, although the years had hardened her face to reflect the imperiousness of her nature. She sat on the couch, her children arrayed behind her, four daughters and a son. Yossi had known the younger ones since they were toddlers. Their faces were ashen, the girls slack-jawed, their eyes wandering in shock. Menachem, the oldest, looked as if he would explode in righteous fury. Miriam was harder to read. If it weren't for the pallor and the torn collar on her black dress he wouldn't know she was in mourning. Her hair was perfect, her voice even. She was ever in command.

Yossi remained standing as Miriam hadn't indicated that he should sit.

"I have a request, Miriam. In homicides, we usually require an autopsy."

"Why desecrate the body even more?" she said. "It's sinful. You know our stance on that."

"It's up to you. I don't like to leave steps undone."

"They will claim credit, they always do. They don't only confess, they boast. And they will kill again and again, as long as they can."

"What can I do, Miriam? We don't know who did this. Maybe they will make themselves known as you suggest. But until then, we are in the dark. We can't wait for them to do our work for us."

"Ask your questions," she said dismissively.

Yossi glanced at the children again, wondering if they should be present, but the girls seemed too traumatized to register what was going on.

"When was the last time you saw him?"

"This morning. He made breakfast. He was a good cook, whatever his other failings."

"What time did he leave?"

"Before eight, like every day."

"Did he say anything about his plans?"

"He told me he had a meeting at the synagogue," she said. "You know he was not religious, so I wondered."

"Do you know who he was to meet? What it was about?"

Miriam turned to her children and said, "Give us some privacy."

The four girls nodded, relieved to be dismissed, but Menachem remained. He was tall and handsome, the opposite of his father in crucial ways, being hard and extreme like his mother and physically impressive. He had done his military service and worked in an architecture firm in Jerusalem, but he was devoted to the same expansionist ideology as Miriam; it was a family trait.

"You also, Menachem," Miriam said sternly.

"I have a right to hear this," he said, but Miriam gave him a look. Yossi could imagine what it would be like to be raised by such a mother. Even this prideful young man bowed to her. "It's a mistake, Mama," he said meekly as he left.

Miriam waited until the door was closed. "Jacob never talked about the job. He did say he would be home late, so I should not wait for dinner."

"Any idea where he was going?"

"I don't want to say what I think," Miriam said. Her lips pressed tightly together in a thin straight line as if holding a door closed against an intruder.

"It's better to tell me than to wait for me to find out."

Yossi discreetly averted his gaze as Miriam weighed this. The room was small, more of a parlor than a full-sized living room. They didn't do much entertaining. The pictures on the wall were prints of Old Masters that Miriam probably bought online. The drapes were frayed. A window looked out on an unkempt lawn. Yossi couldn't bear disorder in his own house, so he made certain judgments.

"He was weak," Miriam said. "Especially with women."

This was well-known, despite Weingarten's attempts at discretion. "What makes you think he was meeting a woman?"

"He was spending time away. He said he was working, but he never worked like that before, often at night, who knows where he was. Naturally I became suspicious. I looked through his desk and found a diary."

"He wrote in it?"

"No, it was intended as a gift. The cover was decorated with flowers. Something for a girl. And when I heard the news, I looked for it, but it was gone." She gave Yossi a hard look. "You know, Jacob never liked you."

Yossi nodded. He knew that.

"He used to say that all those years you spent in the army, the fighting in Gaza, made you too brutal."

"Someone has to do the dirty work," said Yossi. "But we respected each other."

"He was too trusting," said Miriam. "His fatal flaw."

"He lived in a different world than we do. Maybe a better one, at least he thought so."

An unexpected sob suddenly leaped from Miriam's throat. "Promise me, Yossi," she said. "Find his killers. I want them to suffer."

"If they thought killing Jacob would make us relent, they made a mistake," said Yossi. "They should have killed me instead."

Miriam nodded. A groan erupted from some deep place. "And find the head, Yossi," she said in a voice scarcely above a whisper. "Jacob can not be buried without it."

8

The Presence of Absence

Hebron, Sept. 25, 2023

Malik checked in at the Abu Mazen Hotel in the Arab part of Hebron, walking distance from the Old City. It was a midlevel business hotel like so many Malik knew in the Middle East, eccentrically decorated with inlaid marble, affecting a grandeur it was far from achieving, and patronized largely by Chinese and Gulf Arabs. A large curving staircase dominated the lobby, which was filled with faux-leather couches beneath a distant chandelier. On each coffee table was a box of Kleenex. Malik was no snob about interior design; he just felt out of place, trapped in someone else's aesthetic.

From his window, Malik had an overview of the dense, white-stoned city, the offices six or seven stories high, and the green hills framing the horizon. He was tired but too hungry to eat. With a single glance at the spiritless dining-room, chairs draped in purple fabric with pleated skirts like school dresses, he decided to go elsewhere for food.

Evening was falling; the city softened and lights were blooming. Hebron in the sunset seemed at peace, one of the lies the city has been telling itself for millennia. There must have been brief gaps in history when a strifeless Hebron made an illusory appearance, like a mirage. It was nearly October and the summer heat was just now beginning to release its grip.

He walked down Namera Street in the evening gloom. Malik

hadn't checked in yet with his relatives; he needed a night to collect himself and get his bearings. Besides, he had the assignment to meet with the police chief, which had taken place earlier in the day. He should make some notes before that went entirely out of his mind.

Malik had trained himself in the art of seeing what was missing. The presence of absence, they called it at the academy. A few young couples walked by, one pushing a baby stroller. No dogs. In most non-Muslim countries Malik had been in, people would be walking their pets, but a hadith in Islam condemned the animals because of their saliva. Also absent was the sensuality so casually displayed on Western boulevards. Nearly all the women wore hijabs and long dresses, and the men were also modestly attired, with long-sleeved shirts even in the heat.

There was an acceptable spot that billed itself as the Ottoman Restaurant. A spit of lamb slowly rotated beside the door, the chef standing by with his long flat knife ready to shave off the bits of meat. The smell immediately kindled Malik's appetite. The best thing about the Middle East was the food.

It was time for the evening meal but the place was practically empty. Another absence. A waiter brought him a liter bottle of water. The waiter seemed anxious. "Please, mister, we close soon. If you order it should be ready at once."

Malik ordered the shawarma sandwich with fries and hummus, then turned his attention to the television on the wall, which was showing an Al Jazeera news broadcast. A man's face appeared. He looked familiar. It took a moment for Malik to realize that the man on the screen was Chief Weingarten.

Malik walked closer to the set so he could hear.

". . . headless body found in Hebron's Old City . . ."

Malik's brain raced to keep up with the fact that he had met this man before lunch, and he was dead by dinner.

". . . Israeli government spokesman accused Hamas of . . ."

Malik listened for the claim of credit for the murder, but none was coming. That was odd. Such a spectacular crime was usually followed by chest-thumping boasts. Instead the accusation hung in the air. Look for what you cannot see.

He heard the sound of heavy trucks. Suddenly the restaurant went dark. A metal screen slammed shut over the entry, and the shawarma chef switched off the broadcast.

"Sorry, sir, not safe outside now," the waiter said as he brought a candle to Malik's table. "Please wait with us until the Israelis leave. Meantime here is your dinner."

THE NIGHT WAS FULL of raids by the Israel Defense Forces in downtown Hebron and surrounding villages. The IDF soldiers were brisk and efficient. By now the drill was perfected. They arrived in Humvees and armored personnel carriers, with drones watching from above. They blocked traffic so no one could come in or get out. Cellphone transmission was jammed. The building where the targeted persons lived would be sealed off, front and back, so there was no possible escape. The only choices were surrender or certain death. The response to resistance was brutal and unforgiving. That night ten Palestinians were killed and one Israeli soldier was wounded. After the army rounded up their targets they were handcuffed and hooded and thrown into the back of an armored personnel carrier, then whisked off to a detention center in Jerusalem, where the police would finally be brought in to make the arrests, a pure formality. Meantime, the houses of the detainees were blown up and their families cast into the streets.

That evening the entire Hebron police force gathered in the squad room. They were shaken. Keeping peace between the settlers and the Arab townspeople was always tricky. Many on either side hated the cops and longed for the day when peacekeepers departed and all-out violence could have its way once and for all.

The naked disrespect the killers had shown for the beleaguered cops on the hill had its effect. Fear clouded the eyes of everyone in the room. Yossi had to break the spell, and the way to do that was to be as professional as possible—brisk, efficient, all business. He wrote out a basic checklist on a blackboard in the squad room—work your sources, look out for strangers, check rental cars and hotels, and so on. He divided the tasks among the team. There weren't nearly enough officers to do the job properly.

"Did anybody see the chief this morning?" he asked.

A sergeant raised his hand. "I didn't see him, but his cruiser was parked at the bus stop in front of Kiryat Arba."

"What time was that?"

"Around eight. It was gone when I passed by before lunch."

"Did the chief have plans in Jerusalem, Tel Aviv, Beersheba? Anybody know? And why would he take the bus?"

The officers stared blankly. Then Avi said, "Sometimes it's easier to take the bus than to try to park in Jerusalem."

"The bus is safer," Golda added. Vehicles on the main road are frequent targets of stone throwers. The armored buses are old and worn and the windows are practically opaque but they still offer the best protection. Just the week before, Palestinian gunmen had fired on an Egged bus, but no one was harmed.

"Okay, let's find that cruiser. Golda, check the bus schedules and see where Weingarten might have gone early this morning. Berger, go over the security video at the Cave of the Patriarchs. Take Avi," he added.

Berger glanced at Avi, the new guy, the last person he wanted to team up with.

"Ride in pairs," Yossi ordered. "This town can explode at any time. Our job is to work fast and concentrate on the investigation."

"Won't the terrorists who did it be long gone?" asked Golda.

"We don't know what their plans are but we have to assume that they will strike again. Anything you learn, tell me immediately."

"I thought Shabak was in charge," Berger said.

"Shabak will do what it will do," said Yossi. "We don't interfere, but we don't disappear. This is our case, no matter what anyone says."

9

Sara

Kfar Oren, Sept. 25, 2023

Yossi drove out of Hebron on the Bypass Road. He was troubled by many things but above all by Chief Weingarten calling out his name—"Help me, Yossi, they're killing me!"—those words haunted him. Jacob had turned to him in the last instant of life; that had to be honored.

They had been competitors, not friends. Yossi, a soldier for nearly two decades and a cop for fifteen years, brought the experience. He was not particularly skilled, he knew that. His talent was doggedness. He would puzzle over cases long after other investigators had walked away. Among old-timers in the office, he was remembered for solving a crime that had already been solved—the theft of weapons from the IDF base in Hebron by Israeli soldiers that were then sold to Arabs. The IDF had been embarrassed by a series of similar thefts from armories by its own soldiers, a national disgrace. The publicity was horrible, so closing the case at once was a priority. A Palestinian man who bought the arms testified to the guilt of a young officer from Jaffa. The witness got a mild sentence and the young soldier was given seven years. No doubt a deal was made. A year passed. Yossi arrested a settler for money laundering. During a search, he found an IDF weapon that he traced to the Hebron base. It turned out the weapons theft was still going on. The perpetrators had simply bought off the witness. It took another year for the wrongly convicted soldier to be released. Yossi never got credit for the case; the IDF seized control of it and kept it out of the news, but in the police station Yossi was looked upon with new eyes. It was the kind of detective work they longed to do and so rarely got the chance.

Weingarten might have been more generous about it, but he was a political man in a way that Yossi would never be. He congratulated Yossi but there were no awards, no public acknowledgments. It was more important to placate the army, the politicians, Shabak, Mossad—so many entities would be tarnished by the scandal and others by the cover-up that Weingarten kept quiet. Yossi understood, but it annoyed him. Then, at the last moment of his life, the chief begged Yossi for help. If the situation had been reversed—if Yossi were the one with the knife at his throat—it would never have occurred to him to beseech Jacob Weingarten to come to his aid. "Help me, Yossi!"—what could that possibly mean? The chief was far beyond help when he uttered those words. He would have known that the police would be waved off the investigation by higher authorities. Maybe it was Yossi's doggedness he was appealing to.

Other people would be far more obvious candidates for assassination than Weingarten. Yossi, for one. He had a long reputation, going back to his IDF days, of being bloody and cruel. During the First Intifada, when soldiers were ordered to break the arms of the stone throwers, Yossi was a young officer; he could have ordered his subordinates to do the deed, but on at least a dozen occasions he personally broke the arms of teenage boys. He would have one soldier hold the boy and the strongest soldier he could find stretch the boy's arm over a boulder. Then Yossi slammed a large stone on the forearm. This was done with the boy's palm facing down so both the ulna and the radius were broken. Some of the boys would never heal properly. One of the stone throwers was defiant. He didn't scream when his bones cracked; instead, he spit in Yossi's face. Yossi broke his other arm.

He didn't deceive himself. Those boys he wounded so brutally would become the leaders of Hamas.

As soon as he was outside the city limits Yossi entered Area A, the portion of the West Bank run by the Palestinian Authority, including Bethlehem, Nablus, Ramallah—the main cities in the West Bank, about 18 percent of the total territory, none of it contiguous. Area B, which comprised 22 percent of the West Bank, was jointly administered by Israel and Palestine, but in practice was totally controlled by Israel. Nearly three million Palestinians lived in areas A and B—separate atolls adrift in Israeli-controlled Area C, which was everything else, the largest of the three divisions of the West Bank.

Yossi lived in a small rural settlement, Kfar Oren, in Area C, near a nature preserve in the Negev, several kilometers from the Dead Sea. He cherished the quiet. He had a garden and an orange grove. The air from the Dead Sea smelled sour, but when the wind shifted it brought cool Mediterranean breezes. From the rise where his settlement stood he could see the Kingdom of Jordan. Egypt and Saudi Arabia were only a couple hundred kilometers away. Closer by was the village of At-Tuwani—mainly Arab and Bedouin shepherds and farmers, many living in caves. Such an odd country, he thought, empty but intimate, serene but dangerous.

Yossi liked to putter around in the region digging for artifacts. Among the treasures he unearthed were Byzantine potsherds and a spear point from the Neanderthal era. Nearby an expedition sponsored by Hebrew University found a comb used for head lice with an inscription in the language of the Canaanites. There was an unending hunt for anything that would legitimize the Jewish claim on the land that the Bible said was promised to Abraham and his descendants. Despite the legend of Abraham, Isaac, Jacob, and their wives being buried in the Cave of the Patriarchs, there was no evidence of their actual existence. The same was true of Noah and Joshua and Moses and all the major figures of the Old Testament and the Torah except for King David. There is a basalt fragment from the ninth century BCE inscribed in Aramaic that mentions the House of David, and disputed ruins from the same period that could be a part of a modest Davidian empire or could be Canaanite.

Archaeology was frequently used as an excuse to displace Palestinians. There was a dig in Tel Rumeida, adjoining the Old City of Hebron, where, some believe, King David's palace once stood. The only result of that dig was the removal of Palestinians from the neighborhood and their replacement by settlers. A synagogue from the Second Temple period (the early Roman era) was uncovered in the region near Yossi's home, which gave the government the authority to expel the Arabs. Settlers rushed in, planting vine stems

in an appearance of cultivation, which was another way they justified expropriation of Palestinian land. Arabs kept creeping back
to their homes and their caves, despite the ongoing harassment,
which included polluting the Arabs' wells and poisoning their livestock. Nobody restrained the settlers from such attacks, certainly
not the police. In Yossi's opinion, it was all about politics, nothing
that should concern him. It did trouble him, though, that this brutal
campaign was waged against people who were living in caves.

He usually didn't mind the isolation, but his daughter, Sara, was
visiting, taking a break from classes at France's famed Sciences Po
to work on her dissertation. They had less than two weeks together
and Weingarten's murder was bound to blow up their plans.

Sara wasn't in the house when he arrived. Yossi assumed she was
out for a run, usually the first piece of business in her homecoming,
running the wadis and the sandstone ridges, so far from the urbanity
of Paris. Sara was a child of the desert; it was as native to her as it
was to the Bedu.

On the counter he saw a note: "Protesting. Quiche in the fridge or
you can wait for me."

Yossi removed his gun and stored it on a shelf in the coat closet,
then had a shower. He wasn't surprised that as soon as Sara returned
to Israel she leapt into the demonstrations. Half of Israel was protesting against the government's attempt to take over the judiciary
in an effort to consolidate power among settlers and ultra-Orthodox
who backed the Netanyahu coalition. The backlash had begun in
January with a few thousand protestors taking to the streets after
the administration presented a plan to strip the power of the courts.
Week by week the protests grew, from tens of thousands to hundreds of thousands, moving from Tel Aviv to Jerusalem, Haifa, and
Beersheba. The entire country was in revolt—pointlessly, in Yossi's
opinion. He had long since soured on politics. Netanyahu and the
settlers were unmovable. Israel, which had been at war or near to
it with its neighbors since its beginning, was turning on itself. Was
civil war possible? Such thoughts were being uttered out loud and
in the newspapers. *Maybe we can't live without our enemies,* Yossi
mused.

On the other hand, even a cynic like Yossi recognized that this was at a time when enduring peace suddenly seemed possible. Saudi Arabia had signaled that it was open to recognizing Israel—a development that could eventually bring the entire Arab world to the peace table. Yossi never thought he would see a deal between Israel and the kingdom unless the Palestinians' extreme demands were met. After decades of negotiation there was still no peace, but the Palestinian problem had been reduced to a nuisance. Arab leaders were done with them and ready to move on.

Maybe now they would accept their defeat.

SARA CAME IN, talking on her phone and laughing. Her laugh was rich and musical and it immediately made Yossi smile. While she finished her conversation he made cocktails and waited on the patio, watching the sunset begin its big show.

Sara was the only person who still made Yossi feel loved. Soon she would be back to her beautiful life in Paris after her break, and Yossi would return to the grinding existence he had grown accustomed to. He was exhilarated by her visit but dreaded the moment she left—the penalty for his happiness.

Five years ago his life was different. Leah was alive. All the graces that Yossi lacked she embodied. It was Leah who attracted friends, who cared about art and travel, who added delight to his existence. She labored at keeping Yossi from slipping into the hard place where history had steered him. She made him believe that happiness was possible, even for him. Her death plunged him into a depression from which he never recovered. His desperation migrated into bitterness.

In her last years Leah concentrated on taking care of everyone before she died. She had been ill for so long, fighting breast cancer, which left her weak and mutilated but determined to survive until Sara turned eighteen and graduated from high school. For her, that was the finish line. She wanted the two people she loved to survive her death not just united in mourning but thriving in a loving relationship.

That meant getting Sara launched into adulthood. Leah hid her suffering behind a mysterious access of joy, especially in the final months as she was preparing Sara for her new life abroad that was also a life without her mother. She wanted Sara to set aside the grief that underscored the love they felt for each other, but Sara obstinately refused to leave her mother's side. So Leah set her free. She entered the hospital eight days before Sara was scheduled to report to school. She confided to Yossi, "It's a perfect time to die."

And she did.

Yossi had been a bigger challenge. Leah would have played matchmaker for him if he had let her, but he was stubborn and had no interest in pursuing other relationships. His love life ended with Leah. There had been ruptures in their marriage, but the stupendous fact of Leah's oncoming death overrode all that. Those were unexpectedly precious years together, which made her passing even harder.

There was one lingering mystery about Leah. In her final years she turned to religion for comfort, as many do, but the source of her comfort was Immanuel Cohen. The Rav was kind to her. Neither Sara nor Yossi detected anything cynical in his ministrations. He visited often when she was bedridden. "Life doesn't die," he assured her. "Your body will die but your life will continue." The two of them would talk for an hour or more, until Leah's strength ran out. When she died, the Rav recited the prayer for the soul of the departed.

It was not something that Sara and Yossi spoke about. They recognized the fanaticism that the Rav embodied; they also saw the compassion he displayed to the person they loved most. Their understanding of the Rav was affectionately influenced by this experience.

The vacancy that Leah's death caused in Yossi's life would never be filled, but the emptiness did become normal. His existence was smaller. He was stoic by nature, but not invulnerable. He recognized that Leah was right that Sara needed to start a new life, away from the associations of her mother's illness and the pathology of Hebron—but the simultaneous loss of both women in his life left him bereft. He was incapable of filling the emotional space with new sources of love. Instead, he walled himself off and became formidable—except with Sara, who instantly brought him back to life, like water on a wilting plant.

When she came out on the patio, her mood was changed. "Oh,

Abba, I just heard. What awful news!" She sat in the lounge chair and put her hand on his arm. Other than a few handshakes it was the first time he had been touched in months. "You must be going crazy, although you never do, but still. It's terrifying, Abba. I'm worried about you."

"Worry about the killers, they're the ones whose bones should be shaking."

Sara nodded, expecting just such a demurral. In her entire life, she had never seen her father betray a trace of fear, despite living constantly under mortal threat. "Don't pass it off like that. It's scary. Those poor children, they'll be haunted by this ghastly image of their father. And you act like there's no reason to be concerned. Think about what it would be like for me if something happened to you. I'd be devastated! But you never talk about it."

Sara admired his courage, which was so much a part of his nature that it seemed no great achievement. It was a role, she knew. He erected a barricade against sentiments others would feel in his place. His stoicism was wildly at odds with the French intellectuals in Sara's Parisian circle—so censorious and full of themselves, always quick to condemn Israel, which was their right. But she couldn't imagine them carrying the moral burden that her father did, existing in the contradiction that history had imposed on the Israelis, victims with blood on their hands, constantly having to weigh justice against survival.

All that said, Sara was viscerally opposed to the occupation. She rarely spoke about politics with her father. Invariably, it turned into a subtle attack on who he was, although that was never her intention. She saw him as a good man carrying out a morally indefensible job that was also essential to protecting the lives of Israeli citizens. Her real anger was at the government.

"Tell me about your day," Yossi said, changing the subject. "You went to Jerusalem?"

"Tel Aviv. It was hilarious."

"Please tell me."

"I'm not sure you'd find it funny. You remember Sasha, my gay Russian friend from school? He got married with maybe fifty other couples in front of the rabbinate court. We had a giant pink chuppah. It was so much fun, just seeing thousands and thousands of people trying to bring real justice to this country, not the kind Bibi and his crowd are trying to impose. I can see by your expression you don't agree."

"I haven't got any patience for the current government, you know that."

"It's getting so much worse! The fanatics are taking over. We're asking for equality for all Israeli Jews—women, gays, seculars, maybe one day for Arabs too—and most of our society is on our side. I'm hopeful, really for first time since . . ." Her eyes searched the reddening sky. "I don't know, maybe for the first time. It's historic, Abba, you need to pay attention. And don't tell me you're opposed to Sasha getting married or we will have a real argument."

"He's not really married."

"You're impossible."

"Did an Orthodox rabbi officiate the ceremony?"

"Why should they be the only ones to decide who's a Jew and who's not, or who can get married—officially—and who has to pretend to be something they're not? Anyway, you don't believe that, you're just being obstinate. I know you're not happy with the Haredis avoiding military service and enjoying all those government subsidies. It's like we're sliding into Taliban rule—at least, the direction we have been going—but these demonstrations are giving me hope." She paused, then added, "I'm sorry. You've had a shocking experience. You don't need a political lecture."

"You knew him too."

"Not that well. You guys didn't socialize and Mom didn't have the energy. One time he came to sing at my high school. That was odd. His wife is something else."

"Wasn't Menachem in your class?"

Sara shivered. "He's strange. He did once ask me for a date and I had to invent an excuse. It would have been awkward anyway, me dating your boss's son."

Yossi topped up his drink, then offered a toast. "Jacob," he said as they clinked glasses. He had never called Weingarten by his given name in life.

"I felt sorry for him," said Sara. "It was like he walked into the wrong family." She sank into a thought. "It was such a glorious day up until I heard the news, and naturally I'm worried about you. But you make it hard to worry about you."

"I don't want you to worry about me."

"But I should. You pretend everything is under control, but it's not, really. I always have the feeling that something awful is about to happen. Even in the protest, it was exciting, but you could tell that it could go chaotic. I guess that's part of what made it thrilling, being so on the edge. But there's something in the air. Like a feeling that there's somebody out there—" she pointed to Yossi's orange trees that were vanishing into the shadows. "You don't see them yet. But one day everything will turn upside down. Anything could happen. Don't you feel it?"

"I'm hungry," Yossi said.

Sara laughed. "Okay, enough proselytizing. I'll heat up the quiche."

While Sara was in the kitchen, Yossi got a call from Berger. "We found something," he said. "Can you come in? We're at the cave."

"On my way," said Yossi regretfully.

Sara looked up. "You're not going to eat?"

"Later. I'll make this quick. But don't wait on me."

"I'll miss you, Abba. Be safe."

He embraced her. "I wouldn't do this if it weren't really important."

"I know that."

He got his pistol out of the coat closet, then set a Glock on the kitchen counter.

"Stay close. You know how to use this so don't be shy. If you hear something, call security and be ready." He looked at her anxiously. "It's started again," he said.

SARA TOOK A SLICE of the quiche and sat on the patio. Then she went back inside and got the gun. She thought how Israel demanded an allegiance few other countries could match. Even when she hated it, as she often did, nowhere else did she feel so full of life and guilt, the old Jewish paradox. There was a photo beside her father's bed of his parents, both Holocaust survivors. Sara had grown up with them. That history was still so close. Her grandparents were Lithuanian Jews who didn't speak Hebrew; it wasn't a living language when they were born. A whole language was brought back into existence, a language she adored. For that alone, Israel was a triumph. But it also exacted a moral cost no matter who you were. She used to feel that she had a reason to be Israeli. Back then, there was a peace movement. There was a left. Sara still subscribed to the principles that her mother had taught her. People like Sara and Leah were once seen as pragmatists, trying to work out an accommodation that would open a space for Israel to exist with its neighbors. Then she and the shrinking circle she belonged to were labeled idealists. They were irrelevant, the new consensus declared; they lived in fantasyland. And now they were increasingly called traitors. Each time Sara returned to Israel she felt more alone and isolated.

Paris was supposed to be a refuge; that is what her mother promised. But her identity there was fraught. In some ways, she felt more Jewish, more Israeli in France than in Israel. She couldn't wait to come home, but when she was home she couldn't wait to get away. The whole idea of home was losing meaning to her. Home would be the place she felt accepted, where others believed as she did, or at least allowed her to think her own thoughts. She wondered if she would ever be home again.

She startled at a sound nearby and reached for the Glock, feeling foolish but also on edge. Suddenly she laughed. A large, strange bird, a hoopoe, landed on the stone wall next to her, where Yossi had set out some seeds. It was the silliest creature, with white-striped blue wings and an outsized orange crest, tipped in black, like some kind of avian rapper. The Torah specified that the hoopoe was not kosher, which Sara didn't doubt, but every time she saw one she was filled with pleasure at the absurdity of creation. The hoopoe likes to bathe in the dirt and will spend hours with its head flung back, sunning itself. It excretes a foul-smelling liquid that makes it repulsive to predators. As she watched, the hoopoe flew off awkwardly into the gloaming. It was never designed to fly well, or really do anything except scoop insects off the ground or from the crevices of trees. *But it has survived in this harsh land since the prophets of old*, she thought. *And so will we.*

She set the gun down. *So much of Israel is a contradiction,* she thought. *Yes, it was a miracle, the salvation of the Jewish people, but in the process we have imposed our history on another people, with the ghettos, the diaspora, the pogroms—one victimized people subjugating another, helplessly, unable to stop ourselves.* In that instant, alone in the dark, Sara had a sudden flash of identity, like an unexpected reflection in a window. To be Israeli was to acknowledge the implacable darkness of human nature. It was to know the feeling of a weapon in your hand and to be ready to kill without hesitation.

10

Fanon

Paris, Fall 2022

In her second semester at Sciences Po, Sara had enrolled in a class taught by a noted scholar of colonialism, Léo Brisard. He was Sara's adviser for her doctoral dissertation. He had made his reputation writing about the French-Algerian war, and for more than twenty years he had taught the same subject, relying on his scornful account of the conflict, *Le Prix de l'orgueil* (translated into English as *Backlash*), which spelled out the consequences of colonialism on the occupying power. It was admittedly more about France than Algeria. Brisard had a burst of scholarly renown when the book was first published in 1987, then became a familiar presence on French talk shows following the series of terror attacks in Paris in 2015, which he saw as the enduring afterlife of France's colonial adventure. He advocated a brutal response to the Islamic State, which had claimed credit for the bombings, and forceful policing of the immigrant (largely Muslim) population of France. At that time he joined the faculty of Sciences Po.

The class was held in a faded, ill-lit room on the third floor of the original campus on rue Saint-Guillaume. On that first day the room was less than half full, Brisard having fallen out of favor with the left in recent years. He had never been fully embraced by the right, despite his truculent attacks on French foreign policy. He was no longer a figure of controversy and was regarded as a dusty academic with only one song to sing.

Stooped and gray, wearing a tweed sport coat that had been made for the larger man he once was, Professor Brisard entered the class with his worn copy of *Le Prix de l'orgueil* under his arm, prepared to recite his same lectures from decades past. He set the book down on the lectern and finally noticed that someone had written in bold block letters on the blackboard:

"VIOLENCE IS MAN RE-CREATING HIMSELF."

"What a choice bit of propaganda," he said cheerfully, as he reached for the chalk eraser.

A dark young man in the back of the class stood up and boldly walked to the lectern, physically nudging Brisard aside. "You have been teaching a course that misrepresents the true nature of colonialism," he declared. "This year we will teach *you*." Four other students suddenly stood, three men and a woman, arms crossed, scowling. Two of the men and the woman appeared to be Arab. Sara thought the other student was either Indian or Pakistani (he turned out to be from Bangladesh). The remaining students looked about in confusion. At first Sara thought this must be an enactment designed to make the course appear relevant. This notion was supported by the bemused expression on Brisard's face.

"So, Professor," Brisard teased the young man at the lectern, "who may you be?"

"I am a colonized person."

"Can you favor us with a name?"

"Redha Brahimi."

He was an attractive young man, Sara thought, dramatic and slight, his hair black and glistening, roughly cropped but stylish, with a lock falling over his forehead. His eyelashes were so long and dark one might think he used mascara. Sara's French was not so fluent that she could pinpoint accents, but she guessed he was North African.

Brisard turned to the class. "I assume you know the quote—" he began.

Redha cut him off. "You must raise your hand to ask questions or make remarks," Redha said. "You are no longer in charge of this class."

There were about thirty other students in the room who were in various states of confusion or amusement, but there was also gathering hostility—both to Brisard and the usurpers. Two students walked out of the room, but Sara remained, fascinated by the unlikely drama that was unfolding in a classroom at the end of the hall on a warm September day.

"The quote is from Frantz Fanon," Brisard said, refusing to yield. "It comes from *Les Damnés de la terre—The Wretched of the Earth* in English—and it is responsible for more bloodshed than any other publication in the last hundred years."

"If you wish to stay in the class, you must take a seat with the other students," Redha said. "Or you can just leave."

Two of Redha's allies came forward to enforce his demand, grasping the old man by either arm. Brisard looked at them aghast. He wrenched free, then slammed his book on the lectern. "Here is your text," he said. Then, to the class, he added, "I am sorry for you. I really did hope to teach you something." In the silence that followed the students could hear the professor's footsteps as he walked down the hallway.

Redha stood at the lectern uncertainly as the woman in his group passed out a syllabus. It referenced works by Ali Shariati, B. R. Ambedkar, and Emma Goldman, but Fanon was at the top of the list.

Sara raised her hand. "I understand that you want to make a political statement," she said, "but most of us in this class need the course credit for our degree. Do you have the authority to do that?"

Redha looked at her with a stern glance that softened as he took her in. "Sister, we are not interested in credit but in education," he said.

"Then you are stealing the money we paid for this course."

Other students loudly agreed. "Take your protest out on the street," said a stocky German exchange student who didn't appear to be intimidated by the activists.

The discussion quickly became heated. The passionate insurgents had not considered a counterrevolution by the remainder of the class, but students were standing, waving their hands, their voices trembling with anger. "I feel like you are the occupiers of our classroom," a French woman said. "You are the colonists here."

In the midst of the hubbub, Sara walked out. She found Professor Brisard in his office. He was pale and stunned and looked very old. He gave her a wan smile when she knocked on the open door. "Ah, mademoiselle . . ." he trailed off apologetically, not knowing her name.

"Ben-Gal."

"Yes, the Israeli. I was looking forward to hearing your views. Well, what can we say, it's a comedy. They would rather strike than learn. Very French, I admit." He pointed to a chair for her.

"They don't know what they're doing," Sara said. "I suppose they will be expelled and the class will resume?"

"It's not so easy these days. Professors used to have all the power, but now . . ."

"Most of us want you to return."

Brisard took off his glasses and stared at the lenses, then wiped them on his tie. "Quite impossible at present."

"Would you be willing to consider a negotiation?" she asked.

Sara arranged a meeting that evening at a quiet café in the rue de la Parcheminerie in the Latin Quarter. They took seats at a sidewalk table where no one paid any attention to them. Sara was always struck by how quiet French cafés are; Israelis are so voluble that you can scarcely hear yourself shout. She discovered that Redha Brahimi and Léo Brisard had much in common, at least in their obstinate nature and prickly self-regard. The conversation was in French and occasional Arabic. Both men behaved themselves and clearly enjoyed being in Sara's company. What she understood was that neither of them could afford to be humiliated.

Redha's family fled the carnage of the Algerian civil war that followed the end of the French occupation. He held France responsible for the violence. "After you massacred a million Algerians, after the tortures, the rapes, the concentration camps, what destroyed our society even more was your failure to be good colonialists—to teach us, to build institutions. Instead, your settlers stole our land and kept us in poverty and ignorance. This is what Fanon was writing about. It required violence to expel you, and once we became acquainted with violence, we could not stop. And so when we finished killing the colonists we killed each other."

Brisard, the great expert on the Algerian colonization, was impressed by Redha's analysis but thought it was more informed by leftist dogma than by lived experience. After all, Redha had never actually been to Algeria; his understanding was shaped by Fanon's catastrophic views. He was the child of rather successful immigrants—his parents were bourgeois and he enjoyed a generous scholarship to Sciences Po. "I don't reject your views, but you leave out the consequences that befell us," Brisard said. "Algeria ruined France. The war brought down the Fourth Republic and turned the state into the bureaucratic monster you see today. We have been drowned by Muslim immigrants who fill the prisons and fail to integrate into society. This has turned us into a nation of racists. Yes, we were always anti-Semites, but the anti-Muslim virus is killing our soul. We agree. France is guilty of imperialism, but now it is the colonized who colonize the colonizer."

Redha nodded enthusiastically. "This is what Fanon predicted," he said. "The dream of the victim is to become his oppressor. It is not enough for the slave to escape bondage, he must take the place of the slaver. And so you have made us worse than victims."

"But having replaced the oppressor, Algeria and other former colonies have failed to become relevant in the modern world," Brisard argued. "That is not the fault of France—or of England, or Holland, or Belgium. These nations, these colonizers, tried to plant the flag of modernity only to see their efforts devolve into tribalism. You cannot blame all the failures of the colonies on the colonizers."

Sara watched this exchange with amusement. These two men, so in love with their own voices, matched with an adroit antagonist of equal skill, were thrilled by the dialogue, on the edge of their seats, their eyes wide and excited. Brisard had more experience, but Redha's views were more contemporary and his brain was quicker; he was barely able to restrain himself. By the end of the evening they came to an accord: Brisard would return to the class but he would teach Redha's syllabus. "Perhaps I actually will learn something," he generously offered. "But I do not promise to agree with you."

The course turned out to be riveting, the liveliest class Sara had ever enjoyed. Brisard was on fire; reanimated by Redha's challenge, he began making notes for a new book on postcolonialism. And Sara and Redha became lovers.

11

"Just a Name"

Hebron, Sept. 25, 2023

Next to the Cave of the Patriarchs in Hebron was a small police outpost, where tourists checked their bags and weapons. It was a little after midnight; Weingarten had been dead for eleven or twelve hours. Berger and Avi had spent the afternoon going through the imagery on the security cameras. The videos showed what appeared to be an ordinary morning, with a small number of tourists visiting Isaac Hall, the Jewish portion of the building, or the Ibrahimi Mosque on the other half. Yossi was unimpressed.

"Not them—look in the hallway beside the Abraham tomb," Berger said, pointing at the image. "It's the chief."

Weingarten was in uniform. The time stamp was 11:40 a.m., fifty minutes before Avi tried to order lunch. He appeared to be gesturing to another man with his back to the camera. "Who's the guy in the green shirt?" Yossi asked.

"We don't have a good look at him," Berger said. He told Avi to advance the film. They watched as the two men walked out of the synagogue together.

"That's it?" said Yossi.

"No, we pick up the new guy outside, here—" he gestured to another screen, where Weingarten and the man in the green knit shirt walked down the limestone stairs, toward the same modest outpost where Yossi and the others were viewing the footage. Weingarten and Green Shirt shook hands under a palm tree and then Weingarten walked on. Finally, Green Shirt turned.

"Shit, it's Moshe Dayan!" Avi exclaimed.

"He's dead, idiot," Berger said.

"The eyepatch is a giveaway," Yossi said, "but it could also be misleading."

"Look, he's got a video camera!" said Avi.

"That's our guy," said Berger.

"Can you zoom in?"

Avi enlarged the image. The suspect was of medium height, strongly built, wearing a faded red hat with a P on it.

"We got one other shot of him in the distance," said Berger. Avi brought up a clip of the man in the green shirt walking through the parking lot. He got into a white Toyota and pulled out just as Weingarten's police cruiser was leaving.

"There he goes, tailing the chief," said Berger.

"It's a one-way street," said Avi. "What else could he do?"

"Yellow plates," Yossi observed. That probably meant settlers. "Go in closer."

"That's as close as it gets."

"What model?"

"Camry, I think," said Avi. "Or the other one."

"Corolla," said Berger.

"You're sure?"

"Not exactly."

"Are you even sure it's a Toyota?"

"It has the logo on it," said Avi.

"Check Red Wolf," said Yossi, referring to the surveillance system that Israel used to monitor the movement of all human traffic in H-2. "He would have come through a checkpoint. Get an ID and a facial shot."

"Should we call Shabak?" asked Berger.

"Leave that to me," Yossi said. "Your job is to find this guy, quick and quiet. We've got a white Toyota with yellow plates. There won't be a lot of them outside of the settlements. I'll let Shabak know at the right time. First I want to talk to Moshe Dayan."

. . .

EVIDENCE GROWS COLD, people disappear, memories fade. Other crimes intrude and solvable cases dissolve. Speed is essential; you'll never get those first hours back. It's like digging a hole in the sand; after a while it all fills in and you're back where you started. Which is why Yossi rushed to Jerusalem. It's only thirty kilometers from Hebron but the traffic during the day can stretch out the drive to hours. In the middle of the night with the flashers on Yossi made it in no time at all, but once he got to the outskirts of town, another massive demonstration was breaking up. The smell of tear gas lingered in the air. The protesters were returning to their cars or walking home, some of them still wiping their eyes from the gas.

The country was being pulled apart by irreconcilable conceptions of what Israel stood for. The demonstrations tended to have different themes. The one in Tel Aviv that Sara attended was about social equality; this one seemed to be focused on the Kahanist takeover of three significant cabinet posts, another step in turning Israel into a theocracy. Nonreligious Jews and members of other sects were so alarmed that many were leaving Israel, draining the work force, especially from the high-tech sector that had added so much prosperity to the country. Yossi tried not to dwell on politics, but the drift alarmed him. Israel had been created by secular Jews like his parents. His father fought to create a democracy; now it was being taken over by people who didn't serve in the army and many who didn't work at all, living on subsidies by the government. Freeloaders and hypocrites, he thought. What kind of country were they making? He might have joined the demonstration himself; that would have astonished Sara. Yossi recalled something she said during a discussion verging on argument. "Jews are better in the Diaspora," she had said. "When we're all in one place we turn on each other."

Tamar Levin sat at her desk in a windowless office at the Shin Bet detention center in the Russian Compound, close by the Old City. It was the lair of an intelligence professional, absent of personal mementos except for the awards of merit and photographs of the prime minister and the chief of Shin Bet. Everything was so polished and untouched Yossi imagined that he wouldn't even find fingerprints on the desk. Tamar had agreed to meet with him, but she repeated what she said on the phone: "I have nothing to tell you at the moment."

" 'At the moment,' " Yossi said with just enough inflection to surface the true meaning of the phrase, which was "never."

"You know the rules," Tamar said uncharitably when Yossi arrived. "Haven't you got enough problems with the traffic? It's terrible these days."

Yossi bristled but he refused to take the bait. "Any leads you want us to follow up?" he said meekly.

"If we need your help, of course we would ask. I'm sorry you bothered to rush here for no good reason. Now, if you don't mind, I've got a mountain of work in front of me."

"Please, Tamar, just for my education, maybe you can give me some insight. I have to live in this hellhole. I need to know what to look for."

Tamar was a lonely woman in an unforgiving male world, and a little deference softened her resistance. Despite her steely face, her tone became less dismissive. "Have you seen Daesh in Hebron before?" she asked.

"Daesh? Is that what you think? Islamic State?"

"The beheading. The video."

"In Hebron, it's all Hamas," said Yossi, playing devil's advocate. Privately he also thought that there was a new element in town, but Tamar didn't mind showing off a bit, talking down to him like to a cadet.

"Also there's the bomb," said Tamar. "Our guys are lucky they didn't get blown to pieces by that sneaky device under Weingarten's boot." She showed him several photographs of the apparatus. "We had our best guys. First they find the mine, not a Claymore but one of those homemade ISIS varieties. And underneath there is a grenade. So you disarm the mine and lift it, and then the grenade goes off. Right out of Daesh's playbook."

It was as if she had discovered the bomb herself. If Yossi hadn't warned her, she'd be dead. No thanks offered or needed.

Yossi studied the photos. The artistry of the bombmaker was terrifying. "Yes, but Tamar, they copy from each other. I haven't seen the evidence of Daesh in Hebron."

"We arrested three of them already," she confided.

"When did this happen?"

"Last month."

"The raid on Nablus, you're talking about? They're kids, right? Wannabes. Did you find training materials? Videos?"

"We have information," Tamar said vaguely.

"Anyway, it's different in Nablus."

"Yes, but Hebron is closer to Gaza, keep that in mind."

"Are you worried about Gaza?" Yossi asked, a little surprised.

"Not really, but it's a chronic condition, like some virus that pops up every few years, sometimes deadly, sometimes you hardly notice, like the difference between a cold and the flu."

That had the ring of a witticism she had used before, or maybe she heard on a talk show. "You just now rounded up half of my town," Yossi said, getting to business. "Did you turn up anything?"

"We're still interrogating. It's going to take all night." She paused. "I know what you're after, Yossi. This is our work, not yours."

"I would never get in your way, Tamar. You're always ahead of me, you know that. But let me take a look at them. Maybe I recognize someone. You'd want to know, right?"

"You better not be holding out on me, Yossi. Not if you want my support to replace Weingarten."

He hadn't expected that. Such a threat might indicate real fear on Tamar's part, fear that she might fail, and that someone like Yossi would have to be put in his place so that there was a united front, everyone behind Tamar no matter what. No doubt the political pressure on her was crushing. The papers were full of speculation about the apparent intelligence failure to uncover the new Islamist terror group in Judea, although no one knew if there was such a thing. The administration was eager to divert attention from Bibi's attempts to stay out of prison, so the flames were fanned by official accusations and leaked intelligence.

"You mistake me for someone ambitious," he said. "I am counting the days until I can retire to my oranges and tomatoes."

"Don't be cute with me. You know the difference in the pension between an inspector and a chief. Your life would be so much easier.

You've been dreaming about this since the moment you heard the news."

It annoyed him that Tamar read him so easily. "Many would say I deserve the job," he said. "Others would say, who would want it?"

Tamar refused to leave it alone. "There could be better choices for the position. Younger. Fresh blood." She knew how to stick her finger in the wound, a real pro.

"You know the procedure, Tamar. They will find so-and-so's cousin, a promising junior officer who got in a bit of trouble, needs to be sent to a meaningless post where he can do as little harm as possible."

Tamar looked at Yossi with something approaching pity. "You must have pissed off somebody really important in your career."

Yossi gave a slight, breathy laugh. "You show me the detainees and I'll show you the line of superiors I've offended. It's a mystery how I stayed in this job as long as I have." As Tamar hesitated he added, "We're both after the same thing."

Tamar stared at him for a moment, then abruptly rose. "Okay, a look. You tell me anyone that stands out, anyone that crossed your path, threw a rock, said a bad word in your presence. Even someone whose sister you humped. This is your chance, Yossi. Point your finger and we'll get them to talk."

Yossi followed Tamar to a retaining pen outside. Despite the floodlights the yard was dim, as if veiled in smoke. Yossi took his flashlight from his belt and scanned the faces of the internees, dozens of them, none more than thirty, many of them teenagers getting their first taste of Israeli justice. No doubt they saw themselves as heroes, staring defiantly into the beam of Yossi's flashlight like celebrities. No one in a green shirt or wearing an eye patch.

"Let's see the serious ones."

Tamar stood quietly for a moment, her tongue making a discreet circuit across her upper lip, a strange tic of hers, then she turned without a word and walked off. Yossi decided that he was to follow her, as she didn't say not to. They entered the prison the Palestinians called al-Moscobiyeh. It had served various purposes in its history, beginning as a hostel for Russian pilgrims, then as the headquarters for police and intelligence during the British Mandate. In another building nearby many members of the Jewish underground, whom the British considered terrorists, were tortured and confined. The management had changed since then, but the practices remained the same.

They passed through a security station, and a guard instantly joined them. On the elevator he and Tamar exchanged a few remarks about Maccabi Tel Aviv. Some new player had been signed. Tamar's face lit up. She was a sports fan, something Yossi had never guessed.

As soon as the elevator door opened in the basement, a woman screamed. Yossi stopped still. She pleaded in Arabic, then she screamed again. While this was going on Tamar studied Yossi's reactions. "It's chilling, isn't it?" she asked. "We hire actors for this. It sets the table in a way. The men think, 'If they do this to women, what will they do to me?' Of course, sometimes it's not actors. Female terrorists are on the floor above. When they're actually being interrogated, we bring them down and open the doors so everyone can hear. We call it Palestinian Theater."

The prisoners were behind steel doors with small sliding windows. There was no other sound than the actress moaning and the squeak of Tamar's running shoes on the cement floor. She pointed to a cell and the guard slid open a viewing slot in the door. Yossi looked inside. There was a boy, maybe twelve years old, chained to a chair with his hands shackled behind his back. He looked up at them with little interest and then down again at the floor.

"Be serious, Tamar," Yossi said.

"You don't know. This one is from a Hamas house. A stone thrower. They graduate into worse, believe me."

The cells were full of boys and young men. Some of them may have been in the olive grove the day before. Now they had disappeared into the Israeli apparatus. They didn't need to be charged to be held for years, but if charged they would be convicted; Yossi couldn't remember when it happened that a court ruled for a Palestinian defendant's innocence. *Hopelessness is the goal,* Yossi thought, the result of the perpetual Israeli delusion that a population can be suppressed to the point that it finally accepts total defeat. Jews should know how impossible it is to finally extinguish a people. They will inevitably rise again, stronger, fiercer, with history on their side. This tribal knowledge is what fuels the desperation behind the ruthless treatment of the Palestinians.

"You said you arrested three in Nablus. Are they here?"

"In a different wing," Tamar said vaguely.

"Show me."

"These are confidential matters, secrets of state. You need clearances."

"Come on, Tamar, I know what you're doing. I've done it myself. I just need to see their faces. Nobody will know."

"One word of this and your career is finished."

"Tamar, stop with the threats. We both know the score. If we don't work together we may never destroy this gang."

"I don't know, Yossi. Something tells me I can't trust you. Always wanting something and never offering anything worth spit."

"I'm on the ground, I can be places you can't. Maybe you can solve this without me, but you've got a better chance if you let me be your eyes. Look, if we fail, we're both fucked. So let's not waste any more time."

He could see this argument making its way through Tamar's mind, navigating her instinctive distrust. There were reasons for it. Yossi wasn't corrupt, but he had the reputation of playing at the edges, exercising power beyond his authority. His strategy was to keep people off guard, never letting anyone in on his intentions. He had dealt out justice according to his own prejudices, narrowly avoiding scandal or indictment when he played too rough. He could be crude or surprisingly forgiving but always a cipher. He was an unreliable ally but a remorseless enemy. Tamar weighed all this and then walked away without a word. Yossi followed.

The elevator took them to the third floor. The lobby was a sort of museum, small and somber. There was a roll of honor for those killed in action. A wall full of service awards. Photos of notable terrorists that had been eliminated by Israeli intelligence, including the bomb maker Yahya Ayyash. A vase of roses on the credenza. They walked down a hallway of gleaming limestone, past landscapes of Mount Hebron in the spring. High-quality art, Yossi thought, but surprisingly sentimental. Each door was decorated with appealing geometric designs embossed on frosted glass, just obscure enough to prevent one from seeing inside. Tamar tapped on 305. A buzzer sounded and a click unlocked the door.

In a small, dim amphitheater nine or ten people were watching what Yossi at first thought was a giant video screen, but it was a window into another room. The thickness of the glass slightly distorted the view. Tamar gave Yossi a look that said, "Is this what you expected?" She sat in the back row and he sat beside her.

The Palestinian about to be interrogated was naked, suspended from the ceiling by chains cuffed to his wrists. Only his toes touched the ground, and when he lost contact he slowly swirled, like an exhibit on a turntable. There was a brown burlap bag over his head, probably a seed bag, Yossi thought; there was a bright-yellow smiley face on it, adding a morbid bit of humor to the scene.

A man in the front row wearing headphones spoke softly into a microphone and presently two large guards came into the torture chamber. The prisoner obviously heard them enter and his slender body physically shrunk from the sound. But there was nowhere to go. The guards were carrying military batons. Without a word they began to pummel the prisoner, not sparing any part of his body, with blows that left marks and some that drew blood. The prisoner spun wildly back and forth, as if he were on a child's swing, going from blow to blow. At times Yossi thought he heard bones snap. So far not a single word had been uttered, just the moans of the prisoner.

Yossi could feel the contact between the torturers and the prisoner. His hands remembered the sensation of the baton crushing the defenseless body. These men were remorseless. They played to the audience they knew was watching on the other side of the darkened glass. Their goal was to make death real to the prisoner without killing him. They took pride in going to the very edge of mortality.

The man at the controls said something and the beating stopped. Then he said on the PA system so that all could hear, "Ahmed, don't be so stubborn. We don't enjoy this either. But this is your life until you give us what we ask for." The prisoner gave no sign that he heard except for a stream of urine that ran down his leg. "You have been brave, Ahmed," the controller said in a confiding voice. "You don't have to endure this. No one else suffered as long as you. They all talked like little girls. They said so many things about you, how you recruited the guys, how you planned the operations, it was all you. You working with Zayyat, correct? That's what they say, Ahmed. See, we know these things. These charges are serious. If you can't help us, we have no choice but to believe them. So let's just start with that, Ahmed. We'll make it easy today. Just say are they are lying about you and Zayyat, then we'll leave you alone for the rest of the day. How about that, Ahmed? Just nod if they're lying about you, Ahmed."

The prisoner didn't respond. He just hung there, slack.

"So that means they're not lying about you? Can you shake your head, Ahmed?"

Still no response. The controller said, "Take off his hood."

One of the guards removed the hood. Ahmed had a narrow face with sharply defined features and full lips, a real lover boy, Yossi thought. His hair was inky black and clotted with blood. His eyes were rotated up, unblinking. A guard put his hand on the Ahmed's throat looking for a pulse, then shook his head.

"Well, fuck," said the controller.

As Yossi walked to the elevator, Tamar was shaking. "Look at the people they've made us be," she said hoarsely as she pushed the down button.

"You can't fight evil with flowers and chocolates, Tamar."

As the elevator arrived, he asked, "Who is Zayyat?"

"Just a name, Yossi. Just a name."

AS HE DROVE HOME in the dawn, Yossi considered the faces of the Palestinians in the holding pen. Many of them he would see again, if not for this case then for some other infraction. Sometimes when he was tired and frustrated he thought about how he might behave if the roles were reversed, if the Arabs had the power and the Jews were the supplicants. Would the Arabs be half as clement as the Jews? He doubted it. And who would he be in that scenario? Some compromised shopkeeper trying to keep out of trouble? Unlikely. For the most part, Yossi was happy to be left alone. But he had a weakness—pride. He was easily slighted. He could imagine what he might do if he were humiliated, as were the Arabs almost daily. And not just by casual insults but by actual theft of his land and property. Being rounded up, as those young men were, only because he was of an age when anger and heedlessness were at a peak. No, Yossi Ben-Gal would not do well in such a circumstance. He did not like to think about it. He did not like to think about it at all.

Just as he was turning in to his settlement he got a call from Berger. "We went through all the face scans at the cave. Ten green shirts, if you can believe it." Six of them were part of a tour by an Israeli human-rights organization that was a constant irritant to the settlers and the IDF. "The rest we have seen before, with one exception. He's Arab but he has an American passport."

"What's his name?"

"Anthony Abdul Malik."

"He must be part of the *chamula*," Yossi said, using the Arabic term for "clan." "There are a million Abdul Maliks."

"But this one is Moshe Dayan."

12

Moshe Dayan

Among Israelis Yossi's age and older, Moshe Dayan embodied both Israel's greatest triumph and its most colossal failure. Yossi knew his biography well. Dayan was the first child born in the first kibbutz, in 1915, near the Sea of Galilee, in what was then the Ottoman Empire but would become Israel. He defined the sabra—a native-born Israeli, like Yossi. The word "sabra" refers to the prickly-pear cactus, a tough desert plant, thorny on the outside but soft and sweet in the middle. Sabras spoke Hebrew as their first language, not with the thick accents of their immigrant parents. They were muscular, vital, sensual, and overwhelmingly secular, prizing physical labor over intellectual pursuits. Raised in the shadow of the Holocaust, they understood that their only hope to survive as a people was to secure a homeland. Sabras were the ones who would build a nation and defend it. This distinguished them from all the Jews of history.

During the Second World War, Dayan, age twenty-six, was serving under British command. While scouting Vichy French forces in Lebanon a bullet struck his binoculars, damaging his left eye so badly that he couldn't be fitted with a glass eye. The patch, which he hated, became emblematic of Israel's struggle and the wounds the country endured to become a nation.

Moshe Dayan was the man that the boy Yossi Ben-Gal wanted to be. Dayan was famously solitary and unsociable, without close friends, but admired for his aplomb and renowned for his scandalous romantic liaisons. Like Yossi, he was a passionate amateur archaeologist, often found digging up someone's backyard with no apology. He defined the scholarly warrior, while also ruthlessly eliminating Arab villages to make room for Jewish settlements. David Ben-Gurion, the founder of Israel, described his favorite military leader as having "almost insane daring balanced by profound tactical and strategic judgment." Dayan's daughter described him as "a man made for labyrinths." Such statements testify to the charisma that cloaked the turmoil of a personality who knew better than most the cost Israel would have to pay to endure in the Middle East. On this matter, he was a pessimist. "The decisive question is this: Can we implement a policy to show the Arabs that it is better for them to reach a peace settlement or at least a ceasefire because wars with us will cost them dearly and they will not achieve their goal?" It was a question that remained unanswered.

In 1967 Egypt's president, Gamal Abdel Nasser, threatened war. He was almost certainly bluffing—Egypt was already in a war in Yemen, with half its army engaged—but Israelis worried that an attack from Egypt would be joined by other Arab armies. Fears of extinction rattled Jews all over the world, only two decades away from the Holocaust. Nasser boasted that if it came to war he would "totally exterminate the State of Israel for all time."

Dayan became minister of defense only four days before the war began. He proved a brilliant strategist, so persuasively did he give the impression that Israel was in no hurry to engage in conflict that Nasser dropped his guard and lowered the state of emergency. On June 5, at seven in the morning, Dayan ordered his entire air force to take off, flying at different airspeeds from various airfields across the country, and converging in Egypt simultaneously. It is called the Six-Day War, but the Egyptian air force was wiped out in thirty minutes. The war ended with Israel occupying the entire West Bank, including Jerusalem; the Golan Heights, which was seized from Syria; as well as the Sinai Peninsula and the Gaza Strip, which Israel took from Egypt.

As Dayan surveyed the vast amount of property that fell under Israel's control, he contrived to find a way to settle it with Jews and still be compliant with international laws that forbade building for

civilians on occupied land. In July 1970 he met with other government officials and prepared a document called "The Method for
Establishing Kiryat Arba." Land would be designated as essential for
defense, and 250 housing units would be built ostensibly for use by
the military. According to notes of the meeting, "All of the building
will be done by the Defense Ministry and will be presented as construction for the IDF's needs," but everyone knew that it was a lie.
Kiryat Arba would become a model for annexing land for purported
military needs and turning it over to settlers.

Following that stunning military victory was an equally shocking
reversal. Dayan returned as minister of defense in 1973, serving under
Golda Meir. To forestall any future Egyptian attack a seventy-foot-
high rampart, built of sand, was erected along a hundred miles of
the eastern bank of the Suez Canal, fortified with tanks, artillery,
machine guns, mortars, and antiaircraft guns. It was called the Bar-
Lev Line. Reservoirs of oil were available to be poured into the canal
and lit afire in case of assault. To attack would be suicide. Dayan
wasn't unique in believing this; Israeli military leaders were constantly forecasting a future of Israeli invulnerability, a golden age of
total dominance.

Two powerful, self-destructive traits led to the war that followed:
shame and complacency. The shame felt by the Arab world because
of their catastrophic loss in 1967, and before that in 1948, created a
longing for rectification. It wasn't the same as revenge. Nasser's suc-
cessor, Anwar Sadat, offered to sign a peace agreement with Israel if
it returned the Sinai to Egyptian sovereignty and guaranteed a Palestinian state. Meir wasn't interested. Why bother? The Sinai offered
tiny Israel a vast new canvas. Dayan announced new settlements to
be built in the Golan and the Sinai, along with a new port in Egyptian territorial waters.

Frustrated by the failure of his diplomatic offer, Sadat announced
in the spring of 1973 a stage of "total confrontation." He was laughed
at, not only in Israel but in Egypt. The notion that the Egyptian
army, so easily defeated in 1967, could cross the canal and threaten
Israel was too far-fetched to worry about. Dayan's belief, shared by
most Israelis, was that Egypt wouldn't start a war it was certain to
lose. He actually longed for another war because it offered opportu-

nities for further conquests. He imagined "a new Israel, with wide borders," possibly reaching to the Nile.

Dayan paid little attention to the training openly underway in Egypt for a canal crossing. When Egyptian forces moved into position at the western shore of the canal, it was such a pathetic gesture in Dayan's eyes that he reduced the deployment to the Bar-Lev Line and replaced its defenses with dummy fortifications. Military leaders assessed the chance of an attack was "the lowest of the low." After all, the Egyptians would have to surmount the Bar-Lev Line. Artillery was useless against it; the sand would simply absorb the shells. Russian military advisers had told Sadat it was only possible to destroy the fortification with a nuclear bomb. But on October 6, on Yom Kippur, the Egyptians unveiled a new weapon, somewhat more modest than a bomb: firehoses.

The attack began the afternoon of October 6. Within hours, high-pressure firehoses had melted away the formidable sand barrier, creating sixty passageways for tanks to storm through. Israeli jets and tanks were destroyed by sophisticated Russian missiles. These new weapons were devastating, but what impressed Dayan was the Egyptian fighters themselves. Unlike the 1967 war, when the enemy soldiers defending Sinai discarded their uniforms and raced across the desert in their underwear, these forces were tough, ingenious, and courageous—like Israelis, like sabras. In a match of equals, Israel stood no chance against the vastly larger armies of the Arab world. "There is a great danger that a small state with less than three million people will be left powerless," Dayan told the nation on October 10, leaving Israel in shock.

In the face of Dayan's defeatist rhetoric, Major General Ariel Sharon led a blood-drenched counterattack that succeeded in breaking through Egyptian lines and isolating Egypt's Third Army. Cut off from food and water, the army languished in the desert while negotiations to prevent their total annihilation were underway. At that point Henry Kissinger, President Nixon's national security advisor, flew to Israel. Before the war Kissinger had worked with Dayan on a truce proposal with Egypt and was impressed with his "fertile mind." He thought Dayan would be the Israeli best positioned to steer the country to peace, but that man was broken by the Egyptian surprise.

Three thousand Israeli soldiers were dead. The cherished sense of invulnerability, made possible by the hero of the Six-Day War, was exposed as a foolish illusion. Pickets carried posters with his half-blind face inscribed "MURDERER." The 1973 war ended with a new reality. Israel was victorious but chastened. Egypt was defeated but its pride was restored. The feeling of invulnerability that followed the Six-Day War was shattered. The comfortable assumptions about Israel's destiny were swept from the table—and all because of the beloved Moshe Dayan. Yossi was ten years old. He would never put his faith in a hero again.

Dayan's final act was to become a force for peace in the 1978 Camp David summit between Sadat and the new Israeli prime minister, Menachem Begin, hosted by President Jimmy Carter. Dayan repeatedly coaxed Begin to moderate his rejectionist stance to accommodate a real peace with Egypt.

But where the Palestinians were concerned, Dayan remained a pessimist. He understood the tragic embrace Jews and Arabs were locked into. In May 1956, in the kibbutz Nahal Oz, next to the border of Gaza, a young security officer named Roy Rothberg was killed by Arabs who were pasturing sheep in fields that had been appropriated by the kibbutz. Back then, there were no fences; the border of Gaza was marked by the single furrow of a plow. Rothberg had frequently run off such raiders, sometimes killing them. This time the Arabs had laid a trap. Rothberg was on horseback, and as he rode toward them he was ambushed. Shot off his horse, he was beaten, then finished off with another shot. His mutilated body was dragged into Gaza, later to be surrendered to UN troops. Dayan, then the army chief of staff, delivered the eulogy. It stands as the most candid assessment of Israel's historic predicament.

Yesterday morning Roy was murdered. The morning stillness so dazzled him that he did not see those lying in wait for him on the furrow line. Let us not cast blame on his murderers today. It is pointless to mention their deep-seated hatred of us. For eight years they have been sitting in Gaza refugee camps while before their eyes we have been making the land and villages where they and their forefathers had lived our own.

It is not from the Arabs in Gaza that we should demand Roy's blood, but from ourselves. How we shut our eyes to a sober observation of our fate, to the sight of our generation's mission in all its cruelty. Have we indeed forgotten that this young group in Nahal Oz carry on their shoulders—like Samson did—the heavy "gates of Gaza"—and that behind those gates live hundreds of thousands of hate-ridden people who pray that we be weakened so that they may then tear us apart . . .

Dayan went on to remind his audience of the lessons of the Holocaust:

Millions of Jews who were annihilated without having had a country look to us from the ashes of Israeli history, commanding us to settle and build a land for our people. But beyond the furrow border, a sea of hatred and vengeance swells, waiting for the day that calm will dull our vigilance, the day that we listen to ambassadors of scheming hypocrisy who call on us to lay down our arms . . .

This is the choice of our lives—to be prepared and armed, strong and resolute or to let the sword fall from our fist and our lives be cut down. Roy Rothberg, the blond, slender young man who left Tel Aviv to build his home at the gates of Gaza and serve as our bulwark, Roy—the light in his heart blinded him to the gleam of the knife, the longing for peace deafened him to the sound of lurking murder; alas, the gates of Gaza were too heavy for him and they prevailed.

13

A Cup of Tea

The Old City of Hebron, Sept. 27, 2023

Sara was still sleeping when Yossi slipped away. He cursed the fact that the most important case of his career was spoiling the only time all year he would see his daughter. When he got back to the station, he walked down the hill to the Arab souk, which adjoined the Cave of the Patriarchs. Most of the shops were shuttered by the army following the Goldstein massacre. The economic collapse of the market followed, street after narrow street of padlocked storefronts, each the size of a one-car garage, all painted a uniform glossy yellow. The lifeless souk wound beneath ancient stone arches on a path of pale bricks covered with litter. Although the Israelis controlled everything, they failed to pick up the trash. An older section of the souk, painted blue-green and stained with mildew and rust, was papered with expulsion orders. Wire mesh covered the street to catch the stones and trash hurled on Arab pedestrians below by children in the several settlements above the shops.

There was a time, when Yossi first came to Hebron, that the streets were teeming with shoppers. The fruit stands, the camel market, the tailor, women's fashions, one store after another bustled with commerce. Only a handful remained, including a candy store, where a father and son were making Turkish delights. Roosters guarded the caged hens at the chicken market on the corner. A tour guide sat in front of his souvenir shop reading *Al-Hayat*. It was still too early for customers, who never came anyway. Three stores down was the butcher shop with animal carcasses hanging from hooks, trays filled with calves' livers, chicken parts, and sheep's heads with eyes and teeth intact, ready for the stew pot. Yossi knew the shopkeepers weren't making any money; their presence was a silent form of resistance. *No one really wants to be here,* Yossi realized, *neither the Arabs nor the Jews; we're all here to make a political point. We empty our lives for this.*

He had tried unsuccessfully to get transferred to a different post. He suspected there was a notice in his file indicating that he was only suited for duty in Hebron. He could be both brutal and dispassionate, and he knew when to look away when it wasn't his business. His reputation for killing too easily gave him respect among the settlers. Not everyone could be depended on to have such traits, but they were admired in Hebron. He supposed his bosses preferred to keep him in a place where force was valued and hesitation could be fatal. As it must have been for Chief Weingarten.

The truth was that the time had passed when Yossi might have adjusted to life outside the territories. He was proud that Sara lived in Paris. It meant that something good from him could survive in civilization. He often pictured her in the classroom, or walking past shop windows on freshly washed sidewalks, sitting in outdoor cafés, enjoying a concert in some noble building, far from the grinding hatred, the killings, the humiliation, and the endless justification on both sides for actions that were wicked and cruel and intended to be so. The sole point of life in Hebron was to create misery for others. Yossi knew that, but he couldn't break free of it.

One of the shops had been divided in half. The shutter was open and a small, elderly man sat on a stool in a space not much larger than a coffin. He wore a black-and-white kaffiyeh wrapped around his head and neck so that only his face from his eyebrows to his lower lip was exposed. He had on three layers of garments—a dirty brown sweater, a puffy vest, topped by a dark checked sport coat with the name of the manufacturer, Roland, sewn on the cuff. His hands were chapped and a silver watchband drooped from his emaciated wrist. The shelves were mostly empty, save for a few bags of flour, some lentils, chickpeas, and cooking oil. Day after day the old man sat here and watched. He saw everything. He heard everything. He regarded Yossi warily.

"How goes the world?" Yossi asked.

"It is cursed," the old man said.

"We agree on this." Yossi sat in the customer's chair and looked around as if he would never move again. This act of patience was almost physically painful at such a moment of crisis.

Finally the old man offered, "You will take some tea?"

"Why not?"

The old man dug out a box of Lipton Yellow Label, perhaps the most enduring remnant of Britain's colonial adventure in the Middle East. He filled a kettle with bottled water and sat quietly until the tea was ready, all this done with his right hand as his left lay immobilized in his lap. The old man poured one cup and handed it to Yossi.

"Chilly today," Yossi observed.

"It gets in the bones," the old man said. It was not so cold as all that, but old men need to warm themselves, especially if they sit idly hour by hour in a desolate market.

"How is Mustafa?" Mustafa was the old man's grandson that Yossi had twice arrested for stone throwing. The old man had already paid a seven-thousand-shekel fine for the boy's first offense, which must have bankrupted him. For the second offense, the punishment was as much as twenty years in prison. The old man had come to Yossi, begging for his help. Yossi dropped the charges, expecting to be repaid in information. Nothing had to be said. The lives of the old man and his family would always be in Yossi's hands.

"Mustafa is in Birzeit University, thanks to God," the old man said warily.

"This is wonderful news. What does he study?"

"Finance," said the old man. "He will be a banker."

"Last we talked, he wanted to be a movie director."

The old man looked away, chagrined. "When he is rich, he can be a movie person."

"He made a wise decision," said Yossi. Then casually he added, "Tell me about the Malik clan. You are the mukhtar, you know what's going on. I can always depend on you." The mukhtar was the leader of a clan, an honorary post, often accorded to the oldest member of the tribe. The old man was respected and in on the gossip.

"The Maliks are good people," said the old man.

"This I know. They keep out of trouble."

The old man nodded gravely.

"It's a big *chamula*," Yossi observed.

"From Jordan to Lebanon, Syria, Iraq. Twenty families in Hebron district alone."

"And in America?"

"America?" the old man was surprised by the question. "Of course there are Maliks in America. And all places. You will even find in Moscow."

"Perhaps you have heard of someone from that clan who has recently arrived?"

"People come all the time. To visit. For the holidays, for business," he said, guarding his words. "Or so many matters."

"There's something you know and you owe it to me to tell." Yossi didn't have to make the threat more explicit.

"Why do you say the Maliks only? There are many troublemakers not in our clan."

"Only a day ago your people were throwing rocks."

"Yes, we defend ourselves, what else should we do? Meantime you hold the bodies of our young people killed in the grove. Their parents are suffering."

"I made no arrests," Yossi said. "I might have taken many." He paused. "I could still do so. It would be a mistake to make me angry." He could see the conflict in the old man's face and the nervous tremor in his legs. "The best thing is to be honest with me. You know I will help you if I can."

"We are good people," the old man said again.

"And I treat you with respect. But you heard the news."

The old man nodded gravely. "We did not do this deed."

"I haven't accused anyone. I only need information. Let's say a new group has started and they want to make a statement. We need to know who they are."

"We don't agree with this action, not a one of us!" the old man said, as if his furious denial had any weight at all.

"Someone new to town," Yossi said gently. "Maybe he came from Jordan. Maybe Lebanon. Maybe he flew here from America. Who knows. Perhaps someone in your clan is upset about the Rav's people trying to seize your land."

"What happened to your chief has nothing to do with the family."

"I have not said the man I seek is a perpetrator, only that he might have some information. Like you. Maybe you know something you don't think is important. Things will go easier for everyone if you tell me."

"It is nothing."

"You don't know what is important. I decide."

The old man sighed. Something inside him gave way, as it had many times before. He had learned that betrayal was a moral landscape of its own, needing to be measured against the cost of silence or deceit. Just as there were small lies there were small truths that could feed the demands of the occupier. "There will be a wedding," he admitted, "so some people have come for that."

"Which family?"

"Sheikh Abdullah Abdul Malik."

Yossi nodded as if he already knew this. "The same family that owns the olive grove where we had the incident."

"Sheikh Abdullah is an honorable man. The family are teachers and engineers and farmers. They do not do violence, you know this."

Yossi put fifty shekels on top of an upturned fruit box. "For the tea," he said. The old man quickly scooped it into the pocket of his jacket.

14

Stakeout

Hebron, Sept. 27, 2023

Tony Malik picked up a copy of *Al-Quds Al-Arabi* at the front desk. There was a brief account of Weingarten's murder. Most of the commentary was not condemning of the slaughter, casting it as the kind of retribution Israel should expect as an occupying force and promising more to come.

He sat in a purple chair in the hotel breakfast room, staring at the photo on the front page. Yes, he met him in the Cave of the Patriarchs yesterday morning. That was the reason he came to Hebron a day earlier than planned. He recognized the gap-toothed smile. It couldn't have been more than a couple hours before he was killed. But what did he actually say? Did the chief confide the reason for the meeting? Malik was blank. Names of sources often slipped out of grasp but he usually recalled the intelligence they produced. For some reason the meeting with Weingarten fell into the second order of importance. That is, it was forgettable, and therefore, forgotten.

He believed his mind had this executive sorting capacity—remembering the bullet points while losing the details—but maybe he was fooling himself. If something was forgotten, how could he tell whether it was important or trivial? He couldn't. Which meant that he really didn't know who he was, half blind in his mind as well as his body. It was like trying to remember a dream, reaching for ungraspable fragments. The narrative structure of a true memory was absent.

In any case he had the whole day to think about it. He wouldn't meet his relatives until the engagement ceremony—an exchange of gifts between the families of the bride and groom, followed by a feast. It had been delayed until Malik's arrival. Meantime he would go sightseeing in the country where his father grew up. The waiter arrived with buttered toast, drowning the stream of thought.

BERGER AND AVI DROVE through the congested downtown, passing hotels and parking garages. Toyotas were everywhere, different models, different colors, most of them Corollas, although by now they had decided that the model they were looking for was a Camry. So far they all had white Palestinian plates.

There weren't a lot of accommodations in H-1, a handful of guesthouses for the tourists visiting the Old City and a dozen hotels downtown competing for business travelers. These days a lot of them were Chinese who had come for the marble trade (there were more than a thousand quarries in the region); and that, along with the abundant vineyards and olive groves, shoe factories, and handicrafts made Hebron the backbone of the Palestinian economy, accounting for 40 percent of the gross domestic product in the West Bank.

"This is a big fucking waste of time," Berger said. "Guy comes to town, meets the chief, does the deed, will he hang around? No, he will not. He's back across the border in Jordan. We'd have to send a hit squad to take care of him, Mossad stuff." Avi nodded. He tried not to disagree with Berger, who was a bit of a hothead. Moreover he was hungry and needed to pee, a contingency that wasn't covered in the police academy's lesson on stakeouts.

The Israeli police had no jurisdiction in this part of the city, so they used an undercover truck, covered in dust, looking like any other delivery truck that might have been in the fields and no one ever bothered to wash. With stolen plates it was practically indistinguishable in the Hebron traffic. It happened to have an eight-cylinder engine with high-compression pistons and was deceptively speedy.

"Slow down, there's another one," Avi said, pointing at a white Toyota parked in a tight spot beside the curb. "Let's check the plates."

They were on Namera Street, near the Ottoman Restaurant,

about ten meters behind the Toyota. It was parked so close to the other vehicles they couldn't clearly see the plates. Avi got out and casually walked by, phone in hand, pretending to be in an argument with the person he was pretending to talk to, as he videoed the scene, a bit of acting that made him feel like a genuine sleuth. He paused at the rear of the Toyota. There was just enough space for him to make out the yellow plates. And he had it on video. He was ecstatic.

"It's the one," he said, affecting a casualness he didn't feel at all. It had just occurred to him that they might be in danger if the killer's car was so near.

"Okay," said Berger.

"Should I call it in?"

"I'll do it. Not now."

"I thought you were doing the driving."

"We're not going anywhere, we're going to wait to see if our guy turns up. So far it's just a Toyota with yellow plates."

"I still think I should call it in. They might want to see the video I made. They'll send a whole team. That's the drill."

"Let's wait a bit," Berger said. "We might be able to take this guy by ourselves."

"Is that a good idea?"

"Think about it. We'll be fucking heroes."

Avi did think about it. He was the youngest member of the force, the least experienced, but he privately believed he was the most competent, at least after Yossi, who was authoritative but maybe not so skilled as he should be. Avi had studied criminology in the academy and he loved detective stories. This was like one of those stories. If they captured the suspect by themselves, the whole country would salute them. They'd be promoted. They might be honored in the Knesset or shake hands with the prime minister. On the other hand, suppose they failed. Suppose the guy got away. Suppose he was already back in Jordan. And they had failed to make the call. Or worse, the guy wasn't alone, he was with a bunch of terrorist friends.

"I don't know, Aharon, I think we really should call it in," Avi said.

"I say wait."

They waited. Berger was double-parked with the hazard lights on, as if they were making a delivery. They had a clear view of the Toyota.

"He must be in the hotel," Avi said. The Abu Mazen Hotel was across the street.

"In that case he's not Hamas," Berger concluded. Abu Mazen was another name for Mahmoud Abbas, the leader of Palestine and the Fatah party, despised by Hamas. (The hotel had no actual connection to Mahmoud Abbas.) "Could be Islamic Jihad, Lion's Den, Daesh, who knows."

"Or could be deception," Avi suggested. "If he really is Hamas, he might stay here so we think he is not."

Berger chewed this over. "That's not crazy," he conceded.

They waited. Avi was jumpy. He finally confessed: "I need to pee."

"You were supposed to pee at the station."

"I did. I need to pee again."

"We're on duty," said Berger. "You know the drill."

"Yeah, but I really do need to pee."

"Do it on the street."

"I can't do that." Avi thought a moment. "I could pee in the back of the truck."

"Absolutely not."

Avi crossed his legs but that made it worse. "I'm not kidding. I can't hold it."

"Fine! Go in the hotel. But if we lose this guy it's all on you."

Avi started to open the door, then asked, "You don't need to go too?"

"I do but I'm holding it."

Berger watched Avi walk into the hotel. Berger put the binoculars to his eyes to see if there was anyone visible in the lobby, but the glare of the sun blocked the view. It was just cool enough to keep the windows closed, but by now his breath was beginning to fog the windshield, so he let a little fresh air in. That helped wipe away some of the sleep-inducing boredom of a stakeout. Who knows how long he would have to be here, doing nothing but talking to that moron Avi. He was certainly taking his time, the lying little bastard, no doubt he was sitting on the toilet reading his emails. *Yossi must know how I feel about that guy, he just pairs me with him to piss me off.*

These reflections led Berger to remember a scene that very morning when his wife suggested he should find a better job. "It's not just the money," she said, although it was. "You need something respectable. It embarrasses me to see you working for so little. You should be thinking about your family."

"I make a decent salary. You need to do a better job of budgeting."

This inflamed her. "You say you make a living but what do we have to show for it? Where does our money go?" The last thing she said as he left the house was, "You don't want to end up like Weingarten. And for what?"

These were difficult questions. Berger had pondered them many times. He had a few habits that he kept to himself, which were nobody's business, including his wife's. Some things he couldn't talk about with her, and money was one of them. He had a promising deal that brought in a little money and could bring a lot more. Weingarten's death opened up opportunities. So many problems would be solved if he got the promotion to chief inspector. Capturing the terrorist single-handed might make that possible.

Lost in his thoughts, he hadn't noticed a man in a green shirt getting into the Toyota, but suddenly the car moved, just slightly, wedged as it was between two other cars. Berger was startled back into awareness. He could only hope that the Toyota was stuck. Back and forth the car went, nudging the bumpers of the Ford in front and the Volkswagen in back, making incremental progress toward liberation. Berger was going crazy. Where was Avi? He beeped the horn lightly. Nothing. Another forward, another back, and the Toyota pulled out and drove away.

Berger pulled in front of the hotel and honked repeatedly. Berger was just about to abandon him when Avi rushed out, putting on his belt. He was only half in the truck when Berger lurched off with a screech. "Idiot," he said.

"I'll call it in," said Avi apologetically.

"Really? Be sure to tell them you were taking a shit while our suspect got away."

There were no traffic lights or stop signs in Hebron; drivers navigated through negotiation and bravado. Berger was not given to civility, and under pressure he drove even more recklessly. He stuck to Namera Street hoping that the Toyota hadn't already turned off, leapfrogging cars that stood in the way, darting in and out of the oncoming traffic with only millimeters to spare, leaving a chorus of angry horns and rude gestures in his wake. Avi put his seat belt on, something the officers rarely did.

"There he is!" Berger cried, just as the Toyota took a turn to the right. "The fucker! Now you can call the desk. Let them know we're in hot pursuit."

"Got it!"

"And don't use the radio, Shabak will hear. Use your phone."

Golda answered. "We have him," Avi said. "White Toyota. Going south on—wait, he just turned on Ein Sarah Street."

Berger turned the corner so sharply the truck tilted onto two wheels. "Be careful!" Avi cried.

MALIK HAD PICKED UP the dusty delivery truck in his rearview mirror right away. It appeared to be driven by a hopped-up maniac. There must be some emergency, he thought, so he turned off Namera Street. When the truck squealed around the same corner he realized he was being chased.

He cursed himself for not listening to all the nay-sayers who told him that Hebron was too dangerous, that as a highly informed FBI agent with a history of intelligence in his head he was quite a target. Hamas or al-Qaeda or whatever terror organization was at the wheel would be thrilled to capture such a trophy. They would torture him; he would talk, everyone does; and then he'd wind up like Weingarten missing his head.

BEHIND HIM, Berger zoomed past three cars in a row, only just making it back into his lane before a station wagon sideswiped them. "Not so close!" Avi said.

"I'm not losing this asshole again."

"We're passing the Kentucky Fried Chicken," Avi told Golda. "Now he's turning again. He must have spotted us."

"I'm alerting the others," Golda said. "Don't hang up."

THIS WAS a sorry town for a car chase, Malik thought. He had to maneuver around pedestrians, bicycles, and a donkey cart. His pursuer didn't care about the damage he was causing. That was the core of every terrorist; the cause is more important than the casualty list. Malik was handicapped by his humanity. He reminded himself that he had trained for these situations. Now was the time to see if training worked. He turned another corner and hit the gas. The Toyota lurched ahead, then he slammed on his brakes and turned the wheel sharply, sending the car into a skid and somehow avoiding the parked vehicles on both sides of the street.

BERGER TURNED SHARPLY and astonishingly there was the white Toyota coming from the opposite direction. As it passed, the cops got a quick glance at the driver, who wore a green shirt and a red hat and a black eyepatch. He looked directly at them with his one good eye, his middle finger raised.

"Fuck yourself, you son of a bitch!" Berger cried. He turned the steering wheel sharply and slammed into a school bus. The children's shocked faces stared at them. Berger braked and backed up, but by now the Toyota had turned again. Berger raced to the corner and made a sharp left, but nothing was in view. He turned again, right, and there was the Toyota, two blocks ahead. Lucky guess.

"We got him again, but he's going really fast," Avi reported.

So was Berger. Ahead, the Toyota was four cars ahead, slowed by traffic.

"Need assistance, now!" Avi cried into the phone.

"They're coming, they're coming!" Golda said.

Berger was closing the distance when the Toyota entered a traffic circle, so he drove in the wrong direction, scattering cars but cutting off the Toyota, which darted into a narrow side street with Berger right behind him. The cars ahead slowed to a crawl.

"I got you, fucker!" Berger yelled.

Avi closed his eyes as Berger crashed into the Toyota. It jumped the curb and drove around two cars, half on the sidewalk, with Berger right behind, finally ramming the Toyota into a telephone pole. Avi's scream was muffled by the exploding air bags.

For an instant, everything was black. Avi wasn't sure if he had gone unconscious or if the airbag had blocked the light, but he was alive and covered in a light powder and feeling like he had been punched hard in the chest. An unfamiliar smell clouded the air. He looked over at Berger, who was panting, gasping for breath. "Are you okay?" Avi asked. Berger nodded. The airbags draped loosely from the dashboard and steering wheel. Berger suddenly snapped to. "Let's get that bastard," he said.

They got out of the truck. On the side of the street bulldozers were clearing the way for the latest Jewish settlement on the edge of the city, which was endorsed by the Rav's smiling face from yet another billboard, this one looking over the scene of smoking cars and gas draining into the street.

The Toyota was smashed on both ends like an accordion, the hood crumpled and the trunk popped open. The rear bumper lay on the ground. Out of nowhere exhilarated Arab children descended on the scene, and in an instant they were plundering the Toyota with quick little hands, grabbing anything they could reach.

"What are you doing, you little vermin?" Berger said, scattering the children. "Get out of here!"

Guns drawn, the deputies approached the Toyota on either side. The car appeared to be empty, but when the deputies drew closer they saw the driver slumped over the steering wheel. His red hat was missing. One of the children was brazenly showing it off to the other boys, who were ready to finish ransacking the car at any opportunity.

"Police! Hands on the wheel!" Berger said these words in Hebrew. Malik raised his head. He was alive, at least. He looked at Berger in puzzlement. "Do you speak English?"

"We're police," Avi said. "Hands on the wheel."

"You're police?" That was confusing. Malik had assumed they were terrorists. Why else would they be pursuing him? He was still trying to assess any injuries he might have sustained. His midsection felt like he had been pummeled by Mike Tyson. "This is a big mistake," Malik said to Avi.

"Hands on the wheel!" Avi shouted.

A siren screamed and in a moment Yossi arrived, followed by two other police vehicles, openly ignoring the fact that they were in H-1, outside their nominal zone of authority. By now the cars trying to pass the wreckage were slowed by curiosity. One of the police vans moved to block the road and Yossi signaled to the other drivers to move along. He stood for a moment, taking in the smashed Toyota and the now-ruined delivery truck. The telephone pole leaned dangerously over the sidewalk. "What happened here?" he asked.

"This asshole was fleeing arrest and we caught him," Berger said. "We got the chief's killer." He directed this statement to the other officers standing around to make sure he got credit for this historic arrest.

Yossi looked at Malik, who hadn't been able to follow the conversation but had a good idea what they were saying. "Your guys nearly killed me," Malik said, hoping Yossi understood English. "How was I to know they were cops?"

"Are you injured?" Yossi asked.

"Not sure."

"Get out of the car. Keep your hands in view."

Malik tried opening the driver's side door but it was bent and impossible to open, even with two cops on the other side tugging on it. Avi opened the passenger-side door. Malik slid across the seat. It was painful but it didn't feel like anything was broken. Avi stepped back and kept his pistol trained on Malik as Berger cuffed him. Then Avi noticed something.

"The camera," he said.

Yossi looked inside the buckled vehicle. There, on the floorboard, was the video camera that could unlock everything.

15

Milk and Cookies

Hebron, Sept. 27, 2023

A dozen armed and angry settlers filled the police station with taunts and demands. Their faces were inflamed and their voices loud and rude, filled with insinuations of violence. Most of them were Kahanists, but mixed in with the others were a few secular Jews, all drawn together by mutual fear of an onslaught of terror. Golda ordered them to leave, but they had no interest in going anywhere. A bald man, the dome of his head shining with perspiration and his eyes wide with panic and indignation, cried, "We are only a few, but they are everywhere! If they killed your chief, they can kill us!"

"We deserve information," said their gruff leader, Itai Chafets. He had the confidence of a big man, arms crossed over his chest, looming over Golda and speaking in a hoarse whisper that added menace to his words. "We are telling you nicely. If you don't take care of this soon, we will do it ourselves, in our own way. So you know."

Golda backed away. She was alone in the station; everyone else was on the streets dealing with the white-Toyota man. "Better leave now," she said. "You might do something you'd regret."

Itai took a step closer. "Just tell us you have information, clues, something that sets our minds at ease." He was close enough for Golda to smell the garlic on his breath.

"I'm not authorized to divulge any information about this case," she said.

"If you give us reassurance, perhaps we can rest," Itai said. "Otherwise, we feel the need to express our righteous anger. We are grieving for our brother Jacob. We are impatient for justice. A word from you might calm our hearts."

Golda understood the threat behind these words. Itai and his people were preparing a "price tag" attack—the retribution they felt entitled to wreak upon the Palestinians because of the killing. Many of the Kahanists she knew personally. They were her neighbors in Kiryat Arba. Justice was not on their minds; vengeance was. At that moment she had a choice to make: to give them some assurance that there was a break in the case, or to say nothing and set them loose on the town. Not for the first time she had to choose between disobeying an order and deciding on her own authority to compromise to prevent an atrocity.

Golda was spared when she heard the cruisers pull up in the gravel lot.

On either side of the handcuffed prisoner Berger and Avi marched into the station, followed by Yossi and the other police officers. Yossi took note of the settlers and their guns, then cast an accusing look at Golda for letting the situation get so out of hand. That would be settled later.

The settlers pressed in to get a close look. "Is this the terrorist?" Itai demanded. One of the settlers spat in Malik's face. Yossi shoved the man back. "Clear out," he said. "You've got no right to bring weapons into this station."

"If he's the killer, give him to us," Itai said. "Be reasonable. We can save you the trouble. We know what to do with such as he."

"Get out of the station now or we'll put you in a cell," said Yossi. "You're obstructing police business." Itai and the others made no motion to leave. Yossi's threat hung in the air.

"Listen to him, all of you." Benny, the Rav's grandson, stepped into the circle. Yossi hadn't noticed him until now, he had been standing back behind the mob, a hanger-on, but now he asserted himself and the mob quieted. "We can trust Yossi," Benny said.

The dynamics in the room became clear. The boy was in charge. Yossi had seen it happen occasionally in the military, when teenagers are given so much more authority than they've experienced before. Some become leaders, some become killers. Benny was both. A rare specimen. And a dangerous one, empowered by his grandfather's standing. But at the moment he was useful. The settlers listened to him as if he were a prophet. Benny smiled and gestured toward Berger and Avi, saying, "We should thank our heroes."

Immediately, the atmosphere changed. The settlers cheered. Avi and Berger swelled in response, looking the part of fearless guardians of the community rather than the intimidated young men they had been an instant before. The bald settler tried to raise Yossi's arm in triumph, but he pulled it away as he approached Benny. "Ask your grandfather to keep his followers under control," Yossi said. "Tell him I'll handle this."

"Whatever you say, Chief. The Rav will be pleased to hear of an arrest."

It was the first time anyone had called Yossi "Chief." Maybe Benny knew something.

The officers ushered Malik into one of the three cells in the cramped jail in the back of the station. Most of the time there was no one incarcerated here. The settlers had their own ways of handling criminals and rarely let anyone from that community face arrest by other authorities. Either the Palestinian police in Hebron or the Israeli Border Police handled actual crimes in the area. The Israel Police was left with traffic control and counterterrorism, although that duty was typically usurped by Shabak. It was in some respects a suitable arrangement for a group of cops who were not, it should be admitted, of the highest standard.

The prisoner was still dazed from the wreck. He sat on the bunk and stared blankly at the officers, who crowded around to get a look at him.

"Who the fuck are you?" Yossi demanded.

"Anthony Malik," he said. "Who are you?"

"Yossi Ben-Gal, interim chief. You are in the custody of the Israel Police, understand? Where are you from?"

"I'm American. From New York City."

"Prove it."

"You'll find my passport in my suitcase."

"What suitcase?"

"It should be in the trunk," said Malik. "That's where I put it."

"The trunk was empty."

Malik reached for his back pocket. "Shit! Who stole my wallet?" He looked accusingly at Berger. "Where's my phone?"

"Maybe the Arab scum took it," said Berger, who was hovering over him.

Malik looked confused. "I've been robbed," he said. "I need to call my embassy."

"First, we talk," said Yossi.

"I'm an American citizen. I have rights."

"You say you are an American but you have no identification. Even though we don't know you, we treat you well. We merely ask why you are here. We don't feel in a hurry to call Shin Bet, because they won't be nice about it. We do this for your protection. Once Shabak is involved you enter a black hole. So now tell me why you are here."

"It's some kind of family business."

"That's your alibi? Some kind of family business?"

"I have trouble remembering."

"He may have a concussion," Golda said.

"It's a head injury from before," Malik said.

"So you just forget stuff that's not convenient to remember?" said Yossi.

Malik looked at the ceiling, puzzling over the question. "It'll come to me. It usually does. And I'm still a little rattled by the wreck."

Everyone was quiet for a moment until Berger said, "He's conning us, Yossi, come on, he's putting on an act."

"It was for a wedding," Malik said.

"Who's getting married?"

"My cousin."

"Name?"

He paused, again seeming to search his memory. "Dina Abdul Malik."

Yossi exchanged a glance with Berger. "If you come for a wedding, why do you run from us?"

"I wouldn't want to wind up like your chief."

"What do you know about him?"

"I'm not talking until you let me know why I've been arrested."

"We haven't charged you yet, but you violated many laws." Yossi turned to Berger. "He was speeding?"

"Speeding, reckless driving, evading arrest."

"So already we know you are a criminal," said Yossi.

"It was for my own safety," said Malik. He looked at Berger. "I spotted him and his buddy following me. They made it really obvious. I didn't know who they were, and this isn't the safest place in the world. So I tried to get away. Also I don't think you have police authority in H-1, so this is like a kidnapping."

Yossi smiled at this observation. "You know Hebron well?"

"First time here."

"But you know the division of authorities."

"I read the advisory on the internet."

"When did you come to town?"

"You're asking me questions so fast it's hard for me to put it all together."

"You remembered the chief getting killed, so why can't you remember when you came to town?"

"Some things I never forget, others just disappear. You're crowding me. I need a little space to think."

"A very convenient memory you have."

"Head injury. It's a fucking curse." He looked to the ceiling. "I got here Monday. I remember that now." He shrugged. "I guess I'm a little shaken up."

The conditional nature of Malik's responses was confounding. Also probably useless in court, if it came to that.

"Okay, take your time. You're not going anywhere. Tell me about yesterday," Yossi demanded.

"I'm not sure about the order of things but I do remember sleeping late. Jet-lagged. I would've eaten lunch somewhere, probably near the hotel. Don't think I saw anybody. Did some tourist stuff." He looked at Berger. "I was on my way to meet my family when this bozo came after me."

"Give him to me, Yossi," Berger said. "He's playing with us. I will get him to talk."

"Fuck off," said Malik.

Berger slapped him hard. "You killed our chief!" Berger said. His eyes were bulging and his face was red with fury. "Arab pig!"

Malik didn't bother to react to the blow. "Do you do any real police work or just beat people up?" he said.

Berger lunged for Malik's throat but the prisoner exploded into action, suddenly fully conscious and surprisingly swift, with a combination of blows that sent Berger sprawling outside the cell. Yossi thought, *This guy has been trained.* When Malik turned his blind eye to him, Yossi struck him hard in the stomach. He groaned and sank to the floor, gasping for breath. Berger rose and kicked him once before Yossi pushed him back. "Stand outside!" he said. "You," he said to Malik. "You don't react, you just accept. Understand?"

"I'm an American," Malik said between gasps.

"Right now you're just another Arab causing trouble. So you tell me everything and then we talk about embassy business. Understand me?"

Malik nodded.

"How do you know about our chief?"

"Who doesn't know? It's all over TV."

"You met him, our chief."

"Yeah, we met. I don't remember exactly what was said. I remember he was in a hurry."

"You don't remember anything that he said?"

"If it had been important I would have written it down. Or else taped it. I often do that to help me recall conversations or places I have been. Wait, I have some notes."

He reached into his shirt pocket and pulled out a small notebook. "I was right," he said. "Dina's getting married on Thursday. What day is today?"

"Wednesday," said Golda.

"Let me see that book," said Yossi. He took it from Malik's hands and leafed through it. "'Jacob Weingarten,' you wrote that name. It's right here."

"Did I write anything else?"

"'Cave of Patriarchs.'"

"Right. Yesterday morning. I remember that."

Yossi turned to Avi, who was standing in the hallway. "Get his camera."

Avi returned with the camcorder and handed it to Yossi. "It's expensive," Yossi observed. "Canon, professional quality. Your phone is not enough?"

"I started using it to help with my memory but it's become a hobby. I must have offered to shoot a video of the wedding."

Avi brought a laptop from the office and attached cables to the camera. He seemed stymied by the options on the camera.

"Just hit the playback button," Malik told him. "It'll do the rest."

An attractive woman came on the screen. "The rain in Spain stays mainly in the plain," she said.

"My girlfriend," Malik explained. "Ex-girlfriend, now that I think of it."

"She's a poet?" asked Yossi.

Malik smiled. "She works in the mayor's office. In New York."

Yossi twirled his finger, indicating to Avi to move ahead. He paused on a camel strutting through the desert. "Where is this?" Yossi asked.

"Jordan. Camping in the desert with the Bedu. It's really something. You'll see Petra next. I remember that perfectly. Have you been there? Amazing place."

Avi sped through, stopping at a scene on a road through an olive grove. There was a line of cars and police vehicles with flashing lights. "Hey, Yossi, it's the Rav's people at the grove!" said Avi. "Shit, that's me!"

The video showed Avi ordering Malik to get back in the car. The video ducked below the dashboard, as if Malik were hiding the lens, and then rose and focused on the storm of stones from the Arabs and the crazed gunfire from the Kahanists as they raced back to their cars. Then the camera found Benny stalking through the trees, firing selectively, killing as he went.

"Are you kidding me? This son of a bitch knew what was going to happen!" Berger cried. "He was making a jihadi video."

"That's ridiculous," said Malik. "I was just driving around getting familiar with the country. It helps me get oriented. Then I saw this and thought to record it. You could use it as evidence."

The next scene was the Cave of the Patriarchs. The video panned the massive Herodian structure and the security fence outside. Then it entered the richly adorned mosque with red-and-gold carpet under the high-arched ceiling. The camera then cut to the Jewish synagogue on the opposite side of the monument, where Jews were davening. Here were the cenotaphs of Jacob, father of the twelve sons who became the tribes of Israel, and one of his wives. Between the Muslim side and the Jewish side, behind bars and bulletproof glass, were the memorials for Abraham and Sarah. The camera began a slow pan inside the Jewish section. In addition to the library and the historical markers, one could see security cameras on the walls and guards in the doorway.

"Looks like surveillance," said Yossi.

"You think these shots are different from what any tourist would shoot?" Malik asked.

But in the next frame Chief Weingarten walked toward the camera and the video ended on a shot of his face, his eyes widened in recognition.

"Why'd you cut it off?" Yossi demanded.

"People feel strange if you just shoot without permission. He may have asked me to stop."

Yossi stared at the screen and then turned to Malik, his expression hardened. "You lied about everything," he said flatly.

"I'm telling the truth."

"You remembered Weingarten getting killed but you didn't remember meeting him."

"I did remember meeting him but not what we talked about, or if we really talked at all."

"It looks like he knows you."

"Never met him, I swear."

"Why would we believe that? He walks directly toward you. He's expecting you."

"He might have thought I was somebody else," Malik said. "It probably wasn't important."

Yossi snorted. "This is bullshit."

"I want to call the embassy now. I've done what you asked, even if you don't like my answers."

"Where's the rest of the video?" Yossi demanded.

"There's no more, that's it. I went back to the hotel and took a nap."

Yossi looked at Avi. "Possible there would be more on the camera? In the trash or something like that?"

"Maybe on another memory chip."

"I'm telling you, that's all there is," said Malik.

"We've got a stranger," said Yossi, "filming our soldiers, our holy places. He's got no identification. He films a violent encounter in the morning. He meets our chief. He follows him. He runs from the police. He says he doesn't remember all this but he's got video proving where he is. So we are suspicious."

"This is insane," said Malik. "Look, here's what you do. Call the embassy like I've been saying. They'll straighten you out." He looked through his notebook. "Want me to give you the number?"

"We've got the number," Yossi said testily.

"Ask for Steven Greenblatt," said Malik. "He will know who I am."

"Who's he?"

"The legal attaché."

Greenblatt was not picking up, so Yossi left a message that he was holding a person who says he is an American citizen on suspicion in the murder of Chief Jacob Weingarten. The name of the suspect was Anthony Abdul Malik.

Greenblatt called back instantly. "Who am I talking to?" he barked.

"Yossi Ben-Gal, acting chief of the Israeli police in Hebron."

"Let me talk to Malik," said Greenblatt.

Yossi put the call on speaker. "Malik, what the fuck?" were the words that came out of Greenblatt's mouth.

"It's a dumb misunderstanding, Steve. Some weird coincidence. I happened to run into their chief shortly before he was killed."

"Listen, Ben-Gal, Malik is FBI," said Greenblatt. "We've known each other for decades. We worked together in the region coordinating with Israeli intel on terror threats. He got blown up by a bomb little over a year ago, so some of the pieces are scrambled."

Yossi looked at Malik. "The United Airlines bomb?"

Malik nodded.

"He may be damaged but he was the best field agent I ever saw, and he's still got better instincts than anyone I know," Greenblatt said.

"Why didn't he tell us he was in the FBI?"

"We asked him to keep it quiet."

"Does he have official business in the territories?"

"I'd rather not say."

"Well, then, I'll just hang on to him till we straighten this out."

Greenblatt laughed. "Look, hardass, you win. I guess it doesn't matter now. Malik has been working terrorist financing. The man in charge here at the embassy set up a meeting with Weingarten, confidential-like, so we treated it as privileged information. He had reached out. Wanted advice. Didn't trust the locals. I don't know the what or the why of it. Guess we'll never know. We sent Malik, our top man. Weingarten was going around protocol, so sending Malik was a way of putting some official distance between us. He just happened to be coming to the region for a wedding. Otherwise it would have been me and I've got my hands full. Hope they're treating you well, Malik."

"Oh, yeah. Milk and cookies."

"Good to hear. Don't want to piss off our allies, do we, Ben-Gal?"

"Hey, Steve, do me a favor," said Malik. "I need a new passport. And some money."

"Will do. I'll send a car for you and we can meet in Jerusalem. Give me a day to get everything together. And, Malik, keep your head down, they're fucking fanatics in that town. No offense, Ben-Gal."

Family

Sheikh Abdullah's Farm, Sept. 27, 2023

The wedding, this is real?" asked Yossi as he drove Malik to the sheikh's house in the fields outside the city.

"Why would you doubt it?"

"Because you lie so easily maybe you forget the difference."

"I didn't tell you everything but everything I told you is true. Some bits I have a hard time remembering. I can see why it would be suspicious. Also, I was told to keep my mouth shut, so that's why I asked you to call Greenblatt. He is authorized to tell you things I can't."

Yossi chewed over some memories of his own. His department had been on alert ever since the Jordanian bombing. "Did you know Husni Obeidat?"

"We were friends," said Malik. "I saw his widow when I was in Amman. He had four kids. I wondered why I was spared and he died."

"You lose people in this business."

Malik looked out at the terraced hills and the scattered houses, built of the limestone that was everywhere, yellowed like an old man's teeth, the same scene as a hundred years ago, or a thousand—the same vineyards, the same olive trees, the same dwellings. On either side of the road were the carcasses of vehicles, stripped of parts and stacked on top of each other. "One helluva junkyard you got here," he observed.

"All stolen from Jews," Yossi said.

"How do you know that?"

"Usually we don't bother, but if we get a tip, we have to find a Palestinian cop before the criminals take it apart. He makes an arrest, then he lets them go as soon as we return to our side. If we're lucky we get the car, at least some of it. They always take the tires first to make it harder. It's a good business for them. Look," he said, pointing to another automotive graveyard, "here are trucks only. They also specialize in tractors and farm machines, or bulldozers that they take from the road crews. They have balls, these guys."

Yossi cast a glance at Malik, gauging how much of the investigation to disclose to a man he didn't really know and whose purpose was still a mystery. Malik was younger, but obviously he had the respect of his superior. Yossi assumed he knew more than he admitted, but without the possibility of arrest he had little leverage. The bombing added credibility to his memory problems, but the partial nature of the affliction was confounding and, to Yossi's thinking, suspicious. "So tell me the truth, what did you talk about with the chief?" he asked.

"I really don't remember much. If it had been important, I would have remembered it, or at least written it down. A lot of chitchat goes right through me like it never happened. I mean, look at the time stamps on the camera. There were only seven minutes between the shot of Weingarten coming into view and the one outside. We probably said hello, exchanged a few remarks, maybe I gave him my card so he could call me when he wanted to talk. Not much time for anything else."

"I still don't believe you."

Malik shrugged and said nothing, which further infuriated Yossi. "He could have handed you some information. That doesn't take seven minutes."

"If he did hand me a document or whatever, it would be in my suitcase, wherever that is."

"The Shabak says this is just an act of terror, but Weingarten had something he wanted to tell you. Something he didn't tell me. So I have to wonder what this something is—did it have anything to do with his murder? Or were the terrorists just looking for any Jew to kill?"

"If there was something exchanged, I don't remember it. There was no sense of urgency or I'd have written it down. Maybe he had second thoughts about meeting at all."

Yossi shook his head in frustration. "I don't buy this memory bullshit. Your stories are too inconsistent. They come and go. It doesn't add up."

"I'd probably feel the same way if I were in your shoes," Malik said.

When he was confounded or really angry and had to put a cork on his emotions, Yossi ground his teeth. It was a bad habit that cost him a fair amount in dental expenses. Vital truths were being withheld, of this he was certain.

Meantime, Malik contented himself with examining the countryside. It was sunset, time for the engagement dinner. The road passed through a village with a café and a gas station. Men in red-checked kaffiyehs were seated in brightly colored plastic chairs smoking shisha and fingering prayer beads. They noted the Israeli plates on Yossi's personal car and glared at him.

"They don't look too happy to see you," Malik observed.

Out of the crowd of pedestrians a man rushed over and pounded on the hood, then walked slowly in front of the car, daring Yossi to run over him. Yossi laughed. "They like to test us. Even the old men, they play this game."

"Is that what you think, it's a game?"

"It's a cycle. The terrorists stir them up, we beat them back. Mow the grass. Never can we let them win. And they never stop. So it goes on and on till the end."

"Isn't that supposed to be the definition of insanity?"

Yossi shrugged. "I don't ask about mentalities. My job is to keep order."

"Must be hard without justice."

"First order, then maybe justice," said Yossi. "With chaos, you don't get either."

"Did you ever think of trying a different approach?"

"We tried that, many times. What we have learned is your people only understand force."

"My people?" Malik asked.

"Whatever you are in America, here you are an Arab."

Malik looked out at the Arabs in the café and on the street. They seemed a world away from who he was.

"You've been here before?" Yossi asked.

"No."

"So what is your relationship?"

"Sheikh Abdullah is my uncle, my father's twin brother."

"You never met him?"

"My dad came to the US before I was born. He promised that he was going to take me to visit his homeland but he passed away and that never really happened. I forgot all about it till I saw on Instagram that my cousin was getting married. I thought: now or never."

"How did you know about the action in your uncle's grove?"

"I didn't know anything. I was just checking things out. Curious to see where my relatives lived before the big get-together."

Yossi mulled this over. "You know the person your cousin is marrying?"

"His name is Jamal Khalil. Never met him." Malik looked at Yossi. "Something tells me you have."

Yossi shrugged. "Many have this name. The Khalil clan claim to have been here since the beginning of time. In Arabic, Khalil is the name they call Hebron, like if you were named New York or Chicago. They have blue eyes, these Khalilis. They say from when Napoleon was here."

"But this particular Jamal Khalil, maybe you've dealt with him?"

"Maybe."

"Tell me about him."

"If it is the same Jamal Khalil, he has passed through our system many times. A radical."

"Violent?"

"He calls himself a peace advocate but he causes trouble wherever he goes."

"What would you be if you were in his place?" Malik asked.

"We don't ask ourselves theoretical questions."

They rode in silence. It was getting late. Malik worried that the family he had never met was waiting on dinner for him. Or maybe not; maybe they had forgotten he was coming, or else they had simply set a plate aside. He hoped the latter.

They came to a narrow road with the asphalt worn down to the dirt, like an old shoe. The road ascended through farmland and then Yossi turned onto a driveway lined with cedars. Cars and trucks were parked on the road, indicating a large gathering. The night sky was vivid, the moon lighting up the vast vineyard that spread across many acres. "This is the place," said Yossi. "Sheikh Abdullah Abdul Malik."

"Thanks for the lift," said Malik.

"One last thing. Your boss says you're a top man. Tell me, why does a fresh corpse have extreme rigor in his hand?"

"Instant death," said Malik. "Cadaveric spasm. Probably gunshot to the head."

"No, no, they cut his neck. It was on the video."

"The actual murder?" Malik asked.

Yossi hesitated. "Not the actual murder," he conceded.

"Good luck on your investigation."

"Yeah, well, now I lose my only suspect."

"That shouldn't be a problem," said Malik. "Any Arab will do, right?"

"As soon as the wedding is over, go back to America. I don't want to see you again."

THE HOUSE WAS OLD and well used, like farmhouses everywhere. A cistern in the yard caught the moonlight. The vineyard spread for acres, and down the slope Malik could make out the olive groves. His uncle must be a wealthy man, he figured, although how that was accounted in a country so broken was hard to understand. Aside from the land nothing here spoke of money, only of immense unending labor.

His knock was answered almost immediately and there stood his father, or his replica. For an instant, Malik couldn't speak. He hadn't thought about what this moment might mean to him—seeing the embodiment of his father as a white-haired, wrinkled old man. The olive skin, the heavy-lidded eyes, the jutting chin, the prowlike nose were identical in his father's twin. Even the mole on his right cheek. It was eerie. Malik felt lightheaded, overwhelmed by the occasion and the shock of the wreck.

Sheikh Abdullah held him by the shoulders to examine him. "Allah!" he cried. "You look like your father!"

Malik laughed. "I was just thinking the same about you!"

"Cousin Tony!" A radiant young woman came rushing toward Malik. "You're here! You're really here!"

"Dina!" he cried. "Instagram doesn't do you justice!"

"Are you all right? We were worried about you."

"I'm okay. There was a wreck. Nothing serious, just bumps and bruises."

"Your head!" she said, gently touching a knot on his forehead.

Malik hadn't noticed it until now. "Does it look awful? I haven't had a chance to look in a mirror. Maybe I shouldn't, what do you think?"

She got a serious look and said, "Not till after dinner. We're all starving."

Dina was brown-eyed with delicate, expressive brows that seemed to illustrate everything she said, serious or sad or surprising, jumping up or knitting together for emphasis. Her lips were full, slightly turned down at the corners with a tendency to pout, at once sensual and childlike. She arranged her hair in classic fashion, swept back in a bun, so that her slender, lovely neck was fully on view. She took Malik's hand and led him into the dining room, which was filled with family. They cheered when he entered and chattered excitedly in Arabic and fragmented English. "This is the American!" someone said. Another muttered, "Now we can eat!"

Dina introduced him to uncles and aunts and grandparents— a confusing assortment of unfamiliar people gathered to merge the families of the young couple. Sheikh Abdullah's wife, Nirmeen, was a stout woman with a blue hijab and a walker parked behind her chair. Dina's attractive mom, Yasmine, was married to cousin Hasan, who ran a computer shop in Bethlehem. Yasmine appeared not much older than Dina, more like sisters than mother and child. There were too many relationships to take in all at once.

"And this is Jamal," said Dina. "My husband-to-be."

"Congratulations, young man," Malik said, realizing in the same instant that Jamal was not that young, in his mid-thirties probably— Malik's age. He was striking, with the physique of a former athlete, broad-shouldered, his beard closely trimmed, his blue eyes marked with caution. "You are welcome," he said, hesitating just long enough before shaking Malik's offered hand for it to feel insulting.

Malik realized with dismay that he was seated at the head of the table, the place of honor because he was a stranger. Dina sat on one side of him and Jamal on the other. They both spoke excellent English, which compensated for Malik's imperfect Arabic, but no one was talking. They were all staring at him expectantly, as if he were supposed to make a speech.

"I just want to say how grateful I am to meet all of you," he said. "I've always wanted to make the journey to visit my father's homeland. He told me that when I finally came to the Holy Land I would find much of value. Since my parents passed away, I haven't had a family, but now I realize that there was always one waiting for me." Malik looked at the faces, which seemed to be demanding more. "I guess I should tell you a little about me," he said.

Dina whispered, "Actually, they're waiting for you to start."

"Start what?"

"They won't eat until you do."

Malik looked down the long table and saw nothing but platters of dates and pitchers of lemonade. He reached out and took a plump date. Everyone's eyes followed him as he took a bite. Then they ravenously grabbed for dates.

"I thought this was some big feast or something," he muttered to Dina. She laughed—a rich, musical laugh. Dishes began arriving—tahini, yogurt, stuffed grape leaves, falafel, tabouli—filling every space on the table. Malik piled up his plate, feeling conspicuous but also desperate for nourishment.

A young teenage boy hobbled in and sat on the other side of Dina. He affected indifference to the entire tableful of relatives. "You could at least say hello to your cousin Tony," Dina said in Arabic under her breath.

Omar turned to Malik. He was a handsome kid with a feathery adolescent mustache. His eyes were large and expressive. Malik wondered what the injury was to his leg. "Hello," said Omar. Malik held out his fist and they bumped. Omar nodded in approval.

"What grade are you in?" Malik asked.

"Ninth."

"My little brother is a computer genius," said Dina.

"No kidding?"

"Seriously," she said. "He's already coding."

"Wow, I'm impressed."

Omar suppressed a grin. "I'm a hacker," he said.

"Do you do things like rob banks and bring down governments?"

"Not yet," he said seriously. "Mainly I download stuff, like Netflix, Hulu. Everything free! We just binged on the final season of *Game of Thrones*."

"So you're Mr. Robot."

Omar beamed. "Are you like a superhero FBI guy?" he asked.

"Superhero is overstating it by a mile."

"So what do you do?"

"Honestly, not much."

Omar gave him a blank look.

"I got injured last year and I've been in various kinds of therapy since then. This trip is sort of a coming-out party."

"You look like a pirate."

"Omar!" Dina exclaimed.

"That's okay," said Malik. "I'm still getting used to the way people react to me. There must have been a lot of one-eyed pirates in the day."

"Moshe Dayan," said Aunt Nirmeen.

"Yeah, I get a lot of that."

"I found the beheading video on the internet," said Omar. "It's gross. Want to see?"

Dina looked horrified. "Omar, don't say things like that!"

Sheikh Abdullah frowned. "This is a great sadness for us. Weingarten was our friend."

"Why should we call him a friend?" said Jamal. "He was part of the occupation. I do not call him an enemy, but he was an adversary, not a friend."

"He protected us!" Abdullah protested. "Not like this new one."

"We should protect ourselves," an older man said.

"That's a stupid dream," Jamal said sharply.

The whole table was suddenly oblivious to Malik's presence, having plunged into an argument that had been going on, he supposed, their entire lives. It became obvious that the older man Jamal was talking so heatedly to must be a close relation. They spoke with an angry intimacy.

"He was a Jew," the older man said, as if that settled the matter.

"If we call every Jew an enemy we will never find anyone to make peace."

Jamal turned to Malik to explain. "I love my father but he misplaces his faith. He thought the intifadas would bring a solution. Instead, they only fed the violence."

Jamal's father clucked his tongue in disdain. His face was dark and fierce. Malik noticed he bore a scar on his neck, which might account for his raspy voice. "The Jews understand one thing only, when we stand up to them with weapons."

Many around the table nodded in agreement.

"Your way has gotten us nothing!" Jamal said.

"And what have you brought us?" his father snapped. "Only shame."

Sheikh Abdullah slapped the table, bringing the argument to a startled end. "We will not have this in our house. Here we are one family. We disagree but we do not fight each other." He looked around the table to make sure everyone understood, then he addressed Malik. "You visit at a difficult time. Our hearts are heavy because some young members of our clan were killed protecting our land. Three boys, handsome and full of life. They belonged to different families but we all protect each other because no one else will do so. When Weingarten was alive, he tried to help."

"But he didn't, did he?" said Jamal's father.

"Maybe he would have tried," said Abdullah. "Perhaps for this he was killed."

"I'm sorry," said Malik. "I didn't realize you were all grieving."

"We try to be happy because you are here," said Dina. She spoke warmly but her words were solemn. "Our hearts are divided between joy and sorrow. We have so much sorrow we need to make more room for happiness."

"The police refuse to release the bodies, so we are unable to release our sorrow," said Jamal's father. "We only feel anger."

The conversation subsided into side talk until two servants appeared carrying an entire roasted lamb. Now that the curtains opened on the real meal Malik realized how badly he had miscalculated with the mezes. As the sheikh carved generous portions from the lamb, Malik asked, "Have you lived in Hebron your entire life?"

"Our family has farmed this valley for two hundred years," Abdullah responded, passing a plate around to Malik that could feed three people. "Until your father, no one left. Tariq wanted the good life in America, this is understandable."

"And did he have a good life?" asked Dina. "We all wonder what it would be like to live in America or Europe, or anyplace, really, that isn't here."

"He ran a small grocery in Philadelphia. My mom was from Arkansas, a state in the southern part of the US. My parents didn't have an easy relationship and they separated when I was ten. I lived with her in Little Rock and saw my dad during the summers. When he got sick I spent a month taking care of him before he died. That's when I really got to know him. It wasn't much time. But to answer your question, I think he never fully left his life here. He still had his accent, and as he got older he became homesick."

"Homesick?" asked Nirmeen.

"Meaning he really missed his home, this place."

Everyone nodded. This is what they expected.

"Tariq always sent money to the community," said Abdullah.

"That was thoughtful, he didn't have much," said Malik.

"In fact, he built a school," said Abdullah, "the one Omar attends now."

Malik couldn't take this in at first. "He did what?"

"He contributed his fortune to the construction of the boys' school. Many people don't realize this, as he refused to have his name entered. He was a truly great man. I feel pride that he was my brother but also embarrassed that I have done so little in comparison, despite I have so many more years of living. Perhaps we looked alike but his soul was much bigger."

Never had Malik been so stunned by such a revelation. He had looked upon his father with affection mixed with pity—often the case with the children of immigrants who regard their parents as they would a handicapped relative. The idea that his father made a "fortune" in that little shop in Fishtown opened a window on his character that Malik had never imagined.

"Anthony, can I ask you a question?" said Jamal.

"Call me Tony."

"Tony. Are you a Muslim? A Christian? Are you an Arab? An Arkansas person? What are you?"

Malik laughed. "I'm all those things. My mother grew up in the Baptist faith but she didn't make a big deal out of religion. Neither did my dad, really."

"You don't think religion is a 'big deal,' but here it defines us, it orders our lives."

"I guess you could just say I'm an American. We tend to be all mixed up, our genes, our goals, our identities. If you ask me to define myself, I say I love mysteries and the challenges they pose. I'm a huge baseball fan and sports would have been my alternate life. I've lived alone off and on and have become a passable cook. I know religion is a lot more important here than in America, but that doesn't mean I don't respect your beliefs."

"Jamal, he's come a long way to help us celebrate the biggest day of our lives," said Dina, noticing his impatient expression. "Can we leave it at that?"

"Of course, my dear," said Jamal, in a tone that indicated he wasn't done. "I just wanted to know where his loyalties are." He turned to Malik. "Among Arabs, loyalty is second only to religion. For us, this is also a 'big deal.'"

"If I've disrespected anyone, I apologize. We come from two different cultures, two different histories. After you're married I hope we'll have lots of time to solve the world's problems."

"'Different histories,'" said Jamal, once again putting quotes around the phrase and indicating that he was not finished prosecuting his case. "You know that for centuries we have been ruled by Persians, Greeks, Romans, Ottomans, the British—and now by Americans and Israelis. Do you know any of this history?"

"I know you've gotten a rotten deal, but America doesn't rule over you."

"Your government gives Israel nearly four billion dollars a year. Your rich Jews give even more."

"Jamal!" said Abdullah. "He's our guest."

"It is a luxury to know so little," said Jamal.

Dessert arrived, a spectacular pastry called *farareer*, stuffed with pistachios. Nirmeen poured a lake of honey and passed the first dish to Malik, who sampled it gamely, making suitable noises of appreciation. The sheikha pointed to Dina. "Took her two whole days!"

"Dina made this? Amazing!" Malik said.

She nodded, with a shy smile, but when she picked up her teacup, her hands were shaking.

17

"The Rav Is Right"

Kiryat Arba, Sept. 27, 2023

Golda Radidowicz went to the synagogue that night to celebrate a bris for a boy born to her former IDF commander and his wife, Jules and Rose Garfinkle, two of her oldest friends. Golda's circle in the settlement was smaller than most. Not everyone in Kiryat Arba was an extremist, but it was a highly conservative environment that Golda would always be a part of and apart from. Without children or a partner, she was excluded from many social occasions. Her talents as an actress, in the theatrical performances sometimes staged in the concert hall, were appreciated, but she was seen as an odd duck because of her bohemian private life, which was far less scandalous than popularly imagined. When she entered a room, with her blue-streaked hair and nose piercing, heads turned in her direction—and then quickly away.

That was as she intended. One of the consequences of being a police officer is that she engaged with the world outside of the compound, but what set her apart more profoundly was her free spirit. She had a horror of losing herself in the group mind. She was eclectic and curious where so many people around her were simply dogmatic. She was also an attractive woman in a community where women abstained from emphasizing their beauty. She knew that many of the residents—especially women—looked down on her, whispering that she was flaunting her sexuality, and by their standards, she was. Golda deliberately aggravated their disdain with her cosmetic experiments, which would go unnoticed in most of

Israel but in Kiryat Arba stirred intense resentment on the part of the fanatics and those whose world was just a hundred meters wide.

Tonight, because of the shock of Weingarten's death, the bris served as an opportunity for the community to gather and hash over the news, and as a police officer, Golda would be in the center of conversation. There was little she could tell, since the investigation was ongoing and, so far, fruitless.

When she arrived the settlers were singing and davening in the direction of the beautifully wrought ark, its brass doors depicting grape vines and the Hebron Hills beyond. Despite the crowd it was chilly in the stone room. The men were wearing puff jackets and hoodies over their tzitzit—the ritual fringes meant to prompt the remembrance of God's commandments. Some of the other men, including Jules, wore white prayer shawls and tefillin—small black boxes containing biblical verses—that are strapped on the head and an arm for morning prayer and on special occasions such as a bris. Some of the women left their hair uncovered, others wore turbans. Dozens of children scurried around, excited by the ceremony of welcoming a new Jew into the community. It was the eighth day of the baby's life, the age that Isaac, Abraham's son, was circumcised, so the bris had to be on this date, despite the solemn and portentous mood of the colony.

The Garfinkles were Likudniks, like Golda, politically conservative but not so extreme as the leadership in Kiryat Arba. She always felt at liberty to speak freely with them. Jules held his infant son, who was swaddled in a blue blanket on a floral-patterned pillow. Jules's father, Yitzhak, sat in a chair next to the altar, a handsome old man with an untrimmed white beard. Yitzhak was part of the Kiryat Arba leadership. Everyone knew that he had been close to Baruch Goldstein and still prayed at his grave. Golda wondered what it had been like for Jules to grow up under the influence of such an imposing figure, and how he had avoided becoming an extremist like his father. It was said that Yitzhak was not so radical as a younger man; events made him that way. Of course, every extremist has an origin story that makes violence a natural conclusion.

Yitzhak's face lit with delight when his grandson was placed in his lap. The mohel approached with his tools and the crowd pressed closely together to witness the cutting. The baby was sleeping, despite the hubbub in the room. Golda finally got a peek at him. He favored Rose, with her fine cheekbones and delicate nose. It occurred to Golda that this darling boy could be a part of her life. She would sit for him on occasion, play games, watch him grow. She sometimes considered offering acting lessons. Maybe people would be a little more open to her if she had allies among the children. She would have a part to play, the community aunt.

The mohel opened up the baby's onesie and removed the diaper. The boy was suddenly alert and alarmed and began to wail. The mohel worked swiftly and adroitly; it was a performance he had done many times. He spread the baby's legs and wiped his genitals with disinfectant. Jules held the razor as the mohel took his hand in his own, so that it would be the father who made the cut that signi-fied his son was now a Jew. It went smoothly. The mohel squeezed blood from the wound and sucked it into his mouth, his lips over the head of the tiny penis, then Jules dipped a cotton swab in wine and dabbed it on the lips of his child, whom he named David.

Golda wondered about the pain that Jews intentionally inflict on such innocents, a form of disfigurement that God imposed on Moses and the men of his tribe so that they would always be marked as a people apart. The Nazis used to force men to drop their pants so they could identify the Jews.

The dinner afterward was subdued and Golda didn't stay long; she was exhausted by the day. She spent a few moments congratulat-ing Jules and Rose about the bris. "It's a shame it had to be on top of the tragedy," she told them. Weingarten had been a friend of the Garfinkles.

Jules thanked Golda for her sentiments but he was curt. "Some-thing has to be done," he said.

"Jules, we are doing everything possible to find out who did this. And when we do, you can be sure we'll bring them to justice."

Jules had an expression that she hadn't seen in him before. His jaw was set and he wouldn't look in Golda's eyes; instead he stared at his hands as if some answer waited there.

"It has to stop with this," he said. "We're done with waiting for justice."

Rose nodded.

"I watched the blood of my son—Jewish blood—spilled for the sake of the Lord, sacred blood, and I thought of Jacob, our friend, and his slaughter—also innocent Jewish blood—spilled for the sake of—what?" Jules said. "One a holy act, the other a work of terror. We cannot abide this. Something has to be done—now."

Golda was shocked by his vehemence. "Jules, I don't know what you're thinking but restrain yourself. We have laws, we have police, we have an army, and we will find the killers and bring justice. This is not for you alone."

"Restraint!" he cried. "You ask me to tie my hands in the face of this crime against my community? It's not just Jacob Weingarten they killed. They butchered him because he is a Jew. As they would do to any of us. Are we to sit here and wait for them to act again? Do you doubt that they will? And who will they kill next? Would it be Rose? Would it be our precious son, eight days old? You ask me to trust the police and our soldiers and our justice system, but did they stop the murder of Jacob? Did they stop the massacre of 1929? These questions answer themselves, Golda. There has always been persecution of the Jews. The only thing that permits it to continue is the restraint you praise so highly. We cannot afford to be made weak by our supposed high morality. What is it worth if Jews die while we sit on our hands?"

Golda could scarcely talk; she was breathless with anxiety from hearing Jules speak with such cold fury—to her, a friend, who longed to hold his child and be a part of their lives. Jules had drawn a line between them, separating their friendship. "I don't know what you're thinking but be careful, Jules," she managed to say.

Jules shook his head. "It's time for us to act. There is no room in this land for Arabs and Jews together. The Rav is right."

18

Benny

Hebron, Sept. 27, 2023

I need to apologize," said Yasmine, Dina and Omar's mother, as she drove Malik to his hotel in town. She was a handsome woman and he could see her fine features reflected in her daughter, especially her rich brown eyes and sensual mouth. Yasmine talked rapidly and dramatically. She wouldn't hear of him taking a cab, especially after he admitted he had no money or credit cards, everything having been stolen from him. She also seemed eager to talk with someone outside her usual circle. He guessed her anxiety was always present; she fidgeted and had a hard time keeping her hands on the wheel when she talked.

"No need to apologize," he said. "I didn't take offense. He's passionate, that much is clear."

"Passionate?" she exclaimed. "Jamal, he is a hothead, but I admire him. He is not afraid to tell the truth. We all of us live with fantasies, that there will be a solution to our problem or that there will never be, one or the other, we cling to these ideas and fight about them all the time, as you see. But Jamal, he has another perspective, so everyone is angry with him."

"Yeah, what's going on with him and his father?"

"You really don't know anything about these people?"

"Honestly, this is the strangest day of my life. I don't have a clue."

Yasmine laughed. "Okay, I feel sorry for you. I will tell you whatever. As for Jamal and his father, their tragedy begins with his older brother, Nader, one of our famous 'martyrs.' He shot a settler family, killing even the baby in the perambulator. His face was in posters all over the West Bank celebrating this heroic deed. The IDF eliminated him straight away. His parents were broken. They live on subsidies from the PA—the Palestinian Authority—which supports the families of martyrs. All the father wants is revenge, it is the only flavor he cares to taste. And Hamas knows this. The first thing they do is declare Nader a martyr, then they recruit the family. Obviously, Jamal is the prize. But Jamal drew a different lesson. He concluded that violence only creates more violence, which becomes the great excuse the Israelis use to push us off our land."

"The cop who drove me here knows him."

"Of course, he has been arrested so many times. Last year it was for leading protests against the new temple the Rav is planning on the sheikh's land. Jamal is very clever. The Israelis keep inventing new laws to keep him quiet, but until recently nothing has succeeded. The PA also arrested him, because he criticizes their corruption. Hamas hates him because he preaches nonviolence. We don't agree with him about this, by the way. Nothing ever changes in our lives except by violence. That's the only language the Israelis understand. And they say the same about us."

"He sounds like a very brave man but a risky prospect as a husband."

"We worried so much about this! Perhaps you don't know that my first husband is in prison. He was high in Hamas. So Dina and Omar have different fathers. I do not want Dina to repeat the same experience."

"That must have been hard for you."

She waved away his concern. "Everyone here has a story, but in a way they're all the same. Many women live alone because their husbands are dead or in prison. Dina's father is named Ibrahim, Sheikh Abdullah's only living child. People consider him a leader of the resistance, but what kind of leader can he be in prison for eternity? Hasan, Omar's father, he is totally different. He does not let radical thoughts enter his ears. I am grateful for his support, but the truth is he is broken. I think all men in Palestine are one or the other, broken or defiant. When Dina started seeing Jamal I was frantic. I spoke to him privately. He assured me that he is giving up his activism for Dina. He says he will live normally from now on. He has already lost one family. His wife and little boy moved to London ten years ago or so. The wife was not made for the resistance. I also don't want that life for Dina—the resistance or the exile or the broken man."

"Dina is remarkable."

Yasmine nodded vigorously as she fumbled in her purse for a pack of cigarettes. "She's the family secret. Everything she does is perfect! She speaks English better than any of us! She is smarter, she is nicer, the only thing wrong with Dina is that she is perfect! Of course, this is her mother speaking."

"Do you think she's young to marry?"

"She's eighteen. I was fourteen when I married and sixteen when I had her. It's not unusual in our culture for girls to marry young and to marry an older man. For the man to marry, he must have an income and a home, and we have all these young men who can't afford it. Their hormones make them insane. And what do they do? They become radical. It is an occupation for them. Maybe also they think of it like a romance, instead of a wife, something they can afford. It only costs them their life. This is my opinion." She laughed. "You can call the newspaper and give them the news."

"She's still in school, right?"

"Thanks to God, she is at the Hebrew University in Jerusalem."

"That's a surprise."

"You have to understand, Dina is ambitious. Hebrew is the best school, and Dina secured a permit to study. Very hard to get. This is a determined girl."

"What is she studying?"

"She announced she will be a pharmacist. Where this came from we don't know. But in Palestine the pharmacy is a very good job. Of course, we don't expect her to work. Sheikh Abdullah has announced that Dina will be the inheritor of half of his estate. If she marries, she receives the entire property. You can imagine how this complicates matters, with every bachelor in Palestine presenting themselves for examination."

"Really? In that big family there is only one heir?"

"Ibrahim is the only child, and he is in prison. Dina is the only direct grandchild, there are no other blood kin except for you. So if anything happened to Dina, you'd be the probable heir."

"Me?" Malik laughed.

"Seriously. Abdullah has already said that genetically you are his son."

"Well, I hope Dina stays safe, because I don't know the first thing about agriculture."

"Neither does Jamal! I am always discussing this with Dina."

"How does he make a living?"

"Before I say, you should know about Jamal that he is an educated man. His degree is in engineering, with honors. He is intelligent, as you see. This is what Dina loves, his mind. But he works as a butcher. Actually, as a butcher's assistant, in the Old City. And he is grateful even for this."

She offered Malik a cigarette, which hadn't happened to him in years. He shook his head. "I know, you Americans, you insist on living forever, your healthy lives," she said as she took one for herself, rapping it on the dashboard before lighting up. "Here we don't have such expectations. We are distorted, all of us, by depression or rage or hopelessness, you name it, all the bad emotions. And yet . . ." She took a drag of her cigarette and cracked the window. "There's something noble about us, I think. That sounds vain, sorry."

"What do you mean?"

"I don't expect you to understand how the Israelis suffocate us. Imagine you are just a single meter tall, like a little child. You live in this world, but everybody else is bigger and stronger than you," she said, hands flying. "They step on you all the time and then complain that you are in the way, this is their world, so we should pack up and go to some other country, some place for small people. Instead, we stay here. We resist by refusing to leave. We accept the misery they put on us but decline to surrender. After what they've done already it only remains to kill us, and this is what we wait for."

Malik wished she would keep her hands on the wheel while she drove, but forced himself to look away. "The sheikh said that Weingarten protected you. From whom?"

"The people who follow the Rav. They come from all over the world."

"The old guy with the Santa Claus beard? His picture is all over town."

"They say he is a man of God but for us he is of the devil. He wants to buy Sheikh Abdullah's land but the sheikh won't sell."

"So he just takes it?"

Yasmine nodded. "Weingarten stood in the way. He was a friend. We don't trust this new one, Ben-Gal. He works with them. With Weingarten, there were always two sides, not just the fist but the open hand. When Omar was shot, Weingarten provided the pass so he could get treated in Israel."

"Is that what happened to Omar's leg?"

"The Israelis shot him at a protest. He was twelve years old. So first they shoot him and then they kindly give him medical treatment. We live in this paradox."

As they came into Hebron the air was hazy, like fog, which seemed strange, given the dry heat, but then Yasmine said, "They're burning the city. Look!"

It took a moment for Malik to make out the figures in the smoke and shadows a couple blocks ahead of them, darting back and forth in front of the flames inside the windows. He could smell the smoke now.

"The followers of the Rav," Yasmine said. "And look—" she pointed at an armored vehicle blocking the street—"the Israelis have imposed a curfew." She pulled over, uncertain what to do. "I knew this would happen. Please God don't let it stop the wedding."

There was shouting in the distance and then an explosion. "You better go back to the farm," Malik said. "It'll be safer there."

"And what will you do?"

"I'll make my way to the hotel and keep out of sight. It's nearby. I doubt they'll target it."

"These people are crazy, you can't tell where they will go. And what if they see you?"

"I'll be quick."

Yasmine tossed her cigarette out the window. "If they think you had anything to do with the murder they'll kill you instantly." She looked at him intently. "I'm telling you truth. They don't care about your life."

"I'll be careful. You should turn around and go straight back."

"Tony, please come back with me."

"The hotel is five minutes away."

She reached into her purse again and came up with a handful of shekels. "You need some cash," she said matter-of-factly.

"No, please."

"Pay me back when you get your money."

Malik hurried down a dark side street that was faintly illuminated by a burning car in the distance. Without his phone he didn't have a guide to the hotel. He knew it was north, so he turned onto a bigger street in that direction. The walls were covered with graffiti. They said "Price Tag." Stars of David were painted on the shops, a way of claiming credit for the vandalism for Jews in general. Stores were looted; an appliance shop was emptied of anything it was possible to carry.

Malik kept to the shadows, walking quickly, his training kicking in. There was nobody on the street, fear had chased everyone indoors. He was very aware of his aloneness, his exposure. He was going to have a bad case of shakes when this was all over, but he didn't have time for that now.

He had to cross a major street alight with burning cars and buildings. A block away a gang carrying semiautomatic weapons and sidearms was preparing torches and Molotov cocktails. Even from a distance he could tell they were teenagers; they had that manic energy and jerkiness, like marionettes, bouncing and jumping with excitement. Something else he saw that stunned him: a pair of IDF soldiers were doing nothing to stop them. In fact, they were guarding them.

Malik lurked in the shadows until they all seemed focused on a boy throwing a burning bomb through a shop window. The glass shattered and an instant later a bright bulb of flame erupted from the store. As the boys cheered the explosion, Malik walked across the street, trying to appear unconcerned. He made it to the opposite curb when he heard a voice cry out, "There's one!"

As soon as he turned a corner Malik broke into a run. He was not especially fast, nor was he even sure of the hotel's location or whether it mattered. His only goal now was to evade the teenage gang. He could hear their shouts as they raced after him. He turned left at the next block, then immediately realized his error. It was a narrow side street but longer than he expected—long enough that his pursuers who were closing the distance would see him. They were young and fast and propelled by adolescent zeal. He quickly ducked behind a garbage can in front of a Greek restaurant, praying that they hadn't spotted him. He saw them come around the corner, then they paused where Malik had turned. The gang split in half, one going the opposite way and the other coming directly at him.

He could make out four boys. Each of them armed. If he ran now, they could easily shoot him down. Their huge shadows flickered on the walls from the flames of their torches. Malik longed for a gun; the odds would still be against him, but he would have an outside chance. They approached cautiously, suspecting he was hiding nearby; they looked in doorways with their weapons pointed. There was no way they were going to miss him.

Malik stood up. "Hey," he said. He raised his hands.

The boys stopped. Malik recognized two of them from the police station, the young one the others deferred to and the big guy who was the chief agitator. There were no soldiers with them. The big one chambered a round in his Glock and said something in Hebrew that Malik didn't understand, except that he called the younger one Benny. They talked in low urgent whispers.

"You're the American," Benny said. He indicated the other boys. "They say you killed our friend the chief. When Jewish blood is spilled we repay the insult a thousand times."

One of the boys thrust a torch in Malik's face, close enough to singe his eyebrows. Benny made no effort to interfere. "They arrested you," he said.

"They let me go," Malik said, dodging the flames as the boy toyed with him.

"Why is that?"

"Because I'm innocent. I'm just a visitor."

Benny nodded, either because this was information he already knew or because he had weighed it and found it meaningless. He had a feline passivity in his manner, like a cat toying with its prey.

Malik did not doubt that he would kill him without remorse or even curiosity. "The city is burning and you had to take a walk or something? We find this strange."

"I was just going back to my hotel."

"What is your hotel?"

"The Abu Mazen."

"So you are Fatah?"

"I'm not political."

Malik kept glancing at the big guy with the Glock pointed at him, so eager to pull the trigger. "Let's do it, Benny," he said in English. "Why wait around for this guy to unload some of his bullshit." He spoke with a Boston accent.

Benny looked at him, then back to Malik. "Yossi made a mistake, Itai. This one didn't kill the chief. He's an American who doesn't know anything." Then he turned to Malik. "That's true, isn't it?"

"That's true. Absolutely true."

"You are new, so you don't understand shit about our culture. Here in Hebron we struggle for our land. You get it? Arabs are not welcome here. You are an Arab, but because you are also an American we accept you, for the moment. Many of us were Americans once. So we permit you to be here. But listen to me: this is our land, Jewish land. Every piece of it is ours, God-given. Now you understand?"

Malik nodded slowly.

"Enjoy your stay in our country," Benny said, then wandered off with the other boys.

MALIK STOOD IN the bathroom staring at himself in the mirror. It was the face of a living man. Several times in his life he had felt close to death. Ever since the bomb went off he lived with the idea that he should be dead. It colored the way he looked at the world, the way he related to others, always expecting that death would leap out at him again. Now, in a single day, he had escaped mortality again and again. The collision caused by that maniac cop—it was hard to believe anyone survived—his body still trembled from the impact of the wreck. His head throbbed like a tolling church bell. Suppose the police had surrendered him to the mob in the station, he had no doubt how that would have turned out. But the encounter with the boys—they were still children, not one of them more than eighteen, some much younger—they would have killed him for the thrill of it, his death would have been nothing more than a brief amusement, quickly forgotten.

He sat down to make notes about the day so he could fix the events in his memory. He recalled Sheikh Abdullah's revelation about his father. He ran that little corner shop in Philly for decades. It seemed to Malik a sad life, the modest apartment his father lived in, for so many years alone, isolated in part by his immigrant background, his apparent inability to prosper, to find a steady circle of friends. Was any of that true? He had never thought of his father as well-off or generous, and yet he had endowed a school in his homeland, a beautiful gesture, in some respects the pinnacle of the immigrant experience. People come to America from all over the world and send money home to support their families or to build the communities they left behind. His father never said a word to him about his philanthropy. He had said only that he hoped that one day Malik would visit the place where he grew up and scatter his ashes in his homeland.

In the last months of his father's life, Malik returned frequently to Philly to close up the shop. That part of town was being redeveloped and the landlord was eager to tear it down and build condos. There would be no trace of Tariq Abdul Malik in America after that. His father had done a commendable job of settling his affairs before lung cancer carried him away. Even toward the end, his memories of his Palestinian childhood remained vivid and affectionate. The Hebron he recalled was sweet, beautiful, lively, full of intrigue but not violent. If he trusted his father's fond memories, the Palestinians and the Jewish settlers were sometimes at odds but they weren't cruel to each other. Listening to those stories, Malik wondered why his father ever left.

Now his only remaining family was here in Hebron. They were a troubled and endangered clan, his uncle and aunt and cousins, vivid and obstinate, nothing like the freewheeling urbanites in Philadelphia or the soft-spoken, comfortable people he had known in Little Rock, certainly not the cosmopolitans of New York. Although here he was no longer a stranger in their company, he was one of them, in some ways more a part of them than he had felt in his other homes. He felt protective of the family and even the clan, which he had never thought about before. Thousands, maybe millions of other Abdul Maliks filled the globe, his tribe. He had a people.

19

Five Minutes

West Bank, Sept. 28, 2023

Yossi showed his badge to a Shabak officer at the door of an abandoned marble factory beside a quarry in the Hebron Hills. It was at the end of a gravel road, a place few knew about, including Yossi until now. It was peaceful out here—no horns or city noises, the sun just coming up, the air fresh, and fall wildflowers in bloom, phlox and cyclamen and plants his wife would have known.

Inside the ruins of the factory forensic detectives were collecting evidence, dusting for fingerprints, using tweezers to pick up strands of hair—a full-blown investigation of the type that Yossi dreamed of but saw mainly on television. Obviously Tamar was taking the investigation more seriously; the rounding up of usual suspects had produced nothing. He found her standing in front of a Hamas flag on the rear wall.

"Five minutes," she said furiously. "We missed them by five minutes."

"Anything at all?" he asked.

"Shredded documents. Maybe something in them. They didn't have a chance to burn them."

"Still, remarkable work finding this place. And so quickly."

Tamar shrugged, meaning it didn't matter how smart or capable they were, they were also unlucky. "I have a bad feeling about you, Yossi. You're supposed to tell me everything. And then I hear about this FBI person."

"I didn't want to trouble you with needless speculation, and it would have made no difference. Anyway, you're on the trail, just five minutes behind after all. You'll get them, Tamar, you always do."

She looked at him sternly. It was hard for her to see through flattery, she had so little of it in her life. "Everything means everything," she said.

"I understand. I won't make that mistake again." He looked around the room. "You think it's Hamas, no question?"

"Why would you doubt it?"

"I'm not doubting anything. I just want to understand how your mind works."

"It's obvious, isn't it?" she asked, pointing to the Hamas flag.

"It would seem so."

"Yossi, I get impatient with you. Why don't you just be straight and tell me what you're thinking?"

"Just that Hamas doesn't cut heads. Daesh, yes. Maybe Islamic Jihad would think about it. But it's not their style."

"Until now."

"Of course, I'm sure you're right. And the man who did this, you suppose him to be Zayyat?"

She registered that Yossi had done his homework. "That's the working hypothesis. He's the engineer behind the scenes, the bomb maker, the recruiter. Ruthless. Well connected. We think he's hiding in Gaza."

"They come and go, as you know," said Yossi.

Tamar nodded. "The tunnels never stop, no matter how many times we blow them up." She looked at the lake of blood on the floor, now just a dark stain. "They didn't even bother to mop it."

Yossi stepped around the bloodstains to examine the cinder-block wall. Near the base was a neat hole, scarcely noticeable—at least by the team of detectives who were scouring the room. Yossi couldn't help himself. "Tamar, do you suppose this could be a bullet hole?"

Tamar signaled to one of the detectives. He was surprised and chagrined. "Definitely," he said. "We'll dig it out at once."

"Of course, it has nothing to do with Weingarten's death," Tamar said. "We saw what happened."

"But you never know, do you?" said Yossi. "These days, people can fake almost anything. And we didn't see the actual moment of the killing, only the moment after."

"Why is that even relevant?"

"Remember, Tamar, the extreme rigor in the chief's hand. Must have been caused by a cadaveric spasm, set off by instant death, such as a gunshot to the brain."

At this point every detective in the room was looking at Yossi with expressions ranging from curiosity to disbelief. He could tell he made a strategic error by revealing so much. Tamar now regarded him as a competitor.

"It was just a guess," he said, as the detective produced the slug from the wall.

Yossi drove back to Hebron, preoccupied by his conversation with Tamar and the scene of the crime. He couldn't pinpoint the reason for his discomfort. Small things. The Hamas flag was damning, but why hadn't their spokespeople said anything? Ordinarily they would be hammering reporters and bragging about how they humiliated the occupiers once again. At least he had learned more about Zayyat. He was now the main suspect in Yossi's mind, even if he was puzzlingly quiet about claiming credit. There really wasn't anyone else.

20

A Simple Man

Hebron, Sept. 28, 2023

Weingarten's guitar rested in the corner of his office, illuminated by morning sunshine through slatted shutters. Yossi recalled how often he would hear the chief playing folk songs during slow periods. He was not a great musician but he was competent and sincere, popular with the old folks who remembered the words to all the songs. Civic awards and photographs adorned the walls and bookshelves. A family man. A good citizen. That was the story the pictures told. Why kill him? It probably didn't matter that Weingarten was humane in a way that few authorities in Hebron allowed themselves to be. Whoever did this was simply opportunistic. They lured Weingarten into a trap and he was the type who would fall for it. For them it didn't matter who he was, it only mattered what he represented. Weingarten was a simple man in a devious, evil world, killed because of his naivete. That was Yossi's working hypothesis.

He was troubled by the fact that Weingarten's cell phone wasn't on his body, although his wallet was, with cash still in it.

He went through the chief's desk. There was a file cabinet but it was locked and the key wasn't in the desk. He asked Golda if she knew where the chief kept it, but she didn't even know the cabinet was locked or what it was for. No one did, it was an unnoticed piece of furniture. In the back of his mind Yossi had known that the chief kept his own files, but he was never sufficiently interested to wonder why. All other criminal files in the office were stored on computers, except old ones that had never been digitized. Now he was curious. What was the need? He recalled that the chief was worried about hackers. No doubt the ancient police software was vulnerable. That must be the rationale.

There were four drawers in the cabinet and a single lock at the top for the whole thing. It wasn't all that secure; it could easily be drilled; but finding the key became a challenge. Yossi was sure it must be in the room, but there weren't many obvious places to put it. He looked under the desk to see if it was taped to a drawer, or under the chair. *What am I doing?* he thought. *The chief wasn't that imaginative.* He peeked behind an award from the Jerusalem Rotary Club to see if there was a safe in the wall. *This is not Weingarten, he was a simple man.* The best explanation was that the chief had misplaced the key and hadn't bothered to call a locksmith.

Weingarten wasn't much of a reader but there was a shelf of books, most of them on police procedures. A signed memoir by Amos Oz was a surprise, but on second thought Oz was the kind of thinker that Weingarten would have admired, a romantic who spun the tragic history of the Jews into literature. Yossi didn't trust such writers; history was blood and struggle and betrayals, it shouldn't be looked upon kindly. He flipped through the books to make sure there wasn't one that was fake, something with a secret compartment. Nothing, of course. He felt ridiculous.

He made a slow turn around the room to see if there was anything unexamined. He was sure there was a key here. He was sure he had looked everywhere.

He started to leave the room but just as he was walking out the door he thought to look behind it. There was an overcoat hanging on a hook. There were two pockets in the overcoat and inside one was a key.

Yossi paused for a moment to reassess a man he thought he knew passably well. He was a hider. This evinced a certain paranoia in the chief's character, or else a carefully considered precaution. In either case, the chief had his reasons.

The key fit, but the top two drawers were empty, except for a personal sidearm, a ten-millimeter SIG Sauer, an unusual caliber in Israel. Maybe it had some sentimental value. The bottom two drawers contained numbered files, starting with JSW-001 and going through JSW-234. No other information about what the files contained. Once again, a form of disguise. Somewhere there should be an index; meantime, Yossi jotted down the subject of each file in a notebook. He was struck by how random the contents were. Some contained little slips of paper with handwritten observations, others were lengthy memos about individuals. He found information about various Arab families—the Abdul Maliks were in there, as were the Khalils and Tamimis—with amateur attempts to draw family trees and yet making connections that weren't so obvious if you didn't know the players. They could be useful. But there was also a file with pictures of Bar Refaeli, the Israeli supermodel. Nothing pornographic, but many swimsuit shots; it was sweet in a way, a middle-aged man's crush. JSW-60–85 contained song lyrics; JSW-121 was an out-of-date list of members of the Knesset. There was a file on Rav Cohen, which Yossi set aside to read later. JSW-165 contained a list of informants, a dozen of them, most of them well known in the office, along with payments for some; apparently the chief kept a private account. Such a list could get people killed if their names were ever leaked. Yossi also noted that there were files on the other officers in the station, including one that leaped out at him.

YOSSI BEN-GAL

b. 1963, only child of Holocaust survivors, Yechiel and Hassia Ben-Gal. Father with Irgun, received Medal of Valor in the War of Independence. Part of the moshav movement (Nahalal). Yechiel elected to Knesset in 1977–9 with Likud.

YBG joined IDF after high school, 1987. Served in Gaza during First Intifada. Brought up on charges for using unauthorized live fire, charges dismissed in view of his courageous service . . .

Yossi leafed through several pages of testimony drawn from the tribunal, most of which he had forgotten. Memory is elusive and plastic, he knew, but confronted with contemporaneous accounts, Yossi realized how he had purged some of the details and reshaped the events into a less horrible narrative. All those details came rushing back into mind now. He remembered the frustration of having to explain a war against stone throwers and Molotov cocktails. It was all new then, tactics hadn't been established about fighting an entire population. He recalled the panic of the moment when his platoon was surrounded on a nameless street in Gaza, more than a hundred Palestinians throwing anything they could get their hands on, panicked soldiers firing plastic bullets to no effect, until Yossi gave the command to use real ones. The mob fled, leaving the bodies of six teenage boys in the dirt road. In the end, Yossi got off without a reprimand.

. . . studied Archaeology at Hebrew University for two years. Married Leah Kadishai 1993, tax lawyer . . .

Yossi skimmed over the details about Leah, it was still too painful to have her brief life summarized. Although Weingarten had known her only slightly, he referred to her in the file as "gracious." The chief seemed puzzled by the fact that she was married to someone of Yossi's gruff nature. Well, Yossi was, too. Leah was always a gift he didn't deserve. After all the deaths he had seen and caused, only this one death—hers—stirred him. He turned a few more pages containing annual assessments of his work in the police. The reports were largely positive, but his volcanic temper was noted. "Insolent," according to the chief before Weingarten. On the other hand, Weingarten himself assessed Yossi as "reliable" and "intelligent."

. . . applied for transfer in 2010 and 2018, not granted, apparently because of previous complaints of unwarranted force . . .

That first transfer request was because Leah was desperate to escape Hebron. The hostility frightened her, especially when she saw it in Yossi. She believed if she could only get him out of Hebron, and preferably out of the territories, the turbulence inside him would subside, and they could have the quiet and ordinary happiness that married couples aspire to. His unruly reputation prevented that from happening. Yossi would never know what their life would have been like if they lived in Haifa (her dream) or the Golan. Ultimately

Hebron was the only suitable place for him, especially after Leah died. He was too much of a brute to be anywhere else.

. . . YBG politics unclear, perhaps because lack of interest, but somehow allied with Kahanists. Seen with Rav Immanuel Cohen at Leah's funeral. Possible that YBG has provided investigative information to Rav or—

"Did Tamar have anything?" Golda asked as she stuck her head in the doorway.

"Nothing," said Yossi, setting the file aside.

She sized up the situation. "Are those the chief's files?"

Yossi nodded. "There's one missing, do you know anything about it? Number 169. I've got 168 and 170, but where's 169?"

"Honestly, Yossi, I've never looked at them. Is there something wrong?"

"Was he working on something I don't know about?"

"If you don't know, how would I?"

"Never mind, I just thought he might have asked for your help."

Golda lingered at the door. "Anything interesting in there?"

"Nothing," he said. "Nothing at all." He shut the file cabinet and put the key in his pocket. *So Weingarten suspected I was a spy for the Rav*, he thought. *That explains a lot.*

21

In a Natural Area

West Bank, Sept. 28, 2023

Shabak was doing the usual, listening, watching, interrogating any person who happened to fit the profile, locking up hundreds just to get them off the street. The Wise Ones upstairs had settled on the premise that a new group had formed. The beheading wasn't the only novelty. An operation like this was typically trumpeted by the killers, the whole point of terror being to frighten people, to convince them they are not safe—they will never be safe—and that a new round of killing could spring up at any moment. Death is hiding behind the door, slow and painful and humiliating death. Terror attacks have always reverberated with such boasts and threats. It was the silence that unnerved the authorities. Another mysterious absence.

While Shabak was pursuing the phantom terrorists, Yossi and his crew continued with their investigation. The Hebron police sometimes used a Palestinian drone operator for operations involving severe traffic accidents and lost hikers. This one was off the books; explaining it would be too much trouble. Wa'el Hilal was a professional photographer and drone shots were a feature of his offerings. As a Palestinian he kept his work with the Israeli police confidential. Yossi had enlisted him the morning after the murder to conduct a widespread search of the area, knowing that by now the chief's cruiser had probably been stripped for parts and buried.

Wa'el was reconnoitering Palestinian farmland when Yossi directed him to examine the area around the abandoned marble factory and quarry. Within a couple of hours Yossi received a video text showing the cruiser on its side at the bottom of a ditch in a natural area north of town. It was in Area C, about three miles from the murder site.

As he drove through the Palestinian farmland, Yossi thought about the beliefs that operated behind the psychological curtain of the Holy Land. What made a place or a person holy? This land, for instance, so rocky and forbidding in many ways, but so venerated that many were willing to kill or die for it. Yossi's reading of history suggested that holiness was magnified superstition, used mainly as an excuse for savagery. The Holy Land had been fought over through the millennia more than any other acreage in the world, one army after another, one belief against another, all in the effort to own God.

When he got about a mile out of town he came upon a man running. He thought to turn on his flashers but curiosity got the best of him, so he trailed the runner to see where he was headed. Finally he got close enough to realize it was Malik.

"What are you doing?" Yossi demanded.

"I'm running." Malik was streaming sweat. He didn't stop, so Yossi cruised along beside him.

"Why?"

"It's exercise."

"Nobody does that here."

Malik laughed, but Yossi was serious. "An Arab man running, you could get shot."

Now Malik stopped. "You're serious?"

"Get in. You might be interested in some real police work."

Malik wiped his face with his shirt and climbed into the cruiser.

They came to a rutted dirt road that wound back and forth into a pine forest on a steep rise. The land out here seemed so open, but after a few turns the forest was closeted from the rest of the world. The area was a dump for burglars and smugglers, who abandoned several cars that had been stripped of parts. A small safe lay on its side with its door open, serving as an animal nest. "Is this some kind of hideout?" Malik asked.

"Looks like it," said Yossi. "The criminals, they use places like this. Maybe some of your relatives."

"Ha."

Where the trees gave way to a clearing there were remnants of habitation. Yossi parked beside the foundation of what once had been a house. There were remnants of a stone fence, probably a pen for goats or sheep. "Used to be a little town here," Yossi said.

"Maybe some of my relatives," said Malik.

Walking about, Yossi realized there was more to this clearing than he had guessed. Vines and shrubbery covered the half-buried stone tracery of a substantial Palestinian village, bulldozed after 1948 so that no inhabitants could return. Hundreds of such places had been wiped off the map, many of them hidden, as this one was, by forests planted to erase the evidence of another existence. They were officially termed "natural areas." You couldn't even see where the towns had been unless you looked closely. As an amateur archaeologist, Yossi blamed the Israeli soldiers who did this for being too thorough, obstructing the archaeologists of the future who would be unable to reconstruct the society that once occupied this place. The ruins sat on the hilltop against a steep drop, which would have served a defensive purpose; there were still some stones that had been part of a fortification. No telling how old this place was; he guessed it was originally settled in the Canaanite era. He made a mental note to come back when he had time and see what he might dig up.

"Look at this."

Malik was standing on the edge of the precipice. He had found where the village had been bulldozed into the deep gulch. It was full of the rubble of the rustic life of Palestinian shepherds. Even from this height they could see bits of furniture and broken tombstones and what looked like school desks. An entire way of life, a history, had been turned into a dump.

Atop the mound of debris was Chief Weingarten's cruiser, lying on its side like a dead animal.

"You can see the tracks where they drove it up to the edge and then just pushed it over," Malik said. "I'm guessing it rolled over a couple times."

Yossi carefully made his way down the slope, holding on to a vine for support and then sliding on his butt. Malik followed.

Because the cruiser was armored it had suffered less damage than might have been expected. Yossi tried the door but it was locked. He had brought the spare key from the station, so he put on latex gloves and boosted himself onto the side of the car, then opened the passenger side door and looked inside.

"Blood?" Malik asked.

Yossi shook his head. He lowered himself into the cab. The shotgun that Weingarten preferred to the standard-issue carbine was gone. Some gum wrappers had found their way onto the driver's-side window. The ashtray had the stubs of several Noblesse cigarettes, Weingarten's brand.

The radio worked. Yossi called into the station. Golda answered and he gave her the coordinates. He knew that Shabak would be monitoring the call and would be here any minute.

He opened the glove compartment. The extra Glock was gone but there was a surprise—Weingarten's cell phone.

Before they left, Yossi stood for a moment on top of the cruiser and looked around in case the chief's head might have been thrown into the dump as well. There would be flies, but he didn't see any.

Malik was sitting amid the rubble reading something. "It's a schoolbook," Malik said. There was an edge to his voice that caused Yossi to step back.

"We need to go," Yossi said. "Shabak will be on the way."

Malik didn't seem to hear. "It was in a little satchel, maybe that's what children used for their books back then. You can see his name, Mohammed al-Dajani, in his handwriting. He would have been ten or so. This was his village. We're standing on it. A whole way of life."

Yossi braced himself for an argument but he registered the immense sadness in Malik's eyes and his voice. "And where is Mohammed now, Yossi? You took his home, his school, his community, and threw it in the dump. What else have your people done to him?"

There was no answer to the question. Yossi turned and struggled up the hill, losing his footing again and again as the soft soil slipped underfoot. It was good that Malik was with him; the younger man gave him a hand. He wasn't sure how he would have gotten out otherwise. *This is the same as what the Russians and the Ukrainians did to us with the pogroms,* Yossi thought guiltily. *It was the same goal as the Nazis, to wipe out the entire Jewish civilization and bury us under vine-covered ruins.* He did not utter these thoughts aloud. He didn't want Malik to know what he really thought.

On the way back to town they passed a Shabak convoy coming the other way.

22

Golda

Hebron, Sept. 28, 2023

Golda startled when Yossi came into the chief's office where
she was reading the files he had set aside. "I was just looking for that missing file," she said, in a tone that wordlessly
confessed she was lying.

Yossi nodded. "It's all right, I was curious as well."

"He even kept files on us."

"Let's keep this between ourselves, okay? It's not the moment to
pry into the chief's mind to see what he thought about his colleagues."

Avi was collecting the chief's phone records but Yossi was impatient. Despite the chief's fear of hackers he kept a list of passwords
in his office desk, another weird contradiction, as was the fact that
the passcode for his phone was the year of his birth, 1972, the easiest
code to break. "Let's see what the last call was," Yossi said to Golda.
"Maybe his pretty little girlfriend. We'll see who answers."

Weirdly, he heard a ring nearby.

"Allo?" a voice said, which was also near.

Yossi walked down the hallway until he came to Berger's office.
Berger was still speaking into his cell. "Allo? Allo?"

"Aharon?"

"Yes, who is—?" Then Berger looked at Yossi in confusion. "It's
you?" he said. "I thought it was the killer calling on the chief's
mobile."

"You were the last call the chief got."

For an instant Berger's expression froze. "Ah, maybe. Yes. I did call him. Yes. That same morning, you're right."

"Before he went to the synagogue."

"Maybe so, I don't remember."

"What did you talk about?"

"Andrea Bocelli."

"The singer?"

"I had a line on tickets for the concert next Thursday in Jerusalem. Mika was not feeling up to it. So I asked the chief because he likes that stuff."

Yossi started to walk back to the chief's office but turned around. "Did he buy the tickets?"

"He was going to ask Miriam, but then we lost connection," said Berger. "I never heard what happened."

Yossi closed the door to the chief's office and tried to piece together the fragments of evidence. His deductive skills were rusty, since he was rarely challenged by an investigation. Pieces of information surface that may not fit together. Not everything makes sense. The trick is to find a path from one piece of data to another and eventually a pattern emerges. Or doesn't. Nothing defeats a detective like the randomness of human nature.

Miriam had said Weingarten left his house around eight. One of the sergeants saw the chief's car at the bus stop about the same time. The surveillance video placed the chief at the Cave of the Patriarchs at 11:40 a.m. What accounted for the missing three and a half hours? There was a bus to Jerusalem at 8:15, which would have gotten him there forty-five minutes later—plenty of time to do business and return to Hebron. Weingarten got the call from Berger just before 10:30. Is that what prompted Weingarten's return, or was he already back?

Then, at the cave, Weingarten met Malik. They spoke briefly, then walked out together. It was unclear but possible that Malik followed him. At 1:24 p.m. the video of the chief's execution was sent. In the 104 minutes between the Malik meeting and the transmission of the beheading video the chief could have driven to the abandoned cement plant. Someone he trusted must have lured him there, alone, without notifying anyone in the office. Weingarten probably went alone. Maybe Bar Refaeli came along and asked for a lift. You never know. Life was full of inexplicable synchronicities, but it was clear that whoever killed him had planned this. They had set up an execution chamber. A videographer was waiting. The drive from the cave to the abandoned factory would have taken about twenty-five minutes in low traffic. The killers still had time to torture him; hard to say without an examination of the body or an actual autopsy, which Miriam refused.

How was one question; why was another. Suppose Hamas wanted to score a political point—the typical object of such murders—but missing in this video was the chief making some abject statement about the occupation or the treatment of prisoners, the main complaint these days. No chest-thumping boasts from the terrorists. Instead, Hamas kept quiet about it. Lone-wolf killers were increasingly common given the fractures of leadership in the old-guard Palestinian terror organizations; however, this killing was well designed, carefully done, the work of many hands. Few groups could pull it off. They also hadn't bothered to ransom the head. These pieces didn't fit together. What's the point of terrorism if you don't know who to fear?

Another troubling detail: Weingarten's last known contact was Anthony Abdul Malik. Yes, he was an FBI agent, but he was a Palestinian, and Yossi still suspected he was withholding information. Ordinarily Yossi would have detained him and questioned him at leisure, perhaps letting Berger have a few hours to soften him up.

Another question now presented itself: Who was Jacob Weingarten? In death he was revealing himself to be a more complex personality than Yossi had understood, and this thought gnawed at him. His failure to see the hidden depths of his superior had shaken him. What else was he missing?

Yossi called Golda back into the office. "You knew the chief really well, didn't you?" he asked.

"I don't think anyone knew him really well."

"But you lived in the same settlement. You must have a sense of how he was regarded, what his habits were, anything about his life outside the office."

"Oh, you know, music, that was important to him."

"Folk songs."

"And jazz, he loved jazz, but there wasn't a lot of it around. Opera also, big opera fan."

"Weaknesses?"

"Women, yeah."

"How do you know? Did he make a pass?"

"Women just know. He had the aspect of being available. Like, if you made the slightest gesture in that direction, he'd be on you like a bear."

"Was he secretive?"

"Discreet, I'd say. I mean, you recognized his hormones were churning but he kept his actions out of sight. You couldn't see behind the curtain."

"His relationship with his family?"

"Well, he was married to the Ice Queen, so you can imagine what that was like. His children—when they were young I think he was very supportive. Can't say much about them now. He became isolated. It bothered me because I feel isolated in that community too, and I could have reached out to him. But I worried where that would lead. My boss, you know."

BEFORE HE LEFT the office Yossi closed the door and pulled out another file from Weingarten's cabinet. It was surprisingly detailed.

GOLDA RADIDOWICZ

Raised political liberal in J'salem. Radidowicz family involved in the peace movement in 1990s, before Oslo. Sympathized with Palestinians during First Intifada in 1987, seeing it as a rebellion of youth seeking justice and opportunity. Family active in peace marches and workshops at Neve Shalom. Her father Akiva spoke at a council meeting in Rehavia expressing outrage at the treatment of stone throwers—bones crushed by IDF, shot with rubber bullets, some with live ammunition—etc. Father noted 20K+ Palestinian children treated for severe beatings by Israeli troops.

Probable GR shared these views until the Second Intifada. March 2002, older sister Ruth killed in Café Moment bombing. She 18, about to start her military service, went to have a beer

with boyfriend. Same month 100+ Israelis killed in suicide bombings. Turning point for R. family when they watched Palestinians
in Gaza celebrate the 11 Israelis killed in Café Moment.

As he read, Yossi detected in Weingarten's tone a personal interest
in Golda, an attraction. He seemed drawn to her passion as well as
her bohemian lifestyle. He described her as "adorable" and expressed
an interest in her love life, noting several boyfriends—obviously, he
never intended anyone else to read these entries. Despite the pru-
rience Weingarten was clearly intrigued by Golda's transformation
from peace advocate to hardened warrior.

GR friends with Gilad Shalit's family when he kidnapped by
Hamas in 2006. In high school GR active organizing protests, petitions, etc. In 2008, GR joined IDF during Operation Cast Lead.
Excellent record although extreme political views began to be
noted. GR expressed anger that the war failed to rescue Shalit.

The abduction of Shalit was a turning point in Golda's life, as
for many Israelis. The IDF ransacked Gaza, but after five years they
had nothing to show for it. There were clocks in Israeli cities that
ticked off the days, hours, and minutes of his captivity. Marchers
carried cutouts of his face—thousands of cardboard Shalits in the
street, matched by thousands of actual Gazans killed—but none of
it mattered.

GR reenlists. Assessed as having resolve to kill if necessary, placed
in "Spot and Shoot," all-female squad operating machine guns by
remote control on Gaza watchtowers. In 6 mos GR recorded 4 kills
of Gazans who crossed within 300 m of fence. Commended twice.

Yossi hadn't known the details of Golda's military service—she
never spoke of it—and he was impressed by her unexpected steeli-
ness. Killing was never easy.

In 2013, GR marries Amos Yadin. They bought a house in Kiryat
Arba. He associated with Kach extremists. GR politics also hard-

ened, affiliated with Likud. In 2014, Hamas launches massive rocket barrage from Gaza, both GR and Yadin called back to their units. He in the tank corps. She promoted to major, served in strategic ops at IDF headquarters responsible for approving questionable strikes; i.e., danger to the soldiers v. likelihood that action would cause collateral damage or deter future attacks.

Yadin's squad surrounded Jabaliya refugee camp north of Gaza City where rocket fire detected. Unspecified number of children seen on a balcony in one of the camp apartment buildings. Unofficial understanding was to shoot anything that moves, but Yadin's commander hesitated, radioed HQ for guidance. Were these innocent children or were they "spotters," directing fire at the Israeli troops? How to tell the difference? GR rules they take out the apartment. Yadin fires the shell, destroys the apartment. 9 schoolgirls killed who had taken refuge in the apartment after their school was bombed.

Incident haunted Yadin. Blamed GR, although not her decision alone. The seven-week war killed two thousand Gazans, including more than five hundred children. Yadin confided to me that his politics had changed. He had treated Palestinian children in his practice, couldn't shed the shame of having been the instrument of the death of so many innocents. Not the only reason they divorced, but it played a role.

In Kiryat Arba GR seen as eccentric, odd hairstyle, piercings, theater sideline. Occasional romantic attachments of short duration. Depressive episodes, incidents of self-harming. Her rabbi describes her as "good hearted lost soul."

So she was haunted, like Weingarten, like Yossi himself, like so many people who bury their memories and live both courageously and guiltily. *There's something phony about us,* Yossi thought. *We invent the lives we lead but we're haunted by the people we actually are.*

23

The American Colony

Jerusalem, Sept. 28, 2023

Many say Jerusalem is the holiest place on earth. Everywhere Malik looked there were people displaying vestments of their faith, some representing belief systems he had never heard of, but they each had an oar in the ocean of holiness. Priests, bishops, cardinals, nuns, imams, Haredis, all in splendid outfits that adverstised their piety. Brooklyn was also a center for ultra-Orthodox Jews, so they weren't new to him, but in Jerusalem there was a concentration and a diversity that he had never encountered before. Here people were separated not so much by race or ethnicity or even by belief as by civilizational time, with some living at the furthest edge of modernity—computer programmers, international businesspeople, avant-garde musicians—and others in some long-ago Polish shtetl.

The cab dropped Malik at the American Colony Hotel in East Jerusalem, a charming spot made of rough limestone blocks and buried in bougainvillea. The stone floors were polished into an art form, worn and irregularly fitted together but arrestingly beautiful in shades of gold and crimson. He found Greenblatt in the garden beside a pomegranate tree, with another person that he wasn't expecting.

"Frank Clooney," the man said. Tall, lithe, athletic, white-haired, the taint of boarding school and yacht clubs about him, an old-school agency man for sure.

"You finally made it to the Holy Land, buddy," said Greenblatt.

"From what I've seen, it's stuck in the Old Testament."

"You got that right. On the other hand—" he took in the garden, the towering ficus trees, the water lilies in the fishpond—"don't you love this place? It's in the highly contested East Jerusalem and officially we're discouraged from coming here."

"It's called the American Colony, so come on," said Clooney.

"But the food is—" Greenblatt kissed the tips of his fingers. "Lawrence of Arabia stayed here. Everybody does. Bob Dylan."

"Used to be the informal headquarters for the PLO," Clooney added. "It was awkward, but it served as a convenient back channel."

Greenblatt indicated with his eyes. "See the guy in the tennis duds talking to the reporter? Mordechai Vanunu. Like the biggest traitor in Israeli history. He told the world about their nuclear program."

"What's he doing here?"

"He spent like eighteen years in the hoosegow but now he hangs out in the garden of the Colony giving interviews. What a country."

"Imagine if it had been a Palestinian," said Clooney. Eastern liberal, Malik assumed, perfunctory sentiments for the oppressed.

"It wouldn't be pretty," Greenblatt agreed as the waiter approached. "What are you drinking? We're doing beer."

"Whatever you're having."

"A Maccabee for the gentleman. And another round for us."

"By chance, do you have something to nibble?" Clooney chimed in, as if it were the biggest favor of the day. "Some mixed nuts? That would be so welcome."

"We were just talking about how worried we've been for you," Greenblatt continued. "This whole adventure wasn't meant to be like combat duty. Just a quick hello and see what Weingarten had to say."

"Do you have any idea what he wanted?"

Greenblatt and Clooney exchanged a glance. "You don't know?"

"I did meet with him but I don't recall anything significant."

"Huh. You weren't just playacting with Ben-Gal?" said Clooney.

"I probably would have noted anything important."

"Weird," said Greenblatt.

"Sometimes the memories come back. I think it's getting better but it's hard to measure these things. If you give me some more information, I might dredge up something."

Greenblatt and Clooney just stared at him, probably wondering whether they could trust such a broken operative. Clooney pursed his lips, calculating what to say. "I'm the one he called, okay? He asked to talk to the chief of station. Didn't know him from Adam. He said he had information on a big case but he was afraid to run it through regular channels. Corruption or something he was worried about, not sure about that part. He insisted on a face-to-face. Steve—" he indicated Greenblatt—"was going to head down and meet him."

"My plate was full," said Greenblatt.

"So he sent it up the chain to see if someone in the neighborhood could hear his confession," said Clooney. "We were thrilled to pass it off when the report came that you were inbound."

"Seemed perfect," Greenblatt added. "I shined you up good. I bet he was starstruck when you finally met."

"You left out the fact that I'd never been to Palestine."

"You're related," said Greenblatt. "That's even better. Anyway, who knows what he wanted to talk about. Guess we'll never know now."

"Do you know this guy who took over?" asked Malik.

"Yossi Ben-Gal," said Clooney. "Piece of work. Used to be Sayeret. Israeli special forces," he said off Malik's look. "They say he was a real badass until he got too deep in the Manischewitz."

They were discreetly quiet for a moment as the waiter brought the beers and the nuts.

"Whatever the chief wanted to tell us must be connected to his killing," said Clooney, returning to the sore subject.

"Maybe, maybe not," said Greenblatt. "People get killed in this region for damn little reason. I wouldn't put a lot of weight on it. Ten to one it was some nut-bag terrorist. I'm sorry I roped you into this. Now the best thing is to peel you off this case and get you out of the country ASAP."

"This whole episode has kicked up a world of shit," Clooney added petulantly. "Last thing we want is for word to get out about your involvement."

"The agency thinks I'm 'involved'? I met him for a couple minutes."

"It's all interagency bullshit, the usual rivalry with the bureau," said Greenblatt.

It was suddenly apparent that Malik's future was on the table. "You guys could have taken care of this yourselves. I'm sure you would have done a better job." He didn't bother to hide his irritation.

"Settle down. Nobody thinks you fucked up," Greenblatt assured him, "just a series of bad events and now we got Mossad and Shabak and even the prime minister's office kicking sand in our face. Folks back in Langley and the bureau aren't happy, you can imagine. Do everyone a favor and just drop it."

"The message is get out of here as soon as this wedding thing goes down," Clooney added. "Let everything cool off."

"We made you a reservation," said Greenblatt. "The night after the wedding you wing home and leave all this craziness behind. Meantime, here's a passport, government credit card, ticket, and seven thousand shekels to tide you over." He handed Malik a manila envelope. "Don't lose this, Uncle Sam will be really unhappy."

"What about a phone?"

"You could pick up a burner at a pharmacy and just toss it at the airport. Up to you. You're probably not going to be here long enough to need it."

The curfew was lifted during daylight hours, so as soon as he arrived back in Hebron, Malik went shopping. After the theft of his suitcase he needed a new wardrobe, including a suit for the wedding and respectable shoes to replace the joggers he was wearing. He had been in the same green shirt for three days going on four. He couldn't wait to toss it in the trash.

In a city that abjured movie theaters, bars, and almost any form of nightlife, shopping was taken seriously. The gleaming Hebron Center mall offered whatever was needed in its five stories of shops. He grazed through a men's store, selecting a regimental tie, two dress shirts, a couple of knits, and a midnight-blue suit that almost fit. At another store he found discount underwear and socks and a decent pair of jeans. Hebron, it turned out, was famous for its shoemakers, and he splurged on a handsome pair of oxfords. Before he left the mall, he stopped at a pharmacy and loaded up on toiletries and a new razor. He felt a little giddy charging it all to the US government but these were defensible expenses. The pharmacy sported a kiosk that sold phones. He decided it would be a hassle to set up and if he really needed one he could come back and get it. Meantime he could scan through his emails on the hotel computer.

He left the store just as the noon prayer shut down all commerce in the city. He was making his way back toward the hotel, loaded with shopping bags, imagining how pleasant it was going to be to put on new clothes, when a boy passed him on the sidewalk wearing a red Philadelphia Phillies hat. It took a moment for Malik to register what he had seen. How likely was it that there was another Phillies fan in Hebron? When he turned around, he saw the boy staring at him, and then the boy took off running, dodging the slow-moving pedestrians. Malik raced after him, but his flapping shopping bags were like sails catching the wind. In any case, the boy was faster. Malik stopped and watched him run. A block away the boy turned and waved.

24

"Everything Is Perfect"

Hebron, Sept. 28, 2023

Yasmine and Dina stopped at the dress shop for the bride's final fitting. Yasmine had looked forward to this experience since Dina was a child, but now that the wedding was upon them she was filled with unwelcome ambivalence. Her own tumultuous first marriage, to Ibrahim Abdul Malik, haunted her. They had married when she was still a child; if she had waited, if she had been more mature and experienced, if she had extended her education—so many what-ifs—her life might have taken a different turn, one that would have liberated her from the eternal rivalries of Arabs and Jews, Israelis and Palestinians, Hamas and PLO; instead, she had only become more deeply immersed. Her main object was to keep Dina from being swallowed in the quicksand of ethnic hatred.

Perhaps Yasmine's own experience had led her to judge Jamal unfairly. After all, he had pledged to give up his political crusade—swore to her—but she remembered similar protestations from Ibrahim. The very things that had drawn her to Ibrahim—his passion and courage that stood out so starkly in her defeated society—made him impossible to live with. She knew even before her wedding that some catastrophe awaited, but in the nihilism of the moment, with the Second Intifada raging throughout the territories and young Palestinians turning themselves into human bombs, one more sacrifice hardly seemed to matter; indeed, it was a debt owed to the struggle. Her family, in Nablus, did not object. They were all devoted to

Hamas and Ibrahim's politics posed no problem. Her brother had been martyred when Yasmine was in elementary school, and in a way—she now realized—Ibrahim replaced him, not only in her heart but in her parents'. Because of that, she put up with abuse that she might not have excused from another man, accepting his violence as a part of the pathology of occupation.

From the beginning there was an expectation that Ibrahim would also lose his life, through death or imprisonment. It was only after Dina was born that Yasmine realized the catastrophic bargain she had made with fate. She spent two years alone with the baby while Ibrahim was detained without charges. If the Israelis knew the truth about him, they would have locked him up forever. When Dina was five they rearrested him on terrorism charges, this time with a lengthy sentence. Ibrahim did Yasmine the favor of divorcing her and setting her free. That only made things more complicated.

As the probable inheritor of the Abdul Malik estate, Dina became a prize. Such a calculation was made by every family with a marriageable son. Even boys and old men applied for the position. Dina was aware of her bargaining power, but she was under the spell of Jamal's charisma. She believed that if anyone could bring peace, he was the one. In her eyes, he was a Palestinian Gandhi. Yasmine understood her daughter's infatuation. But the price she imposed on her daughter's alliance was that Jamal would give up the one thing that made him a hero in Dina's eyes.

So be it. Jamal would find his place in the community as a sober and noncorrupt farmer with considerable wealth from Sheikh Abdullah's vineyards and groves. Instead of being the butcher's assistant he would be a man of influence. Their children would have advantages. They would travel, receive the best education. All of this would follow from Jamal's promise to Yasmine to forfeit his dream of peace.

The door to the dressing room opened and Dina came out in her wedding gown, like an angel descending from heaven. Tears immediately sprang from Yasmine's eyes.

"Mom, don't cry."

"I can't help it! I'm sorry."

"Can't you just be happy?" Dina asked.

"These are tears of joy. Tears of pride," Yasmine protested. Then she suddenly laughed.

"What?"

"I was just thinking how you used to play dress-up and you loved being a bride. It wasn't so long ago."

The seamstress, well prepared for this reaction, brought a box of tissues. "Isn't she beautiful? We have new brides coming to us every week but this one is special. I hope you have the right photographer."

"Oh, yes, and we have a cousin who will be making a video of the entire thing," said Yasmine. "He came all the way from America!"

"Mom, can I tell you something?" Dina said in a breathy whisper as she turned to see herself in different angles in the triple mirror. "My heart is pounding and pounding."

"Of course it is! I felt the same way before my wedding."

"And look how that turned out." She said this without sarcasm, as if it were a secret between sisters rather than a criticism of her mother.

Still, it stung. "Don't say that. Your father loves you, but there were parts of him I didn't see. Until later."

"You think it's the same with Jamal, but it's not."

"I never said that."

"You know I can read your mind, so you don't need to say one thing or another."

Yasmine sighed. It was a fact that she couldn't keep anything from Dina. She knew things about her before Yasmine knew them herself. She wondered sometimes who the parent was here. "Whatever you think I think, I love you," she said, "and I'm sure you're going to be very, very happy. It's just perfect. Everything is perfect."

MALIK LAY IN BED straining to remember his meeting with Weingarten. Surely something important occurred between them, something that may have led to the chief's murder. A clue was buried somewhere in his broken brain.

He had developed a technique for recreating elusive memories by means of investigating his own behavior. He asked himself, *What would I have done?* The answer might not be accurate, but in Malik's experience the plausible and the truthful had much in common. He knew himself to be orderly and rigidly logical, traits that had been strengthened since his injury because he was always burrowing into his mind for some buried acorn of memory. Over the past year he had trained himself against this relentless adversary, his memory. He watched videos of magicians who could memorize the order of a shuffled deck of cards or the names of everyone in an audience of three hundred people. Those were tricks he never mastered, but he did learn strategies to outwit his disability. He rarely misplaced objects. When he set down his watch, he took a mental picture of it, as if a flash had gone off, but even that gesture was superfluous, because he always put the watch where it belonged—on the bedside table, when retiring, or inside his shoe, along with his car keys, when changing in the gym. His rule was to place objects in places where it was impossible to lose them.

Ordinary events slipped away too easily. He had a better chance of remembering things that were jarring or surprising. His interrogation in the jail was quite vivid in his mind. He thought he fully remembered the engagement dinner at Sheikh Abdullah's, but the maddening thing about his condition was that he didn't know what he had forgotten. It was no wonder that Yossi doubted him, because the landscape of memory was so blank in places and so full in others.

He wrote a list of things he knew to be true:

1. The chief asked for help. It must have been the kind of help that I might provide, probably related to terrorism or crime.
2. For some reason Weingarten couldn't trust his own department to investigate.
3. The meeting lasted only seven minutes.
4. Soon after that Weingarten was murdered.

Thanks to the video he had a clear image of the Cave of the Patriarchs, so colorful and ancient. He remembered Weingarten's beefy face, his toothy smile indicating that the meeting would be a friendly encounter. The smile was a little too broad—maybe it was Weingarten playing the role of an old friend, pretending the meeting was a fortuitous coincidence. Nobody would take notice. The Cave was perfect because any tourist would stop there, and of course it was in Weingarten's jurisdiction, within spitting distance of his station. Nothing to explain.

He imagined them exchanging a few words with those false smiles of delight, offering a few jolly sentences like code.

WEINGARTEN

Anthony, what a coincidence!

Weingarten didn't know him well enough to call him Malik, as all his colleagues did, or even Tony, like his family and school friends.

MALIK

. . . family wedding . . .

WEINGARTEN

. . . How long in town?

MALIK

. . . see the sights . . .

WEINGARTEN

. . . haven't aged . . .

Weingarten puts his arm on Malik's shoulder and steers him toward the barred window that looks upon the cenotaph of Abraham, shrouded in green tapestry with gold trim. Weingarten gestures toward the grillwork while whispering like a tour guide into Malik's ear. There is no longer any pretend chatter. Weingarten has a problem. Maybe four or five minutes of the seven have elapsed. His voice is urgent. No doubt he is afraid. He explains why he summoned Malik.

WEINGARTEN

. . . too dangerous to tell my subordinates. Can't trust anyone in the intel community . . .

MALIK

Why me . . . ?

WEINGARTEN

. . . and you're American, not from here . . . roots in the region . . . will seem natural . . .

MALIK

How can I help?

That's the question. Malik had a long history of working in the region but never in Palestine or Israel. Much of his time he had been stationed in Iraq and eastern Syria, focused on taking down the Islamic State.

WEINGARTEN

You know a lot about the drug trade.

That was certainly true. Terrorists and drug gangs had become indistinguishable in the Middle East.

MALIK

Is that the problem you're having?

Malik lay in the dark waiting for Weingarten to answer. He tried prompting:

WEINGARTEN

I'm being blackmailed. Nobody must know.

Or:

WEINGARTEN

I need someone to carry a message to the highest officials in Washington.

They were plausible scenarios. Malik was handicapped by the fact that he knew practically nothing about Weingarten, his habits, his flaws, his secrets.

Stymied by his imagination, Malik returned to the known facts. The region was drowning in drugs and black-market weapons. Terrorist groups were growing more powerful and aggressive. Right-wing Israelis, especially settlers, were also buyers. The chief of police would have been deeply involved in these matters. But why did he need to reach out—secretly—to the Americans? Greenblatt certainly didn't think it was important; he had roped Malik into the conversation just to get it off his desk. Thanks a lot.

Had Weingarten confided his secret in the seven minutes of their meeting, Malik would have recorded it somehow—wouldn't he? But if he had written a note it would have been in his little notebook, which he still had. It might be on his missing phone, but Malik was beginning to believe that there was no record of the conversation except his own erased memory. These thoughts preoccupied him until sleep finally put his restless imagination to work, like a towel over a canary cage. The last words he heard of his imaginary conversation were:

WEINGARTEN

Trust Yossi.

Or was it:

WEINGARTEN

Don't trust Yossi.

25

Shalit

Gaza, June 25, 2006

Just before dawn, eight men, carrying automatic weapons and rocket-propelled grenades, emerged from a tunnel three hundred meters into Israeli territory. It was the darkest night of the month. There was a watchtower with two Israeli guards, and a Merkava tank parked at the Kerem Shalom crossing, facing into Gaza.

The year 2006 had begun with the prime minister, Ariel Sharon, suffering a severe stroke and falling into a coma that would last until his death eight years later. That same January twenty Israelis were injured in a bombing in Tel Aviv. Hamas won a majority in the Palestinian Authority legislature. Rockets and suicide attacks increased. Tragedy was a daily event in the Holy Land, but the Israelis were stoic. They were used to tragedies. What they feared were surprises.

The invaders came from the rear. They fired on the watchtower and the tank and an empty armored personnel carrier stationed as a decoy. The four soldiers in the tank panicked. One of them fainted (he would be the only one to escape). The others popped open the rear hatch and ran directly into the oncoming attackers. Two were killed. The third was nineteen-year-old Gilad Shalit. The attackers blew a hole in the security fence surrounding Gaza and dragged him into enemy territory. That was the last time he was seen alive until a video surfaced three years later of him holding up a newspaper to provide proof of life. Shalit was pale and gaunt but appeared healthy.

Sara turned seven that year. The abduction overshadowed her

childhood until Shalit was released five years later. She would always remember her father's anger—at Hamas, but also at the fecklessness of his own government, which was caught unawares and humiliated by its inability to free Shalit.

Only a couple of months before, the Israelis had captured a Hamas military commander in Ramallah—Ibrahim Hamed, who was convicted of killing nearly fifty Israelis and planning the Café Moment bombing—but that triumph was eclipsed by the Shalit kidnapping, even in the mind of Golda Radidowicz. She reenlisted and served with distinction on the Gaza border, but her military service reopened a moral conflict with her husband, who still agonized over the abuses against Palestinian civilians.

Other residents of Kiryat Arba, including the Bergers, the Garfinkles, and the Weingartens, were inflamed. In a community that was already radicalized, the Shalit abduction turned them toward the teachings of Immanuel Cohen. The Rav spoke of the weakness of the government and its willingness to hand over land to terrorists—referencing the decision the year before by Prime Minister Sharon to expel Jewish settlers from Gaza. "We are deluded if we think this will lead to peace," the Rav declared. Many Israelis, perhaps most, agreed with him, and some went further, endorsing policies the Rav advocated that had been widely disparaged, such as using Arabs as guinea pigs in medical experiments, deputizing Jewish suicide bombers to defend Hebron, and the eradication and murder of Arabs who stood in the way of Israel's expansion.

The comatose Ariel Sharon loomed over the country's mood.

YEARS LATER, in a paper for Professor Brisard, Sara wrote about prisoner exchanges between Israel and Palestine. She observed that captives play a heightened role in Jewish law. According to the Mishnah—a collection of ancient Jewish traditions—"Every moment that one delays in freeing captives, where it is possible to expedite their freedom, is tantamount to murder." But the Talmud forbids the ransom of captives for more than their actual value, because it upsets the balance of the universe. "And so there is a paradox," Sara wrote. "Prisoners must be redeemed as quickly as possible, but not for more than they are worth, which is . . . what?"

Shalit's captors demanded a thousand Palestinian prisoners in ransom. Eventually Hamas's ransom demand rose to 1,400 Palestinian prisoners and detainees, including 450 who had been convicted of terrorist killings. The most precious commodity in all of Gaza was its only Jew.

"How did they arrive at that figure?" Sara wrote. "How does one measure the value of a human life?" Was Shalit really so much more valuable because he's a Jew? The argument forced both Israelis and Palestinians to evaluate a question that is at the root of their dispute. It also forced Sara to consider her own relationship to Judaism and to Israel.

Although she was not particularly observant, Sara was a proud Jew. She deeply believed that Jews were a remarkable people, which was evidenced by their disproportionate contributions to art, finance, science, and literature. Go into any big town in America or Europe and look at the names on the hospital wings, the university chairs, the museum boards—so often Jewish names. This was true even in France, despite its history of anti-Semitism. Sara felt shy even remarking on the magnitude of Jewish accomplishments. In the year Shalit was taken there were about thirteen million Jews in the world, less than a fourth of one percent of humanity. That was about as many as there are Mormons in the world. Since 1901, 840 Nobel Prizes had been awarded, 181 of them to Jews—more than 20 percent of all the Nobel Prize winners.

Mormons, zero.

Obviously the twentieth century was a period of remarkable Jewish accomplishments, perhaps the greatest era in Jewish history. She compared it to another era, the Middle Ages, when so much of the world's advances in science, medicine, literature, art, and philosophy accompanied the spread of Islam. "It was Muslims who invented the public library, the university; Muslims who pioneered the sciences of chemistry, algebra, and astronomy; Muslims whose banking and trading practices led to the rise of capitalism; Muslims who invented coffee, soap, shampoo, the compass, the watch, and the three-course meal." But the arc of history rises and falls. There are two billion Muslims in the world—a quarter of the total population of the earth—but when Shalit was abducted they were represented by only eight Nobel Prizes.

If such rewards are a measure of worth, Jews must be remarkably valuable people. But what about this one Jewish individual, "this shy boy with a nervous smile and a studious disposition," as his father described him, who loved basketball and excelled in physics—was the life of Gilad Shalit worth more than a thousand Palestinians? The IDF sealed the borders of Gaza and rummaged through the residential areas, searching for Shalit and rounding up males over sixteen. Sixty-four Palestinian officials, including members of the cabinet, were held hostage. Four hundred Gazans were killed in the next several months, as well as six Israeli soldiers and four civilians. The Israelis never found Shalit. Five years after he was abducted, he was exchanged for 1,027 Palestinian prisoners. (Among them was Yahya Sinwar, who would become the leader of Hamas, and a talented young bombmaker named Ehsan Zayyat.)

Sara titled her paper "The Human Scale."

"WHO CAN SAY what is the value of one human life?" Sara concluded. "Perhaps only God."

The scale that weighs the value of human lives goes back to the idea that there is a God who judges some as dear and others as worthless. The God who demands of Muslims that they eliminate Jews before Judgment Day. The God who tells Jews that he has given them land that belongs to others. The God who chooses one people over another.

Sara quoted a biblical story of a Canaanite army that took some Israelite soldiers hostage. "Israel made a vow to the Lord: 'If you will deliver the Canaanites into our hands, we will totally destroy their cities.'" The Lord heard Israel's plea and handed the Canaanites over to them. The Israelites completely annihilated the Canaanites and destroyed their towns; so the place was named Hormah.

The word means "devoted to destruction."

26

Fajr

Hebron, Sept. 29, 2023

At four thirty in the morning Malik awakened to a pounding on his hotel door. He jumped out of bed so quickly he felt dizzy as he cracked open the door. There was Jamal.

"Come," said Jamal. "We'll go pray the *Fajr* together." The morning prayer.

"Jamal, it's awfully early."

"The sacrifice makes the prayer more worthy," said Jamal. He was startled that Malik hadn't yet put on his eye patch and the wound was evident. "I'll wait for you."

Malik dressed quickly. It had been years since he prayed and he had no inclination to do so now. But he would have to be careful not to get into an argument that would create a rift in the family. Given Jamal's reputation as a provocateur, it was dangerous even to be seen with him in public. Malik wondered why he should humor this unwelcome demand, other than to satisfy his curiosity about this headstrong young man, soon to be a part of his family.

Jamal looked at Malik's new clothes and gave a quick approving nod before heading downstairs. Malik grudgingly followed along.

"Dina was angry with me," Jamal explained in an oddly jubilant tone. "She tells me I was disrespectful. And Dina is always correct. So I think we pray together and then I show you about our life here." He added: "This way we begin my wedding day."

Jamal set a quick pace as they walked downhill, toward Bab al-Zawiya square. The streets were strewn with burned-out trucks and cars from the recent rampage by the settlers. It was not just Hebron, the whole country was agitated by the murder of Chief Weingarten and the Kahanist reprisals. In the constant exchange of meaningless violence, a Palestinian teenager had watched a video of an assault by an Israeli soldier on an Arab woman. The clip was fourteen seconds long. Based on that, the young man rushed out of his house and rammed his car into a bus stop in Jerusalem, killing four people and sending a little girl to the hospital, where surgeons had to amputate her leg. In response, a group of four hundred settlers descended on a Palestinian village called Eli, burning houses and assaulting Palestinians. Similar attacks had taken place in seven other towns. Twenty-seven Arabs had been killed overnight, including eight children. A seven-year-old boy was slain with a hatchet. And such assaults were still going on.

Other figures were moving through the early-morning gloom toward the gate into the Old City. There was just enough light in the sky for Malik to make out the security cameras on the rooftops and a sentry in a watchtower above the gate.

"You go first," said Jamal.

Malik entered the turnstile. Behind bomb-proof glass a young Israeli soldier who looked like she should still be in high school demanded his identification paper. He handed over his new passport. She leafed through it. "Where is your entry paper?"

"Stolen," he said. "This is a new passport."

That posed a problem, apparently. The soldier communicated something on her radio. An officer came and took his passport. Malik looked at Jamal, who shrugged; in other words, this is normal. Behind Jamal was a growing queue of Muslims trying to get to the mosque in time for prayer. They were all straining to see who was causing the blockage. Time passed. It wasn't entirely clear if the gate had simply been shut down and no one was bothering to inform them. The soldier at the window was playing a word game. Malik knocked on the window and she shook her head unhelpfully. Finally the officer reappeared.

"What is this?" the office asked, holding up the passport.

"My passport."

The officer looked at the passport photo and at Malik. "You don't have an entry visa."

"No, it's new. I explained to your colleague my passport was stolen two days ago."

The officer walked off again. Presently another officer appeared and waved Malik through as a loud click and a green light signaled that the gate had unlocked. "My passport!" said Malik, but the officer disappeared. Malik walked through the gate. A soldier held his rifle crosswise to block him and indicated a door beneath a set of stairs leading to the watchtower. The door was locked. He knocked. Presently there was another click.

Two Israeli officers sat on one side of a desk. There was no other chair. They were young, like everyone Malik saw in this broken land, a country run by children nursed on hatred. He felt generationally displaced, as if authority decreased with age. The one with the passport said, "Why are you here?" He spoke in Fusha, the formal Arabic used in print. The soldier spoke it beautifully, but it was not a language Malik had ever mastered. His Arabic was from the streets. He imagined this young man slaving over the diacritical markings of the textbooks in order to humble people passing through his checkpoint, showing off his superior command of their own language.

"If you're trying to test my scholarship, you won't get very far," Malik said in English.

"Speak Arabic," the other officer said.

"Look, I'm an American. I'm visiting family. I was robbed of my passport and other belongings. My friends at the American embassy replaced my identification. Is there some reason you feel the need to harass me?"

"We see you are in Judea and you have contacts with Arabs," said the second officer. He had knife-sharp features and a mocking smile. "So perhaps you are a spy or you aid terrorists. We can keep you here for as long as we wish. Only you give us straight answers in Arabic."

It was pointless to debate them. Malik responded in the Arabic dialect he grew up with, "I work for the American government. In the FBI."

"If this is true, show us your badge."

"Stolen. If you don't believe me, call the embassy, they can tell you." He wondered if there was a magic answer that they were looking for. Instead, they suddenly stood up and walked out of the room, leaving the passport on the desk. Malik hesitated, then picked up his passport and opened the door to the outside. He was beginning to realize that things didn't need to make sense. Reason was a useless mental construct in the occupied territories. Contempt was the operative emotion.

Jamal was waiting for him.

"We need to hurry," Jamal said, completely unsurprised by Malik's brief detention. "Because you were with me," he explained. "I hoped if you went first they would not make the connection. They hate me here."

"I believe it."

"I tell them I have quit this work but they think I'm lying."

They walked past the shuttered shops. Alone now, the other worshippers having already reached the Ibrahimi Mosque in the Cave of the Patriarchs, they quickly shed their shoes in the doorway, washed their hands and feet, then entered the vast carpeted chamber. Hundreds of men were lined up in even ranks facing the mihrab, a large niche in the wall, shaped like a keyhole, that indicated the direction of Mecca. Women prayed on the other side of a partition. Jamal and Malik found spaces in the back.

Malik felt like an interloper, but he raised his arms in preparation for prayer and said the words from his childhood: "Allahu Akbar." God is the greatest. The same words that the 9/11 hijackers would have said as they struck America, invoking the blessings of the divine before murdering as many people as possible.

Malik's father had been devout, with the dark callus that marked endless hours of pressing his forehead to the prayer mat, just as Malik was doing, the words of the prayer finding their way into his mouth once again. In this moment at least, he was a Muslim again.

AS A YOUNG CHILD he had not experienced discrimination because of his beliefs. Their neighborhood in Philly was largely Italian

Catholics, and as Tony Malik, with olive skin and Mediterranean features, he blended in. His father worshipped in a small mosque in the neighborhood. When people spoke of American Muslims back then, they usually were thinking of Black Muslims who followed Louis Farrakhan and the Nation of Islam. That was especially true in Philadelphia, a stronghold for Farrakhan's disciples. Malik's father, like so many in his community, kept his head down. Muslims in America were an invisible minority.

After his parents divorced and Tony moved with his mother to Little Rock, he was folded into mainstream America, which in Little Rock was centered on the First Baptist Church. He was never baptized, because he felt it would be disloyal to his father, but he kept that to himself, thinking it was funny that he could be a member of First Baptist without actually being baptized. It was his secret identity, pretending to be a part of the gang while knowing that he was in some hidden but essential way different from them. A spy, in other words.

On 9/11, Tony was twelve. In his brief life no one had ever addressed him as a Muslim, nor did he see himself that way. He had always been a spectator of religion, not a believer, no more a Muslim than a Baptist. Suddenly he was alone in the spotlight, the only Muslim in Little Rock, at least that's the way it felt. The spectacular cruelty of middle-school boys landed on him, with their taunts, their bullying. Along with the welter of hormonal change, the delicious emotion of hatred made its debut, and Tony Malik the Ay-rab was the chosen scapegoat.

Tony realized he needed to become powerful. Physically, he was tall and slight, not strong but quick. He began going to a boxing gym run by a Pakistani, Rizwan Khan. A lot of the boys who went there were marginalized—black, gay, immigrants; there was even a lesbian who would later become a trans man. The youth classes were separate, but after a workout Tony would study the technique of the real boxers. It was inspiring to be in the same environment with muscular adult men, glowing with sweat, as they punched the bags and sparred. They were beautiful to watch. The inevitable element of danger and punishment added to the seriousness of his pursuit.

Until this point in his life Tony Malik had successfully made himself indistinguishable, a part of whatever community he lived in. Now that he had an Arab Muslim identity thrust upon him, he accepted it. Year by year he fought for it in the ring, defending his right to be who he was with every angry blow. He worked out more than the other boys, not just building his muscles but learning the craft, the ancient feints and combinations. He ran, he jumped rope, he was able to work the speed bag like a pro. Rizwan recognized Tony's ferocity; he had his own experiences as a Muslim in a community with very few of them. He also saw Tony as a boy without a father present, and that was a role he filled for many of his protégés.

The day came when after school a couple of boys called him a terrorist. Tony put down his books and walked up to them. His composure was intimidating. "Say that to my face," he said. When one of the boys, Hank Johnson, did so, Tony hit him in the nose. The other boy ran away. And then Tony hit Hank again and again, even when he was lying on the ground, defenseless. A crowd gathered around telling him to stop but he couldn't hold his fists back. Finally a teacher pulled him off. He was immediately expelled.

His mother called Rizwan; she didn't know anyone else who could reason with him. Rizwan drove Tony back to the school. He told him about the history of the place, Central High, one of the first schools in the South to be integrated. The National Guard came to shield the nine Black students who broke the color barrier. "But the guard couldn't be here every day," Rizwan said. "Those children had to learn to conduct themselves with dignity. Do you think the harassment you received is as great as what the Little Rock Nine endured? Not a chance. They won over their classmates because of their courage to be the first, being gracious in the face of hatred, proud of their identities but not resentful of those who oppressed them. Those children changed America. Now it's your turn."

Rizwan asked the principal to arrange a meeting between the boys and their mothers. The principal knew about the harassment Tony experienced, but Hank had never been one of the bullies. Her highest obligation was to protect her students. But she agreed because she had also failed to protect Tony.

Tony was shocked by the sight of what he had done to Hank. His eyes were swollen shut, his face purpled, and a big X of bandages crossed his broken nose. Hank's mother was furious with the prospect of Tony being readmitted to school. "He should be in prison," she said. That seemed to be the reason she had agreed to the meeting, just to get those words out.

"That is a possibility," the principal said. "Assault on school grounds is a crime and can be prosecuted in juvenile court. If you chose to pursue this path, I can inform the police."

Tony's mother cried helplessly. "He's a good boy," she kept saying, avoiding the look on Hank's mother's face, who would send him to the gallows.

And then Hank spoke up. "It was my fault," he said.

"That's not true," his mother said.

"You weren't there, Mom. I heard what some of the kids were calling him, and I knew he wasn't a terrorist, but I thought it would be fun to pick on him." He turned to Tony. "I'm sorry. I know you're not a terrorist. I hope you'll forgive me."

Tony Malik and Hank Johnson kept up with each other for years after that, until Hank was killed in Afghanistan, fighting against Muslims who used their religion to terrorize anyone who believed differently.

WHEN THE PRAYER was over and the congregants dispersed, Jamal and Malik lingered. The mosque was ornate and stately, richly colored in geometric patterns. Malik never cared for the aesthetic of those churches and synagogues designed for people to sit and listen, especially the gaudy ones meant to subdue the congregation with their splendor. Mosques were simpler. There were no statues of saints or frescoes of angels, just a large room covered with rugs. The presence of absence. The purpose of a mosque was to prostrate yourself and bow toward the rock in Mecca that somehow embodied the spiritual force of the universe, just as Jews prayed before the stone wall in Jerusalem. The unifying choreography of Muslim prayer was a part of the appeal, everyone moving together in gestures filled with arcane meaning.

"See that door?" Jamal said, pointing to a beige metal entryway at the back of the mosque. "On the other side is Abraham Hall, where the Jews pray. One day, in February 1994, a man came through that door. His name was Baruch Goldstein, a doctor from Brooklyn, who lived in Kiryat Arba, the settlement on the hill behind us."

Malik knew the story but he could see that Jamal needed to tell it.

"He was wearing his army uniform and he carried an assault weapon. It was Ramadan. Imagine, this entire room, people on their knees, eight hundred people praying their *Fajr*. First he throws a hand grenade, then he starts firing. He shoots through an entire magazine and reloads. And he does this again. Again. Again. Five times."

A group of Muslims gathered around to listen to the story they so often told themselves, nodding in agreement as Jamal continued. "And while he's reloading—*for the sixth time*—the surviving Muslims rush him." Jamal waved to an old man who joined them, carrying a red fire extinguisher. "And this man—*show him!*—he broke the head of Baruch Goldstein." The old man grinned as he relived the moment, pounding the air with the fire extinguisher, a look of fierce joy on his face.

They walked outside into the fresh early-morning air. The sun was low and soft, painting the limestone walls in sherbet colors. Malik thought how beautiful this place must have been, and could be again, were it not so marred by graffiti and litter and the overwhelming apparatus of oppression. He noticed fake trees among the palms, cunningly placed, laden with cameras and communications gear. The Old City was a UNESCO World Heritage Site, but it had the charm of a prison yard.

"Twenty-nine Muslims died," Jamal continued. "What happens after Goldstein is that he is celebrated as a hero, with a massive funeral parade in Jerusalem, an honor guard, people shouting 'Kill the Arabs!' They bring his body to Kiryat Arba, not neglecting to pass through Arab villages along the way. They make a shrine for him. Women who have trouble conceiving go to the grave and pray for a child such as the martyred Goldstein. Till today! His picture is on the walls of many who would follow his example. They believe the only solution to our problem is to kill everyone or push the survivors across the Jordan River. Even people in the Israeli government think this. They may talk about two states but they actually conspire to murder us if we stay, or turn us into slaves. They say Goldstein is in third place, behind King David, who killed more, and Samson, who is number two. Actually, they forget Joshua, who their holy books say killed every living thing when the Jews took possession of the Holy Land. These are their heroes."

Jamal glanced at Malik to gauge his reaction. "I don't say that Muslims are innocent," he continued. "We are equally terrible, but weaker. If we could drive the Jews into the sea, we would do it. After Goldstein, Hamas went crazy. It was then the suicide bombers increased. Killing innocents is forbidden in Islam, and suicide is a terrible sin. The Prophet said that the person who does this will spend all of eternity in the act of killing himself. All eternity! And yet, suicide becomes what you might call the weapon of sacrifice. We are weak so we use the instruments of weakness.

"What you don't understand, what nobody outside understands, is the real enemy is not each other. It is peace we hate. Goldstein was not only killing Muslims, he was killing Oslo. The first real path to a Palestinian state and it had to be destroyed. Among the Palestinians, there is exhilaration. They say Oslo is too hard and it gives us too little in return for dropping the sword. Now we can wage righteous violence on our oppressors. Surely this is better than peace."

Jamal led the way through the serpentine market in the Old City, pointing out the butcher shop where he worked, which was not yet open, and introducing him to the venerable mukhtar of the Abdul Malik clan. "You are welcome, mister," the mukhtar said repeatedly while insisting that Malik take a tin of candies, even offering a sack of chickpeas from the modest store of goods for sale. Meantime Jamal explained how clans worked, and that Malik was actually a member of a vast extended family. Malik smiled at this little man in his negligible shop, thinking how far away they were in so many respects, but somehow the blood of the clan made them kin.

"Look, this was my house." Jamal pointed to the end of a short dead-end street, little more than an alleyway, chaotically crisscrossed with electrical wires, where a three-story fortresslike stone building sat abandoned and decrepit. Dark shuttered windows stared back. Like all haunted houses it had an air of abandoned elegance. Off the balcony on the third story was a dovecote with pigeons still nesting there. Next door was a lot full of rubble from a house the IDF had blown up.

"It's closed to me, even though my family owns it," said Jamal. "When I was a kid here, this street was full, like Times Square." His eyes were alight with the memories. "Here was the barber. This building was the ice-cream store." He pointed to a vacant building on the corner. "My teacher lived here. I spent so many hours on this street! This was a fruit stand. I can see it in my mind. Now they have closed eighteen hundred shops. Their goal is to drive everyone out of the Old City, and after that they will take over all of Hebron. They don't bother to evict any longer, they just make it impossible to live. People don't feel safe because of the settlers, there are no services, no social life, no one can visit—to the point people stop resisting. They begin to think about making a life somewhere else."

"And that includes you?"

Jamal sighed. "I also want a life. I don't need to be a martyr. In the past, maybe yes, I thought about that. Too many people want me dead. The last thing they want to hear about is peace. I call it the Big Peace. Israel and Palestine, problem solved. That was my goal. I was giving my life to this. Now I think only about the Little Peace, that is what is left for me. I will stop worrying about the situation that I cannot solve. I want to find peace for me, peace *inside* me, do you understand that? And so I have surrendered."

"Maybe that's the real victory," said Malik, "to live a peaceful life."

"This is what the word 'Islam' means, to surrender. It is understood as submission to the will of God, not the Jews, but I believe this passivity is crucial to achieving peace. Okay, it is also because Muslims have been trained not to resist that we have such a problem with dictatorships. Everywhere you look in the Islamic world we have them, these monsters, most of them military, some of them religious, but we surrender to them. We talk about democracy, about human rights, but we do not fight for these qualities. Jews we fight against because they are colonialists. We'd rather be governed badly by Arabs than treated well by Jews.

"Even right here, where we stand, they killed a Palestinian youth last month. He was lying unconscious on the street, already shot, and a soldier shot him again in the head. This action is officially condemned but applauded by many. I admit I am tired of being afraid, tired of being beaten. See—" he pointed at his teeth—"my new mouth. Six months ago a soldier hits me with his rifle and destroys so many teeth. But anyway. No more hero. Now I can smile at my wedding."

Malik turned away from the sight of Jamal's gleaming dentures, a memento of humiliation that struck him as unbearable. Jamal immediately acknowledged the emotion and the question it posed. "Of course, I wanted to kill him or at least injure him terribly. For me, the 'resistance' is resisting my own violent nature. This—" gesturing again to his teeth—"was the least of such punishments. When the Israelis killed my brother, it was my duty to avenge him. A matter of honor. My parents expected this, they prayed for it. And of course I wanted to murder. The humiliations pile up to the point that revenge becomes irresistible. They arrested me and did things to me no man should suffer. Humiliating things I have never talked about. It occurred to me that they longed for me to strike at them to justify their own violent response. My only source of power was disappointing them. I admit to you, Tony, part of me despises my pacifism. I could kill without remorse. This is my struggle."

"So what's the answer?" asked Malik. "Does this just go on and on till the end of time?"

Jamal stopped still. They had come to an arched limestone passageway. A drain ran down the center of the walkway with piles of trash on either side. "You ask me seriously, right?" said Jamal. "I will tell you the answer, but you will not accept it. You will say it is impossible, and okay, maybe so. Many years I have thought about this, and I concluded that the Palestinians must surrender and the Jews must forgive. The Arabs cannot win, but their pride keeps them from going to the gates of Jerusalem and begging for mercy. Not just a few. Millions of Muslims on their knees pleading for their rights, for their dignity—this is the only thing that will soften the hearts of our occupiers. Can you imagine the scene? The whole world would demand justice and the Jews would be ashamed. The voices of peace would be heard, not like now, in whispers. Finally the Jews could say, 'At last, we won! Our enemy has given up, he is begging for us to be merciful. And as Jews, we must do this.'

"But they cannot. Just as the Palestinians will never abase themselves at the feet of the occupiers and admit defeat, the Jews insist to hold on to their anger. They are ashamed of their history, of being lambs to the slaughter, and they must prove they are no longer such lambs, they are a mighty people. If you kill one Jew, they must kill a hundred of you. Or a thousand, a million, whatever the going rate. As a Palestinian, you do not own your land, it belongs to Jews because God said so. What is ours is theirs. This is the dynamic. Neither side wishes for the struggle to end, and whenever the possibility of peace seems near the knives come out, the boys strap on their suicide vests, the missiles fly, the bombs fall, and so it goes. No. I have given my life for peace. But I am the one who has been defeated."

Jamal led the way down the portion of Shuhada Street where Arabs were allowed. "One more thing to show you," he said. They came to the Muslim cemetery. The gate was unlocked. Under an acacia tree was a bench surrounded by police tape. "Where they found the body of the chief," said Jamal.

Malik examined the site. He had been to many crime scenes and knew how to read them. What he saw was a mess, footsteps all over the place amid broken plaster molds, fingerprint dust on the ground below the bench, a forgotten tape measure, the residue of haste and people bumping into each other.

"But that's not what I was going to show you," said Jamal. He waved Malik over to the north side of the cemetery. "These," he said, with a sweeping gesture including dozens of headstones, "are your people, the Abdul Maliks, going back for centuries."

Malik was dumbstruck. He was a man with so little family, the connections having been severed by death or carelessness, and to see before him the evidence of other lives somehow tied to his hit him in an unguarded place. He had spent his own life largely alone, strengthening his defenses, becoming self-sufficient and happy in the way of a man who needs no one. If he knew anything about genealogy he would have been able to piece together the lives that somehow led to his, but here they were, his ancestors, his lineage, a vast and interconnected tribe. The main emotion he felt upon seeing the evidence of his people was a profound sense of loss.

27

The Butcher Shop

Hebron, Sept. 29, 2023

As Malik walked back to the hotel for a nap Jamal went to work. It was still early when he unlocked the butcher shop and began the task of carving a side of beef into various chops and steaks. He had a couple of hours before customers arrived. This was Jamal's special day, but he felt obligated to do his job as quickly as possible so that his employer would not suffer his absence.

In the back of the shop, next to the freezer, was the cooler, where a side of beef hung, a sheer white skein of superficial fascia clinging to the carcass like a nightgown. Jamal put on his butcher's jacket with his name embroidered above the pocket and stroked his knife on the honing steel. The ribs of the steer were purple-blue and evenly spaced. The engineer in Jamal marveled at the mechanical efficiency of animal bodies, each designed for different tasks in life, but they were purposeful in death as well. He sliced through the flesh just above the thirteenth rib. There was little more resistance on the knife than a man might feel shaving in the morning, so keen was the blade. He sawed through the backbone then loaded each half of the sundered carcass onto meat hooks attached to an overhead railing leading to the processing table behind the front counter.

He began with the rear leg, severing the tendons that held the rump together. He peeled away the roasts, beginning with the top round, which yielded to the feathery cuts of his ten-inch knife. Beneath it was the eye round, which the butcher traditionally ties into segments. Next he liberated the femur bone, rich with marrow; then came the bottom round, a healthy slab that would serve as a roast beef. Jamal sliced the plump portion known as the knuckle into sirloin tip steaks. His moves were quick and dancelike.

He cleaned the fascia and fat from the flank, scraping out the suet, which would be sold for candles, and then broke the bone separating the loin from the sirloin. By now he had worked up a sweat. He was proud of his meager trade. He was doing something useful, and what else in his life was as meaningful? When he finished carving the chuck and the neck he began laying out the cuts of meat in the window. Other carcasses—lambs and goats—he suspended from hooks in the shop, then he arranged trays of livers and kidneys. He unlocked the freezer and brought out some camel meat to thaw. Tonight he would be married.

YOSSI PINNED a small black kippah to his hair and entered Miriam's town home in Kiryat Arba. He was carrying Weingarten's guitar and a tote bag full of personal effects. The door was cracked open. He touched the mezuzah on the doorpost as he went in. There was no one in the living room and no sounds in the kitchen, and yet the mirrors were covered in black, although official mourning would have to wait until Weingarten was buried. "Miriam?" he called.

She appeared on the stairwell, so pale she nearly disappeared against the white wall, looking as if she had lost ten pounds overnight. Her blouse was torn in mourning. "Miriam, I'm sorry to disturb you, I thought there would be a shiva."

"We can't sit shiva until the funeral, Yossi, and you know I won't bury him until you find the head."

"We will find it, I swear. I won't stop until we do. We will catch the killers and they will produce the head, I promise you." He was still awkwardly holding the guitar and the tote bag. "I brought by some personal items."

"Set them down anywhere," she said distantly.

Miriam had not invited him to sit, nor was she inclined to converse. Beneath her shock and her seeming apathy he detected a volcano on the verge of explosion.

"I'll just put them in his office and be out of the way. Don't bother to see me out."

Miriam nodded and retreated upstairs. Yossi went through the den into the chief's personal retreat, a small room with a pricey music system and LPs on the shelves. He worked quickly, sizing up the chief's retreat. Weingarten was a man of slightly antiquated tastes; both the books and the music on shelves reflected a sensibility that was best expressed in the 1960s. His taste reflected a romantic and compassionate nature; in this struggle those were fatal qualities. But Yossi now knew he was also a man with secrets.

Yossi set the items down and quickly examined the unlocked desk. He knew the chief better now. If the missing file was in this room it would be hidden in some ordinary place, not under missing floor-boards or in a wall safe behind a painting. He would hide it where other people wouldn't be looking, and there in front of Yossi was an obvious, very Weingarten place: the record albums. There were several hundred. Yossi thumbed through them rapidly, he wouldn't have time to look inside one by one. They were carefully alphabetized, typical Weingarten, mainly classic jazz by the great instrumentalists: Louis Armstrong, Chet Baker, Ornette Coleman, John Coltrane, and there it was, lodged between the albums *Bitches Brew* and *Kind of Blue* in the Miles Davis section, File 169. Yossi knew Jacob Weingarten better in death than he had in life.

He noticed a photograph on the wall of the chief posing with a slender white-haired man with closed eyes. He looked closer and guessed that the picture was of Andrea Bocelli, the blind Italian singer with the beautiful voice. Out of curiosity he thumbed through the albums again and found six albums by Bocelli.

He heard the footsteps and quickly stuck the file behind the Bocelli album that he was holding just as Miriam entered the room, along with her son, Menachem. Yossi maintained his pose of being interested in Weingarten's record collection. "You never see such a collection these days," he said, as if to himself, then looked at Menachem apologetically. "I don't mean to pry, but your father and I often talked about his love of music. Something we had in common."

"Really?" said Menachem mechanically.

"Jacob did like to talk about his music," Miriam confirmed. "He was very particular. Not many people shared his taste."

"I'm more interested in the singers," said Yossi, "like Andrea Bocelli." He held up *Concerto: One Night in Central Park*.

"Jacob loved him," Miriam said. "He tried so hard to get tickets for his concert but they were all sold out."

"Too bad."

"As for me, I care nothing for opera," Miriam said.

"Anything you need, Detective?" asked Menachem.

"No, no, nothing at all." He pretended to put the album back on the shelf, then stopped himself. "But would you mind if I borrowed this? Jacob said it was one of his favorites. It would be like hearing it through his ears." Menachem paused, then nodded slightly. "I'll bring it back, I promise," Yossi said.

"Don't bother," said Miriam. "We're going to sell all this on eBay."

THE OWNER OF the butcher shop was Iskander Khoury, a Christian from the southern part of Lebanon who converted to Islam. There were few Christians left in Hebron except for a colony of Russian monks. Some people in town doubted the sincerity of the butcher's conversion, but Jamal thought it unfair to judge any person's faith. Much of the time he thought his own piety was more habit than true belief.

Sheikh Iskander—as Jamal called him because he was his boss but also because of the butcher's sensitivity about his provisional acceptance in the community—had a suspicious manner and was just as judgmental as his critics. He collected gossip and behaved unctuously toward his clients while disparaging them behind their backs. Although he didn't drink, smoking was a vice he couldn't give up. He would sneak into the cooler and smoke among the suspended carcasses until he was too chilled to enjoy the break. He smoked with the passion of a true addict, as if it were inhaling life itself, rather than the opposite. His habit left the cooler stinking of tobacco.

Jamal felt obliged to his boss because he had given him a job when few wanted anything to do with a troublemaker such as he. Perhaps

Iskander identified with Jamal as another outsider and wanted to help him; more likely, he saw him as vulnerable and compromised and not likely to reveal any secrets. Jamal wondered if there was something in the butcher's background that would cause him to abandon Lebanon and change his religion or was the conversion just a convenient way to have more than one wife? Sheikh Iskander had four, the maximum at any one time, and that kept him occupied and constantly impoverished. Maybe he was just greedy—greedy for money and greedy for women—in any case, Jamal quietly observed the little cheats when the butcher weighed the portions, gaining ten or fifty agorot in a sale, so cheaply did he sell his integrity. He had instructed Jamal in the art of butchery, although Jamal also watched videos and taught himself, soon becoming more skilled than his boss. Sheikh Iskander gradually retreated from his duties, knowing that the shop was in competent hands. Some days he didn't come in at all, unless he felt the need to be on the register and make a little more money than he deserved. This was such a day.

"You should be preparing for your wedding," the butcher said, although he would have been annoyed if Jamal hadn't worked all morning getting the shop ready.

"I do need to take off early," said Jamal.

"First do me the favor of preparing twenty chickens while I handle the sales," Iskander said lightly, as if it were of no matter to butcher so many chickens. It would take at least an hour and a half that Jamal hadn't counted on. He set a large bucket of water on a burner and walked about forty paces to the chicken market, where he selected five cages of four chickens each. The birds were old and scrawny, well past their laying days; it had been a long time since Jamal had worked with a plump young pullet. Two boys helped him take the hens back to the shop.

Jamal tried to make the killing as quick and painless as possible so as not to alarm the animals awaiting their turn with the cleaver. He put on a pair of blue latex gloves and set the cages under the processing table. When the water was close to boiling, he grabbed the first hen by its feet and in a single motion, before it had time to squawk, he flopped it on the butcher block and severed its head. Automatically the bird's wings spread. If Jamal let it go, it would fly out of the shop and down the street until the body realized it was dead. As a child, Jamal was fascinated by this phenomenon, but now he dumped the chicken in the scalding water before the wings fully opened. Immediately the body relaxed, the flesh surrendered its grip and twenty seconds later the bird was ready to pluck. Sheikh Iskander was widely known to be stingy, and yet he had invested in a plucker, which was just a drill with a cylindrical attachment studded with rubber fingers that miraculously shucked the feathers. Within a minute the body was entirely naked. Jamal sliced off the feet and carefully extracted the crop and the gizzard. When the chicken was finally prepared, he tied the legs together and placed it in a cardboard basket on a bed of ice in the display case.

Killing one animal after another had never become an entirely mechanical act. Mentally Jamal still registered the action. He held an inner conversation with the beings he killed, sometimes asking forgiveness, sometimes making a little joke when he encountered resistance to the killing, a brief protest that was quickly ended.

Jamal had rarely been outside of Hebron, but he had come to appreciate that the city had a different stance toward the dead than other places. In Hebron, the dead had meaning. They were present. There was an endless communion between the living and the dead—the dead from centuries ago still demanding revenge and the newly slain demanding the same. There would never be enough revenge and there would never be too many dead. The butcher was always at work and the dead were in some way alive.

A customer arrived looking for Sheikh Iskander, who was taking another smoke break in the cooler. Jamal chatted with the customer, a bulky middle-aged man with a guilty look, asking if there was anything he could do for him. There was not, but Jamal knew what he wanted. Every month it was the same: a pork shoulder and a rasher of bacon. Eating pork was taboo, both in Islam and Judaism, but for some people that only made it more appealing—a forbidden meat that was reputedly the tastiest of all, and therefore highly profitable, impossible for Sheikh Iskander to pass up.

Presently the butcher emerged from the cooler. Recognizing the customer, he asked Jamal to bring out the brown bag with the special order. Jamal went into the freezer. Not seeing the bag on the top shelves he looked at the bottom of the freezer and brought out a likely-looking sack.

"Thanks, Iskander, you're the only one in town I can count on," the customer said as he took the bag from Jamal. He looked around furtively to see if anyone in the narrow shopping street had observed the transaction. As the butcher was counting the shekels the customer peeked inside the bag. Then he screamed. With a sudden violent movement he ejected the bag into the shop. As he did so, Chief Weingarten's bald head emerged and rolled across the cement floor, landing at Jamal's feet.

In the confusion the customer rushed away, leaving Jamal and the butcher staring at the frozen head on the floor. Jamal looked up to see Sheikh Iskander pointing at him. "You did this!" he cried.

"What are you saying?" Jamal said. His throat was dry and his words were scarcely audible.

"You have the key!" the butcher said. "I took you after jail and trusted you!"

"No, no, it's not true!"

The butcher fished his phone out of his pocket and began to call. Jamal was paralyzed. He glanced at the crowd of shoppers drawn to the commotion and saw that several were filming him. His image was going to be all over the territories in an instant. The police would arrive. He knew how he would be treated. They would not miss the opportunity to be done with him. Everything he hoped for was doomed. His life was over. He pushed Sheikh Iskander aside and vaulted over the display case, muttering an apology as he knocked over a woman pointing her phone at him. Hands reached out to restrain him but he broke free.

28

"Save Him!"

Hebron, Sept. 29, 2023

File 169 contained some news articles, several intelligence briefs, and a few handwritten pages—random thoughts that Weingarten had been trying to connect. The intel community wasn't paying attention to the drug trade—it wasn't an existential threat, like terror—so the information was raw and unvetted. Diagrams Weingarten sketched linked Iran, Hezbollah, and Hamas—nothing surprising about that—but they contained references to a drug called Captagon, a cheap amphetamine popular with jihadis in Syria that spurred them into battle longing for martyrdom. Weingarten noted that Mexican cartels were breaking into the European market with crystal meth and a form of fentanyl mixed with cocaine to make it extra addictive; the chief found evidence this deadly concoction was making a debut in the territories. The Taliban were funneling heroin and unprocessed opium from Afghanistan through Turkey and from there to Hamas, bypassing the old trade with Hezbollah, which concentrated on cocaine. The picture Weingarten had been assembling was of interlocking multinational drug cartels that were competing with each other while partnering with Islamic terrorists. They were all converging on Hebron and the West Bank.

One of Weingarten's charts showed settlement communities on the West Bank overlaid with deaths from drug overdoses. Yossi could read Weingarten's mind: the deaths were taking place wherever a Kahanist settlement was nearby.

Yossi asked Golda if there was drug use in Kiryat Arba.

"They keep it quiet but we have had incidents, every community does, right?"

"Any drug in particular?"

"The usual, hashish, Ecstasy, nothing to get excited about, but bear in mind this is all under the table and is handled by the community leaders."

"Any unusual deaths—like from overdoses?"

Golda thought a moment. "Two young people died in the last several months. One was an aneurism but they didn't say anything about the other, a girl about twenty. Maybe a suicide, who knows."

The Palestinian police had long complained about drug transactions right in front of Israeli soldiers who did nothing to stop them. If the Palestinian cops tried to intercede, the dealers would just cross into Israeli jurisdiction and that was the end of it. Yossi vaguely recalled that there had been a rise in fatalities from drug overdoses in the territories, but it was a Palestinian problem, not an Israeli one.

So what was Weingarten's interest? And why was he keeping it a secret?

Yossi went back into the chief's office. He put File 169 in its place in the cabinet. While he had the drawer open, he took File 213 into a stall in the men's room, where he could be assured of privacy.

AHARON BERGER

b. 1987, Boston, MA, Orthodox family. Parents known extremists. AB's father followed Meir Kahane, went to prison for bomb making. Family noted for financial support of Kach party. AB identified with his father's hatred v. homosexuals, Muslims, Christians, women, especially liberal secular Jews ("sheep"), became fanatic, dedicated to changing image of Jews as "weak and vulnerable" to "mighty fighters" (language from Kahane).

Yossi was surprised by how radical Berger's upbringing was. No wonder he had migrated into Kahanist circles.

AB made aliyah after dropping out of NYU 2015. Took Hebrew courses in Tel Aviv, worked in a coffee house. Military service in the Galilee. Disciplined for assault on Arab schoolteacher during protest. After service moved to Kiryat Arba to be near the tomb of "martyr" Baruch Goldstein. Politically anti-democratic, aligned with national religious, his goal to get rid of Arabs "once and for all" (Kahane again). In context of the settlement his views unremarkable.

Married Mika Blum, three children, the couple spent a year apart but were reconciled. Strains reportedly continue in marriage. She viciously anti-Arab, was briefly detained after assault on a Palestinian woman in the market. She sees as her duty to drive Arabs from Judea and Samaria. A frequent presence at protests.

Aside from his multiple prejudices AB is a capable investigator so long as he is kept from dealing with Arabs. Hot-tempered and ambitious. Suffered undisclosed health problems that kept him out of office for three weeks just before the pandemic, mysterious absences continue from time to time.

AB and wife close to Immanuel Cohen's movement. He is not to be trusted on matters that touch on the Rav's cause or followers. Came under suspicion in firebombing of Palestinian home in 2022 but evidence—

"Yossi? Are you in there?"

It was Golda, of all people, he recognized her running shoes under the toilet-stall door.

"Golda, I'm occupied. What are you doing in here?"

"We identified the killer!"

JAMAL WALKED QUICKLY through the Old City. As soon as his image was posted it would trigger Red Wolf and every security camera in Hebron would be looking for him. The signal would be relayed to checkpoints. Drones would follow him. If he broke into a sprint, Red Wolf would spot him. Sharpshooters in the watchtowers would kill him on sight. The only way he might evade the intense security of the Old City was to head up the hill of Tel Rumeida, behind Shuhada Street. An olive grove provided meager cover from the drones and balloons. There he might cross the hill and drop into

H-1. His goal, so hastily formed, was to turn himself in to the Palestinian police. They had no authority over the IDF but they might at least give him a chance to tell his story. Although what was the point? There was no reason for anyone to believe him.

He hurriedly glanced back at the Old City. He could see an IDF helicopter taking off from a pad just beyond Kiryat Arba. It was happening.

Now he ran. He stripped off his white butcher's jacket and sprinted through the olive grove. He threw away his phone so he couldn't be tracked. He was breathless when he came to the ridge that dropped off into Qarantina Street, the only possibility of escape, but suddenly there were IDF vehicles screaming alarms as they rushed to cut off every junction. Either he would be killed now or he would race across the street and face the next obstacle to freedom, and the next, and the next, endlessly.

There was a steep dirt path from the ridge to the street. He crept down, hiding in the shade of large clumps of prickly-pear cactus. He startled a pair of rabbits, who hopped farther down the slope away from him. Heavy engines approached and then a procession of Humvees and armored cars zoomed past, machine guns mounted on their roofs. One of them slowed and came to a stop right in front of Jamal, only twenty meters away. The gun turret rotated in his direction. He froze. The slightest movement would awaken the computer targeting system. Could it see his eye between the cactus pads? He tried not to blink.

The gun erupted, exploding bits of cactus into the air, along with pieces of rabbit. Then there was silence as smoke wafted across the path. He dared not look up to see the balloons and drones and helicopters and satellites that were no doubt following his every move. Searchlights from the aircraft probed through the trees. Armed militias from the settlement patrolled the street, ignoring the IDF soldiers who dutifully avoided them. Jamal was known to everyone. His infuriating provocations and his connections to Western media and to sympathetic Israelis had made him a target for years. Every soldier serving in Hebron was given a lecture about how to treat him; he knew all the rules and boldly exploited the loopholes. He had been arrested many times. Rough treatment was officially discouraged, although young soldiers, stirred by nationalist or religious feelings, or simply insulted by Jamal's insistence on claiming his rights, frequently crossed the line. They were furious that he didn't care about his beatings; he was willing to be mistreated if it brought attention to the occupation.

But now he was a wanted man, suspected as a terrorist, and if that description didn't correspond with the peace activist he had long been, little thought was given to the contradiction. People would tell themselves it was a cover. He was Hamas all along.

Even Palestinians were ambivalent about his role. Some would say that Jamal Khalil would better serve the cause as a dead martyr than as a living rebuke to the corruption of the Palestinian Authority and vocal opponent of the violence of Hamas, Islamic Jihad, and whatever new groups were arising to vainly attempt to overthrow the occupation. It would serve a purpose to praise him as Chief Weingarten's executioner. He would be a hero, but first he needed to be killed.

MALIK FINISHED DRESSING for the wedding festivities, and as he came downstairs to order a cab Yasmine burst into the lobby. "Tony!" she cried. "You've got to come with me!"

"Am I late?"

"No, no, I'll explain." She drove frantically. "They are saying Jamal is the murderer," she said.

"Is he?"

"Be serious. Jamal is not a terrorist. Even you must know him better than that." She told him what she had heard, about the head in the freezer and Jamal's flight. There was a YouTube video of him bolting out of the butcher shop. "You've got to help us. They'll kill him, I swear it!"

"How's Dina doing?"

"You will see."

Dina was sitting in the front room with the lights out. She scarcely acknowledged her mother and Malik as they came in. Omar stood sentry. They all had the faces of people who were about to face execution themselves. The room was overflowing with wedding gifts.

Malik sat beside Dina and wordlessly took her hand. At his touch, she began to sob. She tried to form words but she choked on them. "Don't let them kill him," she finally said.

"I'll do what I can," Malik promised, not knowing where to begin.

"He's innocent, Tony, he never did this!"

"Okay."

"Mom, leave us alone, okay? You, too, Omar."

Omar started to protest but Yasmine shooed him out the door.

Dina looked around the room at the flowers and gifts strewn across the tables and chairs. "It's perfect, isn't it? At the moment of maximum hope and happiness. Gone. What a fool I was." She wiped her face with a tissue. "Living here, you always expect the worst. The only surprise is how bad the worst can be. Finally, it becomes impossible. You fill to the top with rage. Depression. Fear. Regular feelings there is no room for. You begin to understand the suiciders who think they can make death meaningful in a way their life is not."

"Don't let that be you."

Dina shook her head. "I don't have the courage of my despair. But I understand the anger. Our lives are not like yours. You are free. You can go where you want, be who you want to be. Our lives are like on a railroad track. We go where we are pointed. There are many stops but only one destination."

Malik was quiet for a moment. "I've known dark thoughts. Hopelessness. Many times I wished I had died in the bombing rather than having to live a life that was less than I had before."

Dina squeezed his hand. Malik continued: "I still think that sometimes. I miss the person I was going to be. But that person had other limitations. If I were ever to recover all that I lost, I'd try to be more like the person I am now. I'm certainly a lot more humble. I'm finding joy from things I wouldn't have noticed before. I know this doesn't have anything to do with what you're experiencing. People will tell you that this will just be a memory one day, a bad dream. It's more than that. It's horrible. I wish I could be more consoling, have something profound to say."

Dina turned her desolate, tear-stained face to him. Until a day ago Malik was an unmet cousin who had rarely communicated with the family; now, suddenly, he was her only hope—a faint, unlikely hope—and who else could possibly come to her aid now?

"I don't need your sympathy," she said. "I need your help."

"What can I do?"

"Save him!"

Malik had no authority in the territories. Nor did he understand the complexity of the struggle that people on both sides were waging. The available evidence against Jamal was incriminating, if not damning. He certainly made it worse by running away. Now he would be hunted down by forces ready to shoot on sight.

"Dina, do you know anything? Was Jamal connected to Hamas? Did he know the chief? Did he ever say anything to you that made you think he could be violent? Where was he at the time of the murder? Anything you think might be even a little bit relevant. Anything at all."

But Dina was mute, her eyes wide with fright.

"Dina, you want my help but you have to give me something to work with."

"They will see me as a—what is that word for the person who helps with a crime?"

"An accessory?"

She nodded. "But I am also the alibi. Because Jamal was with me that day. He pretended to be sick and we spent the whole day together."

"Did anyone see you?"

"No! We were together—as lovers." A shiver ran through her body. "You don't know what it is like in this culture when an unmarried woman is with a man. Instantly she is a whore. Some families would kill the woman because of the dishonor, this stupid custom. So we were careful, like bandits."

"He should have been more cautious with you."

"Don't blame him for that. We had already signed our marriage contract. In our minds we were married, just without the ceremony. When they arrested him the last time, we didn't know if he would be charged or how long he might be held. Suppose it is for years? So we made our secret vows to each other, like children." She smiled at the memory. "You have to find moments of joy when you can. Those were the only times we were truly happy. But in this place such emotions must be destroyed."

Up until now Dina had struck him as still partly a child, and she certainly had the glow of youthful beauty, but he also recognized her as a sexual creature who knew pleasure. Even in her grief she was a desirable woman. Her sexuality was accented by a new maturity that comes from facing life's impossible struggles. Beyond her beauty was a graciousness that would always be present, even as it was wrapped in tragedy. But there were depths to her personality and he sensed there was more to her than what he was being shown. Each new layer promised another.

"Without any witnesses this is just a story, it's not evidence," he said, surprising himself with his harshness. "What am I supposed to do with it?"

Fresh tears came. "I don't know. Why can't the truth be believed when everybody is so willing to believe the lies?"

"I'm sorry, I didn't mean to upset you."

"Please help, Jamal," she said, her face streaming with tears she no longer bothered to wipe away. "There is no one else who can."

29

"Nobody's Innocent"

Hebron, Sept. 29, 2023

Wedding's off," Yossi said gruffly. "The groom can't make it. You should be on a plane."

"I'm leaving as soon as I can," said Malik.

"So you came to say goodbye?"

They were standing in the reception room. Golda was at the desk again. Berger lurked in the hallway, radiating distrust.

"Could you give me a minute? Cop to cop."

Yossi considered this, then nodded curtly.

They went into the chief's old office, and Yossi closed the door. "You were right about the gunshot. Behind the left ear. So I give you five minutes."

"What was the weapon?"

"Nine-millimeter pistol, probably a Jericho. What everybody uses. We found the slug." He said this with some pride.

"Do you have the gun?"

"We have the head and we know the killer."

Malik looked around the office. It had the haunted, empty feel of a missing life, a place once filled with work, memories, enthusiasms. The presence of absence.

"He was a musician?" he asked, picking up a photo of Weingarten playing the guitar before a group of schoolchildren.

"He thought of himself as a singer," said Yossi. "Is this how you want to spend your five minutes?"

"Don't you think it's strange that Jamal would hide the head in a place where it would lead right to him? You've got to wonder what he planned to do with it."

"We think he intended to sell it. Jews believe the body should be buried all together. Every drop of blood even. Animals like him take advantage."

"What about the guy who owns the butcher shop?"

"He's the one who called us. Jamal is the one who ran. What else do you want to know, 'cop to cop'?"

"I have a witness."

"Let me guess. Your pretty cousin."

"I know what you're thinking and why. She says she was with Jamal at the time of the murder."

"And does your witness have a witness to what she says she witnessed?"

"It's possible. They met in a hostel. There should be a record of it. Somebody may have seen them."

"But you believe your cousin."

"I don't believe anything. Just what I can prove."

"On this we agree."

"Look, this guy—Jamal—he's not a part of any group. He's spent his life working for peace and in return everybody hates him. Why would he do such a thing? What is his motive? Instead of bringing peace this murder has set off a firestorm, exactly the opposite of what Jamal stands for. Looks to me like you're just using this as an opportunity to get rid of the guy because he says things you don't agree with."

Yossi stared at Malik for a moment, then called, "Berger!" In a moment Aharon Berger came into the office. "Show him what you found on the internet," said Yossi.

Berger brought an iPad and flipped through screens. "It's on this encrypted site the terrorists use called Arba Arbaeen. I was monitoring it and almost scrolled right past this." He handed Malik the iPad.

It was a photo of a couple at an outdoor café. The name of the place wasn't visible. Small tables with round black tops and wrought-iron chairs with patterned cushions—it could have been Haifa or Tel Aviv. A middle-aged bald man who looked like Weingarten was with a young woman. She was smiling, he had his mouth near her ear, probably whispering something amusing or affectionate. The woman was Dina.

"This is a motive?" asked Malik.

"You think Jamal would be happy knowing our chief is shtupping his girlfriend?" Yossi asked. "He's about to get married and then he sees this on the internet. I don't care what you say about the peace business. Maybe you think he's Martin Luther King. Nelson Mandela. I'll tell you who he is. He's an Arab man. He would go insane if he saw this. So he cooks up this plot and makes it look like a terrorist act. He's clever, but he's also greedy. He hangs on to the head, knowing that there's nothing more valuable than the head of a Jew."

"It's an interesting theory with no evidence. And if he knew where the head was, why would he take it out of the freezer and give it to a customer?"

"Stupidity, incompetence—the main way we solve crimes is because criminals fuck up," said Yossi.

"You don't believe Jamal is stupid or incompetent."

"Sometimes they want to be caught," Yossi insisted. "Or they think they're untouchable. Anyway, the butcher claims there were only two keys. He didn't run, Jamal did. That's the difference. It's not perfect but show me the perfect answer to this one. Every case has loose strings. Remember Sherlock Holmes: 'When you have eliminated the impossible, whatever remains, however improbable, must be the truth.'"

"I wondered where you got your training," Malik said.

Yossi pursed his lips appraisingly. "There's another theory. Also interesting. They are in it together, Jamal and his prospective bride. He knows Weingarten is a sucker for pretty girls. He urges Dina to give the chief a little attention, that's all it takes. When she calls, the chief comes running. He may have told you he had another appointment and had to slip away, that's why your meeting to discuss his big secret only lasted seven minutes. Probably had a hard-on when he told you that. Nothing was going to stand in the way of a piece of Palestinian pussy."

Malik was troubled. Dina had told him she would be accused of being an accomplice. She knew there was a reason—a reason she didn't tell him. "Just check it out," he said. "That's all I'm asking. Keep your mind open to the possibility that he's innocent."

"Here, nobody's innocent."

"Maybe you just can't stand the idea that somebody is trying to find a way to peace and you'd rather see him dead and a young girl's life ruined."

Malik recognized the danger that flashed from Yossi's dark eyes, but then the mood shifted. Yossi took a file out of Weingarten's cabinet.

"What's this?" Malik asked. "I don't read Hebrew."

"It's one of Weingarten's little messages from the Great Beyond. This one is about your cousin."

Yossi read portions of it aloud.

DINA ABDUL MALIK

b. 2003, daughter of terrorist Ibrahim Abdul Malik. Person of interest in the chamula. Probable heir to Sheikh Abdullah Abdul Malik land rights. Although young she is seen as future leader in the family. Highly sought by prominent bachelors.

Became a source in 2021 when half-brother Omar, age 12, was injured by gunshot, possibly self-inflicted. Boy suffered chronic incapacitating pain. Depended on OxyContin and other opioids from Hamas source, who saw him as a possible recruit for suicide mission. Omar is highly intelligent. DAM very protective, was willing to become an informant in return for his treatment in Israel. She was also provided with a student permit which facilitated meetings in Jerusalem.

"He attaches a list of people Dina informed on," Yossi said, indicating about twenty names. "Her own mother, how about that for loyalty. Looks like she betrayed everybody she knows."

"She's trying to save her brother's life."

Yossi shrugged and continued reading.

Like many compromised informants DAM expresses occasional anger at being "trapped" and "tricked," but she also sees advantages in providing information that may aid her family. Her grandfather has been in a lawsuit with Israeli government over a permit for his illegal irrigation wells—lawsuit going on for twenty years now—and a successful resolution of this matter could open new opportunities to deal with this problematic family.

"The chief makes some historical notes in here about your clan, by the way," Yossi said as an aside. "Apparently the Abdul Maliks were among the Muslims who protected Jewish neighbors in the 1929 massacre."

"They did?"

"It is remembered. Hundreds were spared by such actions. Your uncle Sheikh Abdullah served on the Hebron Reconciliation Council, which was established after the Baruch Goldstein massacre." Yossi turned to another section of Weingarten's notes, dealing with Sheikh Abdullah's son, Ibrahim, Dina's father. He achieved high rank inside Hamas. Weingarten recorded that Ibrahim had many supporters in his clan and still exerts influence from Shatta Prison, one of the harshest institutions in the vast Israeli system of confinement.

Yossi continued to read:

DAM highly productive informant but withholds certain key elements. Knows intimate details about Hamas leaders, much of it from her imprisoned father, whom she visits periodically. Her brief engagement to Ehsan Zayyat was sponsored by her father but dropped for undisclosed reasons. This is something that may be elicited in time. She has not seen her father in the last year despite my urging. She continues to provide new insights into Hamas procedures and methods.

Malik was caught short by the offhand reference to Dina's engagement to Zayyat. "What do you know about that?" he asked.

"Nothing more than what the chief says. He had access to intel he didn't feel comfortable sharing. For what reason I don't know."

Observations on DAM character: Intelligent, wary, a talented liar when caught in a contradiction. She is full of youthful passions balanced by need for self-protection. Aware that her fate not in her hands, she resists by cleverly playing off the forces that intend to control her.

DAM will continue to be exploited as a prize informant.

Yossi set the report back in the file.

"It doesn't sound like a man having an affair with his source," said Malik.

"To me it sounds like a man covering his ass in case Shabak might be poking into his investigation."

"I might be wrong about her," said Malik, "but you might be too. If you don't run down this lead, you'll never know."

30

Sweet Dreams

West Bank, Sept. 30, 2023

T he next morning, the Sabbath, they were on the way to the hostel, near Bethlehem, when they passed another billboard of the smiling Rav, a look of ecstasy in his eyes. "He's getting to be a familiar face," said Malik.

"Immanuel Cohen is his name," said Yossi. "A complicated man."

"What do you know about him?"

"You heard the name Moshe Levinger? As a teenager, young Immanuel came to Hebron with his parents. Levinger had just established Kiryat Arba. The Cohens returned to America, but they left their son in Levinger's care for the summer. When he returned that fall he entered the Yeshivah of Flatbush, where Baruch Goldstein and Meir Kahane also attended."

"I know that place. I used to walk by it all the time."

"They all had the same philosophy, one generation after another, each more radical than the last. Throw out the Arabs. Kill them all. Be merciful and allow some to become slaves. So you see Levinger, Kahane, Goldstein, and now the Rav. He is not personally violent like Goldstein but he has the same philosophy and a larger following. What's different with him is that those other guys were seen as outsiders, an embarrassment to most Israelis, but the Rav has influence at the highest levels. This is the main thing. The radicals are in control. Government ministers bow down to him."

"What's it say under his picture?"

"'The Temple of the Messiah,' he calls it. Then it says, 'We will build it together,' It is supposed to be the great temple to bring about the End of Days. This is the goal of his sect, first the Jews are redeemed and then comes the apocalypse. They even talk about provoking a war so violent it summons the Messiah. They're in a hurry, these guys."

"Why Hebron and not Jerusalem? Isn't it supposed to be more holy?"

"Jerusalem is number one, yes, but Hebron is the biblical graveyard, starting with Abraham and Isaac and Jacob and their wives. They even say Adam and Eve are buried here. Then we have minor figures like Lot, the guy whose wife turned into a pillar of salt. Some say Cain is buried in one of these caves—that's the rumor anyway."

"Humanity's first murderer."

"Hebron, home of homicide. Or fratricide. Whatever, it all started here."

"What is it about this place? We've got Arabs and Jews in Brooklyn. Yeah, there are some issues but mostly we manage okay."

Yossi glanced at him, then shook his head. "Here we also have cowboys and Indians, and they get along. Best friends."

Malik grinned. "We've got some history to live down, that's for sure." They rode in silence for a few minutes before Malik asked, "You believe all this? That Abraham and Adam and Eve are real people and their actual bones are in the cave?"

Yossi shrugged. "Believe or don't believe, it doesn't matter, it's what we say. We have a very old joke about this, by the way." He glanced at Malik.

"I'm listening."

"There was a holy man in Beersheba. His job was attending the grave of a prophet, one of the minor ones, but any prophet gets respect if he has a proper tomb. Anyway, a young man comes to sit at the feet of the holy man and serves him for many years. Pilgrims visit. They pray. They consult the holy man. It's a living.

"One day the holy man tells his servant it is time for him to find his own way in the world. He gives the young man a donkey, who is called Enoch, after one of the prophets that got thrown out of the Torah because he was nuts. So the servant mounts Enoch and they wander through the Holy Land for many years. Enoch got old and then he dies. And the young man who's not young now is heartbroken. He buries Enoch and puts a mound of rocks over his tomb and a sign that says "Enoch," so he'll know the spot when he visits again.

"The servant wanders on foot for many years and then he comes back to the place where his donkey died. He's surprised to find dozens of pilgrims who have come to pay tribute to Enoch. It is such a big deal that the old holy man in Beersheba hears about it and decides to see what's going on. There he finds his former servant. They greet each other after so many years, they have tea and break bread together, then the old holy man asks in a confidential voice who is actually buried in this grave. 'Enoch,' says the servant, 'the donkey you gave me.' And then the servant asks, 'By the way, who's buried in your tomb?' The holy man says, 'The father of your donkey.'"

Malik laughed.

"And that's how religions get started," Yossi concluded. He gestured at the rocky hills, a tousled landscape like an unmade bed. "What I really think is that God made this land holy, and then he looked all over creation for the craziest people, and he brought them here."

"You're including Jews in that?"

"Jews can be worse than Arabs. You don't know."

The Sweet Dreams Guest House was an old tourist spa that had long since gone to seed. Built of stones painted turquoise, surrounded by palms, it was a ruined oasis, with a murky half-filled swimming pool and a restaurant of notably greasy odors. "The romantic hideaway," said Yossi.

Inside the lobby patched leather chairs sat among plastic plants. Yossi rang the bell on the unattended desk. Presently a grizzled clerk appeared. Tattoos covered one spidery arm and the other bore the image of a faded blue cross. He was half awake until he noticed Yossi's uniform and fell into a coughing fit.

"What's your name?" Yossi demanded.

"Halbouti."

"Christian?"

The clerk nodded.

"You here last Monday? About this time?"

Halbouti fell to coughing again, a dry hacking cough that he didn't bother to cover.

"Young couple rented a room," Yossi prompted. "Maybe for a few hours. Remember?"

The clerk looked blank. "You have to keep records," Yossi prompted again. "Identification, registration."

Halbouti pulled out the registry under the desk and made a show of peering closely at the handwritten entries. "Nobody like that here," he finally declared.

Yossi took the registry and examined it himself. As he did so, an elderly couple entered the office, chattering in German. The clerk handed them the key to Room 7.

"Maybe they used fake names," Malik suggested.

Yossi was still studying the registry. "Those people," he said, referring to the German couple in Room 7, "they're not in the book. I wonder why."

Halbouti looked trapped. "Why do you ask me these things?" he said.

Yossi grabbed the clerk by the collar, pulling him halfway across the counter. "Don't waste my time," he snarled. "Some guests you don't register to avoid paying hospitality tax. Others maybe as a favor, right?" He released the clerk and cast a cautionary glance at Malik.

"In New York, we call it the Bronx Handshake," said Malik.

Yossi put the identity photo of Jamal on the counter. Halbouti looked at it and shrugged. Then Yossi added a picture of Dina. "What about her?" he asked.

"Suppose she came here," Halbouti said. "You ruin her life for this?"

"What room did she say they were in?" Yossi asked Malik.

"Fifteen."

"Give it to me."

The clerk glumly handed over the key.

Room 15 was sparsely decorated with wildlife prints and a vase of wilted flowers on the bureau. Malik pulled back the bedspread. "Clean sheets," he observed ruefully.

"What'd you expect?" Yossi asked.

"Miracles happen."

"Okay, let's go," said Yossi impatiently. "The only thing this proves is they have excellent maid service."

"We'll see."

Malik dropped to his hands and knees and began running his fingers through the thick, filthy carpet. "How do you control the drugs around here?" he asked as he looked under the bed.

"What drugs?"

"Heroin, for instance."

"This is something Weingarten was looking into. Why are you asking?"

"That desk clerk is a Class A junkie. You check the needle tracks on his arm?" Malik turned on the light in the bathroom and looked carefully at the toilet and the drain around the shower. "Ah, that's interesting," he said. "A bit of lipstick on the rim of the water glass." He found a tampon-disposal bag in a drawer and used toilet paper to lower the glass into the improvised evidence bag.

Yossi peered into a trash can with a pop-up lid. It had a fresh plastic bag inside. "Even if they were here, they probably flushed the condoms," he said.

"Huh." Malik stood straight up, flooded with inspiration. "Maybe not."

Yossi trailed behind Malik as he headed outside. Behind the restaurant was an overflowing, stinking dumpster. "This is a joke, right?" Yossi said.

"Believe me, I'm not happy about it."

"This is something they teach you in the FBI?"

"Dumpster Diving 101. Can't get your badge without it."

"Help yourself."

Malik sized up the dumpster, which was patrolled by hissing alley cats. "First you develop a theory of the case, then try to disprove it," he said. "If you can't, you might be on the right path. In this case, my theory is that while your chief was being killed, our lovebirds were having sex in Room 15. If we don't find anything, it doesn't help one way or the other, but if we do, it makes it a little harder to disprove."

"Even if you find something, it won't be a perfect alibi."

"These days the lab can ID the DNA and even the date of the discharge."

"Maybe in America they do this."

"At least give me a boost up."

Yossi grudgingly cupped his hands into a stirrup. Malik stepped into it and clambered into the dumpster, sinking into the trash up to his belt buckle. He was wearing his brand-new jeans. "You're missing a peak moment of police work," he said.

"You are an insane man."

"Let's make a deal. If I find a condom, you'll let me examine the body."

Yossi thought for a moment, then said, "Out of pity, I accept."

Much of the garbage was restaurant scraps covered with maggots. He ripped into a plastic bag, only to find a wad of fantastically odorous diapers. Despite the flies dive-bombing his head, he attacked the trash methodically, working from one end to the other. To avoid the stench of the kitchen grease he breathed through his mouth, lips barely parted to keep flies from darting in. Much of the room trash was contained in white plastic bags, so he concentrated on those. Used tissues, an unmatched sock, hairspray cans, empty toothpaste tubes—it was a collection of an untidy civilization with an outsized interest in creating waste.

"I'm going back to the office now," said Yossi. It was nauseating just being close to the odors. "Do you need a hand getting out of there?"

"Oh man, oh man, oh man," Malik said excitedly. "You're not going to believe this." He took a photo and then used a handkerchief to pick up the edge of a Trojan, holding it up in the sunlight.

"It could be anybody's," Yossi said.

"Or it could be Jamal's. The lab will tell us." Malik triumphantly dropped it into the tampon-disposal bag.

31

Abu Majid

Mandatory Palestine, July 8, 1948

Abu Majid, the mukhtar of the Abdul Malik clan, trod slowly up the hill to the police station, using his cane to steady himself. He was born in Hamayteh, a little Arab village within sight of the settlement where Yossi lived today. Abu Majid was eight years old when Arab armies from Egypt, Syria, and Transjordan along with expeditionary forces from Iraq invaded the newly created Jewish nation. His family fled their home when the Israelis counterattacked, but Abu Majid—then called by his given name, Hussein—stayed with his grandfather and his older cousins, first at his uncle's house in Beersheba, then in one of the numerous caves in the Hebron Hills. One day an Egyptian infantry squadron came into the area and found Hussein and his relatives hiding there—ten of them; the uncle had snuck back to Beersheba to get supplies but never returned. The Egyptians gave them rations and asked the boys for help in locating the Israeli troops. Four of them hiked along the ridgelines until they spotted an armored formation in the plains north of the hills. They rushed back to the cave to report, but the Egyptians had left and there was no one to report to. Another family had taken refuge in the cave; there was scarcely any place to sleep, and food was scarce.

For three more days Hussein and the other Palestinians hid in the cave. It was midsummer; the weather was warm but the cave was temperate. The children spent their time playing amid the wildflowers in the field or scavenging for acorns and berries. Hussein was as agile as a goat. They could hear sounds of battle and twice Israeli planes flew low overhead; the kids believed they could see the pilot and they waved, even though he was Israeli. It was rare to see an airplane.

On the morning of the third day the artillery was closer. Before noon, Egyptian deserters returned to the field, bloodied and desperate; they had been in a terrible battle and had neither food nor water. The families sheltered the wounded men in the crowded cave and shared their meager provisions.

Late that afternoon, as the sun was casting giant shadows across the field, drawing a dark curtain over the opening of the cave, a column of Israeli tanks and infantry came through the pass in the hills and rolled across the wildflowers. The refugees in the cave held their breath. The tanks and the soldiers appeared in a state of hyperreality as the sunset spotlighted their faces, their uniforms, their guns, extra vivid in the slanting light. A soldier walked up the slope toward the cave to relieve himself. He stood at the edge of the shadow of the hillside, with the cave lurking in the shadow only twenty meters away. They all watched the soldier staring aimlessly as he peed into the shade, then a baby sneezed and his gaze focused.

The soldier called out and a group of his comrades walked up the slope, fanning out on either side of the cave opening. Then the soldier gestured for the refugees to come out. There were eighteen of them plus the two wounded Egyptians. Hussein's grandfather and one other elderly man were with them; the rest of the Palestinians were women and children. Two of the women were old; three were young mothers, one carrying an infant in her arms. The soldier ordered them to line up, then he and another Israeli demanded any jewelry and cash as another pair went through the cave picking up anything of value. The Egyptian soldiers they shot with their own sidearms. When the Israelis had taken what they wanted, they moved aside and a tank opened up with a machine gun, killing children and adults alike, slicing them into pulp.

The Israelis spent the night in the valley, just below the scene of the massacre. Hussein lay in the grass with the body of one of his cousins draped across him. He didn't know if he had been shot; for a while, he wondered if he was actually dead, but the weight of his cousin's body plus the intense metallic stench of blood testified that he remained alive. He was too terrified to move. He could hear the soldiers as they ate dinner, and then one of them played a guitar and they sang a song that was popular on the radio. While the soldiers slept Hussein lay awake through the night, watching the stars revolve in the heavens. He felt very close to God.

At dawn other soldiers walked toward the cave, but they were also relieving themselves. The sun was at their backs and they cast long shadows. Hussein watched through half-opened lids. One of the soldiers peed on the dead Palestinians, which became a game as the others copied him. Hussein felt the urine wetting his shirt and then running across his nose and lips. He wondered what thoughts were going through their minds. He wondered why they had bothered to kill rather than to just move along. He wondered who he would be if he survived and grew to manhood—would he be like the soldiers, indifferent to killing, or would he be a coward? These were the alternatives that presented themselves to his eight-year-old mind as he fervently prayed that no one would come forward to bury the victims.

He heard the cacophony of departure, the tanks spurting into life, the foot soldiers calling to each other, the grumble and roar of the engines, which gradually faded and then dissolved into bird songs and the buzzing of flies. The dead were left behind like litter. And yet Hussein still lay frozen. What if a soldier was waiting for him, intending to finish the last of this family? These thoughts were interrupted by a fly drawn to the urine. It explored his face, crawling across his closed eyes and then entering a nostril despite Hussein's futile attempt to blow him away. He had to move. His left arm was trapped under his cousin's body and he had long since lost any sensation in it. He sat up.

He was intact but his left arm hung limp and pale at his side. He picked the fly out of his nose then looked around. The pasture was scarred by the tracks of the armored vehicles. He was aware of all the death around him but he couldn't look. He called out the names of his cousins: Ibrahim, Yahya, Amal, Marwan. None answered.

He stood and examined himself. He was covered in flesh and brains that weren't his but he was untouched by bullets. He wondered when his arm would wake up. It never did. That was the price of survival. The soldiers had left no food except for scraps of their breakfast in the grass, which Hussein devoured.

He was a shepherd so he knew how to find his way in the mountains. He bathed in a mountain stream to get the stench of urine and death off him, then lay in the grass until his clothes partially dried in the morning sun. He stood and took the first steps of the long walk of his new life. Months later he found his mother and siblings in a refugee camp just outside Hebron. He married at the age of eighteen and fathered five children, starting with his namesake, Majid. For years he operated his little grocery in the Old City; it had been prosperous once, now it had shrunk to little more than a closet and only served to occupy his time. Gradually his peers aged and died but he persisted, until the day he assumed leadership in the *chamula*, respected as an elder who had survived the *nakba*—catastrophe—that led to the flight of 750,000 Palestinians and the elimination of hundreds of villages where they once lived. One people supplanted another.

SEVENTY-FIVE YEARS LATER, at the age of eighty-three, Abu Majid made his way to the Arab entrance of the police station, on the other side of the building from the Jewish entry. He asked to see Inspector Ben-Gal.

Yossi came out of the office and sat with Abu Majid on a bench that overlooked the Old City and greater Hebron. He offered him coffee but Abu Majid declined. He had come for a favor, and like all favors in the Holy Land it would come at a price. First, the affectionate courtesies, the well-wishing for loved ones, the avoidance of the point until it became impossible to stall any longer. "You now have the head of the Jew," Abu Majid pleaded. "Return to us the bodies of our young men. Let the burials begin."

32

The Summons of the Dead

Kiryat Arba, Oct. 1, 2023

Yossi drove Malik through Kiryat Arba, past the supermarket and the concert hall, to Kahane Park, created after the assassination of Meir Kahane in New York in 1990. Here was the grave of Baruch Goldstein. "You see the pebbles they put on the grave," Yossi said. "Every day people come to pay tribute and leave a small stone behind."

Malik could see that it was a well-ordered community—limestone row houses, red-tile roofs—such a regimented environment for a settlement containing so many extreme elements. They were drawn by the values of Kahane and the violent activism of Goldstein, united in their intention to reclaim the land that God gave them. Their goal in living here was to drive the Arabs out. More than angry at their prejudice, Malik was awed by their tenacity.

The funeral parlor was nearby, and adjacent to that was the preparation room. Two men in undershirts were pouring water over the naked corpse of Chief Weingarten on a porcelain bier under a sickly fluorescent light, solemnly singing as they worked. Four other men held a canopy, like a wedding chuppah, above their heads, each of them modestly facing away from the body. A plain wooden casket awaited his remains. Yossi and Malik stood quietly at the door as the leader of the burial society prayed in a loud voice: "Jacob Shlomo Weingarten, we have done our job. If we have done it poorly then we beg your forgiveness." Then they patted down the corpse with towels. The head had been crudely sewn back on.

Yossi was not sentimental seeing Weingarten in this lifeless state. A dead body was just an object, he thought; existence was an off/ on switch, nothing human about it, no more than the clothes in the closet—not like mysteries, which linger, still alive in their own confounding way until they are forgotten or resolved. All that remained of Jacob Weingarten was the puzzlement of why he was killed.

They had never gotten along, Yossi and Jacob, opposites in so many ways, but Yossi wished that he had taken the time to step beyond the insincere pleasantries they used with each other. In some unflattering ways they were much alike—two lonely middle-aged men, they might have been friends. Or perhaps if they had known each other better they would have been mortal enemies. Another riddle he would never solve.

"Give us a moment, gentlemen," Yossi said, as the men were about to place the body in a shroud.

The burial-society men were startled when they saw Yossi and Malik. "You cannot touch him!" the leader said. "He's been purified."

"This is police business," said Yossi. "We will be respectful." He turned to Malik. "Can you do this without touching him?"

The leader of the society wasn't finished. There were rules to be strictly followed. "The body must be covered. You can examine one portion at a time but not the entirety. We do this for modesty, not to be unreasonable. But do not touch him or breathe on him closely."

The body was draped with a sheet. Malik moved closer and asked to view the torso. One of the society men pulled open the sheet to expose only that portion.

"No autopsy," Malik muttered.

"The widow refused."

Weingarten was a heavy man with a hairy torso like a bathmat. He might have been athletic when he was young, there was some residual muscle tone, but his body was largely uncared for. Malik wrote something in his little notebook, then said, "Show me this arm." He stood quietly, as close to the body as permitted. One wouldn't think that Weingarten could have put up much of a fight, but Malik saw evidence of resistance. "Look here," he said, indicating the circle of bruises on the chief's right arm, "you can see the imprint of the killer's index finger and thumb. What does that indicate to you?"

"There was a struggle."

"Maybe that's the reason he was shot. He wasn't going easily."

Malik examined Weingarten's hands and sighed. "They even pared his nails," he said of the burial society. "I bet there was a ton of DNA."

When Malik finished with the arms and hands, he moved on to legs. "The killers broke his knees," he said, pointing at the garish bruises and the visible dimples in the bone structure. "A bat or a pipe, I'm guessing. It's curious. You might think they wouldn't bother if they were just going to kill him. Instead they tortured him."

"Maybe they planned to hold him and this was to prevent him from running away," said Yossi. "They wanted information."

"Could be. They had a plan but it didn't go well."

"Amateurs."

Malik nodded. He silently read the evidence on the dead man's body. More bruises on the ankles. Other men holding him down. He fought. They broke his bones. Still he resisted. They had planned a video of the execution but he wasn't having it. So they shot him and cut off the head of a dead man.

Finally, Malik examined the bullet-entry wound just behind the left ear. The ear itself was covered with tufts of black hair and filled with some kind of waxy substance, as were other orifices, which was part of the ritual. "Was there powder here before they washed it all off?"

"Yes," said Yossi, "we figure the shot was fired from about three inches."

"Now let's see the neck."

Malik peered at the mass of stitches where the burial society had reattached the head. "What a mess," said Malik. "Look—one, two, three, four different cuts. Jagged. Clumsy. Does this look like the work of a skilled butcher?"

"You've made your point."

The two men left the burial society to do its final chores and entered the waiting room, where dozens of mourners were assembled to accompany the body to the cemetery. Berger and his wife were there, and Golda arrived, all of them neighbors of the Weingartens in Kiryat Arba. Golda said hello to Jules and Rose Garfinkle, who stiffly acknowledged her. When she saw Yossi she pulled him aside and whispered that soldiers were waiting outside and they seemed to be expecting trouble. She was pale and grieving and worried. Berger was strangely impassive. Yossi thought how death reveals so much about the living, while also being cloaked in its own unsolvable mystery.

Malik stood aside, knowing he was intensely unwanted. Four days ago he had been suspected of murdering this poor man; now here he was at his funeral. There was an edgy feeling in the room, not just the usual atmosphere of mourning but also of excitement, of anticipation. Something was stirring in the furtive looks people cast in his direction. He thought it best to leave but he didn't know how to extricate himself.

Women crowded around consoling Miriam. Yossi noticed her son, Menachem, standing next to Benny Eleazar. He hadn't realized until now that the Rav had a follower in the chief's family, but it wasn't surprising, the same had happened in Yossi's family as well. Then he watched Berger join them. The three of them were soon deeply engrossed in conversation, which Benny conducted, nodding and saying very little. The men were clearly reporting to him. *So young but already the boss*, Yossi thought. *The future is in the hands of kids like him.*

Benny caught Yossi's glance. He walked over, holding a small knife. He made a neat cut in Yossi's collar to signal mourning. "We were with you in your time of need," he said in a low voice. "Now you bring the intruder here. This at a time when the community is at one in our grief."

"Benny, he's of use to us. He's helping with the investigation. He's a pro."

"We all know who did this action. He's hiding somewhere among the Arabs. We've been patient—with you, with the army—but we are preparing an action. I'm giving you the warning: keep out of it."

How daring and presumptuous this young man was, ordering the police to stand down for whatever fatal mischief he had contrived.

"We're in the middle of an investigation," Yossi said. "You need to give us time. We have no proof of what you're saying. Right now, it's only speculation."

"Then get proof, and quickly," said Benny. "I try to hold the line because I'm your friend, but Yossi, the people are angry. They've grieved enough. They want satisfaction."

Yossi joined the procession to the Jewish cemetery on the west side of the Old City. Jews had been buried in this place for a thousand years. After the 1948 war, when Jordan assumed control of the West Bank, the cemetery was vandalized by Arabs who used the ancient tombstones for construction of homes and businesses. In a separate part of the cemetery were the graves of the Jews massacred in 1929. British authorities made the Arab prisoners who were responsible for the slaughter dig the graves, but the legend Yossi knew was that the prisoners sang as they labored.

The Israeli government eventually shut down the cemetery because it was seen as a provocation, but in 1975 Baruch and Sarah Nachshon, two of the earliest Jewish settlers to return to Hebron, defied the army and interred their six-month-old child, Avraham, there—the same cemetery where the mourners were now headed, through the narrow streets of the Old City to bury the latest victim. The dead continued the struggle through their descendants. They all had a claim on the land.

Malik trailed behind at a distance. He didn't belong here, but he was drawn by the spectacle. The soldiers left him to walk alone. Except for the mourners, there was no one about. It was a beautiful sunny day on the first of October. The leaves of the mulberry and sycamore trees were beginning to turn and they covered the street in hues of red and brown. He could hear the muffled footfalls on the cobblestones. He sensed the antiquity of this place and thought how life comes and goes but the dead are permanent. In Hebron, death exerted a magnetism, it was tugging constantly at your pants leg, like a rabid dog.

As the pallbearers carried the casket, new people joined the silent procession on the narrow street, two or three at a time, then tens of them, swelling the marchers so that they stretched more than fifty meters and then as long as seventy. When they arrived at the graveyard a crowd was already waiting. People stood on the slope or around the improvised podium, where a microphone had been set up. Some were armed with automatic weapons or sidearms. Malik sat under an oak tree on a hillside to watch.

Yossi had not meant to come to the burial either. Although he had seen a lot of death he avoided funerals, and yet once he was caught up in it, he understood that it was mandatory to honor his chief, the man whose murder he was determined to solve. Those who are killed deserve a reckoning, and it was on Yossi to provide it. He would not fail.

The first time he came to this place was when his mother died. She had lived too long, but he had been dutiful to her, paying visits to the memory ward several times a week. Perhaps her dementia was a blessing. Haunted all her life by the Holocaust, she had remained a kind mother, but given to fits of depression, disappearing into herself. Yossi often wondered if that was also his destiny. Sometimes he felt that he already had too many memories.

One of the young rabbis in Kiryat Arba led the service. Yossi stopped paying attention. He hated showing emotion and distrusted the revisionist eulogies that dressed up ordinary lives in the garments of heroes and saints; indeed, he hadn't been to the graveyard since Leah died. She was also buried here. People were standing on her grave. It was pointless to shoo them away so Yossi decided to join them. He could be closer to her, as if something of Leah would rise through the dirt and stone and he would enter her body once again.

The crowd stirred as an old man with a white beard and a broad-brimmed hat approached the podium. It was the Rav. Yossi had no idea that he would even be in attendance. He was small, somewhat stooped; he accepted a hand to step up to the platform. A brief spate of applause started, only to be hushed into silence; this wasn't the place for that, but people were thrilled to see him. In this world the Rav was a star, but that he would be summoned to speak at the funeral of Jacob Weingarten was unexpected. Yossi supposed that Menachem had planned this.

"We stand on this ground where the prophet Abraham, the father of the Jewish people, spoke with a broken heart about the loss of his beloved wife, Sarah," the Rav began, his gaze taking in the horde of mourners among the graves and on the hillside. "I do not attempt to surpass the words of our great ancestor in that first Jewish eulogy, only to remind us all that the children of Israel have been living and dying in this land for thousands of years, since the Lord told Abraham—then called Abram—'to you and your offspring, I give this land, from the river of Egypt to the river Euphrates.' Our land, Jewish land, the Lord declared, 'for an everlasting possession.'

"And they call *us* colonists!" he suddenly erupted. "They call *us* settlers! *They*—" here he pointed to the Palestinian houses on the hills beyond—"*they* are the foreigners, the occupiers, the illegals, not the Jews. We gather here to reclaim our birthright. We are not like another nation. The land of Israel is essential to the preservation of the whole world. Our purpose here cannot be compromised. The fate—not just of Jews but of humanity itself—depends upon our commitment. When politicians speak of 'diplomacy' they cynically lead us away from our divine mission. Our job—our sacred mission—is to reclaim the land. God has chosen us for this task because the Jewish people are holy and supreme. It is only our prayers, our continuous study of the Torah, our continuing sacrifice that preserves the Jewish people. We wandered in exile for two thousand years, blaming the Lord—yes, we did, we refused to accept the responsibility for our dispossession. But we returned, at first a few, now a flood of Jews from around the globe, to our ancient home, coming with the divine purpose of redeeming the Jews so that our Messiah can arrive and bring on the End of Days. It is for this purpose we vow that for every drop of Jewish blood shed, they will pay many times with their own blood. They will pay also in land! All that you see before us, all the land that reaches from the Nile to the Euphrates, is promised to us. And we will claim it!"

These words tumbled out of the mouth of a man whose aspect seemed so calm and certain. There was no raving, no waving of the hands, no red face, no pounding on the lectern. Yossi saw that this conviction moved the audience, their heads nodded in assent. If they hadn't been followers before, they were his now.

Here the Rav paused and looked directly at the widow and her children. "Jacob Weingarten was one of us," the Rav said. "We did not always agree with him, but we loved and respected him because he lived his life as a practicing Jew, a Jew on the front line, in the final messianic era. Yes, he was perhaps too kind for the task we are given, too trusting. God has repeatedly told us to expel the enemy, to kill without pity. But it is our enemies who kill. They killed a Jew! One of our beloved rabbis once said that the difference between a Jewish soul and the souls of non-Jews is greater and deeper than the difference between a human soul and the souls of cattle. Who among us can doubt that when God chose us, he exalted Jews among all peoples! And so you do not kill a Jew without retribution that equals the difference between the soul of a holy Jewish man and the soul of a lowly beast. The soul of Jacob Weingarten will not find peace until his murder is avenged—ten times, a hundred times, a thousand times over!"

As the service concluded the crowd lined either side of the road so that the family could walk between. People called out greetings and cried for justice. They were full of righteous fury, their faces set, as they joined the walk behind the family toward the Cave of the Patriarchs and from there up the hill to Kiryat Arba for the shiva. The crowd was like a cloud charged with electricity, waiting to hurl a lightning bolt.

Malik walked several blocks ahead of the mourners, not wanting to get caught up in the procession. He had no business here; he was headed to the police station as quickly as possible to wait for Yossi. His walk took him past the Muslim cemetery—where his ancestors lay, where Weingarten's headless body had been dumped—and as he walked he heard something weird, an uproar, sounds of chanting and moaning and then the distinctive ululating of Arab women. Then there they were, thousands of Palestinians filling the street. The bodies of the three young men killed in the olive grove were borne on the shoulders of pallbearers wearing green bandanas, defiantly marking them as members of Hamas.

Malik froze. Instantly he foresaw the catastrophe that lay ahead and his own helplessness to prevent it. The soldiers who had begun the march with Weingarten's mourners had disappeared. Malik stood to one side as the Palestinian mourners moved past. Hamas flags flew in the procession and draped the bodies of the dead. In a watchtower across the street an Israeli soldier stood guard behind the bulletproof glass, a perfect vantage to see the mourners from Wein-garten's funeral approaching this same spot. Was he doing nothing? The soldiers' barracks were nearby, but they stayed inside. Where were the riot police or a battalion of soldiers to stand between these colliding forces stoked with grief and longing for revenge?

As the corpses of the young were being carried into the graveyard, Weingarten's mourners came into view. They had been marching silently and no doubt they heard the uproar of the Arabs headed in their direction. Menachem was at the head of the procession with Benny at his side. He raised his hand to halt the followers, and as he did so, the Hamas pallbearers also came to a stop. Some of the young Arabs in the crowd ran into the graveyard, where they were protected by a high stone fence, with the advantage of being elevated above the crowd.

Yossi pushed his way through the Jewish mourners to the front, where Menachem and Benny were waiting for the moment of igni-tion. "Don't do this," Yossi said. "Turn around, we've had enough death already."

They didn't hear him, they were living in the future, seconds ahead, when the clash had begun and weapons were firing. Benny was grinning, moving in agitated motions, sheer excitement shoot-ing through his body like electrical charges. He had convened this moment when he shot the young men in the olive grove. "What's the point, Benny?" Yossi asked but even as he said it he realized that the object of the burials was to bring the violence to a climax, a debt of the living demanded by the dead. There had to be a bloodbath.

A single stone flew over the fence into the crowd and a volley fol-lowed, raining stones on the settlers. One of the Arab kids—a child, maybe nine years old—stood on the fence with an exhilarated look on his face, but before he managed to throw his stone into the crowd he crumpled and fell in a swan dive over the wall. It was hard to tell where the shot came from, from the soldier in the watchtower or one of the armed settlers, but immediately the mourners on both sides rushed at each other, heedless, starved for combat. The clash came with the explosion of gunfire and the flash of knives, fists swing-ing, stones flying. Benny crouched behind a wall and fired into the melee, even though it was nearly impossible to separate the Arabs from the Jews, they were fighting face-to-face, beating and choking each other, banging heads on the street and the curb.

The female settlers standing behind Miriam rushed toward the Arab women. There were few weapons among them so they fought with their hands and fingernails, with a ferocity that astonished Yossi. He had never seen women tear at each other with intent to kill. Nor did the Palestinian women restrain themselves. Years of rage and hatred obliterated all thought of modesty or humanity. Mourning clothes were ripped asunder. Stones were used to club with lethal force. Even children tried to enter the fray but were knocked aside as mothers fought to kill mothers and young women sought to murder their counterparts. Over all this Miriam stood watch, as if in some way she were conducting the deathly purge.

Still the soldiers were nowhere to be seen.

Yossi spotted one of Benny's sidekicks, Itai, gouging the eyes of an Arab boy, and pulled him off, but the boy's eyes were already streaming and destroyed. He found Menachem bleeding profusely through his shirt, shot or stabbed, Yossi couldn't tell. He remembered Menachem as a child; now this stern young man with his stiff-necked posture was hunched in pain. Yossi lifted him to his feet. "Let's go," he said, half-dragging him to the sidewalk and onto a side street.

Malik was there. Wordlessly he put Menachem's arm around his neck and helped Yossi walk him to the IDF barracks. The screams and cries of the warring mobs followed them.

Menachem's face was as white as his shirt. "Keep pressure on your wound," Yossi told him. "We'll find a medic, they'll take care of you."

At the barracks, they had to pass through a security turnstile one at a time. Menachem weakly held on to the bar of the gate and made it through. Inside about fifty soldiers in riot gear stood at ease, still marking time, waiting for the order to end the slaughter.

"Where's your medic?" Yossi asked a young captain, who indicated a door leading to the clinic. A female soldier was already rushing toward them. "In here," she said.

Yossi and Malik steered Menachem into the clinic and laid him on the gurney. The doctor ripped open the shirt to expose the wound. It was round and neat, a small-caliber pistol shot, Yossi figured, dark blood was spurting, indicating that the shot had pierced the liver. A nurse placed a vapor mask over Menachem's face and he was instantly unconscious. *I'm going to have to tell Miriam,* Yossi realized. *She'll have to prepare for another loss.*

The soldiers, donning gas masks, finally left the barracks, carrying riot shields and batons. They moved in formation. Yossi and Malik walked cautiously behind them. On the street in their funeral shrouds were the bodies of the three boys killed in the grove; around them lay the bodies of the freshly slain. Still the mourners on either side continued the fight, slipping in puddles of blood as if they were on ice, a murderous comedy. A strange yellow cloud appeared overhead, dimming the sunlight—a drone spewing tear gas. As the cloud engulfed the rioters they began an awkward dance, pawing the air and running into each other. Ambulances had arrived but the attendants remained in the cars, waiting for the gas to clear.

"THAT WAS PLANNED," Malik said furiously. "You knew about it."

They were standing on the Arab side of the police station. Both of them were dappled with blood and bits of flesh. The air had been so charged with slaughter that everyone was bathed in it.

Yossi looked at him evenly and didn't respond. A strange energy that they experienced as shivering coursed through their bodies.

"I don't know how you people can stand being who you are," Malik said.

"You mean Jews."

"Both of you! Arabs and Jews, the same thing. You both think it all belongs to you. God gave it to you or whatever. Such bullshit. And you know it! If you were one of those Haredi zombies I'd say what a shame, a mind gone down the drain into some cultish swamp, but no, you're not even a believer, so what does that make you?"

"You're the one with the answers," said Yossi.

"A fucking hypocrite."

"Is that all?"

"A thief. A killer."

Yossi stepped closer to Malik so that their noses nearly touched. "You Arabs, you come out of the desert," he said in a low voice, "you know nothing of civilization, of government, not even of agriculture. Jews have to show you everything and still you don't understand. Leave God out of it—we *earned* this land. For thousands of years it was useless, uncultivated, good only for goats. You should go back to the desert where you belong. Yes, we wish to be rid of you. All you live for is destruction and terror. We Jews have a civilization to build and you only stand in the way."

"That's the same fascist language that Hitler used," Malik said. "You're just like them. A fucking Nazi." He spat the word out.

Yossi's eyes narrowed. His hand automatically touched his pistol. "That word can get you killed."

"Go ahead, I bet you got a lot of practice in that."

I could do that, Yossi thought, *I could fucking kill him.* "You don't know," he stammered. "You can't know." And then he suddenly collapsed onto the bench.

"Yossi?" Malik could see that Yossi was flushed and perspiring and his body now visibly trembled.

Yossi waved him aside. He was clutching his chest in obvious pain and he struggled to catch his breath. "Just leave," he gasped.

"I'm getting a doctor."

Yossi shook his head furiously.

"Listen, I'm sorry. I was out of line. Let me call someone. One of your cops."

"Absolutely not."

"I think you're having a heart attack."

Yossi shook his head again. "Happened before. I'm okay." He ran out of breath.

"I'm gonna call a doctor."

"They're busy."

Malik realized that every medical facility within miles would be treating injuries from the riot. Yossi handed his phone to Malik. "Call Sara," he said. "My daughter."

The phone rang six times before Sara answered. "Hey, Abba, sorry, I was just doing laundry. How are you?"

"Is this Sara?"

She immediately froze. "Who am I speaking to?"

"Anthony Malik. I'm working with your dad."

"Is he okay?"

"He's having some kind of attack."

"Let me talk to him."

Malik held the phone to Yossi's ear. "Abba, what's wrong?"

"I'm fine. I'll be fine."

"You're not fine. It's angina. You need medical assistance."

"Bring me something," Yossi said. "The pills. In bathroom."

"Your heart pills?" She paused. "I can't hear you."

"Yes."

Malik took the phone back.

"Where are you?" Sara asked.

"Behind the station."

"I'll be there in twenty minutes."

Malik sat on the bench beside Yossi. They stared out at the Old City, neither clear about what had happened and how to call back the words that could not be unsaid. "You should put your head between your knees," Malik advised. Yossi complied. His breathing began to even out.

It took Sara more than an hour to get through the blockades the army erected after the violence was finished. She arrived with the meds—beta blockers—and made sure Yossi swallowed them. Then she turned to Malik. "What went down here?" she demanded.

"There was a clash," he said. "Two funerals. Lots of people killed and wounded. Yossi was in the middle of it."

"Was he harmed? You both have blood all over you."

"Not that I saw. He was trying to stop it, but things got out of hand. It was ugly."

While he was talking Malik took note of Sara, her long oval face, gray eyes, hay-colored hair, so unlike Yossi. There must be a rather smashing mother involved, he thought. He also perceived that she didn't trust him.

"What's your relationship with my father?" Sara asked in a tone meant to be neutral.

"We don't have a relationship, exactly. We're on the same case."

"Chief Weingarten's murder? So who are you working for?"

"I'm with the FBI."

"That was quick. He's been dead less than a week."

Malik didn't respond. She clearly suspected there was more to the story. "Something went on between you?" she asked.

"We had words," Malik admitted.

"What words?"

"I called him a Nazi."

Sara took this in. "That would do it. What did he call you?"

"From what I gather, he just sees me as a know-nothing Arab terrorist bent on destroying civilization."

"You're lucky you walked away from this."

"The thing is, we both said things we didn't believe. I did, at least. I didn't know he had heart problems."

"He wouldn't want you to treat him any different. He's the most obstinate man I ever met."

A smile crossed Yossi's face.

"See?" said Sara. "He's proud of it."

In the hazy mentality that Yossi currently resided in thoughts crossed his mind like a slow-moving caravan. *He sees me as I really am*, was the first regretful realization to present itself. His self-image ranged from a stalwart hero of the Jews to being a heartless killer in the service of a cause he no longer believed in. These opposing identities were always at war but came to a climax in the events of the afternoon. Malik was right. Yossi had seen how it was going to unfold when Benny confided that there would be an "action," and Yossi obediently followed orders. He did nothing. And he realized the truth: *I am working for him, that twisted little*—the word "Nazi" had come into his mind at that moment—*and if that's true of Benny, then who am I?*

33

Red Hat

Hebron, Oct. 1, 2023

The curfew was in effect at night, so Malik rushed to Yasmine's house before dark to talk to Dina. Yasmine answered the door and pulled him aside. "I fear for her so much," she whispered. "She would have been married. And now . . ." Yasmine's voice drifted into a long exhalation. "Really, I think she may be going mad."

Dina was alone in the front room, hair awry, eyes drifting, as if she hadn't moved since they saw each other the night before. Her wedding dress was draped across her lap. She had sunk so deep into a dark interior space that she didn't register when Malik came in.

"You should have told me," he said angrily.

Dina looked up, startled, as if Malik had suddenly materialized in front of her like a ghost. "I dreamed you were Jamal," she said distantly. "It was confusing. We were young, like children. But then you or maybe Jamal ran away. I was lost, a dog was chasing me, people were laughing—"

"Dina, look at me. I can't help you if you don't tell me the truth."

"The truth," she said to herself, silently laughing and shaking her head.

"Is it funny? Do you understand what I'm saying? They think you were the chief's lover."

These words shocked Dina back to reality. "If you believe that, you must consider me as a whore."

"Don't turn it on me. Is it true?"

She retreated again into delirium. "It's too much," she said, talking only to herself. "It's too much . . ."

"Dina, *stop.*"

"Why do you have to ask this?" she said in a little girl's voice.

"I need to know everything."

Dina covered her face. "Please don't hate me," she moaned.

"Listen, whatever it is, I promise I'm not going to hate you. But if I don't know the whole truth I can't help Jamal—or you."

"You're wrong. You will hate me. Everyone will."

"Dina, I know you were a source for Weingarten—"

Dina cut him off. "I was a *spy*—" she spat the word out in a harsh whisper—"an informer. A collaborator. I betrayed my people. This cannot be forgiven. Even Jamal would condemn me."

"Tell me."

"Not here," she said under her breath, "not in the house." She stood up, letting the wedding dress fall to the floor with no more thought than if it had been a table napkin. She led Malik outside, to a small garden where Yasmine grew hibiscus and geraniums in pots. Bougainvillea twined around the window shutters. Avoiding Malik's inquisitive stare, Dina picked a blue plumbago blossom and spoke as if she were confiding in it.

"Two years ago, Omar decided to become a suicide bomber."

Malik waited, speechless.

"His pain was unbearable. One stupid moment when he was sleeping a bullet changed his life. Who knows who did this to him."

"Your mother told me the Israelis shot him during the intifada. Weingarten thought he shot himself."

"Everybody has a story. Each is better than to say the bullet came through the wall and we all lay on the floor hoping that they didn't shoot again. They, whoever."

"What led to the idea of suicide?"

"Always there are these vultures looking for people ready to kill themselves, and we have so many like this in our society. You become a bomb of hopelessness and you want to explode. The vultures make this dream possible. They knew Omar was suffering. And they chose him—him, a child, in pain, so defenseless, so hopeless. They brainwashed him. They tell him this action will bring meaning to his life. And it will end the pain.”

“Weingarten knew about Omar?”

Dina nodded. “That’s when we met. Hamas was preparing Omar’s martyrdom. Then the army raided and many were killed. Weingarten arrested Omar. He could have sent him to prison. Instead he brought him home. And he asked me to talk. That was the trade.”

“Talk about Hamas?”

“About Hamas, al-Aqsa, Fatah, Lions’ Den, they’re all here. He demanded I tell him about members, about plans, many other things.”

“Such as drugs?”

Dina nodded. “He was particularly interested in drugs. He wanted to know what Omar was taking for pain. It is difficult to get pain relievers in Palestine except on the black market, and so many people here are addicted to a drug we call Tramal, also named tramadol, it’s like morphine, you become addicted so easily. To get good medicines you have to go to Israel for treatment, and that requires a pass only the Israeli authorities provide. Weingarten arranged for Omar to go to a hospital in Tel Aviv. He now receives a drug called Dilaudid. It’s safe. I think it saved Omar’s life.”

“Tell me the words Weingarten used when he asked about the drugs.”

Dina thought for a moment then said, “He said he wanted a list of all the drugs being smuggled into Palestine, where they came from, who were the people doing this. Of course I didn’t know everything.”

“But you told him something.”

“I said I knew about the heroin.” She was still talking to the plumbago, as if she was confiding a secret that no one could hear. “Another called crystal meth, this is a big problem here. You’ll see people—young people—on the street, they’ve given up, they’re sitting on the curbs, doing nothing, their eyes all crazy. Some are taking one thing, some another. Marijuana, hashish, these are common, but they don’t kill. Much of it comes through the tunnels from Gaza, which means that Hamas controls it. This is a huge business that is destroying our young people. Everybody knows, not just me.”

"Dina, when was the last time you saw the chief?"

"About two weeks ago."

"Look at me," he said, his face hard and cold. "I know that's not true. You have to tell me exactly what happened or I can't help you at all."

She was once again a child, frightened and alone. She glanced up at him, then quickly looked away. "Why don't you believe me?"

"You saw him the morning he was killed."

"No, I was in classes at the university."

"If you don't tell me the truth I can't help you. I'll fly home tonight."

Dina's breath was shallow and her voice, when she finally spoke, was a hoarse whisper. "What chance have I if they know I met him before he is killed?"

"The police already know. They think you lured him to his killers. That's their theory. The only way to change their minds is to come up with a better story, one they can't disprove. And your only chance for a better story, no matter how risky, is the truth."

He could sense her resistance crumbling. Malik was her only chance, they both knew that, but they also knew that he was a slim chance at best, and he might make things worse by getting her to confess she was with Weingarten the morning he died.

"We met on the bus," she said in a trancelike voice that he could scarcely hear. "We did this sometimes. Many go to Jerusalem on the bus every day, so it is not suspicious. We exchange notes. We had some talk, as if we were being polite to each other. When we got into the city he wanted to talk more, and I had some time before class. We met at the famous café where you see us in the photograph. Someone must have known we were going to be together. This time he gave me a little present. It was not very discreet."

"What did he give you?"

"A diary. Maybe he had the idea that I would record certain actions. Instead, I use it for writing poems."

"What did he want to talk about?"

"He wanted to know where my information was coming from."

"And what did you tell him?"

Dina pursed her lips and shook her head. "I said no, I can't, but he was being very threatening, like I haven't seen before."

"Say the words and you'll be free of the fear."

"I'm so ashamed." Her voice quivered.

"Just let it out, exactly as you told Weingarten."

"It was Jamal. He knew I was going to meet him."

Malik absorbed this. Everyone he met seemed to have a secret life and now the door opened on Jamal. "He was in Hamas?"

"No. His cousin Ehsan Zayyat, they grew up together. They were always close even if they are so different in their politics. They talk. Then Jamal would confide in me. He needed someone he could trust and he thought that was me. But I betrayed him." She threw the plumbago blossom into the garden and sobbed.

Malik put his hand on her shoulder. "Maybe he wanted you to tell what you knew."

Dina shook her head vigorously. "He was always demanding never to say a word, that it was too dangerous."

MALIK HURRIED BACK toward the hotel before the curfew fell.

As an investigator Malik was used to deception, but in Hebron it was as if people weren't purposely lying so much as they were conforming to a warp in reality. There was a day-to-day Hebron that people like Malik, passing through, might experience; but there was also a covert, underground world, an unseen presence that ruled the imagination. The shifting stories about Omar's injury, for instance. Malik wasn't sure if he had gotten to the bottom of it, but Yasmine's version—that he had been shot by the IDF—corresponded to the preferred Palestinian narrative. Weingarten's theory that the wound was self-inflicted, possibly an accident, was plausible, but conveniently placed the blame on a Palestinian—it was Omar's own fault. The story that Dina told—of a random crippling shot in the middle of the night—reflected the aimless chaos of the life they were living. Any of these things could be true, but each folded the story into their theory of how the world really worked.

Malik was beginning to see how both societies drew meaning

from death—the creation of martyrs, the veneration of lives lost to the cause, the need to avenge those losses, even the longing to die. In Hebron the shadow of death eclipsed life itself, and why not? Life was degraded and mean, fueled by the absence of justice, the ambition to kill, and the collapse of hope. Death was noble, death was grand. Death ruled.

The American side of Malik believed that most problems were solvable, a theory that included the subconscious illusion that he was a hero who could rescue Dina from the dangerous forces that ensnared her. He rushed toward her fragility. With that intimate picture of her and Chief Weingarten on the internet, she might be in mortal danger. People would see her as a traitor. Jamal would certainly feel that way. Danger was all around her.

Dina described Jamal as a neutral force between the Israelis and Palestinian terrorists, but was he? Was that even possible? Her confession that she was with Weingarten the morning of his murder made any triumphant resolution of the mystery so much more difficult. It would fit right into Yossi's theory. She and the chief meet on the bus, they rendezvous in Jerusalem, she agrees to a tryst after class in a secret place only she knows. Weingarten would be excited, what man wouldn't be? He rushes back to Hebron in time to keep his appointment with Malik, then drives to the abandoned quarry to meet Dina. His killers are waiting. It was a workable theory. Weingarten had a notable weakness for women. If Hamas wanted to get to him Dina would be attractive bait. And she had a tie to Hamas through her father and possibly Jamal as well. Maybe she was still attached to Zayyat in some way.

He tried to envision another way of looking at it: Dina and Weingarten ride together in the bus, as they have before, spend time at the café, then the chief gets back on the bus and arrives in Hebron a few minutes late for his appointment with Malik. He apologizes, saying that something had come up. But what could that be? Something more important than talking to the FBI agent he had summoned to Hebron? For a man like Weingarten, the prospect of sex might trump any other considerations. Dina had been so evasive about her relationship with the chief that Malik had no idea how much he could believe. If he looked at the evidence with a cold eye it was easy to believe that Dina set him up. Nothing else made any sense, unless there was something else that Yossi hadn't told him.

As the sun was meeting the horizon and the hotel was only a block away, Malik noticed a boy standing across the street smiling at him. He was wearing a red Phillies hat. The boy walked away, turning at the corner. Malik followed him, annoyed that he was being taunted again by this same youngster, who was probably eleven or twelve but already invested in a malicious personality. It wasn't enough to steal Malik's property, the boy had to rub it in, delighting in his criminality, teasing Malik's fruitless anger at being victimized by children.

Malik ran to the corner, then slowed to a casual walk as he turned onto the street, so that he didn't appear to be chasing the boy—a race he wouldn't win. So far, the boy did not seem to notice that he was being tailed. He was a stocky kid with a big head—the hat almost fit him. He paused and looked in a shop window, then stopped to tie his shoelaces. Malik hung back, telling himself it was not worth getting into a confrontation with a child over a hat that would be easy to replace. More important than the hat were his passport and wallet and suitcase with personal items that he hated to lose. This boy probably knew where they were. Malik could offer him a reward. The kid was a thief and would do anything for money.

There was a narrow driveway between two buildings leading to a loading zone for a furniture store. The boy turned in to it. Maybe he was planning to slip through an unguarded back door and rob the place. Or maybe it was a shortcut that only natives knew. When Malik entered the darkened drive he saw the boy standing against a concrete wall with no place to go. Trapped. He banged on the door of the warehouse, but it was already curfew time and no one answered.

"Calm down, I'm not going to hurt you," Malik said as he cautiously approached the boy, who was as wild as a stray cat. "Look, I'll give you a reward if you return my stuff. I'll make it worth your while. More money than you'd get if you tried to sell it on the street. Do you understand me?" But the boy pounded harder on the door as Malik came closer and reached for him. Then a red light illuminated the boy's face and Malik heard the sound of a diesel engine. He turned to see a bulky panel truck backing up, brake lights glaring, blocking the driveway. At the same moment he noticed this, the boy raced past him, laughing. Two hooded men got out of the truck and opened the rear hatch. They both carried automatic weapons.

Malik shook his head. "No, I'm not gonna play this game. Nobody's gonna make videos of me, understand? If you're going to kill me, do it now. I'm not getting in that truck."

One of the men fired a shot between Malik's shoes. He thought for an instant, and then climbed into the truck.

34

Sir Charles

Kfar Oren, Oct. 1, 2023

The kitchen showed signs of cooking; there were pots on the stove, the source of a celestial aroma that suffused the air. Yossi's senses instantly came to attention. He looked around but didn't see Sara. He found her in the garden. "It was driving me crazy with all these oranges everywhere," she said. "So I bought a duck for dinner."

Sara handed Yossi an apron, an artifact of his marriage that he hadn't even known he possessed. "You're going to make the sauce," she said, as she took the roasted duck from the oven. It was crusty brown, its breast crosshatched with neat incisions like a photograph in a food magazine.

"I can't cook," Yossi solemnly declared. "I'll ruin the meal."

"I've known you to make toasted cheese sandwiches. This is easier." She directed him to squeeze the juice from two oranges into a saucepan, then reduce the mixture with rosemary and mustard. In France she would have added butter, but in Israel she used schmaltz. "See, you did it," she said.

"That's all there is to it?"

"Congratulations, chef," she said.

"Are you studying how to cook in addition to all your courses?" Yossi asked.

"The thing is that you simply can't live in France without learning to love food," she said as she garnished the dish with orange slices and sprigs of rosemary. "You should try it, at least for a vacation. You'll find there are other things to eat than frozen dinners and chicken nuggets. Heart-healthy things. I'm making you a list. The duck is an exception." She sliced off a bit of meat and fed it to her father. "What do you think?"

"It's the best thing I ever put in my mouth."

"See? There's a huge part of you that needs to be reacquainted with pleasure. Imagine living in a place that is as full of joy as this place is stuffed with gloom. You don't have to subject yourself to it. You deserve a break."

"I'm not sure how that would work."

"Abba, you're still young enough to have another life. It's not healthy to be always fighting, always living with this hatred. It's taking a toll, you know that."

Yossi cut her off. "This is for you, this nice life. This is what your mother wanted for you. What I also want for you. But for me, it's too late. I can't leave. It's my duty to be here."

Yossi had never said these words before, but as he spoke he realized that they defined who he was. He couldn't tell Sara how, despite the misery that suffused every pore of life in Hebron, he was needed, and that feeling was more important to him than mere happiness.

"You're a hard case, but now it's time to eat." Sara raised her glass of Chianti. "First, a toast. To Mom. We miss her."

Yossi toasted but he was unable to speak.

Lulls in the dinner conversation could turn into long stretches of glum silence, so Sara equipped herself with conversation starters. When she noticed Yossi's gaze drift away from the table, she supplied a sure topic of debate. "I suppose you've seen the news," she said as if it was a matter of little consequence, adding, "Pass the carrots."

"What news?"

"The American secretary of state is going back to Riyadh."

"What a waste of time!" Yossi said, unable to disguise the cynical pleasure he took in disparaging any attempt to create peace. To him it was all for show and nothing would ever come of it. Hopelessness was a kind of consolation. In such instances his vehemence would usually squash any feeble attempt to raise a flag for a peaceful outcome, but with Sara it was a different matter. She was, after all, studying politics at one of the world's most esteemed institutions. He had to be cautious or she would run chapter and verse and even footnotes into the conversation. It pleased him to see her be so informed and adroit, even if he profoundly disagreed with her.

"It's all about the Iranian attack on the Saudi refineries in 2019," she said. "You remember what a trauma that was, drones and cruise missiles coming from Yemen, some of them apparently unarmed just to show what Iran could do through its proxies, in this case the Houthis. Iran showed that it could have destroyed the largest oil-processing facility in the world, and the Saudis were totally defenseless. But the real question for the Saudis is what did America, their great protector, do about it? Absolutely nothing."

"That's why they're demanding that the Americans sign a defense treaty with them," said Yossi.

"You're right, Abba. But they also want something else. The bomb. The Saudis are demanding that the US sign off on their nuclear-enrichment program. MBS already said that if Iran gets the bomb, the Saudis must have one as well. This is the deal. The Saudis will recognize Israel and in return they build their nuclear capacity to match the Iranians step by step."

"Bibi will never agree to this," said Yossi. "The Saudis to have the bomb? Unthinkable."

"There's something he wants more. Under this deal—at least, what has leaked out of these talks so far—the Palestinians would get essentially nothing. After the Saudis recognize Israel, what other Muslim country will remain with the Palestinians? It is Bibi's way of imposing peace on them, even if it means that the most important country in the Arab world can one day destroy Israel."

"Is this actually happening?" Yossi asked.

"It's a real opening to an accommodation with the Arab world," said Sara. "Too bad that it will come once again at the expense of the Palestinians."

"Well," said Yossi, shrugging, "what can they do?"

.   .   .

IN HER CHILDHOOD ROOM were the artifacts of Sara's youth. They might have belonged to another person. The room seemed so small and childhood so distant. She flipped through an old sketchbook with landscapes and portraits of school friends and secret drawings of boys she had been interested in. Among the stuffed dolls was one she slept with until she went away to school. It was a strange little primate-like object she had named Sir Charles. She wondered now where that name came from. Sir Charles had red ears and whiskers and was missing a plastic foot. Leah had sewn up his wound before all the stuffing fell out. There was a photo of Sara and her beloved collie, Babka. Sara was probably eight when it was taken.

Each time she returned to Israel she found that her life had receded further from the person she had intended to be. It wasn't just a matter of becoming adult. She was becoming less Israeli. The country's politics were impossible to defend, as she was constantly demanded to do in Paris, and in any case no non-Israeli could begin to decipher the complexities and many layers of grief and defiance and pride that set her people apart.

In her heart she was saying goodbye to Yossi. If she made a break with Israel, she would also leave him behind. As much as she loved him, Sara knew that Yossi was poisoning her life. There was a passage in Frantz Fanon's psychiatric notes in Algeria that deeply disturbed her. He was analyzing a young Frenchwoman whose father was a civil servant in charge of a rural area. "As soon as the troubles broke out, he threw himself like a maniac into a frenzied manhunt for Algerians," the patient said of her father, who tortured those he captured in the basement of their house. "Every time I went home the screams coming from downstairs kept me awake." She moved to town. "Eventually, I never went back. The few times my father came to see me in town I couldn't look him in the face I was so horribly frightened and embarrassed. I found it increasingly difficult to kiss him." She was afraid to go out on the street because she felt surrounded by hatred. "Deep down I knew the Algerians were right. If I were Algerian I'd join the resistance movement."

Sara had often wondered who she would be if she were Palestinian. It was a taboo topic among her Israeli friends. Basically, the question was about the justification for Palestinian resistance. During a discussion in Brisard's class, Sara referenced Hannah Arendt's critique of Fanon, who worshipped violence as a path to liberation. "Liberation is indeed a condition of freedom," Arendt wrote, but "freedom is by no means a necessary result of liberation." History was marked by resistance movements that succeeded in throwing off the colonists only to institute regimes as brutal as that of the occupier—Algeria being a case in point, a country despoiled by colonization but ravaged by civil war. Sara observed that Arendt's analysis at least opened the possibility that a Palestine without Israel could be worse than the occupation. She was surprised that Redha agreed with her and Brisard did not.

Sara felt like a coward. Leaving Israel was running away from the conflict. She didn't know how to integrate it into her life. There was no longer a peace movement in Israel. The Palestine Authority was corrupt; Hamas was bent on genocide; the settlers were continually squeezing Palestinians off their land and gaining more power as they did so; and the government under Netanyahu was taking the country in a direction that was, in her opinion, fascistic—a word that she never imagined could be applied to the Jewish homeland. Religious extremists were a minority in Israel but they were at the helm. How could she live in such a place that had become such an ideological prison?

She crawled into bed with Sir Charles and wept—for her country, for her father, and also for Redha. In one of his classes, Brisard had discussed the lingering effects of colonization in France. Muslims accounted for about 12 percent of the French population, but more than 60 percent of the prisoners. Now there was one more. Brisard had called the day before to tell Sara that Redha had been arrested for some terror plot yet to be revealed.

Redha had shifted Sara's perception of religion and gender and masculinity. He was prettier than she was, something other than handsome in the male fashion. He wore his beard closely trimmed, outlining his features in a wash of blue-black stubble. Each morning he splashed himself with a musty sandalwood cologne. He shaved his armpits and pubic hair. In the bedroom the fiery Algerian revolutionary faded away, revealing a true French intellectual. They were living in a fourth-floor apartment she rented on rue Saint-Jacques. He hadn't offered to share the rent.

Redha saw her as a colonizer; he scarcely disguised it. She had been in the army and he assumed she had killed scores of Arabs, but this was part of her appeal. In various ways he signaled his desire for her to dominate him. He would lie on his back and let her please herself on top of him. Sara felt like she was raping him. It was unsettling how powerful it made her feel.

Now she would be returning to Paris and he would be gone. She wept because she was glad.

35

Zayyat

West Bank, Oct. 1, 2023

Malik lay on the floor of the truck blindfolded, his hands bound behind his back with flex cuffs. It occurred to him that this is what they did with Weingarten. It was so easy. If only there was a checkpoint, Israeli soldiers would demand to look in the truck. It was after sundown; they would be stopping traffic in town. But as the road smoothed out Malik guessed they were on a highway. How long would his disappearance go unremarked? Greenblatt and the embassy crew would assume he had boarded his flight and left the country the night before. His friends back in New York weren't expecting him. Yossi didn't seem likely to seek him out. Dina and her mother, perhaps they would inquire, but in truth a week could go by without anyone raising a flag until the hotel clerk asked for payment—stark evidence of how alone he was in the world, how unneeded.

Helplessness was a feeling Malik despised. His entire life was a struggle to overcome it—when he could do nothing to keep his parents from divorcing, when he was bullied for being an Arab in school, when 9/11 happened and he felt in some way responsible because he was a Muslim—all of these emotions had led him to fortify himself. He became strong. He was good at math and a college counselor advised him to study accounting—a profession that guaranteed security. He went to work for Ernst & Young, one of the Big Four accounting firms, which offered the best hiring package. The work was fine, the life was a continual party, women were surprisingly available. It was more than he expected or hoped for. His suits and shirts were tailor-made. He kept fit at a boxing gym where future Olympians trained with the pros. He felt invulnerable.

He thought he was set for life, but then the firm was investigated for cheating on qualification tests for its auditors. (EY later paid a $100 million fine for obstructing the SEC investigation.) Malik wasn't as shocked by the scandal as he was intrigued by the investigation. EY was supposed to have the best talent in the business, but the firm proved no match for a group of young government auditors with subpoena power and the law on their side. Once Malik began to consider alternatives, he realized that in the pursuit of security his life had become dull. Always frugal, he had built up his retirement account with sensible investments. When he decided to join the FBI he took a meaningful salary cut, but he knew that when the day came to leave the bureau, lucrative employment opportunities awaited with international security firms. Meantime there were other rewards. Pursuing terrorist financing was fascinating, and he was good at the job. It was true that his profession sometimes led him into danger but he had impressive resources to call upon. His badge said that this man is not to be trifled with. He wasn't rich but he dwelt in a rarified neighborhood of highly potent individuals. And he carried the passport of the most powerful country in the world.

None of that mattered now. Since the bombing his life had come unsprung. The assumptions he had made about his future were pitiable, from the perspective of a man who had lost everything that mattered to him and was now being driven to his death. He might have been living in that apartment in Manhattan with Lucy, watching the ships traversing New York Harbor. He might have gotten Tommy Cantemessa's old job after he moved up the ladder. All that was gone, the job, the apartment, Lucy, the future he might have had.

He counted seconds by tapping his fingers like a drummer keeping the beat. Presently the truck slowed and turned right, onto a graveled drive. He heard a garage door opening, then the truck moved forward and stopped. The garage door closed. Malik did the math: a little over eleven hundred seconds, about eighteen minutes. He guessed the truck had been traveling at an average of forty miles per hour, which was three quarters of a mile per minute, which multiplied by eighteen would be a little over twelve miles from the point of origin. When he got out of this, if he got out of this, he would draw a circle over a map with a radius of ten to fifteen miles and examine every turnoff to the right with a gravel drive. He was always good with numbers.

The doors of the truck opened. Malik heard their footsteps as the men walked away. Distant conversation, not quite in range of hearing. Then nothing.

Malik cursed himself for being such an easy target. He knew better than to expose himself as he had, alone in a city where factions fought over trophies such as a kidnapped American agent. It was especially galling to have fallen into a trap set by a child, but it was also, he had to admit, a very clever deception. He was in the hands of people who knew how to find human weakness, who could hide the play until it was too late to make a break. This was not likely to turn out well and it was entirely his fault. If he was going to die he hoped it would be quick and merciful, but that wasn't the nature of this group. He had seen what they did to Weingarten. There was no reason to think his own abduction would be different.

He rolled himself up into a sitting position.

He would not beg for his life. They didn't care and his pleas would only make the video more humiliating and more likely to go viral. Nor would he express sympathy for the goals of the group. At best that would gain him but a few more minutes of life. These were promises he made to himself, just as he had vowed not to get into the truck in the first place, but one bullet at his feet changed his mind.

He had time to consider the irony that Israel's enemy was his enemy now. The age of terror had harvested so many lives; his would just be another brief sensation in the press, soon buried in memory by the passage of time and the bodies that would inevitably follow. But he was also an Arab, a Muslim, and he had come to identify with the deprived lives his people were experiencing, the all-consuming helplessness of being in the hands of others who despised your very existence. The clock on his last seconds of his life would begin to tick the moment the truck door opened.

He had to at least try to escape. If he was shot and killed in the process, well, better that than being tortured and humiliated on video prior to having his head cut off.

The room had sounded large for a garage; maybe there was another exit than the closed overhead door. His best chance would be to run and hope there was a way out, but first he had to get the blindfold off. It was just a kaffiyeh tightly tied around his eyes. He explored the space in the truck with his head and found the back of the passenger seat, which he used to try to scrape off the kaffiyeh, but he couldn't get traction on the slippery leather.

Footsteps again. The door opened. He was pulled onto the floor, then suddenly he was freed from the cuffs. The kaffiyeh was unwound and Malik was staring into the face of small, handsome man, about the same age as Malik, with stylish black glasses and a light dusting of freckles. He offered a hand to help him out of the truck.

This was the moment to flee. Malik could see in a flash that it wasn't an ordinary garage, it must have been an auto-repair shop, there were hydraulic lifts on the floor. He noticed a camcorder on a tripod. That was as much as he could deduce in the time it took him to bolt from the truck to the overhead garage door and fail to lift it. He looked around, puzzled that he hadn't been shot as he tried another locked door. He could hear the laughter as he hurled his shoulder into it.

"Won't you join us, Mr. Malik?"

Across the room was a table with three men, including the man with black glasses. They were all grinning at Malik's pathetic attempt to escape.

"Ehsan Zayyat, I'm guessing," said Malik, gathering his dignity. "I've been looking for you."

Zayyat's expression slightly changed; he was now not only amused but also intrigued. "And yet you run when you find me," he said. "Please, have a seat. I'm sorry for the rude manner of bringing you here, but there are reasons I can't just call and invite you to dinner. Please, help yourself." A substantial meal was spread across the table in carry-out cartons.

Zayyat was clearly in charge; the other two were the muscle—big men, scruffy, not so carefully dressed, but there was also something normal about them. You wouldn't think they were terrorists if you ran into them in a café.

"I took the liberty of examining your suitcase," Zayyat said, indicating Malik's stolen Travelpro carry-on beside the table. "I found this." He held up a weathered Quran.

"It was my grandfather's, a wedding present for a relative."

Zayyat dipped a piece of pita bread into a tub of hummus. "Are you a believer?" he asked casually.

"Not according to your standards."

"Don't worry, we don't kill people for being impious."

"What do you kill them for?"

Zayyat paused as if giving the matter real thought. "Jews we kill when we get the opportunity. Also Americans and Europeans who come to their aid. Sometimes we kill those who sell Arab land. And of course collaborators. Like your precious cousin Dina." Zayyat took a bite of the pita. "Of all Allah's creatures, women are the most clever and deceitful. Is this not true?" Zayyat's companions nodded. He added, "And they call *us* terrorists!"

Although his mouth was dry and his appetite diminished by fear, Malik served himself ample scoops of whatever was in front of him, a form of bravado. He took a bite of the meat and dismayingly realized it was lamb tongue. Zayyat smiled at his expression. "You have much to learn about Palestinian cuisine, my friend. This is a delicacy we serve to certain people who talk too much."

Malik defiantly took another bite of tongue. In the subtle tug-of-war of intelligence, it was best not to seem eager or intimidated. Indifference was a useful goad. Any question asked or answered too readily reduced the leverage. So Malik was in no hurry to probe. He would let Zayyat make the first move. The ultimate object of this meeting was to leave alive. The ticket to survival was convincing Zayyat to allow him to exist. The only way Malik could see of doing that was to awaken Zayyat's interest in the one subject he would find irresistible: himself.

"You have some personal reason to be interested in me?" Zayyat finally asked.

Malik looked at Zayyat and then shrugged. "Is this where you killed Weingarten?" he asked.

"If we did this, we would have claimed credit," Zayyat said, annoyed at Malik's evasiveness. "In fact, we thought about doing so because we applaud this action, but we waited to see who came forward. We supposed it was Daesh. They do this beheading thing. But then we heard about Jamal."

"You don't actually believe he did the killing."

Zayyat picked a morsel of food out of his teeth. "You pose a problem for us, Mr. Malik. You try to help our friend Jamal prove he is innocent."

"I think he is."

"We prefer that he is guilty."

"Do you have him?"

Zayyat laughed, a cruel and hollow sound. "If I had him, he would be joining us for this feast. I miss his company, believe me." Under the thin garment of amiability with which he began the conversation, Zayyat's volatile emotions were strangely untethered to the words coming out of his mouth. He reminded Malik of ISIS figures he interrogated in Syria. Like Zayyat they were at peace with the suffering they caused—not just in the West but also in the Muslim world. Sitting in their cages, they still had visions of subjugating America and the sinful Western world.

"But you would let him die for a cause he doesn't believe in."

"Jamal is the bravest man in Palestine. We are all cowards compared to him. No matter that he is wrong about peace. It will never come. Here we have war all the time because Allah wills it. If he wanted peace in the Holy Land, he would surely anoint Jamal to bring it. But he did not. Jamal has no power. No one believes him. No one follows him. Only some liberal Westerners who want to feel good about themselves. But everyone has a breaking point, and perhaps this happened with him." Zayyat speared a small potato and examined it with cold curiosity, much the same way he regarded Malik. "People said he retired from peacemaking. Maybe he creates such a story when he decides to do this action with the police chief. The people with the skill and intelligence to carry it out is not a big number."

"But you know he didn't kill the chief, and you claim Hamas did not, so who did?"

Zayyat shrugged. "Who knows? As for us, we don't care who did it, but of course we approve. The big cop is dead and events have begun to follow their course. The Israelis wish to martyr Jamal. So let them. This will give meaning to Jamal's life. 'It's a good thing,' as Martha Stewart would say."

"You're a little out-of-date on American culture."

"Really? I need to make another visit. America is where I became a true believer. Among the gamblers and pimps and whores and drunks and addicts of your wonderful country, which spreads its sinful message to the world without embarrassment. But the next time I come with bombs."

"They say you learned from the master."

"Sheikh Yeyha Ayyash was my mother's brother," he said, his face lit with pride at the recognition. "I was too young to know him well but I always knew I would emulate his example. This is something they teach in the FBI? Tell me, do they have a big file with my name on it?"

Malik shrugged. "Possibly," he said as if it were of little importance. "There are billions of files."

"And how did my name appear? I have always been 'under the radar,' as you say."

"You tripped a wire when you went to North Korea."

Zayyat set his bread down and cursed under his breath. "They are so proud of their fucking security, but one visit puts my name on the list."

"Three visits, I think it was."

Zayyat nodded in tribute to the thoroughness of the intelligence that implicated him.

"We assumed you were interested in acquiring a nuclear weapon," said Malik.

"Not on offer, unfortunately."

"There must have been a negotiation. Three visits."

"We talked. But this is not your business," Zayyat said impatiently. "Let's discuss what brought you to the Holy Land."

"The wedding."

"As you said already. For your cousin and my cousin Jamal. But this is not your only motive. Why were you looking for me? I'm just one of your billions of names."

"I have a special interest in bombs."

"Ah, well," Zayyat said, "we have something in common."

"In my case, it was a particular bomb placed on an American plane in Amman."

"Oh, yes," Zayyat said. "A great disappointment. Such a beautiful bomb, meant to take two hundred lives but only five in the end. And few even heard of this. I'm surprised you know of it. The Jordanians keep such things quiet. Even here few ever spoke of it."

"Bombing innocent people on an airplane is not an act of heroism. If you were a true Muslim you would know this."

"This morning we lost the lives of nineteen of our citizens. This in addition to the three young men murdered earlier. Every week the settlers slay so many. So we just let this happen? No response? Do you think justice waits for us if we behave ourselves? Believe me, there will be a response. Not only Hebron, the whole of Palestine is coiled and ready to strike. This time we will not stop."

They all believe in their inevitable victory, Malik thought. *Time is on their side, even if it takes a thousand years.* He judged that the Palestinian armed groups were far from being able to do anything other than provoke more punishment on their own communities. But that hadn't stopped them in the past.

"The world will see the Zionist project for what it is," Zayyat continued. "The Jews devour our land piece by piece, pushing, always pushing us out of our homeland. For years we've been cautious. We tried diplomacy. We kept the hotheads under control as much as possible. All this has only made it easier for them to take the totality of Palestine—and after that, they look to Jordan, Lebanon, Sinai—you've seen the maps they proudly display of the land they say their God gave them. But we are the ones who will create a new reality."

"Can you tell me where Jamal is?" Malik asked, ignoring the boast.

"I could." Zayyat tore off another piece of pita bread.

"Is he safe?"

"Soon no one will be safe."

"Why don't you be straight with me? So far you've hinted that you're going to kill my cousin, that you've hidden Jamal, and that something big is going to happen. It's all a riddle."

Zayyat smiled again, his habit when making a threat. "I can tell you the truth in every detail, but there is a price for this knowledge. If you learn it you will not live to repeat it."

These threats were curiously conditional. In the dim light it wasn't easy to see Zayyat's eyes behind the lenses, which complicated Malik's ability to assess the danger. "I agree Jamal is a brave man," Malik said, "but he's also innocent. If we can prove that, he can come back. He can get married. Dina is wild with grief."

"Do you think he would have her now, after what she did? No, he despises her. His only wish is that she is dead."

"I doubt that."

"Believe what you wish, she betrayed him—and worse, she betrayed her people. Yes, Jamal is a man of peace, but he is also a man. In our culture, these are grave offenses."

"Don't harm Dina. Please. She only did what she had to do."

"It's interesting, this phrase, 'what she had to do.' We all say this. It's our excuse, fits all sizes. We don't kill for pleasure, Mr. Malik. We do this to make our society stronger. We must protect ourselves against infiltrators and traitors. Like you. We know what Arabs do in the FBI, going undercover into Muslim communities, spying on believers. We can make an example of you. For your crimes, you deserve to die. And still you don't say why you look for me."

"I came to kill you."

Zayyat's eyebrows raised in surprise. He looked to the ceiling as if a memory waited there. "They say there was a survivor in Amman," he said, "So it was you. How amusing. Please tell me how you were planning to accomplish this task?"

"I'm still working on that."

Zayyat laughed deeply, and cast a glance at his goons, who also burst into laughter. "I like your honesty," he said when he recovered.

"To admit this, knowing that you are only alive because I will it, either you are crazy or very bold to take this risk."

"Because of the life you've forced on me, death is not as unwelcome as it used to be."

Zayyat stared at Malik uncertainly, as if he recognized him from some past experience. "It's foolish to try to understand the ways of the Almighty. He brought us together. Why is a mystery. I long for death, but not yet. There is much to do before I become careless and let someone like you surprise me with martyrdom. You don't have the hunger for this, killing and being killed. If you were one of us you would understand. You would have a meaning for your existence. Death would no longer frighten you. You become at peace. It is as if you have a different set of eyes. You see beyond. You see the centuries stretching out before you, and your own existence is a part of the inevitable glorious triumph of Islam. You become a hero to your people instead of the traitor you are. I give you this chance. Join with us. Palestine needs crazy people like you."

"I would never be what you want me to be."

Zayyat nodded as if he expected this. "We recognize two kinds of death. I am offering you the martyr's way, to fight in the righteous call of liberation. No doubt you will die in this cause. We all expect this at any moment. But you will go straight to Paradise. The other death is horrible. The instant you pass into the next world, the angel of death comes to rip your soul from your body. It is just the beginning of your torment. Perhaps this is why you were spared, so that you could return to the true religion."

Malik considered for a moment the offer Zayyat presented him with. All he had to do was to declare the Shahada: "I bear witness that there is no God but God and that Muhammad is the Messenger of God." He would be a Muslim again, although one owned by Hamas. If he said those words, he might escape. That had been his only intention when he was abducted.

Zayyat rose and came toward him, carrying the silver knife, which he wiped on a napkin. "As a brother Muslim, I give you this chance. You can save yourself from damnation if you accept my offer." He used the point of the blade to raise Malik's eyepatch. He studied the empty socket. "I wish I could see your soul in there. If I kill you now, you will instantly begin the suffering that never ends."

Malik's entire body clenched as the blade lightly scratched across his neck, but he refused to beg. "Do hypocrites go to Paradise?" Defiant words Malik supposed would be his last.

Zayyat shrugged. "I gave you a chance. Your life would be useful to us, but death would also serve our purpose." He looked at his companions, who stood ready to carry out the murder; then he walked away. "You're a very annoying person, Mr. Malik. Because Jamal is my cousin and he would be angry with me, we will send you home with your suitcase, your backpack, wallet, phone, is that everything?"

Malik nodded in answer to Zayyat's question, but then muttered, "I had a hat."

Zayyat looked at his accomplices with a grin. "Remember that joke?" he said, then turned to Malik. "A Jewish joke, I love them. A grandmother takes her little grandson to the beach. She dresses him in his swimsuit. She rubs the lotion on him. She puts a little hat on him. She lets him walk into the water. Then a huge wave comes and picks up the child and takes him far out to sea. The grandmother can't even see him. She cries out to God: 'Please, return him to me! Anything you want from me I will do. I will give away my jewels, I will work for peace, I will praise your name each day!' Immediately a big wave arrives and there is the baby, safe and sound, deposited at the feet of the grandmother. She looks up to heaven and says, 'He had a *hat*.'"

Zayyat's bodyguards laughed as he looked meaningfully at Malik. "You see, we recognize the humanity of our enemy. When we kill, we acknowledge the loss. The Quran tells us that to save one life is to save all of mankind. So it is when you take a life, all humanity is lost. We will answer for our sins. But we kill to save our people. We do what we have to do." Zayyat put the knife away. "We've treated you as a guest, but your time in our country has expired. I tried to kill you once, and you survived. I won't fail again."

The bodyguards took Malik by either arm and led him back to the panel truck. Before he was forced onto the floor, one of the men clubbed him in the kidney with the butt of his gun—a parting gesture. When the door of the truck slammed shut, Malik found his phone, which still had enough battery to bring up his navigation app. He set a pin in his location. To hell with Zayyat. He would not give him another chance to kill him.

36

The Letter

Hebron, Oct. 2, 2023

Malik fell into bed, exhausted and confused, his mind aboil with images and memories that flew by, unattached to any coherent line of thought. He was thrown back into the turbulent weeks in the hospital when it seemed the bomb had just exploded and particles of his identity were scattered into the universe. He shouldn't be alive. The angel of death should be ripping his soul from his body to begin the eternal torture. He plummeted into sleep only to awaken a few hours later drenched in sweat. He hadn't been like this since that first night back in New York after the bomb.

When he awakened the next morning, he looked through the messages on his phone. He kept a journal on the cloud that functioned as a memory aid, but when he opened it he found the last entry was in New York five weeks before. He wrote about the breakup with Lucy. He couldn't read it without weeping. His emotions were rioting. He longed for a pill that would put him to sleep until he could face the life he still had and be thankful for it.

He had voicemails from friends with nonurgent messages, but not many. Apparently he was not the kind of friend people checked on. Of the hundreds of emails, and dozens of texts, none merited a thoughtful response. Everyone has to deal with an onslaught of meaningless chatter, but it was demoralizing to realize there was so little reason to even look at the communications. He could easily cut his ties to the virtual world and cultivate a kind of benign ignorance. His faulty memory did that in any case.

Before he set his phone aside he noticed he had a message on Signal, the encrypted platform he sometimes used in the bureau. Perhaps one of his old buddies was concerned. That possibility made him hopeful; then he thought, *That's exactly the narcotic of social media: there's always the possibility that a message will arrive that will change your life, but you know in your heart it will never happen.*

This time it did.

The sender was Jacob Weingarten, sent exactly a week before, a little after noon, the very day they met.

Anthony, thanks for your trouble. I owe you an apology and an explanation. I had an urgent communication just before you arrived so I couldn't explain why I sought your assistance. Greenblatt said that you were involved in the bureau's terrorist financing unit. I have uncovered a ring of drug smugglers tied to Hamas. I have reason to believe that this group is officially protected, even by my own department. There's no one I can trust, including my top lieutenants. The corruption may extend into the government. I'm just a cop, I don't have the authority to arrest people at that level and I don't know enough about organized crime. I was hoping that Interpol or some outside investigative agency like the bureau would take an interest without my name being involved. I know how that sounds but I think my life is in danger and I don't know where else to turn.

Sorry to be so brief. Can we talk tomorrow? Something unexpected came up at the last minute.

That was it. No wonder Malik didn't remember the conversation: it had never occurred.

Malik read the letter again several times. His mind was clearer. He realized that, had his conversation with Weingarten happened, it would have been a lengthy one. Even before ISIS the world of terrorism relied on drug smuggling to finance its bloody campaigns. Before he was injured Malik had been tracing funds passing from Mexico's Sinaloa Cartel through Turkish middlemen. Hezbollah was dealing directly with the Taliban in Afghanistan, which not only was supplying heroin but now included coke and crystal meth. Syria was turning into a narco state, bigger than Mexico, while Mexican cartels returned the favor by entering the Middle East. Russian mobsters were everywhere. Smugglers traded drugs, weapons, gems, and humans. The Middle East was a carnival of crooks and terrorists and smugglers and cosmopolitan racketeers from all over the world—the dark matter of civilization, emboldened by the chaos and supported by tyrannies. If Weingarten had confided in him during that brief encounter Malik could have been helpful. In return, Weingarten might have pointed to elements in Hebron that were joining the parade. Somebody figured that out and killed him before he had the chance to talk.

None of it was Malik's business now. He was not authorized to pursue an investigation. He couldn't save Jamal if he was in the hands of Hamas. But Dina was in danger and he needed to help her before he left.

He had a favor to ask of Yossi Ben-Gal. He didn't know how much to tell him. Yossi had made it clear that he and Weingarten hadn't gotten along, and in his note the chief had written that he had no one to trust, "even in my own department." How deep did the antipathy between these men go? Deep enough to kill?

One of the first lessons Malik learned in the FBI was that no one is immune to the power of organized crime. It is a cancer that grows and adapts and metastasizes as money takes over and moral considerations crater. It can be found in any society or organization. The mob bosses persuade you with money and influence, and if those don't work, threats and murder will do the job. Entire countries are run by sham governments that are nothing more than fronts for drug lords. They are like termite-ridden houses that appear intact but if you tap on the wall your knuckles go right through the Sheetrock.

Every society has an underworld. Actions that don't make sense on the surface might be understood by entering the taboo zone, where disowned desires and prohibited behavior flourish. Crime was the door in. Cops live between these worlds. The opportunity to cross over is always there, so every day, every minute, you have to lean away from temptation. Those who have never surrendered were often recognizable to each other, but not always, and that was the mortal risk. He had to consider which side of the line Yossi Ben-Gal was on.

"IT'S ANNOYING TO admit this but you were right again," Yossi grumbled when they met in Weingarten's office.

"So you got the lab results."

Yossi nodded. "They were able to match the DNA with a swab we took after Jamal's last arrest. The results are conclusive. No date on the discharge, so we can't say it categorically establishes innocence."

"Does it change your mind about him?"

"Let's say it proves nothing but it complicates everything."

"Maybe the junkie clerk will talk."

"I doubt it," Yossi said. "But speaking of the clerk, you were right about something else too." He showed Malik the secret file that Weingarten had hidden in his home office. "I had to piece together bits of the intelligence the chief was assembling. He was working on a case nobody knew about, a drug ring operating here in Hebron. Heroin, fentanyl, the real killers. The chief believed the drugs were moving through the settlement communities in Ramallah, Jericho, Nablus, and especially here in Hebron."

"How much money involved?"

"Hundreds of millions of dollars. We've never seen that kind of money around here."

"Is there a reason he didn't share the information with you?"

"It's no secret he thought I was too close to the Rav and his movement."

"Are you?"

"Maybe I was."

Malik made a decision. He was going to trust Yossi—to a point.

He related the story of his abduction. He had let his guard down in the most unprofessional manner, which Yossi would immediately grasp. As Malik revealed the events of the night before, Yossi repeatedly shook his head, his dark eyes wide, the nostrils of his impressive nose flaring like an angry stallion's. "The sons of bitches operate like they own the place," he said. "You shouldn't be alive. Why would they let you go?"

Malik shrugged. "I have no idea. I really thought they intended to kill me. Zayyat promised they would if I stuck around."

"And you say they had the video camera already set up."

"A bit of theater, I suppose, to scare the shit out of me, which it did. I still haven't figured all this out."

"Maybe something you said changed his mind."

Malik avoided mentioning Zayyat's invitation to join Hamas because that would have explained everything. He knew that he would always be under suspicion because he was a Palestinian. His American citizenship did not balance his ethnic background in this region and never would.

"I think Zayyat wanted to send a message. He claimed they didn't kill Weingarten, even though they would be happy to take credit."

"Did you believe him?"

"On this, yes. Even more than killing the chief they would like to say Jamal was in Hamas. It would be easy to do if he were dead. But why tell me if that's their plan?"

Yossi shook his head. He had no answer.

"They gave me back my stuff," Malik said, taking his phone from his pocket. "And I found this letter. It's from Weingarten."

Yossi read the note on Signal, staring at it for a moment as the significance sank in. "The poor bastard was really alone. Didn't know where to turn. I wish he had told me." He glanced at Malik, then looked away. There must have been reasons Weingarten didn't confide in him.

"If Weingarten didn't trust his own department, why didn't he go to Shabak?" Malik asked.

"I imagine Weingarten believed he couldn't afford to expose what he knew. That much money can create a lot of corruption no matter who's involved. Too dangerous."

"Maybe he wanted in on it," Malik said.

"Then why wouldn't they just cut him in? A little slice for the chief of police seems like an excellent investment."

"Or they're greedy and didn't want to pay him off."

"Or they had the police covered already," Yossi said. "Little to be gained by adding the chief. Not worth the gamble."

"Suppose that's true, do you have any suspects in your mind?"

"Nothing solid. If the drug ring that Weingarten was investigating was in Kiryat Arba, we've got two officers who live there—Aharon Berger and Golda Radidowicz. Of course, Weingarten lived there as well. I haven't seen any evidence of sudden wealth."

"If the operation is carefully run, they would find a way to wash their fingerprints and make it appear like an honest business."

"We don't have any new enterprises in Palestine, everything in this country is two thousand years old."

Malik picked up the file that Yossi had taken from Weingarten's home. He couldn't read the Hebrew but he saw the sketches Weingarten made to follow the drug traffic and what looked like a flowchart of financial transactions. "Do you think he was close to making an arrest?"

"He would be all by himself. Scared. He had dangerous knowledge, the kind that can get you killed. It was too big for him. He didn't know where to turn."

Malik touched the scar on his forehead, as he sometimes did when he was struggling to tease apart a mental knot. "Let's suppose that this hypothetical drug gang killed him. What's the point of beheading him, making a video, all that?"

"In the territories, we say there are two different categories of crime. There's ordinary crime, which if you talk to Jews in Hebron we have none of. It's all the other kind of crime—terrorism. Anything that involves Arabs—terrorism. The law doesn't really count if you cross that line. You just round up people and lock them in detention. You don't bother to charge them, but if you do, you'll get a conviction 99 percent of the time. If the bad guys make it look like terror they can expect there's no real investigation. Automatically everyone will be looking at Arabs."

"So you think that settlers could be behind this?"

"I don't know what to think. Or maybe I'm afraid to think what I think I think." Yossi laughed. "This is a fucking mess." He looked at Malik. "When are you leaving?"

"Tonight. I already missed one flight."

"Don't go."

Malik looked at Yossi, who was staring out the window, as if he couldn't face what he was asking. "You're a better investigator than me and I don't know anyone else I can trust." Yossi glanced directly at Malik, then quickly turned away. "I know I'm asking too much. You could be in more danger than me. But right now I'm in the same spot as Weingarten, and look what happened to him."

"I'll make you a deal," said Malik. "I'll work with you if you protect Dina. Everybody wants to kill her, the settlers, Hamas, maybe even Jamal, all because she helped your chief. He made her an informer and now her life is in real danger."

"Is she willing to accept my help?"

"She's hardheaded, I don't know."

"Are you sure you want to do this?" Yossi asked.

"No, but I do have a score to settle. Meantime, I know someone who might be able to help."

YASMINE WAS SURPRISED and frightened when Malik knocked on the door and she saw Yossi standing beside him. The police were never good news in this part of town, and that included the Palestinian force as well.

"He can be trusted," Malik assured her.

Yasmine bowed wordlessly.

"We need to talk to Dina, but first we'd like to see Omar," Malik said.

Yasmine looked stricken. "He's not involved in anything, I swear! Can't you just leave him alone?"

"He's not in trouble, we are," said Malik.

This made no sense to Yasmine, but she led them to Omar's room. Lebanese hip-hop blared. The boy hid his surprise with that air of teenage diffidence he had perfected. His room was overrun with computers and parts. Omar had a flush of acne and a pimple with a spot of blood on his nose from being recently popped.

"You have so much equipment and computer things," Yossi said as they entered. He was never comfortable around technology, well aware that he was being supplanted by younger detectives who were native to the tech world. And Palestinian teenage boys in general were problematic.

"My dad gives me stuff from the computer shop," Omar explained. "Broken stuff. I can fix anything."

"I told Detective Ben-Gal about your hacking skills," Malik said. "We need your help."

Omar nodded. It wasn't surprising to him that fully grown men had no idea how to hack into a computer, but in his mind it diminished their standing as trained investigators.

"Is it against the law?" Omar asked.

"We can make an exception in your case," said Yossi.

"I have to warn you that this could get you in trouble," Malik interjected. "But it might help us protect Dina."

"What can I do?"

"To start with, can you find out who posted that picture of Dina and the chief on Arba Arbaeen?" Malik asked.

"I already did that," said Omar. "It was easy. A cop. Named Aharon Berger."

"No, he's the one who found it," Yossi said dismissively.

"He also posted it, so I guess it wouldn't be hard for him to find it."

Yossi started to say something but words didn't come out of his mouth.

"That's very important information, Omar," Malik said. "There's something else I'd like you to look into. You know that temple the Rav is planning to build on your grandfather's land? See if you can find out where the money is coming from, and how much. Is there a pattern of deposits and withdrawals? Just about anything you can find would be helpful. In the US this would all be in the public record but I'm guessing they may be hiding something. It's just a hunch. But it won't hurt to dig around a little and see what you find. Sound okay?"

DINA WAS MODESTLY DRESSED, with a floral hijab, looking like any young Palestinian woman, although prettier than most. Normally, she did not attract so much attention, but when she ventured into the street earlier that morning she registered the stares aimed at her like rifle shots. Everyone must have seen the photo online of her with Weingarten. Perhaps some looked on with sympathy for the public tragedy that had fallen on her like a stone from the sky, but the words she heard in her head were "There goes the traitor, there goes the whore."

Malik explained what was happening. Dina didn't protest. He told her to pack a bag with a few essentials, so she knew she was in for a stay. They took the car to the police station. Yossi escorted her to Golda at the desk. Dina moved as if she were twenty meters underwater with weights on her ankles. "This woman is turning herself in," Yossi said.

"What's the crime?" Golda asked.

"Vagrancy."

Golda looked at each of them for a clue. None was coming, but Dina was scared and disoriented. She looked down, afraid to confront the authority that could easily lock her away for years without notice or charges. Sensing the young woman's fear, Golda put a comforting hand on hers. "We'll take care of you, don't worry," she whispered. Then she ordered a sergeant to fix up the storage room with a cot and chair. "Make it comfortable."

Yossi motioned to Malik. "Time to go to work."

37

The Way of the World

West Bank, Oct. 2, 2023

Sure you're up for confronting this guy?" Malik asked, as Yossi parked in front of a fortresslike building on a hilltop campus with an encompassing view of Sheikh Abdullah's vineyards. During the Ottoman era it had served as a military school, and there were remnants of the old parade ground and a decrepit barracks that was slowly collapsing. A pair of nineteenth-century cannons sat in front of the gate near an empty flagpole. The land the Rav was attempting to seize would be a natural extension of his holdings. If he were able to take Sheikh Abdullah's entire property with its vineyards and olive grove, he would have most of the valley under his control.

"Let's just see what he has to say," Yossi said. "It'll give him something to think about. I need to look in his eyes."

Armed guards stood sentry. One of them was Itai. As soon as he saw the police cruiser coming through the gate he raised his weapon. Another guard approached Yossi. "What are you doing here?" he asked.

"Police business," Yossi said gruffly.

The guard went into the fortress and in a moment an officious little man, dressed in a worn black suit—the leader's secretary— marched to the police cruiser in deliberate, mincing steps, like an artifact of the Ottoman army. "Call for an appointment," he said as if he were speaking to a door-to-door vendor rather than an officer of the law. He handed Yossi a business card, then pirouetted and pranced back to the fortress. Yossi made no attempt to leave. He had a newspaper on the dashboard, which he opened and appeared to read with great interest.

"So we wait them out?" Malik concluded.

"It won't take long." Yossi calmly turned a page of the paper. Malik put in his earbuds and listened to Springsteen. He had really missed his phone.

The secretary opened the door and waved the back of his hand to shoo them away. "Go!" he cried. "Call for an appointment!"

The secretary scurried back inside. Yossi raised his window and turned on the flashers and the siren. The noise reverberated against the stone walls of the fortress creating an awful din, but inside the cruiser with its stone-proof windows the noise was curiously dim. Malik hadn't even finished the live version of "My Hometown" before the secretary returned and said that Immanuel Cohen had graciously agreed to meet.

The building was old and ill kept. Malik supposed the place hadn't been painted in a century. The secretary led them around a corner into a yellowed hallway, marked by water stains and woodwork cracked and blackened by time. Photographs of white-bearded old men lined the walls. Rabbinical students were loudly reciting prayers and shuckling in one of the classrooms. The secretary opened a massive carved door into a library of dusty volumes. Motes floated in the narrow streams of sunlight slanting through the window blinds. "Wait here," the secretary said, summoning his wounded self-regard.

Yossi had a sneezing fit almost instantly. "The books," he said between sneezes, waving at the shelves filled with ancient tomes, their spines cracked. No doubt the pages were yellow and brittle and infested with mites.

Spanning the length of a library table was an architect's model of a gigantic temple in the classical style. The building it represented appeared larger than the Vatican, its vast courtyard filled with fountains and palms, a grandeur that seemed out of place in this humble farmland. "I wouldn't have thought there were enough Jews in the whole West Bank to fill this place," Malik mused.

"There will be." Cohen entered the room. His resonant voice was tinged with a faint Brooklyn accent but distinctive in the way that people who are cloistered in their own communities often sound when talking to outsiders; that is, with precision and caution reflecting a deep suspiciousness. "We are preparing for the day when the Jews of the world return to the Holy Land. On that day, this temple will be full—more than full!" With this, he leaned over to kiss the balsawood model.

"Thank you, Rav, for seeing us," Yossi said. Malik noted the respect in his voice, a tone he had never heard from Yossi.

"My Yossi," Cohen said, grasping both shoulders and gently shaking him, "you always bring trouble."

"It's the way of the world."

"We think of you often, especially since the loss of our beloved Leah. We pray for you."

Yossi made a slight bow of acknowledgment. Malik detected an emotional tie between these men that was unnervingly deep.

Cohen was wizened but still clear-eyed and vital, his face full of conviction. Malik could see why people elevated him into a semidivine status; although physically, except for his massive beard, he was not imposing, being slight and short. His deep, melodious voice broadcasted authority. His eyes did not belong in an old man's head; they were not rheumy or weak, they were hawkish, predatory, restless, missing nothing.

Cohen removed the dome of the model, revealing the sanctuary inside and a room with a golden throne. The entity that would occupy this seat would look upon thousands of subjects, the Rav explained; his voice would carry over the walls, beckoning to untold numbers of followers, stretching on and on, until they fulfilled the biblical commandment for the gathering of Jews in the Holy Land. "By purifying this sacred land, we are inviting the *Mashiach*"—the Messiah—"to return and rule over the End of Days. And it will be here!" Cohen pointed past the dusty windowpanes toward Sheikh Abdullah's groves. "Once again Hebron will be the repository of glory, the very place where humanity began with Adam and Eve, where the Jews began with Abraham and Sarah. In the next stage of human life, the *Mashiach* will spread blessings all over the world."

"Why that particular spot?" Malik asked. "Aren't there other places that would be suitable?"

The Rav smiled but his expression was wary. "This is not an arbitrary decision. The land was chosen because of its association with one of our prophets."

"Which prophet?"

"You wouldn't know him. We venerate our forebearers. They are what makes this land holy."

"Is holiness something you can just declare—this plot of land but not another?" Malik asked.

Cohen stared at Yossi. "Did you bring him here for a theological discussion?"

"He's related to Sheikh Abdullah," Yossi explained.

Cohen tilted his head as if to see Malik from a new perspective. "You have influence over this stubborn old man?"

"I wouldn't say so. The land has been in his family for many generations."

"We have made him a fair offer."

"And if he doesn't want to sell?"

Cohen shrugged. "This is his choice. We try to persuade him."

"Yes, I saw what your people did, destroying his trees, ruining his livelihood. I don't see holiness in your dealings with Palestinians. It looks more like ethnic cleansing."

Cohen shook his head sadly as if he were bearing the weight of a great injustice. "You call them 'Palestinians' as if they were a real people," he said. "Historically, they are not."

"What part of me is not real to you?" Malik demanded. "I am as much a Palestinian as you are a Jew. Our peoples come from the same roots. It doesn't mean the land belongs more to your people than it does to mine."

Cohen's hawkish eyes examined Malik as if he were a pigeon he could finish off for a snack. "Our progenitor, Abraham, bought the cave of Hebron from Ephron the Hittite for four hundred silver shekels, a fortune at the time. It is in the Bible, in Genesis. Proof!

Documented proof! Now we have also offered the sheikh the great kindness of paying him for the property. I do not say 'his' property because it has been stolen from the Jews. All of Israel is God-given Jewish property. We only offer money out of kindness."

The secretary entered again, holding the door for Benny, who was carrying a silver tray with glasses and a pitcher of lemonade. He glanced at Yossi and Malik with an expression that revealed nothing. He poured a glass for his grandfather, who gazed at him adoringly. "Bless you, child," Cohen said. He prayed and took a sip as Benny poured glasses for the visitors.

"The reason we came is that we're investigating Chief Weingarten's murder," Yossi managed to say before he was overcome by another series of sneezes.

"You question me?" Cohen said. "But you know already the killer."

"Why are you so sure of his guilt?"

Cohen looked to Benny, who was kneeling beside his chair, holding his hand. "Remember, Grandfather, the head was in the freezer at that man's work," Benny prompted. "He had the key. What more evidence would you need?"

Yossi gave Benny a long, searching look, as if something had just occurred to him, but he let it go and turned his attention to Cohen. "We've had a sharp rise of drug overdoses in Judea and Samaria. Some of these drugs we've never seen before in the region."

"Terrible, terrible, so much suffering because of these things."

"Do you have any knowledge of drug use in your community?"

"In our community? It doesn't exist. Our faith forbids it."

Yossi pulled out a map with handwritten notations on it. "I found this in one of the chief's files. The deaths follow a pattern. They occur wherever there are outposts of your community."

The Rav studied the map for some time. When he finally looked up, his expression was worried. He cast a sharp glance at his secretary and Benny, then asked Yossi. "Does this have anything to do with the death of the chief?"

"The chief was looking into it personally," Yossi said. "He wanted to know how this is happening and who is responsible."

"We also want to know this," said Cohen. "Our people have nothing to do with drugs."

Malik listened with mounting frustration to Cohen's blithe assertions. "That's an impressive building you're planning," Malik said, as he examined the balsa-wood model. "I was wondering where the money comes from."

Benny stood and looked at Yossi. "Why do you bring this goy here?" he asked in a voice that was low but meant to be overheard.

"He is an American agent, FBI. He has experience in these things."

"He is an uninvited intruder in our community and yet you bring him here," Benny said, his voice rising, "to make accusations against our beloved leader."

"We're not accusing anyone," Yossi said in English, "but wherever this investigation leads, we have to follow."

"Such words have a bitter history behind them," Cohen observed.

"It's a simple question," Malik repeated. "Who's funding this project?"

"We have supporters all over the world."

"How many of them deal in narcotics?"

"I believe we are finished here," said Cohen. His face was flushed and he gave his hand to Benny. "It's time for my nap."

Benny helped his grandfather to his feet and led him out of the room. "God should have pity on such as these," Cohen muttered as he walked by.

"I guess we'll see ourselves out," Malik said.

WHEN THEY WERE back in the cruiser, Malik asked, "Who is Leah?"

"My wife. She died several years ago."

"Did she have something to do with Cohen?"

"In her illness, she turned to his teachings," Yossi said. "I believe they gave her some consolation. Even now, I'm grateful to him."

Malik absorbed this, wondering how much Yossi's grief for his dead wife might have affected his investigation. "So you looked in his eyes. What did you see?"

"I saw a man who might do anything for his dream." Yossi was quiet for a moment, then said, "Benny knew about Jamal having the key. We kept that confidential. No one outside the department was supposed to know."

"So Weingarten was right. There's a leak inside your office."

"There is something I have to do on my own," Yossi said. "I'll drop you at your hotel. Keep out of sight until you hear from me. If Zayyat learns you're still here, he'll act. You can count on that."

38

The Ghost of Ahmed Yassin

The Old City of Hebron, 2004

Jamal Khalil and Ehsan Zayyat grew up together in the Old City. As boys they played endless games of hide-and-go-seek, learning the passageways and secret spots, of which there were many until the IDF sealed off the ancient mews and alleys. But the Israelis didn't find everything. Some places were known only to those who grew up there.

Settlements were present in those days but the Arab shops were still open. After school, the boys entertained themselves by throwing stones at an IDF barricade. Journalists came to film them although the barricade was on the other side of a house and well out of reach of the stones. When the older boys used slings, soldiers immediately confiscated them. Settler kids also threw stones at the Palestinian kids, but the bored soldiers did nothing to stop them. It was all theater.

When Jamal was twelve it stopped being a game. His older brother, Nader, got hold of a Kalashnikov, a very expensive piece of contraband in the territories, evidence that Nader had formally affiliated with Hamas. By itself, that wasn't unexpected; the Arab population in Hebron was full of Hamas sympathizers. It was the gun that signaled Nader's commitment went beyond politics. He was undertaking a suicide mission.

Jamal would always wonder what had driven his older brother to destroy himself and other lives. Nader was not rebellious. He didn't nurse his rage like so many young people confronting the hopelessness of their existence. He seemed uninterested in politics—or was that a pose? He was about to graduate from high school and intended to study computer science at Birzeit University. He talked about the future in a way that implied he was going to be a part of it, his own hands would shape his destiny.

Something shifted inside him. There wasn't a moment of trauma that suddenly made him vengeful, or any more so than most Palestinian teens. This was a young man everyone believed had designed a path through his life ahead. His confidence created hope in others close to him. If Nader could find a way to succeed, perhaps they could as well.

Not like Jamal, who gave his parents more cause to worry. Jamal was prideful and inclined to argue, dangerous qualities in an occupied land. Even Nader tried to moderate Jamal's temper, teasing him that he was going to lead the revolution—watch out, world. While Nader humored Jamal, he also mentored him, dampening his rage, guiding him through the taunts and daily humiliation of the occupation.

And then one day Nader climbed up to the flat rooftops of the Old City. Most of the houses were connected, so he could walk above the town, jumping over places where there was a slight separation between the buildings or a variance in the height. Residents did this all the time; it was a way of evading the checkpoints, although soldiers frequently patrolled the area as well. Carrying his weapon under a winter coat, Nader skipped across the rooftops until he came to a spot with a clear view of Beit Hadassah, one of several Jewish settlements in the Old City.

Beit Hadassah had a history. It was built as a charitable medical center for Jews and Arabs in 1893, but after the massacre of 1929 most of the Jews fled the city. Fifty years later, ten Jewish women, along with forty children, took over the building, refusing to be evacuated. At first the Israeli government quarantined Beit Hadassah, regarding it as an illegal settlement, but the women were persistent, and a year later the government changed its policy. In May 1980, a group of rabbinical students came to Beit Hadassah following Friday services at the Cave of the Patriarchs. As the men were dancing in the street to celebrate, a grenade landed in the middle of the circle and automatic weapons opened fire. Six Jews were killed and more than twenty injured. The perpetrators were members of Fatah. (One of them, Tayseer Abu Sneineh, would later be elected mayor of Hebron.)

Jamal knew about that event—everyone did—although it didn't rank as a historical massacre, just another murder in a place where blood flowed easily. It must have meant something to Nader because he chose the same spot for his attack. He lay down behind the stone façade and slipped the barrel of his rifle through a gutter spout. He was not an expert shot but with a Kalashnikov there was little need to aim. He pulled the trigger and eliminated a Haredi family—husband, wife, and ten-month-old infant in a stroller. He shot up the front of Beit Hadassah without injuring anyone else before the Israeli army managed to kill him. His body was never returned to the family.

Jamal's parents were stoic, at least on the outside. Representatives from the Palestinian Authority came and gave them an award and a monthly stipend. Jamal's tuition was covered. Although friends congratulated them on Nader's martyrdom, they all knew other emotions were being suppressed: they only had to imagine what it would be like if their own son's picture appeared on billboards and in the hallways of the school and on the walls of a coffee shop with martyr pictures surrounding the tables like glamour shots of movie stars. It was a pretend world where the cause mattered more than the life, and the mourners consented to it because the pointlessness of the sacrifice was too great to bear.

Consequences followed, both official and not. A group of Kahanists calling themselves Tears of the Widows and Orphans began shooting at Palestinian cars, in one case killing a three-month-old baby, which they celebrated. They also plotted to blow up a girls' school with the goal of provoking a third intifada. Elements of both sides longed for a war to the finish.

Usually the army destroys the homes of Arab terrorists to punish the family for failing to prevent the action. Because the Khalil home was in the Old City, a World Heritage Site, there would be an international outcry if the house was torn down. Instead, the family was expelled, the doors and windows barred and welded shut, and it sat vacant for more than twenty years.

But it wasn't wholly unoccupied. Two years after Nader's death, Jamal was working at an auto-body shop owned by Ehsan Zayyat's father. Mainly, the shop cut up stolen cars and sold the parts. Taking a car apart required removing spot welds, just like the ones that shuttered the Khalil family home. It wasn't hard. It could be done almost instantly with a plasma torch, or with a little more effort by a simple electric drill with cobalt steel bits. One afternoon after work Jamal stuck a battery-powered DeWalt drill in a trash-filled sack and walked to the house his family was renting in Tel Rumeida. That night he snuck out and met Zayyat in the Old City. No one else was about and the few guards were easy to evade. Slipping through the shadows, the boys reached the corner of the old neighborhood where Jamal was born and turned down the dead-end street that led to the house. A small alleyway ran along the east side of the house, with a low concrete wall separating it from the neighbor. The boys waited in the deep darkness. It was too quiet yet to attempt a break-in. When the sky began to lighten and the muezzin sang his call to prayer, Zayyat helped Jamal mount the wall.

The boys were giddy with excitement and fear. They were both fourteen, too young to fully grasp the consequences if they got caught. Because of Nader's action, Jamal's family would be severely persecuted and he would be pinned as a terrorist and locked up for years. The boys knew this, but they thrilled to the act of defiance, as if this would make a difference in the occupation, while also knowing that nothing they did or would ever do would change a thing.

The bars, rough with rust, formed a cagelike grid over the windows. One of the east-facing windows had only two welds, which Jamal drilled, but when he lifted the bars the window itself was locked. Jamal took a penknife and ran it between the sashes to open the lock in the center, but it was stuck and more trouble than the weld. He wished he were stronger. Zayyat couldn't open it either. Nader would have been able to.

Jamal moved to another window. Morning prayers had awakened the Old City; roosters crowed, shops were beginning to load their stock for the day, so the drill only added to the morning cacophony. This one had four welds, and Jamal had to set a cement block on the wall to reach the top ones. When he lifted the bars, he found that the window wasn't locked at all.

He pulled himself through the narrow opening and landed on the rug in what had once been the dining room. Zayyat tumbled in after him. They spent an hour wandering from room to room as Jamal told the story of his family's life there. He was in a strange numinous state, experiencing a sense of loss and revelation, despite the flat tone of his narration.

Jamal's family had been forced to leave so quickly they hadn't had a chance to say goodbye to the life and the objects that attended their existence. In his memory it had been a rather luxurious home, but now he saw that the house and its furnishings were quite humble. The furniture was in place; there was even food in the pantry, although it had fed many generations of rodents. The boys could hear them scratching behind the walls. On the ground floor was the diwan, the open space with low-slung couches pressed against the walls where Jamal's parents entertained, although they did so rarely. The middle of the house was the living area, with the kitchen and dining space and a living room. The old black-and-white television was still there, an antique even at the time, with its rabbit-ears antenna adorned with tiny flags of aluminum foil to aid reception. The bedrooms were upstairs, one for the parents, one for the little sister, Nihaya, and the third one for the boys.

Nader's bed was made like a soldier's, still neat, the corners crisply folded, and except for the dust it was just as it had been the morning he took his Kalashnikov from under the bed and went to murder Jews and destroy his family's future. There was a Quran on the bedside table between the beds, but it was Nader who read it. Jamal's bed was unmade, reflecting the fact that he was still sleeping when the army arrived. The family was evicted at once, without proclamation or ceremony, just thrown into the street with practically nothing. Jamal's old bureau was in his room, filled with childhood clothes. On his wall was a poster of Arnold Schwarzenegger as Conan the Barbarian.

That youthful excursion with Zayyat changed Jamal's life. In the cobwebbed rooms he saw the ghosts of a life that might have been. He wondered what Nader was thinking when he destroyed their alternative existence by his suicidal action. What made killing a few Jews more important than the security of his own family? Jamal examined the artifacts of the life they had left behind: his mother's cookware, his father's suits, the board games he played as a child—their normal life buried in this house that had been home to three generations of Khalils and who knows how many other families over the centuries, now a nest for rodents and spiders.

Zayyat was light-skinned and his freckles were more prominent back then, marking him as exotic. It annoyed Jamal that Zayyat admired Nader and praised his martyrdom. His family had endured no such sacrifice—his father made a decent living, they had Jordanian passports, so they could travel. Zayyat could have done well; he was a scholarly type with excellent grades. His intelligence lured him into political ideology, an intellectual pathway that drew him into abstractions and further and further from moral scruples. He had not yet become a killer but he gave himself over to hatred with the same intensity most teenage boys apply to love.

Like Nader, Zayyat idolized Sheikh Ahmed Yassin, the quadriplegic schoolteacher who founded Hamas and served as its spiritual leader. He was an oddly compelling figure, like a dead body with a living head. Although he couldn't move his limbs and could only drink liquids with assistance, he was the galvanizing force behind the Second Intifada. Yassin always dressed in a white robe, like a shroud, reinforcing the aura of death. His incapacity and rage precisely embodied the Palestinian predicament, although he smiled frequently and seemed encased in joy. When he spoke, he had the high voice of a child, but his words were full of thunder. "What was taken by force can only be restored by force," he declared. That became the motto of Hamas. He vehemently defended suicide bombings, which he personally authorized. "Without blood we can achieve nothing," he said. Such language intoxicated young men like Zayyat while also justifying the remorseless Israeli response.

Jamal and Zayyat drew opposing lessons from Yassin. Zayyat responded to him more as a religious figure than as a political one. "Martyrdom or victory" was the slogan that Zayyat clung to. Jamal looked past the rhetoric and studied the nuances in the sheikh's positions. Yassin claimed that he loved Jews, as he did all people, and that the conflict was entirely over land. He repeatedly offered truces that would be based on the borders before the 1967 Six-Day War and the Israeli conquest of the West Bank. The Israelis imprisoned him several times, once for murdering Palestinian collaborators. They would kill him with a missile in 2004 as he was being wheeled home following dawn prayers.

The night when the boys slipped through Israeli security to enter Jamal's abandoned house, Zayyat disclosed that he was also going to be a martyr. "I intend to offer myself to the sheikh," he said. "Allah willing, he will accept my sacrifice." He planned to do this on his fifteenth birthday. It seemed so far away.

"Don't you want to have a life?" Jamal asked. "Allah gave you this existence, isn't it a sin to throw it away?"

"I am not throwing away my life, I am using it for the good of our people!" Zayyat replied, his face reddened with indignation. "You think only of living for yourself, but dying for others, this is the greatest gift we can give."

"And what did Nader achieve for his people? Here we sit in what was once my home. My family lives like beggars, taking handouts from corrupt politicians. Did anything change because of his death? Nothing, except the punishment of our family."

"He killed Jews."

"Yes, a family of three. Were they responsible for being Jews? They were born into their tribe, as we have been into ours. Tell me how Nader's action made any difference in the life of Palestinians."

This was a question Zayyat couldn't answer at the age of fourteen. (Later, he would become a brilliant debater, able to frame arguments in a way that justified unimaginable violence.) Jamal was just beginning to acquire the ambition and self-knowledge that, together with his obstinance, would make him the singular figure he became. If he had said at the time that he was going to devote his life to peace, Zayyat would have considered him a traitor. Of course, Zayyat never fulfilled his pledge to become a martyr. Instead, he led many others to the fate he said he adored.

When the boys were done congratulating themselves for their daring, they slipped out the window, carefully replacing the steel bars. Jamal figured that no one would notice the broken welds, and if they did, what would it matter? When they got home, they told their parents they had gone to pray.

39

Same Old Story

Hebron, Oct. 2, 2023

Yossi pulled into the police lot in a spray of gravel. "Berger in my office, now!" he said to Golda as he entered.

Aharon Berger appeared with a fixed grin on his face. "Hey, Yossi, what's going on?"

"Give me your phone."

"What?"

"May I take a look at your fucking phone."

Berger hesitated, then handed it to him. Yossi held the phone in front of Berger's face, unlocking it. He scrolled to recent calls, then looked at his watch. "Last call from Benny Eleazar three minutes after we left the Rav's compound. Your buddy didn't waste any time. He warned you, didn't he?"

"What?"

"That I would guess you told him about the key to the freezer locker."

Golda and Avi followed the commotion and stood at the door. "Is it okay?" Golda asked. "Should I close the door?"

"No, you should hear this," said Yossi. "How your colleague betrayed us."

"So? We talk, Benny and I," Berger said defiantly. "He thinks you've lost it. I'm doing us both a favor."

"You talk all the time," said Yossi, still scrolling through the calls. "More than once a day."

"We're friends, so what?"

"You say 'friends.' Maybe also collaborators. How much did he pay you?"

"Don't be absurd. Benny's just a kid. He's got a lot to learn. I give him advice on stuff. The kid has a huge responsibility."

"You seem to know all about him, so tell me where his parents are."

Berger relaxed. The interrogation had wandered into neutral territory as far as he was concerned. "You know, it's a sad story, Yossi. Benny's mother broke with her father, many years ago, before the Rav came here."

"Yes, the chief had something about that in his files."

Berger gave him a quizzical look. "Files?"

"We all thought the chief wasn't much of a detective, right? We didn't give him enough credit. The file on Cohen is a revelation. Did Benny talk about the sex abuse?"

Berger shook his head.

"Same old story, you hear it all the time. Holy man with dirty hands, in this case raping his daughter."

"Yossi, you shouldn't say things about the Rav that you don't know."

"Here's what Weingarten knew." Yossi handed Berger a file labeled JSW-104. "You'll see the restraining order filed nineteen years ago. The upstanding Immanuel Cohen came to Hebron in order to leave his reputation behind."

Yossi noticed Berger studying the court order. "You're doing the math, aren't you? Maybe he's not just Benny's grandfather."

"We don't know any of that, Yossi. And if it's true, why would Benny even be here?"

"See the death certificate? His mother died of an overdose when he was five. No evidence of a father, so Cohen claimed him."

Berger held out his hand for his phone but Yossi wasn't done with it. "Just as I thought," he said as he scanned the photo app. "You didn't find that picture of Dina and the chief on Arba Arbaeen because of some coincidence. You took it yourself." He held up the phone so that Golda and Avi could see. "You followed them to Jerusalem the morning he was killed."

"Nonsense. You're just busting my balls."

"Shabak traced the post to your computer," Yossi said, taking a blind stab.

"Tamar would never have told—" Berger suddenly realized what he had said.

"You spy for her too? What did Tamar promise you? My job?"

"Fuck you," said Berger, reaching for his phone.

Yossi held it tight. "Fuck yourself. It's evidence of obstruction of justice."

"You must be kidding. You have nothing on me. Just a conversation with a friend."

"Weingarten was onto you. He discovered that Cohen's people were running drugs and using the temple fund to wash the money. But somebody knew that Weingarten knew. It cost him his life."

"This is insane."

"The only way to stop Weingarten was to kill him. That call you made to the chief the day he died, was it to lure him into a trap? Did you pull the trigger?"

Berger's eyes were in slits and a smirk ran across his lips. "You've got nothing, Yossi. So what are you going to do? Put me under arrest for making a phone call?"

"That's exactly what I'm going to do. We can't conduct an investigation when our own officers are communicating with the suspects." He looked at Golda and Avi. "Obstructing justice! Lock him up!"

40

Sympathy

Hebron, Oct. 3, 2023

Dina slept well, knowing that she was safe, although she was disgraced, her wedding abandoned, her future blackened by scandal that she would never escape. Sleep was her respite from hopelessness, a nest that cradled her in the branches high above the forest floor, but as soon as she opened her eyes the nest disintegrated and she plummeted helplessly into the thorny truth of her life.

Remorse and feelings of worthlessness had accompanied her since her fateful arrangement with Weingarten. Her only hope had been that marriage to Jamal would rescue her from the scorn that condemned her. She had allowed herself to imagine that they would live a quiet and meaningful family life, prosperous and respectable. Jamal would protect her, that was her dream, although the occupation would always distort their existence.

She hadn't spoken to her family since she moved into the jail. She worried that Omar was thinking it was his fault that she was in this predicament. He was the one who had become addicted to painkillers, the one who would have become a suicide bomber if Dina hadn't struck a deal with the Israeli police chief. She didn't blame Omar, but she knew he would be blaming himself.

She was shaken out of these thoughts by the sound of a knock on the door to the storage room. She sat up and quickly put on her hijab. Golda brought her breakfast.

"I'm sure you're hungry, you didn't have any dinner last night,"

Golda said. She sat a tray on the desk. There was pita and yogurt and Egyptian beans, along with a cup of muddy Turkish coffee, which filled the room with its heady aroma of cardamom. Dina realized she was ravenous.

"Do you mind if I sit with you for a moment?" Golda pulled up one of the discarded office chairs in the storage room. "You're in a terrible mess, pardon me for saying so," she said. "I feel bad because I know our chief was using you to get information and that put you in a compromised situation. That could be what got him killed, but you're also having to suffer."

The last thing Dina expected was sympathy, especially from a cop she knew lived in a settlement.

"It has to be hard, all this happening around your wedding day," Golda continued. "What a sad time for everyone. You shouldn't let me distract you from eating. Speaking of eating, I wonder what they did with all that food!"

Dina muttered a thanks to Allah and took a bite of the pita. "You say it's sad even though you believe that Jamal killed your chief?"

"It hasn't been proved, so I keep an open mind. It didn't help his case that he fled."

"What good would it have done if he stayed? There would be no justice for him, even you must admit this."

Golda paused. "We are not a fair people," she said. "This is a burden on our conscience. We have learned to protect ourselves from you but we don't know how to protect ourselves from us."

"Why are you being kind to me?" Dina asked.

"I'm not kind, I'm curious," said Golda. "You seem so innocent, but you're also complicated in an interesting way. I understand what the chief saw in you. He was a bit forward in the female department. I wouldn't put it past him to take advantage of you. If that happened, I'm really sorry."

"What can we do?" Dina said bitterly. "We have no power as Palestinians, especially as women. Our men are bent with hatred, like yours, but at least you have the power to protect your reputation. Maybe you don't understand how much that means in our society. Without respect, you are alone, cast out, there is no one who will befriend you, no one to marry. I know such women. They either leave or live in disgrace, always sinking deeper in condemnation. This is what I think of as hell. And now this is my life."

Golda was moved by the utter wretchedness of Dina's situation. She wasn't even a proper prisoner, more like a bird in a cage. "How did it come to this, that we would be enemies?" Golda said. "I mean, of course I know. I have killed four Palestinians, me, just one Israeli. It was my job. One of them was a child, a tall twelve-year-old girl who crossed the unmarked boundary in Gaza where I was authorized to shoot. And so I shot. Those were the orders. I learned her name but I never say it aloud, it fills me with shame. The rabbis told us that this was a sacred action and we shouldn't hesitate to kill. And I never hesitated, never. I got medals for this."

Dina looked at her. She wondered how two women living in the same city could be so different—she, the traditional Muslim girl, modest, compromised, endangered—and Golda with the blue hair and diamond in her nose, a weird hybrid, free to take what she wanted from her culture and from Dina's culture as well, just as she had picked up the pita and beans from the Arab market this morning. Perhaps Golda was victimized by the occupation as well, made to be someone she detested being.

"I have to say this," Golda said. "We can make your life easier. There are ways of protecting you, of putting you in a safer place, even in another country. You can receive monthly payments. It's not a fortune, but it's not nothing. You can live on it, and if you have a regular job, you can live well. I know what you're thinking," she said as Dina turned away, "and I hate to be so crass, but you and I know that from now on your existence in this place is risky. You understand what I'm saying? If you help us find Jamal we can help you."

Dina set the bread back on the tray. "I'm not hungry," she replied.

41

"As for Motive"

Jerusalem, Oct. 3, 2023

Haven't I told you to back off?" Tamar said when Yossi entered her office late at night. He had come as soon as she summoned him, despite the hour and a powerful rainstorm. "And what does this mean?" She waved a copy of Jamal's lab results. "Am I supposed to be impressed by your police work? We don't know when this sample was created. Okay, maybe Jamal and his girlfriend have fucked, big deal, but in no way does this tell us he's innocent."

"It's information, Tamar, a bit of evidence to consider. By itself, you're right, it doesn't tell a new story, but it could be a lead. Maybe there is more to this case than we know."

"Maybe that Arab detective planted it."

"He's an American."

"I know what the fuck he is. But you've forgotten who the fuck you are."

"That's not fair, Tamar. I'm a cop doing my job."

"You keep treating this case as a crime. It's terror, Yossi. The whole spectacle. You make it more complicated than it is. We know there were multiple players in the killing. Where are they? Who are they? Why haven't they claimed credit? Why did they pick Weingarten? Do they have a list of other assassination targets? Until we get Jamal, we don't have anything solid. All we have is a single perpetrator. Aside from this dirty condom you turned up, the evidence is that he had a key to the locker where the head was kept, and he ran away from justice. What else do you need?"

"Tamar, about the key. Jamal wasn't the only one who had it. The butcher did also."

"Of course, it was his shop."

"This butcher is old-school Hamas, once arrested for smuggling. Don't you think these are incriminating factors?"

"Did he run?"

"No."

"Did he report the crime to you?"

"He did," Yossi admitted.

"Does that sound like a terrorist? Why would he do that?"

"As for motive, Tamar," Yossi said hesitantly, "you might look at drug trafficking. There's a huge rise in overdoses and deaths in the West Bank. Somebody is supplying them, somebody who could have a reason to kill." He stopped short of implicating Cohen and his people. If Weingarten didn't trust his colleagues or his superiors, there was little reason for Yossi to risk divulging more information. But if he couldn't trust Tamar, where could he turn?

"There are always drugs," Tamar said dismissively.

"More than ever, is what I'm saying. Maybe a new provider, someone we haven't dealt with before."

Tamar stared at Yossi impatiently, clearly done with him. "Yossi, if you insist on pursuing this, give me more about Jamal and his associates, his past history, his plans for other attacks. What I don't need are confounding hints and tidbits that don't answer any of those questions. We know who's guilty. The only thing is who else is involved. We'll pick them up on terror charges or kill them. Destroy the cell, that's the goal. It's not something that's going to court, do you understand? We don't need witnesses and motives. These are terrorists and we treat them appropriately."

"I haven't heard of any new groups, and nothing that would put Jamal at the center of a terror cell. Have you?"

"Frankly, no. It's worrisome," Tamar admitted.

"There's one more thing I can offer," Yossi said. "Jamal was a childhood friend of Ehsan Zayyat. They're cousins. It's not clear but we assume they remained in contact. Each had an interest in keeping their relationship quiet. Their goals couldn't have been more different, and yet my source said that they had an understanding that neither would attack the other. If it was more than that, who would be surprised?"

Tamar looked at him appraisingly. "At last, you give me something useful. Who is this source?"

Yossi wished he had shut his mouth the moment he uttered the word "source." He should have known Tamar would pounce on it. He was only hoping to impress her and now he had stepped on a land mine. "I can't say," he said haltingly, thinking of Dina in the storage room and his pledge to Malik to keep her safe.

"What does that mean? You can't or you won't?"

"It doesn't actually come from me, Tamar. It was in Weingarten's case files. He didn't tell me the source."

That was partly true, but not the whole story, as Tamar evidently guessed. A look of concentrated fury formed on her face. "You're saying that there are files that Weingarten kept separately? And that he hid the names of his sources even from his own officers? Am I correct about this? Because if that's true, Yossi, you have been lying to me from the start of this investigation. Produce those files for me right away, that's an order—and anything else you've been hiding while you step all over my investigation. You're out of this, understand me? I'm going to speak to the commissioner about removing you altogether. We're done here."

42

Rain

Hebron Old City, Oct. 4, 2023

It was the first rain in weeks. Jamal stood at the window gazing at the storm over the Old City. If anyone saw his countenance in a lightning flash they would surely say it was a phantom or a jinn. He stood in that position for nearly an hour before it occurred to him that he was parched, his lips were chapped, his throat was raw, and there was water right outside, coming down hard. In the kitchen he found dusty glasses in the cupboard. He cracked open the window and pushed the bars far enough away to hold a glass out into the deluge, letting it cleanse the glass before filling it. Within reach was the spill from a broken gutter. It took longer than he thought even in this downpour, but he had the time. He had never imagined that water could be so delicious. He filled another glass and drank it off. Then he went back into the kitchen to gather more glasses, slowly filling one after another, then setting them inside the stove. The refrigerator contained food artifacts he didn't want to face.

He went back upstairs to his bed, immensely pleased with himself. He slept for a couple of hours, despite the thunder that sounded like the sky was breaking. He remembered moments like this as a child, when he would slip into his parents' bed, on his mother's side. She would make room for him without waking his father, who never approved of any show of cowardice, although he was not so courageous himself. Nader was unflinching, of course. He would chide Jamal, saying the Quran was clear that Allah has already written the moment of one's transition into the unseen world and nothing we do will change that. So why tremble in a storm?

His mother was mainly interested in keeping peace in the family. The slightest argument would have her wringing her hands, or more commonly, a white kerchief she kept in her pocket that she produced in moments of anxiety. She understood fear, and she was more forgiving of those childish moments when the perils of life leapt out in tears and screams. Words of reassurance didn't come easily, but she would offer an embrace, or a hand on his shoulder, little moments that made him feel safe.

There would be no such moments now. If the lightning did break through the roof and thrust itself into his heart, that would be a far better death than being hunted down by the Israeli soldiers, or shot by a helicopter gunship, or slowly starving in an abandoned house. If Allah had written his moment of death for this day, in this storm, then Jamal would welcome it.

He heard something other than the rain, something quiet, singular, not a footstep but not thunder or pounding rain. He lay there waiting but the sound didn't repeat. It was in the house. He guessed it was a rat gnawing on the beams behind the walls. He quietly got out of bed and put his ear to the wall and waited. Suddenly the room lit up with another lightning flash, immediately followed by a thunderbolt like a howitzer. But there was no more noise in the wall.

Could there be somebody in the house? Somebody who needed to hide, just as Jamal did? There would be footprints in the dust. The furniture would have been moved around. The bed would have been slept in. Still, he crept down the stairs as quietly as possible, on guard against surprise. *It's a game I'm playing,* he thought, *hide-and-go-seek with nobody.*

Nothing had changed. The photo album rested on a chair next to his father's rocker. Seven glasses of water were still in the oven. He stood for a moment watching the rain. Obviously he hadn't heard what he thought he heard. It was only the storm. He was disappointed. Something might have happened but hadn't. He had seven glasses of water and nothing but empty time until death.

That was something to do, count the days of his imaginary future, but he decided he would have none of that, he would put his mind on higher things. He would write an account of his life—there must be paper and pen somewhere in the house. One day, when his remains were found, his story would be waiting. He became excited by this prospect. He rushed into the living room—suddenly, he had reason to hurry—and looked through his father's desk. Occasional lightning strikes helped him search. There was a fountain pen and an inkwell but the ink had hardened into something like coal. No paper except his father's checkbook, but on a shelf he spotted his father's ledger of accounts covering years of his law practice. It was written entirely on one side of the page, leaving the other unmarked.

Jamal went back upstairs to his room, the darkest part of the house. It was where he used to do his homework. There would be a pencil at least. He opened the drawer of his schoolboy's desk and felt inside until he found it. In the dark he remembered exactly what it looked like: green, with "FREE PALESTINE" in capital letters, the same type of pencil he always had in those early grades. He inserted the pencil into the sharpener on the wall, knowing exactly where it would be. It made the same sound it always had when he turned the crank. Memories were flooding in now. There was so much to write.

He went downstairs to the dining room, where the light was best. The rain let up a bit and scraps of sunlight peeked through the clouds. He opened the ledger and looked at the blank page. It stared back at him. What was he going say? Where should he begin to explain his life? He sat there, frozen, tapping his pencil eraser against his forehead. Should he write about peace, what caused him to become a lonely advocate for such a cause, one that he no longer believed was possible? He might also apologize to his parents for the hardship he had given them. And there was Dina. He wanted to say something to her but he didn't know what. They would have been married now. One day children would come. They would giggle when he played with them, tickling their tummies; he would brush their teeth and hair, get them ready for school. So much happiness awaited. History did not have to determine every minute of your life.

But that was with a woman who was an imposter, a traitor. He had not had time until now to consider the depth of her treachery. Everything he confided she passed to Israeli intelligence. His complicated friendship with a leader of Hamas was revealed. His life's project was a wreck because of her. And yet he couldn't escape the cruel paradox that this very minute he would have been enjoying Dina's companionship in the marital bed, not furtively in some dismal tourist hostel on the outskirts of the city.

Love had been a happy illusion. Part of him had known that all along. He had loved his first wife and adored his son, who was now eleven. It had been six years since he last saw them, when they visited her parents in Jenin. His son did not recognize him. Maybe he had just forgotten him or maybe he harbored resentment at the abandonment. It was just as well.

He had not been a good husband or father in that marriage. A tyrannical side of him emerged when he decided that his wife, Farah, was too progressive. It began with her going without her hijab. Some of her friends did so as well. While he understood and sympathized with her position, he also felt that she undermined his standing in the patriarchal society in which they lived. He told himself he needed to protect his image as a traditional Arab man in order to do peace work. There was some truth in that, but it came at the cost of peace in his own family. Farah chafed at his dogmatic pursuit of an impossible dream. One evening she teased him in front of friends for pretending to be a hero, and he slapped her. That moment had been a revelation to both of them. He begged for forgiveness but she seized the opportunity to leave. His dangerous work was already cause enough to send his family to safety, to give her a divorce, even to surrender the child that, according to custom, he had the right to claim for himself. He consoled himself by knowing that his family would be free and fulfilled in London as they could never be in Palestine.

He was stupefied by hunger and regret.

He looked up at the ceiling for answers, then stood and went to the window. And then he saw it.

At his feet was a parcel wrapped in butcher paper. He froze. Someone had dropped it through the window. Someone knew he was here. He picked it up and carefully peeled back the butcher paper. Inside was a falafel sandwich.

He collapsed into a chair. Tears spilled from his eyes. Somebody knew. Somebody wanted to help. He stared at the sandwich in wonder. He took a bite. *There is reason to hope.* He thanked Allah for that. When he peeled back the wrap to take another bite he noticed something written on the inside:

"Mouse Arch."

He knew it well. It was in a bend in one of the main market roads in the Old City, at a place known to locals, called the Mouse Arch because it was shaped like a giant mouse hole in a Disney cartoon. Shoukry's Tailor Shop was there. Shoukry was long dead, but his grandson Ashraf was running it now, solely as an act of resistance, refusing to surrender the shop that had been in his family for a century. Jamal didn't know Ashraf well but he knew who did.

So many thoughts rushed in but the overriding one was how to get there. Checkpoints lined the way, along with cameras and drones. Red Wolf was constantly on the prowl. Still, he had managed to reach his old home, as did this mysterious courier, so there must be a path through the surveillance that would take him to the Mouse Arch.

The rain gave him an idea, but he would have to hurry as it was letting up. He found candles and matches in the kitchen. He went into his parents' closet. His father's clothes were there—suits and jackets that were much posher than the cheap replacements that he wore after the expulsion. Back then he had a taste for style. Now those fine jackets were shredded by moths, some had fallen off the hangers they were so ravaged.

His mother's dresses had survived in better condition, except for the embroidered gowns she was once so proud of. Jamal remembered moments when she looked quite glamorous. Her jewelry box was on the counter. He thought about taking some of her prizes to her, if he ever saw her again, but that possibility perished as soon as he thought of it. Instead, he found an old black abaya, which he put on over his clothes, and a hijab that he wrapped around his head. He used one of his father's shirts to wipe the dust off the full-length mirror and sized himself up in the flickering candlelight. It wasn't bad, he thought. He had shaved for the wedding, but a close examination would reveal the stubble. That problem was suddenly solved when he uncovered a niqab in one of his mother's drawers. It would cover his entire face except for his eyes. His mother had probably purchased it when his parents went on hajj to Mecca. He added an old pair of his mother's cat-eye glasses. At the last minute he stuck a handful of jewelry in his pocket, having no idea of its value but figuring he would need something to exchange along the way.

The entire plan rested on a single irreplaceable item: his mother's umbrella. It was made of a tough material and had survived the years intact. He tested the mechanism to open it, which was sticky, but worked. He went back into the dining room, then sat down to finish his sandwich.

43

The Queen of Hamas

Hebron, Oct. 4, 2023

Yasmine wanted to visit Dina but she was humiliated and afraid of being seen. Life had slammed a door in her face. She was to have been the mother of the bride; instead, she was the mother of the traitor—such was the term people used to describe her now that the photograph of Dina and Weingarten was all over the internet and even in one of the Arab papers. Dina's disaster reflected on Yasmine and always would. That was the price one paid for living in such an intricately related community.

She was also fearful of leaving Omar alone. He was in crisis, too young to endure the complexity of the life that had been forced on him. She worried he would retreat again into the fog of narcotics. Sometimes she imagined that the flood of drugs into Hebron was a plot to further defeat the Arabs. Why kill them when they willingly turn themselves into zombies? Omar had come so close to letting that happen. What kind of future would he have—lame, dependent on painkillers, overly bright but also susceptible to depression and suicidal thoughts? At this very moment he had buried himself in his room and wouldn't open the door. She was frightened for his safety. The pharmacy in Jerusalem had refused to refill his prescription for Dilaudid, so he must be in pain again. Without Weingarten there was no one to turn to.

Dina might well be killed if she were on her own, but for how long could she remain in hiding? Yasmine's husband, Hasan, closed his computer shop for the week and left for Ramallah. The marriage had been rocky before but now it was going over a cliff, taking with it her hopes for a respectable life. Jamal had disappeared with the entire Israeli military and intelligence agencies after him. Her family and her future were collapsing. She wanted to be strong for her family, but she felt hopeless and defeated. And the rain would never stop.

Malik appeared at the door. He instantly saw how fragile she was. Her hair was loose and tangled and her face was ashen. She startled when she saw him, self-consciously running her hands through her hair and fecklessly straightening her dress. "Oh, oh, oh," she said in a distant voice, and then opened her hands as if she had just dropped something.

"Dina's okay," Malik said. "She's safe."

Yasmine looked at him distrustfully. "She's in jail."

"For her own protection. It's for the best."

"How long will she be there? Is it ever going to be safe for her?"

"I don't know the answer to those questions. I think she is in the best place for now. It's not as if she's behind bars. She's in a quiet room with a nice cot and a desk. She's comfortable."

"I need to visit her."

"I'm sure she wants to see you."

"But I'm afraid."

"If you like, I can escort you there."

Yasmine nodded but her mind was far away. "You might wind up with it, you know."

"Wind up with what?"

"The vineyards, the groves, all the Abdul Malik holdings."

"Yasmine, Dina's going to be fine."

"Abdullah may change his mind. If he learns Dina is an informer, it will be a disgrace for the family if she got the land."

The last thing Malik wanted was to be a farmer in Hebron. If it were left up to him, he would sell it off to the Rav for the highest price he could get. But that would be a betrayal to the larger family. He felt the pressure of their expectations, their need for loyalty and sacrifice.

"Yasmine, I came to talk to Omar."

Her face opened in relief. "He's in his room, he won't let me in. But he will for you. He looks up to you, I don't know if you realize how impressed he is by who you are."

OMAR'S HAGGARD FACE shone in the computer's ghostly light.

"Any luck?" Malik asked.

"It's a little crazy." He gestured toward the screen. There was an artist's rendering of the future temple painted in the warm glow of a Renaissance landscape, with rays of sun breaking through the clouds, illuminating the golden dome. Oracular photos of the Rav. Highlighted texts of his sermons. The spectacular hall with the throne for the Messiah, wildly out of scale, with humans penciled in the size of house flies.

"I found the organizational chart for Messiah Temple," Omar said as he flipped to a new screen. "It's registered in Mauritius."

"Money-laundering paradise."

"Here's what's really confusing. Look at the list of the board of directors."

There were ten names on the list. Immanuel Cohen was at the top. At the bottom was Benny Eleazar. "Who are these other people?" Malik asked.

"That's the thing. I can't find that they actually exist. I mean, some of them have very ordinary names, but nothing in common with the temple or Cohen. Like, take this guy." Omar clicked on the name Robert Friedman. "It says he's the CEO of EcoGreen in Copenhagen. There is a company named EcoGreen, but in Sweden, not Denmark, and the CEO is a woman named Hanna Ljungström. Same with these others. Maybe they exist but I can't find them."

"Do you have records of contributions? Board members are usually the main sponsors."

"Okay. Like with Friedman again. He's listed as a 'Gold Star,' meaning that he contributed over three million shekels, but there's no way to verify that. One other thing about Robert Friedman. That was the name of Itai Chafets before he made aliyah."

Malik looked through some of the pages that Omar had downloaded. "You've got two real people and eight shadow figures. What do you make of it?"

"I think Benny did this," said Omar. "He's an amateur. I mean, this is embarrassing. Even I can see it's a fraud."

Malik studied the charter for the organization. "According to this, aside from his grandfather Benny is the only person with authorized access to the money."

"Is the money real?" Omar asked.

"Without bank transactions it's hard to tell. But suppose you have a lot of cash and you need to make it appear legit, putting it into a nonprofit religious foundation is a classic fraud."

"Do you think this could have anything to do with the chief's murder?"

Malik smiled. "Omar, you are a first-rate investigator. You ask all the right questions. The answer to this one is I don't know but it's at the top of my list to find out."

"Have they found Jamal yet?"

"No, he turns out to be quite a disappearing act."

"I hope they get him," Omar said.

That surprised Malik. "Do you think Jamal is a killer?"

"Yeah, I do."

"Because of what you heard or what you know about him?"

"Because he's close to Hamas. His cousin, right?"

"Zayyat."

Omar recoiled at the name. "That man can make you do anything. If Jamal hasn't killed anyone already, he will if Zayyat gets to him."

"And you've had experience with him."

Omar nodded, looking tired and grim, older than his age.

"Help me out, Omar. I don't understand the culture and the relationships here like you do. How does Zayyat do it? I know he's smart and people are scared of him but tell me how he stays in control."

"Do you believe in the devil?" Omar asked.

"I believe in evil."

"Just add a *d* to that and you've got the devil. He can see inside you, like he's looking through a window, reading your thoughts. I was in pain. I mean, that was all I could think about. There were drugs that would help but we couldn't always get them. When we could, I'd be okay, when we couldn't I wanted to die. He knew that. He got me drugs that made me feel like nothing at all. But it was a deal. He'd make the pain go away, but I had to do something for him. Something for my country, he said. Just put on one of their vests and walk up to an IDF post. They'd do the rest. Zayyat was like, 'You'll be in Paradise.' " He snapped his fingers as Zayyat must have done.

"Did you believe him?"

"I wanted to. I was an addict, man. If I didn't have the drugs, I'd rather die."

"Would you have done it?"

"Absolutely. Those days when I thought I was going to blow myself up and go to pain-free Paradise were the happiest I've ever been. He made you believe it. They put the vest on me just before the army came in. I was ready to go. I'm surprised they didn't set it off right then. I guess they didn't want to go down themselves. That was all because of Dina, you know."

"She told Weingarten."

"Yeah."

"And he saved your life."

Omar shook his head violently. "No! Dina saved my life, Weingarten was just like Zayyat. He saw people hurting and took advantage of them. Look at what he did to Dina. Her life is ruined because of him. He's as big a devil as Zayyat. We don't have angels here. Two devils, that's what we choose between. I told Dina if she married Zayyat, I would kill him or kill myself."

Malik absorbed this. He hadn't really explored Dina's politics, she kept a distance from such talk. "Did she want to?" he asked.

"There was a lot of pressure on her. Even our mom, she was okay with it. You have to understand, our family is deep into Hamas. If Dina married him, she would have been like the queen of Hamas. It's fucked up." Omar winced and quickly turned away.

"So then she hooked up with Jamal, and who knows who he really is."

"You're in pain now, aren't you?" Malik observed.

"I can get through it. But sometimes . . ."

"I'll call the embassy and see if they can help. Just hang on and don't do anything stupid."

44

Dead Man

Hebron Old City, Oct. 4, 2023

Jamal tossed the umbrella out of the window and crawled through awkwardly. It was raining hard again. The unfamiliar loose garment that had once encased his mother kept catching on splinters. He dropped to the ground, his shoes landing with a splash. As soon as he opened the umbrella he was shielded from the drones and the cameras on the watchtowers. He only hoped that the soldiers in their outposts were taking shelter and would be unwilling to face the elements to interrogate one old Arab lady in the rain. Everything depended on that.

The Mouse Arch was close by, but to get there he had to go in the opposite direction, on the street where Arabs were allowed. The checkpoint at the corner was unmanned and there was no one in sight. This began to seem easy. Jamal kept his head down to dodge the puddles. A shallow runnel in the brick pavement was rushing with rainwater carrying litter and garbage.

His mother's glasses were giving him a headache. In his peripheral vision he could see the yellow-fronted shops on either side of the narrow road, nearly all of them shuttered. He was within thirty meters of the Mouse Arch when he noticed two soldiers coming toward him, one short, one tall, wearing hoods against the rain. Jamal prayed that they would walk by but they were headed directly toward him, blocking his path.

"Your identification," the tall one demanded in Hebrew. Rain spilled off the soldiers' hoods and onto their boots. Jamal waved his finger to indicate he didn't speak that language, although he was fluent. He pulled the hijab tight around his face and looked at the ground. The soldier repeated the order in Arabic.

"I lost it," Jamal said in a whispery voice. He noticed a shop-keeper peering through a doorway at the scene. If it weren't raining, Jamal might have counted on a crowd of defenders. But nobody was going to come out into this downpour. He considered making a run for it.

"You *lost* it?" the short soldier said incredulously.

Jamal nodded. "The boys stole my purse," he added in what he hoped sounded like a woman's voice, pointing up the hill at Kiryat Arba while coughing and sniffing as if he were suffering from a bad cold. He wanted to seem pitiable rather than terrified.

The soldiers looked at each other. They were under orders to check everyone's papers. Anyone without identification was to be taken into custody. The soldiers spoke to each other in Hebrew. "Thieving little buggers," the tall one said.

The short one was suspicious. "Let us see your face," he demanded.

Jamal hesitated, then pulled down the niqab, hoping that the rain would obscure the stubble that would be so obvious in sunlight. He decided he would run and take his chances that they wouldn't shoot him.

"What do we do with this person?" the short one asked.

"Let's go get a coffee. This one is not worth our trouble." The tall one then addressed Jamal in Arabic, "Do you want us to show you where to make a report? The police station is nearby."

"I did already," he said.

"Well, then. Get out of the rain is my advice."

The tall one gave a friendly salute. "She reminded me of my mother," he said as the two of them walked on.

Jamal was still getting his breath back. *They were actually nice boys*, he thought.

The tailor shop in the Mouse Arch was closed, but the door quickly opened when Jamal tapped. Ashraf, the tailor, looked at him with a puzzled expression, then with a big grin of recognition when Jamal removed the niqab. "Come in! Come in!" he said, quickly closing the door behind them. Another man in the shop was also expecting him. The man grinned, showing gaps where teeth had been.

Ashraf grabbed Jamal by the arm and ushered him to the back of the shop. "Our mutual friend arranged for us to take you to safety," he said, sounding calm and unworried but clearly in a rush to get Jamal out of his hands. "The only matter of concern was how you would get to us. But you had a stroke of genius!" he said, touching the abaya. "The concept is perfect. Anyway, we do need to hurry, best to get you going while the rain is still on. By the way, this is Montasser." Abdul gestured toward the toothless man. "He's going to be transporting you to the next station on your journey."

Jamal nodded at Montasser, who displayed his frightful smile again.

In the back of the shop was a changing curtain, and behind that, a full-length mirror. Ashraf pushed on the edge of the mirror and it opened onto the old passageway that the Israelis had sealed off. It was made of beautifully crafted limestone blocks from the biblical era. Ashraf was using it for storage—rolls of fabric and plastic boxes of buttons and belts and other items it was too dark to see. The only illumination in the room came from the dim light leaking through cracks between the planks of a garage door at the end of the passageway. Jamal could just make out a long black car with the swooping landau bars marking it as a hearse.

Ashraf turned on a light, a single bulb dangling from the ceiling that did little more than cast shadows, but now Jamal noticed the figure of a man standing beside the fabrics, his glasses reflecting the dim beam. The man stepped forward. "Hello, Cousin," he said.

Jamal had been expecting this. They moved out of hearing from the other men. "How did you know?" he asked.

"I know you, so I knew."

Zayyat produced a bag of almonds. "While we talk, you eat. You've got a journey ahead. First, I ask a favor. You could claim credit for the killing of the Jewish cop. Many would applaud this action."

"I didn't do it."

"We know this," said Zayyat. "But it does no good for the killing to go unclaimed. People see this as a bold strike against the occupiers and naturally they give you the credit. We have discussed among the leaders and we want to say Hamas is responsible. Best would be for you to say you did it working with us. We would use this for our recruitment. You would be a hero to your people."

"You would make my whole life a lie."

"There is another way of looking at it, Cousin. We can provide meaning to a failed existence. Your struggle for peace is an excellent cover for a Hamas spy. Did you achieve the peace you sought? You did not, but you could still strike a blow for the struggle. Your picture will be on martyr posters across Palestine. Children will learn of you in school. Whether or not you agree, this is how you will be remembered. The Israelis will kill you anyway, so why not accept the role that we offer?"

The reality of Jamal's life—the uselessness, the delusional idealism—all of that could be wiped away with a single act of denial of what he stood for. It would be the one meaningful action of his life. He would be redeemed in the eyes of his countrymen—and in his father's eyes as well—vaulting over the martyred Nader into a modest immortality.

"I can't," he sputtered. "I can't be someone else."

"Give it some consideration. You have incurred a debt by coming here. We have saved your life, at least for the time being. You will be a hunted man all the days that remain to you." Zayyat's eyes bored into Jamal's wavering will. "We help you now because we love you. You can help us in return." Then he embraced Jamal and cracked open the garage door and disappeared into the rain.

Ashraf came forward and took his arm. "Here, my friend, you must lie on the table," he said, ushering Jamal to a workbench. "First you must remove your clothes. For this part of your journey you won't need them. This preparation may be unnecessary but if the worst happens and they decide to investigate closely, you must make a convincing corpse."

Still disoriented by his conversation with Zayyat, Jamal wordlessly stripped off his clothes. His life had turned eerie and dreamlike. He had thought death was near, and now he was enacting the ritual of the dead. Ashraf and Montasser politely engaged each other to avoid watching Jamal strip off the abaya and the clothes underneath, folding them neatly into a little pile on a chair. He felt exposed and absurd. He lay down and focused on the stone arch above him.

"Wait," he said, then got back up and went through his pants pockets to find his mother's jewels. "Can I take these? It's all that I have."

Ashraf nodded at Montasser, who put the jewelry in a ziplock bag and placed it in the glove compartment of the hearse.

Jamal lay on the bench atop a length of white cotton. "Don't worry, the shroud is sheer and you can breathe through it. Hands across your chest, right over left," Ashraf instructed. Then he and Montasser began the intricate process of enclosing Jamal in three cotton sheets. It was touching how respectful they were in this counterfeit ritual, as if Jamal were truly dead. The men tied ropes around the fabric above the head and below the feet, then two more ropes around the middle. Jamal fought off panic as he realized how incapacitated he was, naked and bound.

"We're going to set you on a wooden slab," said Montasser. "It's not comfortable, I'm afraid, as it is not meant for living people."

"Where are we going?" Jamal asked through the fabric.

"Montasser is taking you as far as Sderot," Ashraf said, naming a small Israeli town directly west of Hebron. "That's all I can tell you now. You'll be met by friends who will take you on the next part of your journey. These people are putting their lives at risk for you, so we are cautious. It's best to limit your knowledge in case the plan is compromised."

"Will there be clothes for me where I'm going?"

He heard the men chuckle in response. They lifted him onto a slab in the back of the hearse and then belted him in. The slab was flat and hard as a strip of concrete. He felt like a side of beef on the cutting table about to be carved into steaks and chops. A powerful perfume made of agarwood suffused the hearse, meant to cover the stench of death.

"Remember, if you are stopped, don't breathe," Ashraf said. "It would be your last breath."

"Understood."

"Then Allah be with you on your journey."

Jamal felt the hearse back out of the garage and then nose onto

Shuhada Street. They went over a pothole and his head bounced on the hard slab. He heard traffic slushing through the flooded streets. The windows of the hearse were curtained so little light got in, and the shroud covering his face darkened even that, but it was not absolute blackness—not exactly like death but eerily near. Presently he heard the rain coming to a stop. The absence of noise was also like death.

45

The Waiting Game

Hebron, Oct. 4, 2023

I thought you had gone," Greenblatt said irritably on the phone. "What are you still doing here?"

"Just tying up a few family matters," Malik assured him. "I'll be headed back soon."

"When is soon? Did you remember that Hamas wants to kill you?"

Greenblatt reluctantly agreed to secure a prescription for Omar's pain medication—"anything to get you out of here"—but it would have to wait until the next day. Impatient, Malik got a cab to Ahli Hospital in the Farsh al-Hawa district. There was a queue out the front door. Some were elderly, some in wheelchairs, some had bleeding wounds. Malik resigned himself to waiting for hours.

A woman several spaces ahead of him fainted. No one rushed to help. "She's a faker," an older man on crutches confided to Malik.

"You've seen her before?"

The man nodded. "She hopes they will move her ahead in the queue. Some are fooled but most of us have been here many times. Waiting in line is our occupation. My wife's job is to wait for groceries."

A man next to him nodded. "Also my wife."

"Who waits for you?" the man on crutches asked Malik.

"Nobody."

"My wife would be available."

"Also my wife," said the other man.

"Thanks, I don't need such help now."

The two men stared at him. "You are very rich or very poor," the man on crutches concluded.

"I'm not either. I'm a tourist."

"A tourist! From where do you come?"

"America."

The men seemed dazzled by this. "I have never seen a tourist standing in line," one of them marveled.

"Especially an American," the other said.

"Why are you waiting here?" the man on crutches demanded. "If you have money, you go inside. They welcome you."

Malik was seen right away. A nurse took his vital signs even though he said there was nothing wrong with him, he only wanted a consultation. Presently a young doctor appeared. Her name was Samira. "You come to the hospital and there is nothing wrong with you," she observed.

"It's for a friend. He's in pain and he needs medication."

"Why does he not come himself?"

"He's a child. Young teenager. He's been seen before and was told there were no suitable drugs available."

Samira didn't dispute that. "And you think they will be available to you?"

"I'm willing to pay. Whatever it is."

"Bribe me," she said flatly.

"If that's what you want to call it."

"You're not from here, I can see that. Here, when you bribe, you go to the politicians, and then we get the orders. But I can't help you anyway, we have nothing to offer in that department. This hospital is filled with people in pain and all we can do is sedate them. Sometimes we get shipments but for two weeks we have nothing." She looked at him appraisingly. "Since you get nothing for your payment, I will show you something."

The morgue was in the basement. It looked like any other morgue that Malik had seen, rows of drawers like filing cabinets filled with former human beings. "They're children, many of them," Samira said. "They die of disease and trauma but mainly they die of despair.

For two years now, every month we have more overdoses and accidental drug deaths. Here, look at this, the people we don't have proper spaces for." She opened a large door at the rear of the morgue. It was crowded with bodies, many of them strangely contorted by rigor, randomly piled onto the floor. "We pick them up on the street. You see them frozen in their last struggle. Heartbreaking, isn't it? I hope your young friend doesn't wind up here."

46

Habib

Negev Desert, Oct. 4, 2023

Y ou can call me Habib," said the Bedouin sheikh after Montasser dropped Jamal off in the desert. Habib must have been in his middle seventies but was strong as stone and erect as a fence post. His eyebrows were black and severe, his nose hooked and powerful, a figure from the ancients. A few meters away the other men were striking their tents and rolling up rugs. Jamal noticed women and children and a herd of black goats. The boy tending the goats was sulking because he wasn't allowed to go on this great adventure.

"Do you know how to ride the camel?" Habib asked.

Jamal shook his head no. When he was a child, caravans still crossed through the Negev, but gradually the Bedouin way of life diminished, either disappearing altogether or dissolving into urban life. Lately his only contact with the beast was as a butcher, when those customers who still had a taste for camel meat placed an order.

"Then today you learn." Habib turned and walked toward a herd of the ungainly giants and almost magically persuaded them to kneel by tugging on the guide rope and uttering some imprecation they understood. Those long, spindly legs lurched forward and then snapped back like a mechanical toy. Within a minute the camels were all kneeling on the ground. The other men strapped tents and rugs onto their animals' backs and then gracefully hopped into the saddle atop the hump; even the children were mounted in no time. Leaving one camel.

It didn't look difficult, and Jamal had noted the technique the riders used, which was to put one foot in a stirrup and then vault upward in a single powerful motion. He tried, but his leg didn't clear the hump. Again he failed. He was dressed in Bedouin clothes but the camel wasn't fooled. She turned and hissed at him, showing her massive yellow teeth. Habib dismounted and walked over, uttering another curse in the camel's ear. Then, as Jamal put his foot in the stirrup and made his leap again, Habib shoved him forcefully up in the air and he plopped into the saddle, which was a slender frame with horns front and back atop woolen saddlebags, brightly colored, with streaming tassels.

"Lean back or you will fall when she rises," Habib said as he tugged the guide rope. Suddenly the camel's rear end rose and the world tilted forward. Jamal would have been pitched over the animal's nose if he hadn't leaned back as far as he could go. Then the front legs unfolded and Jamal was aloft. He noticed the other riders had one leg wrapped around the saddle horn in front, which he copied uncertainly. He was unsteady and sure that the mean-spirited animal yearned to throw him and stomp on him if she possibly could.

"Do not try to control her," Habib said. "You cannot. Sorry, no time to go slow and learn. We have to move quickly." Habib slapped his camel with a quirt and the animal lurched into a jog. The other camels followed as well, at a quickening pace across the flat and featureless desert. The children were exuberant, leaning forward and urging their animals on with their reins, faster and faster, the women ululating with excitement, everyone bouncing madly.

Jamal clung desperately to the saddle horn, so jostled and worried about falling he could scarcely think. But he studied a wild-eyed boy nearby and noted how gracefully he swayed with the camel's motion. Jamal tried to imitate him by surrendering to the rhythm. After several kilometers in which he had not fallen he began to relax. He pretended he could ride and that helped him do so.

No one told him anything about what lay ahead and he didn't care to ask. He trusted these people who took him in hand without question, unafraid of the consequences. They were the Arabs of legend reincarnated, the Arabs who erupted from the Arabian Peninsula in the seventh century and formed one of the great armies of history.

Courage and bold action marked the Arab people then, along with piety and scholarship. What had happened to those people, Jamal wondered, when and where did the lamp of greatness drop from Arab hands? It was especially bitter to be under the thumb of the Jews, who demonstrated again and again their superiority in learning, their mastery of the arts, the raw power of their military forces.

Racing the camel through the desert made him feel at one with those Arabs of old, his ancestral holy warriors, heedless of death, waving their blood-soaked scimitars and praising Allah as they charged the infidels. They weren't weakened by doubt. They dreamed not of peace but of conquest and subjugation. They weren't a collection of individuals, they were a horde, trailed by clouds of dust from thundering hooves across the desert floor.

THE BEDOUINS CAMPED without a fire, making a meal of protein bars. The colors in the twilight were sharpened, the sky inky blue and the desert chocolate brown. The shabby but capacious tent was a mishmash of frayed blankets and rugs tied to a rough wooden frame. A mild breeze caused the canvas sides to billow dreamily.

Jamal leaned against a saddlebag. He was more than relaxed, he was serene. Perhaps this was just an interlude between perils, but the bare simplicity of the surroundings calmed him. In the distance, shimmering in the last rays of sunlight, was a wall, about fifteen meters high, and a watchtower. Between Habib's camp and the wall stood a lone house with an old jeep parked beside it.

He learned that the group he was with—twenty altogether, not counting the boy goatherd left behind—was a single family, headed by Habib, with his three wives and their assorted children. "We live in one of the unrecognized villages near Rahat," Habib said. He complained that the Israelis were razing such villages to consolidate the Bedu in planned communities with industry and utilities. "It's not all bad, the plan," Habib admitted. "We prefer to live in our own communities among the graves of our ancestors. All this is the same that happened to the Indians in America, they take away our land and push us into small areas. We are a traditional people but we are not primitive savages who need to be told how to live. Look at my wife Nour—" The women and children were arrayed on rugs in and around the tent, some others preparing to sleep under the stars. Nour was in jeans and a green hijab, stroking the head of a curly-haired boy in her lap. "Nour works as a hairdresser in Rahat," Habib said. "Amal—" who was next to Nour, wiggling her bare feet with pink toenails "—started her own business making perfumes. Fadel works at Starbucks." Fadel, the youngest wife, raised her hand. "And our oldest boy is Burhan." Habib gestured toward the young man whose camel-riding Jamal had attempted to emulate. "He is study-ing biological sciences at the technical university in Beersheba."

"And what is your role?" Jamal asked.

"I'm a beggar," Habib said dryly.

The whole family broke into hysterics. Nour finally spoke up. "You have to understand, our husband is the sheikh of our tribe, the biggest in the Negev. It is like being the governor. When we negotiate with Israel, he is the one. Always asking for this or that."

"I've done a bad job of it," Habib confessed. "Even though we are full Israeli citizens, we are the poorest people in the country. And the most depressed, with the most crime. The only people who make money are the smugglers."

The light dimmed and the stars burned holes in the sky. As it dark-ened, Habib strummed an oud and one of his boys played a flute made from a length of plastic pipe. Another child tapped a hypnotic rhythm on a metal can. These humble instruments cast a spell over the children. One by one the mothers sent them off to pee in the sand, then they settled into sleep. Jamal was suddenly exhausted. All he needed was to put his head on the rug and he fell asleep, too worn out even to dream.

HE FELT A HAND on his shoulder and startled awake. "Shh, mis-ter, time to go," Habib whispered. He helped Jamal to his feet and led him outside the tent through the array of sleeping bodies. The desert glowed as if lit from below rather than by the stars. He could see a light in the watchtower and the spectral movements of soldiers inside.

Wordlessly they trekked across the sand, which was soft and yielding, making for sluggish footing. Habib led the way, pointedly keeping Jamal just behind him, in his star shadow, so that if they were observed there would be an image of a single person rather than two. Even with infrared this trick worked passably well if they kept their heads aligned and their arms crossed. Jamal walked carefully in Habib's footsteps.

They were headed for the lone house, a dark and mysterious dwelling. Jamal wondered who would live out here, and how, with no utilities or electricity. Of course, many of the Bedouin existed without such amenities. As they got closer he noticed the stars reflected in solar panels on the roof, so it wasn't entirely unused. On the other hand, the tires on the jeep were flat and half buried in the sand.

The window shades were closed. Habib produced a key and unlocked the deadbolt and pushed open the door. He guided Jamal into the room, which was so dark that his eyes had to adjust to perceive anything at all, and when they did, he sensed only shapeless structures around him, not furniture, just piles. He reached down and touched the mound in front of him. It was sand.

Habib sang one of his Bedouin melodies, and in an instant a light glowed in another room. Habib led him toward the source, past piles of sand, some as high as his shoulders. When they came into the room Jamal saw an opening in the floor where the light emerged.

"Habib?" a voice called out from far below.

"I'm here," Habib said, "with our passenger."

Above the gaping hole was a pulley hoist and a thin cable attached to a playground swing seat dangling above the abyss. Jamal took a closer look. The hole was perfectly round and reinforced with concrete slabs. He peeked over the edge and then drew back, stunned by how deep it was. A man at the bottom waved to him. "Hello," the man cried. "We must hurry!"

Jamal had never thought of being frightened of heights, but the highest he had ever been was atop the roofs of the Old City. As he looked at the swing seat his breathing became shallow. Habib grabbed him by the elbow. "Many feel this nervousness when they see how dangerous it appears. But it is totally safe. No one even gets a scratch. You can relax. And if you fall, Mohammed will catch you. This is true, Mohammed?" he said loudly into the hole. "You will catch him if he falls?"

Mohammed's laugh echoed off the concrete tiles that encircled the hole.

Habib pressed a switch on a post and the swing lurched down about a meter, just enough for him to lean over the hole and grab the frail cable above the swing. He pulled it to him and handed it off to Jamal. "Don't think, just sit," he said.

It felt like suicide. With one hand Jamal held the cable and with the other he guided the swing under his buttocks. When he hesitated Habib gave him a gentle push that sent him off the ground and over the abyss. The momentum carried him across the span of the opening, bumping into the other side. He didn't feel secure on the seat and worried he might slide out, but even as he was thinking this Habib hit the switch again and Jamal began to descend while slowly spinning and colliding with the side walls. "Goodbye, mister! You'll be safe now," Habib assured him.

47

Purim

Kfar Oren, Oct. 5, 2023

When Malik called Yossi he was surprised that Sara answered. He asked how Yossi was doing. "He's drunk," she said. It was four o'clock in the afternoon. "He lost his job," Sara said, "thanks to you."

"What did I do?"

"You got him involved in this investigation that led him into conflict with his superiors."

"Is that what he's telling you?"

"Not directly, but I pieced it together. He seems to think you're some kind of supercop, but so far you've got nothing to show for it. Is that correct?"

"Mostly."

"Tell him to come over for a drink," Yossi said in the background.

"Can you put him on the phone?" Malik asked.

"He's not very presentable."

"Tell him to come over for a drink," Yossi repeated.

"Tell him yourself," Sara said.

"Today is holiday," Yossi declared in a slurred voice when he had the phone.

"Sounds like you got an early start," Malik said.

"You should also be drinking. Special day for drinking."

"Okay, I'll let you get back to the party."

"No party. Only my daughter and she does not approve."

"Put her back on the line."

Sara came on and said, "Do you want to come over for a drink?"

In the Uber on the way to Yossi's settlement, Malik considered all the things he didn't know. Was Jamal innocent of Weingarten's murder? He didn't know. The head in the freezer was damning evidence, but it was also suspiciously convenient, an ideal plant. Jamal represented himself as a man of peace, but was he? Suppose he was working in tandem with his cousin Zayyat, what a perfect cover! What about the burgeoning drug trade, was that at the root of the crime? He didn't know. Violence always surrounds the movement of illegal narcotics, it's one of the first principles of law enforcement, as sure as thunder follows lightning. But who was behind it? He didn't know.

What about the temple fund that Omar unearthed? It was clearly a scam, but how big and for what purpose? Did it play a role in the chief's murder? Suppose Weingarten had found the same damning information Omar had—where had it led him?

A thornier question: Was Dina telling the truth? He wanted to believe her, but the more he knew the less he trusted her. She was a beguiling mystery—so young, so lovely, and so full of secrets. Was she Weingarten's mistress? An Israeli asset? A Hamas spy? What was her connection to Zayyat since their broken engagement? He didn't know.

He also didn't know what to think about the feud between Israel and Palestine. From afar, as an Arab, it was easy to make the judgment that it was a simple case of colonialism. But on the ground, it didn't seem so simple. Jews had been here for centuries, they had a legitimate claim on the land. So did the Palestinians. What did it matter who was here first? He despised the violent aggression of the settlers, especially the Kahanists, but he also recognized the threat posed by jihadist groups. He didn't see a moral difference between them, only a power imbalance. The settlers didn't represent all Israelis, nor did Hamas represent all Palestinians, but neither side worked to eliminate the violent actors inside their communities; instead, the extremists were tolerated, even elected to high office. They served a purpose, and the purpose was to prolong the conflict, justify the hatred, and rid the land of the other.

The Uber dropped him off at the settlement gate. Sara buzzed him in and he walked past the guardhouse down a palm-lined row of town houses. Like other settlements, it was built on a hilltop, the settlement serving as a barricade. Odd little makeshift shacks appeared here and there, with tapestry walls, like children's forts. Some of them were roofed with palm fronds. He saw families taking meals inside their huts.

Sara was waiting at the door. She had no perceptible resemblance to her father, who was built like a massive block of ice, with his heavy-lidded eyes and that prowlike nose, as if he had been sculpted by a chainsaw; no, she was slender, fair, nearly as tall as her father, and moved with athletic grace, whereas Yossi was a plodder, powerful but stiff in his joints.

Yossi was in the living room nursing a bottle of Polish vodka. When he saw Malik he waved his glass. "Jewish holiday!" he cried. "Muslims welcome to become drunk also. Best day of the year."

Malik took a quick look at the living quarters. The front room was covered with archaeological artifacts—ancient pots, coins, mosaics—all lovingly displayed. "It's a museum in here," he observed.

"A national hobby," said Yossi. "In this country, you dig, you find history."

"What are you looking for?"

"Evidence."

The vista through the patio doors stretched all the way to the Dead Sea. On the terrace was a small orange grove, and within it was one of those puzzling huts, with a table and chairs set for dinner.

Sara brought Malik a glass and he poured himself a small shot. Yossi held out his glass, and as soon as Malik poured he downed it and held out his glass for another. "Whoa, I'm just getting started and you're already a mile down the road," Malik said. "What's this holiday you're talking about?"

"Explain," Yossi told Sara. "It's complicated."

"My father celebrates only one Jewish holiday. Every holiday he says is Purim, the most ridiculous holiday on the calendar, when Jews are commanded to be happy and get drunk. Unfortunately, it's the only holy day my father takes seriously, so they are all Purim to him. The actual holiday of today is Sukkot, a harvest festival that lasts for a week. He told you it was complicated." She excused herself to take something out of the oven. Presently an intriguing aroma drifted into the room.

"Your daughter said you lost your job," Malik said, in part to slow the drinking, which looked more like despair than happiness.

"Not yet. Five days to appeal." His eyes were bobbing.

"Because of me?"

"They know I have been working with you. They don't trust this. And I don't report it to them because Weingarten believed there was a traitor in the ranks. So I am under suspicion."

"Can I help somehow? Give testimony or whatever?"

"They will never listen to you. It's like you are watching us take a crap, not something you should see."

"Why don't we sit on the porch?" Sara asked as she came back into the room, wearing an apron. "By the way, I hope you'll stay for dinner."

"I was wondering what that delicious smell is."

"Must be the rosemary and garlic on the lamb. There's also a special marjoram you only find here."

Yossi staggered a bit as he stood up, hugging the remaining vodka to his chest. He sat heavily in a chaise lounge and made a grand wave at the view. "The Promised Land," he said.

"Much too promised, from what I hear," said Malik.

Ever since he arrived in the region, Malik had been puzzling over the source of the religious mania that caused bloodshed throughout the ages. It was the land, he decided. "Everything is reduced to its basic elements, the earth, the stars, the stones. It's got some eerie quality I can't quite name."

"'Ineffable,' 'sanctified,' 'venerable,' all the different words for 'holy,'" said Sara.

"I don't know if I believe that one place is holier than another."

"I don't *believe* it, exactly, but it does cast a spell. I love Paris, it really is the greatest city in the world, but I can't help feeling that it's all superficial. It makes you forget what is real." She gestured toward the shadowed hills. "*This* is real."

"Like the world stripped of civilization," said Malik, "or what we think of as civilization—cities, technology, history, the noise of society. Here you are with the world as I guess God created it, and humanity is irrelevant, just a footnote."

They were quiet for a moment and then Sara noticed her father deep asleep in the chaise. "Well, I'm glad I have at least one companion join me for dinner," she said.

"You don't think we should wake him?" Malik asked.

"If he wakes up he'll just drink more. I don't want him to suffer the consequences more than he has to." Sara draped a blanket over Yossi and left him snoring on the patio. "You'll have to help me carry the meal to the hut. It's silly, but I compensate for my father's heresy by observing the holidays properly." She explained that during Sukkot observing Jews construct the huts to honor the harvest. "It's intimate in a way. Like camping in your backyard."

Sara served a fine Israeli wine from the Galilee. The lamb was perfect, as were the roasted carrots with purple onions, along with a salad of pomegranate, apples, and cauliflower, the meal spread across a narrow table made of cedar planks, with a vase of wildflowers. The simplicity was part of the charm. They sat across from each other, their heads nearly touching.

It was the best meal Malik had enjoyed in months, but it seemed so effortless. He was a little overcome by Sara's accomplishments; for instance, her linguistic ease—she spoke English flawlessly, along with Hebrew and Arabic, and evidently French as well, because of her studies in Paris. She was one of those people at home anywhere in the world, with a mixture of lightness and humor that naturally inclined people to lean in her direction. Malik ruled out any romantic possibility; she was too attractive and far too refined to take an interest in him.

At the end of the slender table, propped on the arms of a chair, was a portrait of a beautiful woman with an oval face and eyes that spilled over with intelligence and compassion. "Your mother, I'm guessing," he said.

Sara sighed. "Leah. On holidays, my father likes to take her down and seat her at dinner because we're supposed to be happy on Purim, even when it's not actually Purim, and nothing makes him happier than the memory of her. That's what he says. In truth, it makes him miserable. He's not happy, he's assaulted by the memories of her. He's never been truly happy since she died. He is not a man who seeks out relationships, no old girlfriends or the like. When he was at a marriageable age my grandmother—his mother—got impatient and sought a matchmaker, an old-world Jewish thing to do. These days they use dating apps. Fortunately, my other grandmother was also of an old-world mentality and she did the same for Leah. Honestly, I don't know what the matchmakers saw in either of them that would suggest they were perfect for each other. It's an art, they say."

Sara looked at her father sleeping on the patio, with the hoopoe proudly perched on his chest. Sara smiled sadly. "I feel like I've abandoned him. And it's true. He's got no one else, and I don't want to give up my life to become the portrait of my mother."

"You were going to tell me about Purim."

"I'll try," she said, brightening. "Well, it's in the Bible, the Book of Esther. It's a crazy legend but it actually tells you a lot about Jews and our supposed history. Also about men and women, if you look at it closely. So . . ." She leaned back and folded her napkin. "There was a king in ancient Persia we call Ahasuerus, probably the historical figure Xerxes. He really enjoyed drinking. He summoned his princes and satraps to the capital for a feast lasting a hundred and eighty days."

"That's quite a feast."

"Well, that's how they did it in the days of old. So, during one night of revelry the drunken king orders his wife, Queen Vashti, to display her beauty to all the nobles gathered there, wearing her crown. According to legend, that was all she was to wear. She says screw you, I'm not doing any such thing. Now you don't tell a king what he doesn't want to hear. Plus the men in the court worried she was setting a terrifying precedent. How might their own wives behave if the queen herself defies her husband's commands? So the king agrees to retire this disobedient queen and find another. Naturally this is decided by a beauty contest, the only quality the king, like most men, actually cares about. All the pretty girls are lined up and one of them catches the king's eye, an orphan named Esther. She lives with her uncle Mordecai, although it's also possible he's her husband, the scholarship on this matter is a little shaky. Wouldn't you know she's Jewish, like Mordecai, who advises her it's best to keep that matter to themselves.

"Now we meet the villain, a proto-Hitler named Haman. He's the king's adviser, very important man. When he walks by everybody bows to him, except Mordecai, who refuses to bow to anyone but the king. This fills Haman with rage. He decides he's going to kill Mordecai and while he's at it he'll exterminate the entire Jewish population. When he has the ear of the king, Haman uses the language that Jew-haters have employed ever since. 'There is in our kingdom a certain people with their own set of laws who don't obey the king,' he says. 'It's not in your interest to tolerate them. Let's wipe them out.' The king thinks this is a wonderful idea and signs the paperwork.

"When Mordecai learns about the scheme he reaches out to Esther and beseeches her to intercede with the king. No one is permitted to approach the king without being invited, she reminds him—under penalty of death. Mordecai says. 'Don't fool yourself, darling, you may be a queen but you're still a Jew. The anti-Semites will come for you eventually. Who knows, perhaps God put you in this very spot so you could be the salvation of your people.'

"Esther gathers her nerve and goes to the king. Fortunately he's happy to see her. He assures her that whatever she requests, it will be granted. Her simple wish is that he come to a dinner she has prepared, and by the way please bring along your absolutely brilliant adviser, Haman. She makes sure they have a lot to drink. Then at the right moment she springs her big surprise. She's Jewish. Moreover, there is a plot to exterminate her and her entire tribe. The king is surprised. Horrified. Who would do such a thing? he asks. 'Who else but the wicked Haman!' she cries. And so the king hangs him and appoints Mordecai in his place.

"And that's where the story usually ends, but there's more. Suddenly everybody in Persia starts identifying as Jewish, worried that the real Jews will come after them. Which the Jews did, killing seventy-five thousand Persians. I can tell you, ours is not a win-win history. The Golden Rule in the Middle East has always been 'Do unto others before they do unto you.'"

"I still don't understand why you're supposed to get drunk because of this story."

"Oh, I should have explained," she said, rolling her eyes at her discursiveness. "It's the best part of the story for me. The whole point is that you're supposed to get so drunk you can't distinguish between 'Arur Haman'—that is, 'Cursed is Haman'—and 'Baruch Mordecai,' 'Blessed is Mordecai.' In other words, you can't tell the difference between good and evil. You're spiritually blinded. The Jews were endangered because of drink, but drink was also their salvation. So we celebrate the complexity. That's my version, anyway."

"I'm beginning to like this holiday."

"Well, then, you should know something else about Purim. It was on Purim that Baruch Goldstein murdered those people in the mosque. After that, everything changed. Until then, people on both sides thought we were headed toward reconciliation. All hope died. It's not a happy day anymore."

"Happiness seems to be the one emotion completely lacking in this place."

"It's so true but nobody ever admits it. They're too passionate to be happy. Happy is not big enough. Not like hatred. I suppose you've noticed that this is the world capital of hatred. Everybody hates something, somebody."

"What do you hate?"

"I hate the hatred. Honestly, I can't stand it. Every other emotion gets squeezed out. Do you know why? Because there's an even bigger emotion inside all of us—on both sides, Jews and Arabs—an emotion we're all afraid to express." She was quiet, as if the answer was charged with some kind of power she was reluctant to release. Finally she spoke, her voice thick with emotion. "Grief. Israel was created by a grieving people. If we had dealt with that, if we had accepted our suffering, we might have found happiness, if such a thing exists for a nation. But we let our grief define us. All this rage, this depression, shame, this insistence on revenge—they are expressions of a grief that is too big for us, too big for any people. And then we made the Palestinians in our image, a grieving and dispossessed people." She looked apologetically at Malik. "I shouldn't speak for you. Is that how you feel as a Palestinian?"

Malik took another sip of wine. The conversation was taking him into deeper water than he had expected and his head was already clouded by drink. "The longer I'm in Palestine, the more American I feel. But something has changed. It's deep. I'm getting acquainted with where I came from, or at least part of me, the Palestinian half. I can see what I lost, the connection with my roots, but I haven't been able to—" He hesitated but he felt propelled to explain something he didn't fully understand. "I spent months interviewing members of ISIS at an American base in Syria. My Arabic wasn't perfect but there weren't that many of us in the bureau who spoke it at all. Our assignment was to find out what made these guys become terrorists. A lot of them were well educated. They had a grudge against America and I understood that. They all said Islam was under attack, even though they were the ones attacking Muslims. With al-Qaeda, the big promise was that you'd be rewarded with virgins in Paradise, but with ISIS you didn't have to wait, just sign up and they'll issue you a sex slave. This was a huge motivator for a lot of lonely young men.

"There was this Iraqi kid—we called him Howdy because he had big eyes and red cheeks and he reminded some of the old guys of *Howdy Doody*, this television show they watched when they were children. Howdy was twelve when I talked to him. Friendly. Smart. His parents took him to Syria when he was nine 'to liberate Muslims,' they told him. He became a part of their youth group, Cubs of the Caliphate. I saw a video of this same child assassinating ISIS captives. They were lined up on their knees blindfolded and he walked behind them with a handgun and shot them each in the head, eleven of them, one after another. He never hesitated. An absolute stone-cold killer.

"Howdy was fixed on the fact that I was Palestinian. He couldn't understand how I could also be American. He told me, 'We're doing this for you!' For Palestine, he meant. And I thought, is that what Palestine really is, an excuse to turn children into barbarians?"

Sara wandered into the kitchen and returned with a bowl of chocolate balls. "I also feel this guilt about the history of my people. Are we to be understood only as victims or oppressors? What should I think about the violence of the settlers? These questions are put to me all the time in Paris. The hostility, the disdain you feel all the time because of being Jewish. They can't believe I defend Israel or maintain any religious feeling. We could be sitting in one of those lovely cafés in the Place de la Concorde, looking out at the giant pharaonic obelisk in the center of the plaza, and I remind myself that this is where the guillotine stood. Housewives of Paris would sit beside the scaffold, knitting, as the heads of the aristocrats plopped into the basket. I imagine these charming streets, with their cafés and bibliotheques, running with blood. And I think, who the fuck are you to judge me? We are all barbarians in our time."

48

Salma

Gaza, Oct. 5, 2023

Welcome to Gaza," a woman said as Jamal emerged from the tunnel in what looked like a kindergarten classroom. Childish pictures covered the walls, along with the Arabic alphabet and photographs of the current leaders of Hamas. She was in her late thirties, he supposed, short and round, with merry eyes, wearing a blue hijab, and noticeably pregnant. Her name was Salma Khalil. "I am your cousin," she said, part of the vast Khalil *chamula*.

Jamal asked Salma if this room was actually used for class, despite the gaping hole in the floor where the tunnel ended. He envisioned children tumbling into the abyss. "No, no," she laughed, "this is no longer a school, although we say it is. It was bombed in 2021 during the crisis, and workmen come and go, pretending to be rebuilding."

"Looks like it was a nice school."

"I taught here myself when it was a real school. I loved my classroom. I'll show you what it is now." She crossed the hallway and opened the door. Inside, six men were fashioning rockets. "These are the Qassams," she said in a neutral tone. "The new ones can reach Tel Aviv." One of the men held up a completed example, crudely fashioned of steel pipe, nearly three meters long, painted green, looking like a child's science project. As Salma closed the door she muttered, "They shoot them in the air and who knows where they land."

Jamal immediately liked her. She was frank and intelligent and behind her ready smile was a woman with independent views. "Hamas insists on hiding arms and rockets in our public places to make it harder for the Israelis to bomb," she explained. "'Harder'— I should say 'morally more complicated.' So when they bomb, we say they bombed a school and children were killed. Of course, they do bomb schools and kill children, so it is true enough. Sometimes I think this whole conflict is about public relations."

Jamal's stroll through the tunnel had taken him nearly an hour. He guessed it had spanned about three kilometers. The guide operated the tunnel as a smuggling concession, charging the equivalent of thirty dollars per trip. It had been built as a military tunnel, the guide explained. Most of the commercial tunnels were on the Egyptian border, having survived extensive bombing and being flooded with sewage, thanks to the Egyptians. Many essential products, including food, medicine, electronics, even cattle and vehicles, were still being smuggled through the tunnels into the Gaza Strip.

Salma drove an old Czech sedan, a Škoda, which had been carefully kept up long after its expected useful life. "We share it with our neighbor," she said. A sprig of jasmine hung from the rearview mirror but it didn't override the odor of rot and salt water that suffused the early-morning air. Salma provided cheerful commentary. "This is Salah al-Din Road," she said as they rode through downtown Gaza City. "It runs the entire length of the Strip." The Strip was a narrow coastal region where two and a half million people were forcibly confined in an area twenty-five miles long and no more than seven miles wide at any point.

Men had already begun to populate the coffee shops on the sidewalks in the early morning. Jamal studied the chaotic commercial buildings and apartments that lined the road. "I'm surprised by the traffic."

"Oh, wait a couple hours. Even though we don't have that many cars in Gaza, we still manage to have traffic jams, especially with the tuk-tuks, those rickshaws you see all over the place. They're noisy and they stink. The Israelis not only limit the cars, they limit the donkeys! So you see such terrible sights," she said, gesturing to a cart stacked nearly four meters high with cotton bales, the driver riding atop this towering construction, which was being pulled by a single small white donkey staggered by the load. "Shame!" Salma said as she passed the poor creature. She added, "I shouldn't blame the Israelis entirely, but sometimes they make us all feel like donkeys."

Salma and her family lived in Jabaliya, the largest of the eight refugee camps in the Strip. "They say it's the most densely populated place on earth, or one of them. That'd be hard for me to judge, as I haven't been out of Gaza in twenty years, since the blockade began. Our kids have never even seen the West Bank. Only this—" She gestured at the unbroken string of shops and offices and shoddy apartments. "Our lives are lived on this street. Restaurants, dentists, food, offices, shoes, appliances, you are here at least once a day or you are in the cemetery."

She turned on al-Quds Street and entered the refugee camp, a warren of half-built apartments, built so closely together that the balconies were jumping distance from each other. Gray-blue UNRWA tents, shaped like igloos, shouldered together in the sandy fields, along with ramshackle constructions fashioned from cardboard and sheets of plastic. Houses were roofed by sheets of corrugated asbestos weighed down with cinder blocks or worn-out tires. A stretch of apartments had burned to the ground in a fire that ravaged the camp two weeks prior. A tent in the middle of a field served as a refugee office, with a tattered Palestinian flag flying from a rebar pole, surrounded by strands of barbed wire that served no obvious purpose.

Children were headed to school, hundreds of them. The boys wore jeans and light-blue shirts; the girls also wore jeans under dresses the same blue color. They all carried backpacks, some with superheroes, some with *Frozen* characters. "Yes, we love children," Salma said, responding to Jamal's unspoken thought.

"How many do you have?"

"Four living," she said. "So far."

"Oh, when do you expect number five?"

"In six weeks, Allah willing, one more cousin for you."

"I can't wait to meet the ones I already have."

At the end of the street was the beach. The same coast ran to Egypt in one direction and Israel in the other. Across the Mediterranean Sea were Europe and Turkey. They might as well be in different hemispheres. The only part of contemporary Palestine touching the water was in this overcrowded internment camp that was Gaza. Jamal felt so constricted it was hard to breathe.

Salma parked her car in the ruins of a bombed-out medical clinic, which had been cleaned of rubble to serve that purpose. What remained of the structure looked as if it could collapse at any moment. "Let me prepare you," she said, wiping dust from the dashboard of the communal car. "I'm telling you this because our place is small and we live shoulder to shoulder. The kids are wonderful, you'll love them, but we're all a bit—I guess the word is 'distorted.' That's true of me, too. Mood problems, anger, we have these moments where everyone goes crazy. It's like a virus that runs through the family and then we're fine. I hope you don't have to deal with it, but everybody in Gaza suffers with this."

Jamal was embarrassed that he had given so little thought to the burdens his escape would impose on his hosts. He imagined Zayyat ordering Salma to make room for her very distant cousin; after all, Zayyat was a high official in Hamas and could force people to do things like clear out a bedroom for a fugitive. It didn't matter how much danger this already highly stressed family was facing.

He followed Salma up several flights of stairs. "I'll just be a day or two and I'll find someplace," he promised.

Salma took a break to catch her breath. "No, no, we're excited to have you. Nothing happens here between catastrophes. We're excited to have a visitor! Here we're incarcerated. Every few years we are bombarded and invaded. The children see things. They have lost friends. Their teacher was killed. We try to make normal lives in an abnormal environment, but people act out. Even me, I'm not normal. I take pills that help, but not too much because of the pregnancy."

Salma labored up the last flight of stairs. Just before she opened the door to their apartment, she stopped and whispered, "I haven't spoken like this to anyone. Everybody has their problems, they don't want to hear about yours. But you come from outside, without the history that we have with each other, and for some reason I can't shut up. So please forgive me. Now, here we are."

The children were in school, but Abdul Wahhab, Salma's husband, was sitting on the couch with his feet curled under him, watching television. He looked up when his wife walked in. "This is our cousin Jamal," she said.

Abdul Wahhab nodded. He was plump and gray, white-bearded, nibbling potato chips. His eyes registered little; it was as if the motor inside were idling, he couldn't even bring himself to stand and greet his guest.

"What are we watching?" Jamal asked.

"The daily indoctrination," said Abdul Wahhab.

"Is she still napping?" Salma asked. Abdul Wahhab shrugged in response. Salma went into another room. Presently she returned holding the hand of a little girl in a pink dress with tiny pearl studs in her ears. Jamal smiled at her, and she regarded him with an unnerving gaze. He had never seen such a mature face on a child, who he guessed was not yet three years old. Her face was round, like her mother's, and her small mouth turned down at each end, not quite approaching a frown but adding to the unnatural gravity of her expression. Like her father's, her hair formed a V-shaped widow's peak between the hemispheres of her forehead above her sharply arched brows. Her brown hair was tousled from her nap, creating even more drama in her aspect. "This is Maya," said Salma. "Give Mr. Jamal a kiss, Maya."

Jamal dropped to his knees as she kissed him on the cheek. It felt like a benediction.

49

Showdown

Hebron, Oct. 5, 2023

Tamar Levin entered the police station in Hebron, shooting a look at Golda, who instantly buzzed Yossi. Tamar walked past without waiting for his response. She found Yossi in his office going through papers.

"Those are the files you promised me?" she said.

"I made no promise," he said.

Tamar stared at him until he looked up. "What a waste, Yossi," she said. "Too bad it turned out this way." She paused again but still he offered no reaction. "You might have been useful."

"Get out of my office, Tamar, I don't need to take your crap anymore."

"I'm not leaving without the files."

"Let's see your warrant."

She laughed. "You're being absurd. You know how easy that would be. I could have one in a heartbeat."

"Nobody is stopping you. Of course, you'd have to put your name on it and describe the reasons you need the material. Why it might be relevant to a terror investigation. And let's suppose you have the files and they contain information you might not want to have generally known. Information that might even compromise your office. Information you would have to act upon or suppress. You'll have to decide, Tamar. Do you really want these files?"

Tamar closed the door behind her and leaned against it. "What are you afraid of, Yossi? That I'm corrupt? That I'm serving some special interest? Or is it the whole Zionist enterprise you're fighting—the occupation, the settlers, the politics, and yes, the corruption? You probably believe all of that. You think you're the last honest man in Israel. We're not perfect, Yossi. I made peace with that a long time ago. I thought you did, too. We all have blood on our hands. We're not the people we'd like to be—"

"Is this a civics lecture?" Yossi said, cutting her off.

Tamar stiffened. "I had you removed because you're insubordinate. You're obstructing a terror investigation. I could still have charges brought."

"Go ahead, Tamar. Then I can feel free to talk to the press about these files. How Chief Weingarten concluded that there was corruption in the police, in the intelligence agencies, in our political leadership. You're right. I don't know if I can trust you. Evidently the chief also did not or he would have asked for your help. He must have known that you placed a spy in our office."

"Berger is not a spy. He does exactly what he should do—what you should do: report any information that might be useful to the investigation. Instead you arrest him for doing his duty."

"It goes around the circle, doesn't it, Tamar? Berger talks to you and you report to the Kahanists. No wonder the chief thought he couldn't work with you if the case had anything to do with Cohen."

If Tamar was shaken by this charge, she hid it well. Her chin jutted in defiance. "Yes, I brief community leaders, as Weingarten would also do. You make it sound as if I betray secrets of our investigations. Never have I done such a thing."

"Weingarten didn't trust you," said Yossi. "He didn't trust anybody. He kept the information to himself. And that's why he was killed, to keep him quiet. But I'm not dead, Tamar. Not yet anyway."

"You've crossed the line, Yossi, and for what? You'll be out of your job in a couple days, Berger will be free, I'll have the files, and you'll be alone and disgraced. If you had only trusted me none of this would have happened."

"The chief knew something, and he wanted me to find out the truth. 'Help me, Yossi!' Those were his last words. And that's what I'm going to do."

"You're a fool."

"That's what everybody says."

"Anyway, we don't need your help anymore. We know where Jamal is."

MALIK RUSHED TO Yasmine's house as soon as she called. He found Omar on the floor, his eyes glazed, his pulse hard to find. "Call the ambulance," he said.

"I called," Yasmine said. She was leaning against the wall, quivering in fear but her face stoic. "We are waiting. I think there is a roadblock."

Malik lay Omar on his back and opened his mouth and probed with his finger to see if there was any blockage. He gave two quick breaths and began rapid compressions. In the bureau they were taught an ingenious method of establishing the correct tempo, which was the chorus of a Bee Gees song—"Ah, ha, ha, ha, stayin' alive, stayin' alive!" The tune came immediately into his mind and played over and over like a stuck needle. "C'mon, buddy, wake up!" Malik muttered. The boy was inert. Death had gripped him and was pulling him away. Yasmine was praying, her voice strange and distorted like something shattered inside. Malik heard the pounding, which he thought was his own heart, but then two men burst into the room and pulled him off the boy. One of them sprayed naloxone into Omar's nose and within minutes focus crept back into his eyes.

50

Histories

In her second semester at Sciences Po, Sara went through the stacks of the research library searching for books on Israel's origin—the subject of her dissertation. She knew the biblical accounts but had never explored the independent scholarship of the founding. For such an esteemed university, the available primary documents at Sciences Po were slight, with little in Hebrew. It occurred to her that she might have to switch topics for her dissertation, but the sheer absence of material indicated a need for more research.

As she was back in Israel for a few more days, she drove into Jerusalem to prowl through the libraries. After lunch she found herself in the Ben-Zvi Institute on Ibn Gabirol Street. She immediately felt at home among the books and manuscripts and oral histories, many of which Yitzhak Ben-Zvi had gathered personally. She knew who he was, of course, mainly from the many streets and boulevards named after him and his face on the hundred-shekel bill. She discovered that he was a scholar activist, much as she hoped to be. The more she learned the more she warmed to him.

Ben-Zvi was born into Jewish politics, in 1884, in the region of the Russian Empire that is present-day Ukraine. His father, Zvi Shimshelevich, organized the first Zionist Congress with Theodor Herzl in 1897, which announced the intention of establishing a Jewish state. Shimshelevich would be the only one of the original Zionists to live long enough to see the dream materialize. His son would become a prime mover in the creation of Israel and serve as its second president.

Ben-Zvi's lifelong passion was the study of diverse Jewish communities before the founding of Israel. He rented a room in Jaffa in 1908 from a member of the Samaritan community, which he later described as "the most unhappy of the sects in Israel, a sect that led a separated existence for millennia and trod its own way." There he learned enough Arabic and Samaritan Hebrew to begin his studies. He wandered among the Arab villages in the hills of Judea, marveling at the correspondence of Arab place names to Hebrew, noting the joint Muslim and Jewish graveyards, seeing the similarities of worship to Jewish ceremonies. More than two hundred Palestinian villages bore Hebrew names. These observations would lead him to a profound insight that would counter many of the legends of Jewish history.

He left Jaffa to study law in Constantinople, but he and his friend David Ben-Gurion, who would become Israel's first prime minister, were expelled from the Ottoman Empire, along with other Zionists. They found their way to New York City, where they collaborated on a book, *Eretz Israel in the Past and the Present*, which contained a frank examination of the legend of the Jewish Exodus. Ben-Zvi's studies of the ancient Jewish communities convinced him that most Judean farmers who inhabited the land during the Roman era never actually left. This remnant was forced to convert to Christianity, or later to Islam in order to avoid paying the tax imposed on Jews and Christians. Ben-Zvi's thesis was that the core of the peasantry was not composed of Arab immigrants who seized the land when the Jews fled; they were the same people who had always been there.

Ben-Gurion and Ben-Zvi believed that, because these two populations were historically one, they should be integrated into the workforce so that both could contribute to the future of Israel. But the Zionist movement collided with Arab nationalists who sought to create their own homeland after the collapse of the Ottoman Empire and the creation of the British Mandate to rule over Palestine. Neither side was willing to concede that they were the same people. Sara read this history with a feeling of loss and anger. After so much bloodshed, had there been another path available? Could the founding of Israel have been a family reunion rather than a perpetual war between relatives?

The 1929 massacre in Hebron and Arab riots in Jerusalem and other cities prompted British colonial authorities to restrict Jewish immigration into the Mandate. By 1937, Hitler was in power in Germany and the Arab population of Palestine was engaged in a bloody revolt. Ben-Gurion understood the tragedy about to befall both populations. "Another World War, and an attendant holocaust, hangs over our head," he prophesized. He also recognized the dilemma facing the Palestinians. "We both want the same thing. We want Palestine," he wrote. He added that if he were an Arab, "I would rise up against immigration liable sometime in the future to hand the country . . . over to Jewish rule. What Arab cannot do his math and understand that immigration at the rate of 60,000 a year means a Jewish state in all Palestine?"

IN 1987, three years before Jamal was born, Sheikh Yassin and other Islamists in Gaza published a charter of the Islamic Resistance Movement, which is what the acronym Hamas stands for. It opens with a quote from Hassan al-Banna, the founder of the Egyptian Muslim Brotherhood: "Israel will exist and will continue to exist until Islam will obliterate it, just as it obliterated others before it." The document quoted Muhammad, the Prophet: "The Day of Judgment will not come about until Muslims fight the Jews, when the Jew will hide behind stones and trees. The stones and trees will say O Muslims, O Abdullah, there is a Jew behind me, come and kill him."

The intellectual isolation of the movement is reflected in the bigotry and conspiracy thinking that decorate this manifesto. "With their money, [Jews] took control of the world media, news agencies, the press, publishing houses, broadcasting stations . . . They were behind the French revolution, the Communist revolution, and most of the other revolutions we hear about . . . They formed secret societies, such as the Freemasons, the Rotary Clubs, the Lions Club . . . They were behind World War I . . . they were behind World War II . . . there is no war going on anywhere, without having their finger in it."

In 2006, when Jamal was sixteen, an election took place in the Occupied Territories between Fatah and Hamas, perhaps the freest and least fraudulent in the entire Arab world. Given the opportunity, Palestinians made a fatal choice.

Why did they choose Hamas?

Fatah, the main force in Palestinian politics for four decades, was so incompetent that it ran multiple candidates against each other for the same post. It controlled the territories like a mob gang. Instead of negotiating peace with Israel, it walked away from a workable deal at Camp David in 2000, then fecklessly stood aside as Israeli settlements pushed deeper into the West Bank and walls went up all across Palestinian land. Fatah was a proven failure.

So when people had the chance, they voted for the opposition— Hamas, an Islamic movement that had spent years providing social services that the Fatah government failed to offer.

For months, Fatah refused to concede, which led to bloody anarchy. Finally, in 2007, Hamas forcibly evicted Fatah from the Gaza Strip. That snapped it for the Israelis. They declared Gaza a "hostile entity," as if the people of Gaza and the terrorists of Hamas were one and the same. Israel imposed a blockade on the entire population, which was already impoverished, isolated, and traumatized by years of occupation. Food and medicine were tightly restricted. A vast black market sprung up, relying on tunnels into Egypt, that brought in cars, cattle, clothes, and, of course, arms. Hamas supported itself by taxing the underground imports. The Israelis bombed many of the sports facilities and banned children's toys. Meantime, the Islamists burned down all the movie theaters. Practically the only entertainment in the Strip was the zoo, which featured a donkey painted with black and white stripes, posing as a zebra. Boredom and misery ruled.

There were no more elections in Palestine. Neither Jamal nor any other resident of the West Bank or Gaza his age or younger had ever had a say in their future.

WHEN JAMAL WAS A CHILD, he visited Gaza with his father, who had legal business there. This was during the Oslo era; peace seemed to be almost achieved, only a handful of details remaining. Workers crossed freely from Gaza and the West Bank into Israel every day. Peace crept in disguised as normal life.

Back then it took less than an hour to drive the forty miles from Gaza to Tel Aviv on roads without checkpoints. Hamas existed but it was not the government, it was simply "the resistance." Jamal remembered the place as being poor but not abject. While his father conducted a business meeting Jamal went to a drugstore and got a fountain drink. It was normal.

Jamal had several Christian playmates. They told him stories from the Bible, for instance the tale of Samson, the legendary strongman of the Old Testament and the great liberator of the Israelites. Although the Bible claimed that "the spirit of the Lord was on him," Samson was a kind of monster, tearing a lion to pieces with his bare hands, murdering his wedding guests, laying waste to the fields, and slaughtering an army of a thousand Philistines with the jawbone of an ass.

Samson used to visit the whores of Gaza, until he fell in love with Delilah. The Philistines bribed her to learn the secret of his uncanny strength. When Delilah cut his hair while he was sleeping, Samson became an ordinary man. The Philistines blinded him with a hot poker and turned him into a draft animal in a grist mill in Gaza.

But God got back into the act. When the Philistines brought Samson out for a little sport, tying him to the pillars of a temple, God answered Samson's prayer and returned his superhuman powers. According to the Bible, three thousand Philistines died in the rubble of the temple—the 9/11 of its day.

Another giant of legend was Goliath, the Philistine warrior, who was clad in iron armor while the Israelites were still in the Bronze Age. He spread terror across the land until a boy named David managed to slay him with a sling and five smooth stones. One account in the Talmud relates that David reminded his giant adversary, "You are actually my uncle." And then he cut off his head and left his body for the crows.

51

Birthday Girl

Gaza, Oct. 5, 2023

In the late afternoon Jamal went for a stroll on the beach with Salma and her children. Abdul Wahhab begged off, saying he was "too tired" to walk. The Mediterranean was the color of green olives, not from the fruit but from the raw sewage that drained into it. "Last year the water was blue, and it was safe for the children to swim, but now the electricity is off and on, so the treatment plants are not fully functioning," said Salma. "Once again—*akkh!* The smell!" Ruined fishing boats were dragged onto the sand and salvaged for spare parts. "We used to call this the boat harbor, but now it is the boat cemetery."

"What happened?"

"The Israelis won't permit the items needed for repairing motors. Even paint, they restrict the colors. Now we receive only blue and yellow. When the boats work, the fishermen can only go out so far. It used to be six miles, now it is fifteen, which has helped, but under Oslo it is supposed to be twenty. You see fishermen on paddleboards catching tiny fishes in this filthy water. Not for years have I dared to eat a fish."

They weren't aware of the drone tracking them, so high it was scarcely visible, like a fragment of a cloud or a star left over from the night.

Gaza didn't feel so much like a prison as it did a zoo. The human animals moved about without destinations. Idleness created a torpor that acted like increased gravity, each movement a struggle against this heaviness. After a couple hours Jamal became accustomed to the monotonic mood of the place. Voices were subdued, possibly drugged. Few other consolations were available.

As they walked, they tried to work out exactly how they were related through the Khalil line, but they could never pin it down. Abdul Wahhab's grandfather came from a little Palestinian village near Jerusalem called Deir Yassin. It stood beside one of the major roads into Jerusalem. In 1948, when Palestine was still under the British Mandate, a coalition of Zionist paramilitaries decided to seize the village and force the Arabs out of their homes. They expected to scare off the residents with a few explosions, but when they met resistance, their tactics changed. They went from house to house throwing grenades into windows. The death toll was never clearly established and both sides exaggerated the fatalities for their own purposes, but according to various accounts the number of Palestinians killed was in the hundreds. Only seven died in combat, the others in their homes. Five attackers died. Arabs who survived were loaded on a flatbed truck and driven to Jerusalem, where they were jeered and spat upon. Then the men were taken to a quarry and executed. Stories of rape and torture in Deir Yassin terrorized the Palestinian population, leading to the diaspora a few weeks later. The Palestinians who were expelled or fled in terror and were not allowed to return—the fatal moment in the future of both peoples.

Abdul Wahhab's grandfather was a boy when he stood on that flatbed truck with his father. He did not go to the quarry to be executed with the grown men; he was left on the street by the Jaffa Gate with fifty-five other children. Hind al-Husseini, a Palestinian woman, built an orphanage for them. Three years later, Abdul Wahhab's grandfather was reunited with his mother in Gaza, where she had taken refuge, living in a hole in a sand dune for the first year of her exile.

The spiral of revenge demanded equivalent suffering by either side. A month after the Deir Yassin massacre, Kfar Etzion, a Jewish settlement near Hebron, surrendered to an Arab force. The settlement's defenders, waving white flags, gathered at a school, but they were shot down by Arabs crying "Deir Yassin!"

Like many of those who fled, Abdul Wahhab's family kept the key to their house in Deir Yassin. It was one of the few Arab villages to remain intact, now serving as the picturesque grounds of a psychiatric hospital. Perhaps the ancestors of Jamal and Abdul Wahhab had met somewhere in the past, Salma speculated. "He would know better."

Her children ran ahead in the sand, seemingly unaffected by the seaside stench. "And here they are, the fourth generation of this family to be living in this prison," she said. She pointed to Adl, the eldest, who assumed a parental air, although he was only fourteen. "He's the one who worries me the most. His seriousness. He feels responsible. Now he thinks he must be the man of the family. I tried to tell him he is too young for this, he should enjoy his life, learn about the world. But I am talking to the wind. Sometimes I search the boys' room to see if he has hidden a farewell note."

Adl looked back at them, as if he was aware his name was mentioned. He was a handsome boy, already the tallest member of the family.

"Iyad, he is eleven, our little athlete," she said, indicating the boy who balanced on the seawall. "He cares only for sports, and I am grateful for this. I hope he never becomes a part of our national drama. He is the happy one, always smiling, although he lost teammates in the bombings of 2021. He is living in a dream world, and I don't wake him from this dream."

Salma turned to her daughter walking beside her, absorbing the conversation. "Amira, she's eight. She's the bright one, aren't you?"

"Adl is also bright," Amira said.

"Yes, he is," said Salma. "You are all bright children, but you especially, Amira. You have intelligence and you must use it. We agree on this, right?"

Amira nodded.

"I have so many hopes, but realistically, what will become of them? Okay, my parents and my grandparents surrendered their lives to this trap they fell into, and yes, my generation as well, living meaningless lives, unable to be the people we might have been. We live with this knowledge every minute. But to look at our children and think that their lives will also come to nothing, this is what breaks me. I can't dwell on it without wanting to scream."

It unsettled Jamal that she was speaking so openly of her desperation in front of Amira, who missed nothing.

"What would you do if you could leave?" he asked.

Salma laughed bitterly. "Let's not fool ourselves into thinking that the problem is only Gaza, or the West Bank. I would go far away from this region. Where among the Arabs is there real freedom, real achievement? Here we are ruled by Hamas. Israel did not force us to do this, we did it to ourselves, our Palestinian democracy. We are ruled by thugs and religious idiots. All we have to do is look at the example of Israel to see what our own societies could be if we were liberated from these tyrannies and the religious dogma that imprisons our minds. How long must the Arab world be a graveyard for youth and talent?"

Jamal was silent. These were questions that he had lived with but never faced as squarely as Salma did. Suppose the occupation ended tomorrow, would Palestine be better off? Or would it become just another Arab country without the resources of the Gulf or Saudi Arabia, a thwarted and corrupt country like Syria, Iraq, Egypt, Lebanon, Libya, Yemen, Algeria, Sudan? The list goes on. It was easier to blame Israel than to accept the failures of Arab society.

"One child you didn't mention was this one," Jamal said. Maya was holding his little finger as they walked. He was moved—thrilled, honored—by her trust. It had been a long time since he had been around such a young child. He still remembered when his son would hold his finger in this same fashion.

"Is she bothering you?" Salma asked.

"Not at all. She's charming."

"She takes to you. She can be so—I'm not sure how to express it—she lives inside herself. We don't know her thoughts. In fact she still hasn't said her first word. She makes no noises at all."

"She's a mute?"

"Not because of anything physically wrong with her. She used to—at least when she was teething—she would cry, but then that stopped, and what we get now are these looks of hers, like some angel with an important message from Paradise but she won't let us know what the message is. Maya," she said, "do you want Mommy to hold you?" Maya nodded, and Salma picked her up. "When we're talking about her she wants me to hold her."

"She's a most unusual child."

"Oh, in so many ways."

"And very striking, with that grown-up face of hers."

Salma was quiet for a moment, then said, "Her face is not hers alone. Before this one was born, there was another sister, our oldest, Fatima. The same round face, the same solemn black eyes, same everything. From the beginning, Maya stole our breath because it was as if Fatima had returned and we had another chance to save her. I know you think this is a mother's fantasy, but I could show you photographs. I mean, who looks like this? Fatima did, exactly. It's uncanny. I don't want to say it is like a ghost come to life, but her spirit is here, I feel this."

"What happened to Fatima?"

"She died in the 2014 war. Her school came under attack, and the girls were evacuated to an apartment building just a few blocks from here, where her teacher lived. This was the plan, in case the school was bombed the girls would be waiting for their parents in Miss Nadine's apartment. It was high and we thought it would be safer because the fighting is on the ground. I don't know why the girls were allowed on the balcony. The soldiers could see them plainly with their binoculars, but they had orders to shoot anything that moved. Later, the Israelis claimed the girls were 'spotters'—they were directing the Hamas fighters. Anyway, a tank fired a shell and nine girls were killed, including Fatima. They were some of the five hundred Palestinian children who died in that war."

As Salma talked, Maya stared at her with an expression both absorbing and inquisitive, as if there was a question on her tongue that could not escape her mouth. She put her tiny hand on Salma's cheek.

"Today is her birthday," Salma said.

"How old are you?" Jamal asked.

Maya held up three fingers.

"I've got a present for you," he said, and handed her his mother's necklace. Maya's eyes widened in what looked like joy.

52

An Ideal Lover

Hebron, Oct. 5, 2023

From the moment he arrived in Palestine, Malik had been confused, assaulted, and culturally at sea. He had imagined he would understand it instantly. He was an Arab, he spoke the language, certainly he would feel at home. Instead, he was in a state of constant revelation, learning things about his background and himself that he had never imagined. Part of him couldn't wait to leave it all behind; another part wanted to dive in deeper. Although he was an outsider he could sense the tremors underfoot, as if a great eruption was about to take place, and yet the Israelis were so complacent and the Palestinians so paralyzed by depression that he distrusted his instincts. He wondered, *Am I the only one who feels this way?*

He spent the first hour of his morning trying to reconstruct his thoughts about Sara and Yossi from the notes he made the night before. The visit to Yossi's house had been discouraging. Yossi had been fired because he and Malik were unofficially working together. Other factors may have gone into that decision. Yossi was headstrong and probably insubordinate. He had a problem with alcohol. No doubt he was unreliable in other ways, but Malik sensed that official powers wanted Yossi out to protect themselves.

He had known Yossi only briefly, and it had been a rough start, evolving into an understanding teetering between friendship and enmity. Malik recognized that however fierce Yossi appeared to be, he was caught like a lion in a leg trap—the unresolvable conflict—and his cunning and thrashing about did nothing but sharpen the indignity. Yossi's predicament touched a button in Malik's psyche. He had always been susceptible to certain wounded personalities.

Sara was much in his mind. He had awakened with the remnants of a still-dissolving dream of her in his arms. In his notebook he described her as "lovely" and "bright" and "amusing," a word portrait of an ideal lover—"ideal" in the sense of being both perfect and unattainable. He vividly recalled the candlelight on her face as the sun set, her face so close to his, and every word of the conversation between them, a conversation he wanted never to end.

He considered the hilarious complexity of courting Yossi's daughter. Nothing about it made any sense—the Arab-Israeli issue being just one of a million obstacles, led by his own inadequacy. His life since the bomb went off had been a struggle to hold on to his identity. He worried constantly that his memory was failing, fearing that he wouldn't detect from day to day the incremental loss of his mentality. He was swimming against a powerful current that was pulling him toward oblivion.

MALIK BROUGHT CROISSANTS for Dina. She had a decision to make and the alternatives were ominous. "I'm not sure how long you can stay in jail," Malik told her. "Yossi is the only one protecting you, and with him gone, I don't know who will take over or what they will do with you. I can't leave you in danger but I'm not sure what the next step is."

"You are disappointed because your expectations are too high," Dina said. "If you lived here, you would adjust. This is normal. Have a croissant. You brought too many."

Her tone struck him as annoyingly neutral when her life and freedom were at stake. Maybe she didn't grasp the peril she was in. "Dina, I'm serious. We need a plan, but you've got to help me. Be totally honest and don't leave out any important details. You don't appreciate how dangerous your situation is."

"I don't know what you want from me. I've told you everything, even the worst things that I thought I would never tell anyone." She took another bite of the croissant.

He could see that his stern tone was scaring her but she spoke with an impassivity he regarded as dishonest. "Okay, let's start with your relationship with Chief Weingarten. Do you have proof that you assisted him as a source?"

"I confessed this already."

"If there is some kind of formal agreement, perhaps the police will protect you. This is what we do in America when our sources are in danger because they worked with us."

"Like what proof?"

"Did he pay you? Do you have a receipt, an agreement, anything? Did you have a lawyer help you?"

"Everybody knows I was a spy, everybody!" she burst out. "And now you ask me to prove it!" She added: "The cop with the blue hair already tried to bribe me to find Jamal. They expect me to help them kill him. Maybe you also hope for this."

"Other than the photograph of you with him in the café, was there other evidence? Did you take a room together, for instance?"

Dina went pale. "You also believe this?" she asked.

"Dina, I know you hate these questions. I'm not condemning you in any way. I don't care if this rumor is true or not true. But if there was something that showed a transaction between you, it would help our cause."

"In other words, if I can prove I was his mistress and took money from him, the police will protect me?"

"They might."

"Why do they think only I confided in him and he did not talk to me? Maybe we were both traitors."

Malik was shocked. She had jumped onto a track he had never considered. "Did he? Did he talk to you about his investigation?"

"I don't know what I should say."

"Dina, if there's something he told you that would help me understand why he was killed, it might help you. And Jamal."

"He just complained that he was an honest person and that people around him and above him were corrupt. He said he wept because of the things being done to the Palestinian people. He proposed he and I would be a secret something, like a spy business but not for either side. We would help each other. I didn't know if this was true or he was pretending so he could get me to talk more."

"What did he tell you?"

"Like I said, there was corruption. Money was changing hands. Mountains of it. He was making notes. One day he would be like Samson and bring the whole thing down, like you know, this hero thing of his."

"Did you believe him?"

"Some of it, why not? We tend to believe the worst about other people. So when the chief of police tells you that there are corrupt Jews, this is easy to accept. We knew that already, right?"

"Did he say anything about Cohen?"

She nodded vigorously. "He was obsessed with this person. He said that all the bad qualities of the Jewish people were in this man, but also some of the good ones. I think he secretly admired him."

"Before the chief helped you get pain medication for Omar, it was all black-market narcotics, right? Did you talk about this with Weingarten?"

"He asked me where the drugs were coming from in Hebron."

"What did you say?"

"I bought from the Palestinian police. They had the best quality. That wasn't the only way of getting drugs but it was the safest. He specifically asked if the dealers were being supplied through the settlements. Questions like that I would take to Jamal. Honestly, despite what people think the chief was not really interested in me. Oh, he was flirting, yes, but I was like a go-between."

"Jamal knew about this?"

"I think so but I don't know. I had to be so careful to keep him from being suspicious, but then he would tell me things that I didn't ask about, as if he wanted to send a message. It was strange. One time I made like a joke that we were helping the Israelis and he became violent with me. I was shocked!"

"He hit you?"

She pursed her lips and looked into her lap.

"Let me ask you another question. I'm sorry to be personal so don't answer if it offends you. Suppose Jamal returns and we prove he is innocent. Do you still accept him as a husband?"

Dina did not respond. She kept her face averted. When he realized she was weeping he handed her a napkin.

"He will not agree," she said. "No one will take me now, no one, never!"

"You're young and smart and beautiful, you shouldn't worry."

"And you're naive and I think a little foolish. You have a big heart, which is a problem in this place. People who try to do good cause the most problems. This is the world I know. We are not in America. Here, good people are bad luck. They are the ones who get killed or get others killed. If you try to help you will only make things worse, not just for me but for everybody."

Malik hadn't really taken the measure of her cynicism until now. "From where you are, the future must seem completely hopeless. It's not. You have a chance for a happy life. It doesn't all have to end here in Hebron. Something will come along, I promise."

"Like what?" she demanded. Her face was flushed and she didn't bother to blot the tears streaming down her cheeks. "Even my family, they will disown me or suffer the consequences. I have nothing on my own. I am destitute. I don't have an education or a trade. Who would give a job to the traitor girl? They prefer to kill me, to make an example. Sometimes I think this is okay. Better that than to live always in humiliation. So tell me, what will come along that will make all this disappear?"

"I can take you to America. I've got connections at the embassy. They owe me. I'll get you a student visa and you can start a new life."

53

The Promise of Virgins

Gaza, Oct. 5, 2023

Abdul Wahhab finally roused himself to invite Jamal to share a hookah at a stand on the beach. Jamal had gotten somewhat accustomed to the stench of the polluted seawater, which the shisha tobacco helped mask. "On the one hand, I feel myself a victim," Abdul Wahhab admitted. "Even talking to you in honesty could result in—let us say—an unfortunate result. Everywhere your mind wanders you bump into laws and restrictions, so many you begin to imagine ones that don't exist. Then comes the point that it doesn't matter. What they do to me they will do. All this is the result of the occupation. We are prisoners of the Jewish entity, this is what we are told to believe. And it's true, we are. But even with the little plot of land we have been allowed, we have ruined it. We elected these fanatics that now control us and will never let us vote again. They have only one goal, to drive the Jews into the sea. It's a fantasy, but we surrender our lives to this."

A hookah attendant came to refresh the coals and Abdul Wahhab fell silent until the attendant was done. "I am a businessman, or was," he continued. "I look at Gaza and see potential. It is small and poor, yes, but so was Singapore, so was Dubai, so was Hong Kong. We do not need to be a democracy—these countries are not, at least in the Western sense. We do not need to be resource rich. Singapore has nothing. Japan has nothing. If you ask me as a businessman what do I absolutely need to succeed, there are only two things: a just legal system and competent governance. Yes, there are other desirable factors. Free enterprise. Fair taxation. Security. But if you have just and enforceable laws and a government that works for the people, businesses will prosper and the wealth of the people will grow.

"So, is this Israel's fault that we are governed by religious fanatics who enrich themselves and do not provide for the people? I will say yes, in the sense that the Israelis humiliate us so much that we do such things to ourselves. They make it impossible not to hate them and we act out of rage. But we always had a choice. If we accept defeat, we could turn our faces away from the past, where there is nothing but loss and shame, and allow ourselves to dream about a Gaza we are proud of, one that is a part of the world, one that raises our children on a diet of hope and possibility instead of meal after meal of despair."

Jamal was impressed by Abdul Wahhab's passion and his unexpected eloquence. "You would have made a wonderful politician," he said. "People need to hear your voice."

Abdul Wahhab shook his head. "I don't believe in politics anymore. We have plenty of it in the Arab world and it only harms people. We pretend to have democracies, but the politicians and the armies only exist to steal the wealth for themselves. I make a confession. I am sorry to see the way Israel is going. They often boast they are the only true democracy in the Middle East, but they value it so little. Let them have a taste of life in an Arab democracy and maybe they will be more careful with their own government." He set aside his pipe and stood awkwardly. "Saying such things could get me killed but I don't care enough to be careful."

LATER THAT THURSDAY MORNING, Jamal accompanied Adl, the oldest child, to a class devoted to memorizing the Quran. It reminded Jamal of the madrassas of antiquity, a sheikh in a white turban instructing a group of teenage boys sitting on the floor, legs crossed. These boys were all wearing green caps, the insignia of the Hamas youth organization that was sponsoring the class. They rocked back and forth reciting verses from chapter 8, "The Spoils of War." Jamal vividly recalled the immense effort of memorizing the six hundred pages of the holy book. It taught him that he was capable of accomplishing a task that seemed utterly impossible. It also instructed him on the divine insistence on violence:

> *Your Lord revealed to the angels: I am with you,*
> *therefore support those who believe. I will cast*
> *terror into the hearts of those who disbelieve. So*
> *strike off their heads and strike off every fingertip.*

After the class, Jamal proposed to buy an ice cream as a reward for Adl's proficiency. The boy led him down an unnamed street where several small shops—a barber, a women's clothing store—were open but untended. A couple was playing backgammon at a plastic table nearby. The ice-cream shop around the corner was surprisingly well supplied with about twenty flavors. Jamal congratulated the young man who ran it. "We make it all ourselves using goat milk," he said proudly, adding, "We are famous here." The fruit flavors came from the apple and citrus orchards, but some of them were wildly improvised—pickle and octopus flavors were strange enough, but there was also a cricket-infused concoction that was truly revolting. Jamal got vanilla, it seemed safest and turned out to be quite delicious. Adl chose ketchup-flavored.

Jamal noticed a knot of people standing nearby looking at an immense excavated space, larger than three soccer fields. "I want to show you this!" Adl said excitedly. "This is where the *shebab* train."

Jamal walked with the boy to the edge of the sunken arena. A mock village had been constructed in the pit, with artificial houses and a cardboard tank. Dozens of young men—the *shebab*—carrying AK-47s and RPGs, darted in choreographed movements past obstacles made of concrete boxes, towers of old tires, and cement blocks. Jamal and Adl joined the other spectators, many also eating ice cream, watching the tableau unfold. "The enemy is inside the buildings," Adl said enthusiastically. "This one—" he pointed to a militant who had made it to a window—"he will throw the grenade!" Everyone seemed to know the drill and they cheered when a cloud of smoke from a dummy grenade billowed out from the window. Presently the militants emerged, with some playing the role of captives, wearing IDF-like uniforms with their hands cuffed behind them. On top of one the houses, a Hamas warrior broke the staff holding an Israeli flag and hurled it to the ground, signaling the end of the exercise. The audience cheered.

"That one is my brother," Adl said in an awed whisper.

Jamal looked at him in puzzlement. Was this a child Salma forgot to mention? A son from another wife? "I didn't know there were other children in the family."

Adl spoke quietly, as if people around them would betray his confidence. "We don't talk about him. Hani is the fighter. People know him. He is with the resistance. I spoke to him and he agrees to meet you. Please do not mention this to my parents."

Hani came round to a café that had been empty during the military exercise but now was overfull with excited participants and members of the audience. He looked to be about twenty, physically striking, with a deep chest and broad shoulders—scarcely the look of so many undernourished Gazans. For years, Israel had estimated the minimum amount of calories needed to avoid near-starvation in order to determine how much food aid to allow into the Strip, but Hani obviously had the benefit of a healthy diet and access to a gym. His jutting chin was like a rock that the rest of his face was built upon, with prominent cheekbones and brows that formed ridges over his eyes. He radiated health and power. He wore a camouflage uniform and the green headband that signified his membership in the al-Qassam brigades, the military arm of Hamas. He lightly touched Jamal's palm with his and then placed it on his heart.

Hani ordered tea, which he sweetened with three sugars. "May I ask how are my parents?" he said in a surprisingly soft voice.

"They seem well."

"But how are they exactly? You must have an impression."

"Your father is very depressed," Jamal said, "but you probably know this better than I. Your mother is harder to diagnose because of her charm."

Hani laughed. "Oh, I miss them so much."

"You can't visit?"

"I can, of course. It's allowed. But we have a problem. They are ashamed of me, and I of them. They do not endorse violent action. They come from an older generation that was repeatedly defeated so they think there is no hope. They no longer pray for freedom. Maybe they don't pray at all. So we travel on different roads."

Jamal could see the idealism and piety burning in the face of this muscular young man, like some kind of superhero toy forged in the oven of Gaza's fanaticism. He thought once again how weakness becomes dangerous when it seeks strength as a solution. Victims of oppression believe that their salvation is to become stronger than their enemy, more committed, more pious, and more ruthless, until they turn into the pitiless enemy that lives in their imagination. Lambs turn into lions. Jamal's mission had been to intercept this progression. Real peace doesn't come through strength, he believed, it comes through forgiveness and accommodation and the renunciation of absolute victory. Peace is the acceptance of mutual surrender. Anything less is merely a truce.

One other thing about Hani that Jamal recognized: he longed for death. He knew it was near and he glowed with anticipation for the long-sought prizes of martyrdom. At the first drop of his blood, all his sins would be forgiven and he would be instantly transported into Paradise, along with seventy members of his family who will be saved from the suffering of hellfire. A crown of honor will be placed on his head; the finest wine—taboo in life—will be at hand. He will be attended by seventy-two dark-eyed virgins, with "appetizing vaginas." The martyr's penis will remain erect for all eternity, and after each act of intercourse virginity is restored to his partner. How many young men like Hani—virgins themselves—had been drawn to this vision of a life without the prohibitions of their religion? Many of these legends arose from hadith—the sayings, often disputed, of the Prophet Muhammad and his companions—and dangled before young men as rewards for their sacrifice. Similar thoughts must have been in the mind of Jamal's brother, Nader, when he took his AK-47 to the rooftops of the Old City and murdered that Jewish family. What kind of God would endorse such an action? Who could believe

Nader is in Paradise now, with his crown and his virgins and his eternal erection?

As Jamal walked back to Salma's apartment with Adl, the boy confided, "This will happen soon. I only wish I could join them."

THE NIGHT OF OCTOBER 5, Jamal slept on a mattress between the two sons. They had both fallen asleep instantly, but Jamal lay awake, stirred by the events he had experienced in the last several days. He remembered being in his childhood home—it seemed like a fantasy now—where he was born and where he expected to die. And yet he had escaped. He could not get out of his mind the sensation of being wrapped in the funeral shroud, suspended between life and death like a zombie aware of his own demise. His thighs were still raw from riding the galloping camel. He imagined the primitive certainty that the warriors of past times must have felt as they raced through the desert, with cries of conquest and vengeance and no thoughts of peace. Part of him yearned for that certainty, the willingness to kill or die for a cause, to see life in bold contrast between good and evil and to know which side he was on. Not to reason with his enemies but simply to destroy them.

He understood the fallacies of such thinking. Reconciliation demanded strength he didn't have. He had relinquished the struggle for peace for what he hoped would be a quiet domestic life, but he was not to have such a life. He had thought of himself as a warrior who fought against violence, including his own shameful urges. What good had his struggle done anyone? Here were his cousins, imprisoned in this claustrophobic ghetto, one generation after another, as periodic peace talks took the stage, then dissipated like mirages in the desert. Was he insane to continue to struggle for peace? Would the Holy Land always be the field of battle in the name of God?

In this confounding state of mind, he got up to pee. He had memorized the path to the toilet, and he threaded his way between the sleeping boys, then tiptoed through the hallway, hearing sounds of slumber from the other rooms. These were his benefactors, fighting to keep from being utterly defeated. He owed them his assistance.

But what, really, could he do? *May Allah bless them for their charity,* he prayed.

As he quietly entered the bathroom he heard another noise, the distant metallic roar of a helicopter, the Israelis making a nightly patrol. It occurred to him that they might be looking for him, but he was here, safe with his sleeping tribesmen.

And then the world exploded.

THE PAIN EVENTUALLY WOKE HIM, a sharp ache in his side. It was pitch black and he was deeply confused. He touched the walls closely surrounding him, recognizing a sink and a toilet. That was all. He fumbled for a door and found the knob, but the door refused to open except for a crack. A bit of daylight streamed in. He heard voices and other sounds he couldn't make out. "Hello?" he cried, but his voice was weak and it hurt when he spoke. "Hello!" He shoved harder against the door, and it moved a bit more but not enough to get his body through. He managed to wedge his hand through the crack and waved frantically. He heard a cry, "Look! Look! Someone is alive!"

It took an hour before the door finally opened and Jamal stared into the remains of the apartment, a mound of blasted concrete, with blocks of plaster and shattered furniture scattered about and strewn into the street below, and the astonished faces of his rescuers. Half of the apartment was missing and open to the air. The couch was upside down and balanced on the edge of the gaping ruin.

White dust covered the faces of the rescuers, like cartoon ghosts. One of them helped Jamal into a basket attached to a boom from a firetruck far below. Jamal was shaky and uncertain when he got into the basket, but he had already evaded death for the day. Once outside he could see that the rest of the building was intact. The bomb or missile or whatever it was had been precisely aimed at the apartment—*at me,* he realized. *I brought this on. It's my fault.* He could see people below him cheering, "A survivor! Praise Allah for his mercy!" He didn't feel like thanking God, but he prayed for the salvation of the family he had put in mortal danger. *Don't let them be dead,* he pleaded. He was also praying for himself, that he wouldn't have to live with their deaths on his conscience.

An EMS truck was parked in the street and a medic removed Jamal's shirt and bathed a bleeding wound on his abdomen, which he said was not serious, but ribs had been broken, accounting for the pain. Jamal stared into the street, dazed. The sound of voices, of motors, of children—all new, but also familiar, as if life were a country of his youth and he had only just returned for a visit. Then he noticed the corpses on the ground. He abruptly stood and walked to them, ignoring the medic who wasn't finished with his examination.

There they were. Abdul Wahhab, the broken father; Salma, the mother who carried the family on her shoulders with another baby inside her; Adl, the teenager who ate ketchup ice cream and longed to join the radicals; Iyad, the dreamy, athletic one; Amira, the smart one; all dead, lying in the street in their nightclothes, their grotesque fatal wounds exposed, crushed and broken and soaked in blood. All dead—except for one.

Jamal climbed back into the basket and demanded that the crane take him up again to the mangled apartment. The rescuers were still digging through the scree, dutifully but aimlessly, sure that they had found all the corpses.

"Where is the little one?" Jamal demanded.

"There is another?" said a man with a hard hat and a yellow vest.

"A small child, you may have missed her."

"Do you know where she might have been?"

"She slept in a crib in their bedroom."

The rescuer pointed out a section in the rubble of the apartment where the parents had been found. Huge blocks of concrete lay like fallen pillars. No one could survive such crushing beams. Jamal reached with his bare hands into the scree, tossing the rough shards aside and raking the smaller pieces out of the hole he was making. He hoped this was where the wall had been, next to the crib where Maya had slept, but he didn't really know. Nothing familiar remained.

"We've been through this already," the chief rescuer said gently.

"She's here!" Jamal insisted. "Somewhere she's here!"

He continued to rake through the broken concrete with bleeding hands. "Look!" he said. He found a piece of polished wood that might have been a part of the crib. "Quick, help me!" His lungs were full of dust. Two other men began to dig. One with a shovel gave his gloves to Jamal.

He was looking for a miracle. He began praying aloud, unconsciously, prompting the other men to pray as well. He couldn't spare his hands to wipe the tears from his eyes. *Amid so many deaths*, he thought, *why does one life matter more?* And yet he believed that if he could save Maya his own life might achieve a purpose.

He uncovered spindles from the crib. He was lucky, he told himself, there must have been a reason why he picked this spot out of the chaos of debris. The reason was that Maya is alive and she is here and he will rescue her. Surely there were pockets of air, it wasn't impossible that she had been surrounded by protective stones that kept her safe. It had happened before. They had all seen such scenes in Syria, where children were saved from the ruins where so many others died. Infants like her.

The men had now made a hole deep enough that Jamal could fit into it. They reached what had been the floor. Jamal faced the wall of debris in front of him. He called her name. Then he saw a piece of material that he recognized as her little nightgown.

"We need to open a space for her to breathe," Jamal said. But when he took a rock from the rubble in front of him, more rocks fell into the space. There was nothing to be done but to dig again from the top, removing another layer of plaster and broken concrete to reach the point where she might get air. Jamal became even more frantic, knowing that she was right in front of him. More rescuers arrived to clear the debris. The men worked silently, as if words would slow them down.

And then they found her hand. Jamal grasped it with his fingers and felt a faint squeeze. Or perhaps he imagined it.

"She's alive!" The cry went through the shattered apartment and into the street. Jamal tried not to think about what he was actually going to find. Whatever Maya had been, she would be something different now.

Bits of her gown came into view and pieces of the crib. The men were working carefully, knowing that her little body awaited them.

Her chin appeared in what seemed to be a slight pocket of air. Jamal removed a rock and saw her face, intact and still eerily beautiful, despite the pallor caused by dust and the loss of blood. Her gown was running with blood and her body below was broken and strangely arrayed, as if the pieces had been cut apart and rearranged in ways that didn't fit.

Her eyes fluttered and she looked at him. "Jamal," she said. The only word she would ever speak.

54

Jericho Wall

Jerusalem, Oct. 5, 2023

The IDF announced that Jamal Khalil had been eliminated by a Hellfire missile from an Apache helicopter that had also killed the five Hamas supporters hiding him. No further word was given about the identity of the victims. Hamas issued a statement from Ehsan Zayyat confirming the deaths.

The rockets flew at sunset, Hamas's answer to the Israeli attack. It was beautiful in its murderous way, bright traces across the darkening sky, the rockets on their murderous mission and Israel's Iron Dome responding with dancing missiles to intercept them—a routine desultory exchange, a conversation that Israel and Hamas had been engaged in for decades, a feature of the changelessness that both sides had become accustomed to.

Tamar received credit for the intelligence that led to the strike. It had taken less than an hour in al-Moscobiyeh to break Ashraf, the Mouse Arch tailor, who gave away the particulars of Jamal's escape. From there the network of informers in Gaza made the connection with the Khalil clan. It all came together quickly, a textbook operation.

To celebrate, Tamar was given a dinner at the Notre Dame of Jerusalem Center, a lavish Catholic retreat originally built for pilgrims. Well-heeled tourists filled Cheese & Wine, the restaurant on the rooftop, along with potentates of the church, their immaculately tailored garments designating their offices. A cardinal in a scarlet cassock with a red skullcap was entertaining a party of acolyte priests

in black, like a flock of crows. The restaurant was spartan but taste-
ful, with warm wooden floors and blue Jerusalem tiles, quoting the
severity of the monastic life while transforming it into high fashion.

Getting a table at the best restaurants in town was never a problem for Shabak. Tamar was pleased to find her colleagues seated in
a quiet alcove behind a limestone wall, the hefty blocks artfully dappled with chisel marks contrasting with gleaming floors and table-
tops that looked almost wet to the touch. Nir Gallant, the chief of
Shin Bet, stood up when Tamar arrived. He had a broad smile on
his face as he raised a glass in her direction. Everyone did the same.
Tamar fought back a sob of gratitude.

Nir ordered mezes for the table and the conversation became
relaxed and self-congratulatory. Chief Weingarten's murder had
been a stain on Israeli intelligence, but thanks to the quick reaction
of its officers, combined with the awesome capabilities of the IDF,
the perpetrator had been eliminated in surgical fashion. The fact
that he was a notorious peace advocate, now revealed as a Hamas
operative, made the resolution of the affair even more glorious.
Smiles and admiring glances in Tamar's direction, as well as some
envious remarks, marked her entry into the elite inner circle after a
long marginal career. On the advice of a colleague who once spurned
her, she ordered an appetizer of grilled shrimp on rice noodles. "The
Catholics know how to do shellfish," he told her, happy to evade the
Jewish dietary prohibitions, which was not so easy to do in Jerusalem. Tamar rarely ate red meat but for her entrée she treated herself
to the lamb medallions, matched with a glass of Masada red wine.
It was all so perfect.

Cheese was the specialty of the house, and after the meal Nir
ordered a selection of platters to accompany their desserts, then
motioned to Tamar to follow him. Nir was in his mid-sixties, with
beautiful white hair handsomely set off by his deep olive complex-
ion. They each took a glass of cognac onto the balcony surrounding
the restaurant on all sides. The Notre Dame Center stood atop the
highest point in the Old City and nowhere else had a more glorious
vista.

Tamar imagined Nir must have been quite a dashing young man, the scion of generations of military leaders and, before the establishment of the state, members of Jewish resistance movements. None of them had achieved the pinnacle of influence and trust that Nir had done. He was revered for his clear-eyed guidance of the nation into a period of stability. Despite the annoyance of settlers continually stirring up the West Bank, killing more Palestinians than at any other point in Nir's illustrious career, the recent rocket attacks from Gaza in response had dwindled to an acceptable nuisance, quickly dying out, as this recent one had.

"You can't get more historic than this," said Nir, gesturing toward the Mount of Olives, which he described as "one giant Jewish cemetery. When the Messiah comes they'll be the first to arise. The Christians say it is where Jesus ascended into heaven. Who knows how these stories arise, but the city is built on such narratives. Believe them or not, they make us the people we are."

Jerusalem glowed in the night like a fire reduced to its embers. Below the mount was the Garden of Gethsemane, and rising from the valley was an intriguing hill known to Jews as the Temple Mount, the holiest place in Judaism. To Muslims it is the Noble Sanctuary, the spot where the Prophet Muhammad visited heaven riding his winged horse, Buraq. Legend located it as the place where God created Adam, where Cain killed Abel, where Abraham brought his son Isaac (Ishmael for the Muslims) to be sacrificed. In that instance, God spared the child because of Abraham's devotion, but that was the last time the divinity stepped in to prevent bloodshed. Two mosques occupied the spot where the Jewish temple stood until it was destroyed by the Romans in AD 70. Its absence has defined Jerusalem and Judaism ever since.

Tamar waited, assuming that Nir hadn't called her aside for a history lesson, one that she knew quite well. Her own father had been among the paratroopers who liberated the city in 1967. They had burst through the Lions' Gate on the eastern side of the Old City and raced down the Via Dolorosa. When they came to the Kotel—the Western Wall—her father, a secular man, burst into tears and fell to the ground, overcome by a feeling that he described as being in the presence of God.

"It may be holy, like they say, but it's also the most dangerous spot in the world," said Nir. "Someday, maybe soon, one of our lunatics is going to blow up the mosques and start a war such as we have never seen."

"Do we have any intel of new activity?" she asked.

"Nothing new, but it's always on their list. We have so much action by the settlers already that we expect something dramatic, a big blow. We have put many resources on these people, but we stop short of actually restraining them. And so they drag us after them, who knows to what end." He paused and they enjoyed the mild October air. "You did well, Tamar," he said. "You'll be rewarded as soon as I find a place for you. Meantime, there's something else. It's an unlikely something but maybe you could look into it. We have a report, poorly sourced, supposedly a Hamas document about an attack on Israel."

"An attack like a rocket attack?"

"No, it's wild and ambitious and maybe fantastical, but some army analysts are taking it seriously. 'Jericho Wall,' they call the plan. Maybe you could look at it when you have a moment. Meantime, the cheese has arrived."

55

I Am Not Worthy

Hebron, Oct. 6, 2023

Yossi was on suspension as temporary chief. Soon he would be formally booted out of the force because of Tamar's complaint that he had interfered with the Shabak investigation. An indictment wasn't out of the question, although the assassination of Jamal Khalil might have sated the bureaucratic desire to put somebody's head on a pole. This was the day he would finish packing up his office and say goodbye to his colleagues. What he would do tomorrow was an unanswered question.

Sara thoughtfully made him a breakfast of poached eggs and potato latkes, topped with a spicy Yemeni green sauce called schug, which Yossi adored but ate only if Sara made it.

He always sank into a bleak mood when Sara was about to leave, which colored their last days together. Even when he rallied, his good humor was a mask that made their time together false and laden with blame. From the moment of her arrival he was mentally marking off the days of her stay, steadily growing grumpier. Yes, there were sweet moments together, but Sara treated him like a fractured egg, too fragile to be handled. She made plans to go camping on her last night so she wouldn't have to deal with his grief, which was harder to bear than his rage. *I shouldn't have to be in charge of his happiness*, she told herself, but she knew there was no one else in his life that he could cling to. *At the very least he should take his antidepressants.*

The only person she had heard her father speak of with any curiosity was this American, Malik. Yossi may have subconsciously seen him as a safe Arab, not his enemy but a kind of intermediary. They were a lot alike, she thought, loners who keep to themselves. Malik was softer and more sophisticated, but they were both wounded in ways that would break her heart if she thought too much about it.

She was intrigued by Malik. Her studies abroad had opened her mind to the way outsiders viewed Israel and Judaism. When she returned home it was like going into an echo chamber where different opinions collided but they were all debating the same question: Who are we? Having a knowledgeable outsider in the conversation added a new perspective. She could talk freely with Malik in a way that seemed impossible in Israel, at least in Hebron. He was disfigured but there was something dashing about the eye patch and also mysterious, as if he was hiding a secret behind that vacant orb. The evening she had with Malik while her father slept had been invigorating and left her wondering if that was all there would be. She would return to Paris, he to New York. There wasn't even a photograph to mark their meeting.

"I've got an idea you're going to hate, Abba," she said as she gathered the dishes. "Come with me to Paris. You've lost your job, there's no reason for you to remain. I have a small apartment, but it has a little office we could make into a bedroom until you find your own place. There are a million reasons not to do this but two million better ones to come. We'll have fun there. You'll make friends. You can travel. You were going to retire in a few years anyway."

"I don't speak the language and I would be a burden on you."

"Not at all, I'd love the company."

Yossi didn't know how to respond, but her suggestion upset him. Sara was asking him to turn away from everything he stood for—at least that was the way he heard it.

"Really, Abba, why not make a break and try a new life? You'd be safe. We'd be able to spend time together." She smiled. "I could teach you how to cook."

"I just can't."

"Why? Tell me what's stopping you."

"I'm Israeli," he said. "It's my choice. Like me, you were born Israeli, and Jewish, but you didn't choose to be either of those things. I did. When you make the decision I have, you accept the moral complications. You understand what the world thinks of us, and why. The others don't have our history."

"Abba, you don't have to be Israeli to be a Jew. Jews live all over, especially in America. They live with the same history we do. Just because they don't fight Palestinians doesn't make them less Jewish."

Yossi hated this argument. He recognized the truth of it but that didn't change his allegiance to Israel. It was Sara's truth, not his.

"Sara, just look at the world. You see so many countries for Arabs, for Muslims. So many for Spanish. Look at Africa for the Black people. They have many places to choose from. All those countries where they speak English. But there is only one country that is truly Jewish. Only one place where the people speak our language. This is Israel." He started to say something and a sudden rush of emotion from some deep ancestral horror stopped him.

Sara took his hand. "What were you going to say?"

"You forget your grandparents, what they went through in Lithuania," he said in a choked voice. "They were young, just married, they knew many in Vilnius who were not Jews. Friends. Neighbors. Came the Nazis with their death squads, but those same friends and neighbors did the job for them. They killed Jews in the town square. They killed them in their houses. They tied them up and drowned them in the river. They made the Jews dig pits and then shot them in their graves. Those few who tried to protect the Jews were also killed. They taught the Nazis not to neglect killing the women and children. They called this slaughter de-Jewification. Nowhere in Europe was the killing so complete. There were two hundred thousand Jews in Lithuania in 1941 and four years later only a handful survived, including my parents."

"I know the story, Abba."

"Maybe you know but don't understand. What did they have, these poor, terrified survivors? Imagine, my father—broken, penniless, ashamed. They hid their concentration-camp tattoos. You can't make a nation from such material. So what did they do, the Israelis? They gave my father an Israeli name. They gave him a gun. They called him a New Jew. He joined Irgun, that Menachem Begin created. Yes, you can call him a terrorist, but now he stood for something! And people like my father, Yechiel Ben-Gal—Jews—they drove out the British, they fought off the Arab armies, they made a new nation.

"And yes, Jews live well in New York and maybe other places. We have seen how that can change. There is only one place on the globe where Jews will always be welcome, and that is here, in Israel. And it is my job to keep them safe. This is what I do."

"I know what you do and how well you do it," Sara said quietly. "I honor that, I truly do. But this is not the country that your parents built after the Holocaust. You've said it before, I've heard it from your lips. You see where this is going, I know you do. Ask yourself, is this the Israel your parents intended? To be divided by religion and constantly at war—even though we're the same people! You know this! You've seen the menorahs on the ancient Arab tombstones, the Star of David even in the Cave of the Patriarchs. You've read the DNA studies that show we're basically the same people. And none of it matters! Both sides are content to fight each other generation after generation and to hell with anyone who stands in the way, not because we're different but because we're the same. It's a sickness! And Abba, you don't have to be a part of it."

Nothing he could say would keep her here, he knew that. This recurring argument was exactly what was driving her away again, away from the only person in the world he felt truly close to. She had always planned to go back to Paris to finish her degree, but this break had the air of permanence.

MALIK ASKED his sources at the American embassy to rush a B-1/B-2 visa for Dina to enter the United States. His plan was to get her out of Palestine as quickly as possible. There were many details to be worked out before he could safely extricate her, but Yossi's imminent departure forced a new deadline.

Malik found Yossi in his office. "Twenty-seven years and this is all I have to show for it," Yossi said, indicating a banker's box with a few mementos, some photos, souvenirs from his army days, and a handful of books.

"What's next for you?" Malik asked.

"Here is my last day and I still haven't thought about it. What do they do in America?"

"There's a big industry in security and intelligence, they're always looking for ex-cops. Lots of money, they say."

"Maybe I move to New York and become rich."

Malik could see this wasn't meant seriously. It was clear that Yossi's mind was elsewhere. "I can't guarantee your cousin's safety once I'm gone," Yossi said. "As for the investigation, nobody will follow up. They will let Berger go, maybe even charge me with false arrest, that's what I'm hearing. He's got more influential friends than I do, and this is a case some important figures don't want solved." He looked around the room for a final sweep. "I'll tell you what will happen. In a few years, maybe less, there will be a big scandal. The drugs will kill too many people, corrupt too many politicians, and finally there will be an investigation. They will come after me because I was the cop who let it happen. I bet they're already planning for that. I'm their escape hatch." He paused. "So goodbye. I suppose that's why you're here."

Malik thought a moment before he spoke. Calamity and death awaited any false step. "I know where Zayyat is—at least I think I do," he finally said. "That might make a difference with your job, right?"

"You have an address?"

"It's marked on my phone. I can't guarantee he's still there."

"Why didn't you tell me this earlier?"

"I intended to the other night but you were occupied with a bottle of vodka."

Yossi's mental calculations were manifest in his distant stare. "I thought you were leaving."

"I am. But I've got a score to settle, so it's personal," Malik said.

"That makes two of us. But there won't be any backup."

"If you trust me to try it, I'm here," said Malik.

"In this entire country, you're the only one I trust."

. . .

MALIK WENT UP to the storage room where Dina was being held. "I've made the arrangements," Malik said. "We will have a visa for you tomorrow." He thought for a moment. "Have you ever actually been outside Palestine or Israel?"

She nodded. "We went to Jordan last year."

"So you have a Palestinian Authority passport. Never on an airplane?"

She shook her head. Once again Malik thought how young she was, innocent of the rest of the world. He wondered how she had developed such grace and self-possession, unusual for any young woman her age, when all she had ever known was conflict.

"Listen, Dina, I can imagine how unsettling things are for you. You haven't had time to even think about what has happened to you and what your life will be like when we get to America. Do you have some questions?"

"Are there Arab people there?"

"Yes, especially in Brooklyn. And Jews, too, but it's not like here. Arabs and Jews are more like each other than they are like a lot of other Americans. You'll see them in the same grocery stores and restaurants because of the halal food. My next-door neighbor is Jewish. You'll like her. She's got a very warm heart. You'll make lots of friends. Your mom said you'd like to pursue your education, and I want that, too. Are you still thinking about pharmacy?"

"Is that a good job in America?"

"I think so. But if you want to do some other studies before making up your mind that's fine too. Any other questions? I'll pick you up Sunday morning and we'll fly to America. That night we'll have dinner in New York."

MALIK TOOK A CAB to Sheikh Abdullah's home. No one answered the door. He walked out on the terrace, then heard a voice calling from somewhere above him. "We were hoping to see you today," said Aunt Nirmeen. Malik looked up. She was on the roof fixing a hole in the water tank. She had left her walker on the grass.

"Are you safe up there?"

She laughed. "I may be old and fat but I've still got work to do. They shot a hole in this tank. Third time this month. Every time we have to drain it and start all over, waiting for rain."

"Do you need help?"

"No, no. Maybe hold the ladder when I get down. Are you looking for the sheikh?"

"Actually, I came to say goodbye. I'm headed home soon. Things have been so busy I haven't had the time to visit with you that I hoped for."

"You should stay for lunch. I've got a nice lentil soup on the stove."

"I'd be happy to do that."

"Would you go to the olive grove and get Abdullah? Tell him lunch is almost ready." She stood and looked out past the vineyard to the olive trees to see where he was. "What is that?" she said. "There's some big machine. What are they doing?"

Malik couldn't see, so he climbed the ladder and looked out over the vineyard. A bulldozer had driven right through the fence and was knocking over trees to make a road for a giant cement mixer.

Malik ran through the vineyard, an immense labyrinth of grapevines, thousands of them, covered by a wire mesh, head-high, the rows broken up by stone terraces. He couldn't see the sheikh until he broke free of the vineyard and came into the grove.

Sheikh Abdullah was standing in front of an olive tree waving his arms but the bulldozer simply dodged him and knocked down a tree next to him. It seemed to be some kind of game, as Abdullah rushed to another tree. Men were laughing at him. Benny Eleazar was there, directing the operation, along with five armed members of his gang. Two were carrying chainsaws but the trees weren't the object of this invasion.

Suddenly Sheikh Abdullah realized what was really happening and ran back toward the house where the irrigation system was connected to a pumping station. Nirmeen hobbled over to stand beside Abdullah. Neighbors began arriving as soon as they saw the bulldozer. Their faces were full of horror. "You can't do this!" they cried out to the settlers, but still the bulldozer continued straight to the well, crushing irrigation pipes as it rolled forward. The neighbors picked up stones but Benny and his gang pointed their weapons, daring anyone to be the first to hurl a rock in their direction.

Then the soldiers arrived. Like the members of Benny's gang, they were all in their late teens or early twenties; some of the boys didn't have whiskers yet. The leader was a young woman who spoke to Abdullah in Hebrew. He opened his palms helplessly, not understanding what she was saying.

"Do you speak English?" Malik asked.

"Yes, of course." Her English was lightly accented. She had hazel eyes and her skin was darkened by the sun.

"These people just broke onto this property and started destroying trees and irrigation equipment," Malik said, expecting the officer to immediately evict the intruders.

"We are here to protect them," she said.

Malik didn't understand at first. "Then you should stop them!"

"Sir, we're here to keep this from becoming an incident."

"An incident? They are destroying private property. What right do they have to do this?"

"The Arab people here, they do not have a permit for this well. So it must be destroyed."

By now Sheikh Abdullah was standing next to Malik, trying to understand what was going on. Malik asked if he had a permit for the well. "Twenty years we have asked for this, but the government refuses," he said. "We have sued eleven times, but the Israelis will never grant water rights to Palestinians. They even confiscate rainwater. They shoot holes in our water tanks, they put dead animals in our cisterns. This well has been on our land since our great-grandfather's time—and before!"

Malik relayed much of this to the woman officer, who listened impassively. "Yes, it's sad for them," she said, indicating Abdullah and Nirmeen without looking at them. "But the water belongs to the Jews. Anything these people take is stealing from the Jewish people. And so we enforce the rights of the lawful owners."

Benny interrupted this exchange. "Are we finished talking?" he asked. The officer nodded, and the work began. It was not careful. The bulldozer attacked the pump house, which crumpled under it. The pump and attachments were simply scraped away, leaving the well itself. Benny dropped a stone into the hole to see how deep it was. There was a distant *plunk*. His followers picked up pieces of the shed and irrigation pipe and stuffed them into the hole. The soldiers stood about casually, smoking and talking on their phones.

Abdullah and Nirmeen sat on the ground, watching as the concrete mixer backed up to the hole and filled it to the brim. Many of the neighbors drew water from the same source, about twenty families altogether. There were two more wells on Abdullah's property and the process was repeated for each one. Few words were exchanged among the Arabs as Benny and his gang began to sing.

"We are destroyed," Abdullah said.

There was nothing Malik could have done to save Abdullah and his family. He truly knew now what it felt like to be a Palestinian—powerless except to sit and watch the ruin and utter humiliation of a decent family. He was repelled by what he witnessed and disgusted by his inability to protect them. He told himself that it was not his fight, but he couldn't separate himself from the harm done to his kin, who had none of the authority that he normally enjoyed. He felt himself to be a child again, not a man. He was seized by the urge to get out of the country as quickly as possible to flee his powerlessness, his Palestinian-ness, and be an American again, with all the comfortable assumptions of privilege and justice that come along with that.

The experience was even more galling because he identified far more with the Israelis than with the Palestinians. The Israelis were like him, or the person he used to be, powerful, polished, and urbane. The Palestinians were crippled and resentful and impotent. He regarded them as he supposed the Jews did. As a lawman and an American, he related more to the moral complexity of power than to the abject dispossession of what he had superficially thought of as his people. Now he felt ashamed to be reduced to their level, to be no longer a peer of the Jews he admired.

He said goodbye to Sheikh Abdullah and Aunt Nirmeen. He would never see them again. They were lost, futureless, and he had no power to change that. And yet when he embraced Abdullah, it felt so much like being again in his father's arms that he wept. Abdullah and Nirmeen were dry-eyed, too traumatized to find the tears. As he rode back into town the thought that repeatedly came to mind was *I am not worthy of them.*

56

Stones

West Bank, Oct. 6, 2023

T hat evening Malik followed Yossi to his personal car in the parking lot, a ten-year-old white Mazda. Yossi opened the trunk.

"Holy shit, what were you preparing for?" Malik said as he stared at the arsenal Yossi kept there.

"War," he said. "You have to be always ready in this place." He handed Malik a Kevlar vest. "Try to not get yourself killed. I don't want to have to explain this. I've got enough trouble."

They drove west out of town, following the GPS guidance on Malik's phone. It was twilight. The bumps and turns in the road felt familiar to him. At mile fifteen they passed an auto-repair shop with a graveled drive. "That's gotta be it," said Malik.

Yossi drove on to avoid suspicion, then did a U-turn another mile down the highway. He turned off on a small road near the shop and parked behind an abandoned tractor. "Now we wait. It'll be dark soon."

They had a clear view of the front of the garage with a tin roof and a sign in Arabic advertising auto repair. There were two cars parked in front but no indication that anyone was inside. A large gate enclosed a side yard filled with car parts. *There must be more cannibalized vehicles in Palestine than the entire rest of the world*, Malik thought. He also spotted a rented van from Budget behind the fence. "Two cars, so we can guess there are at least that many inside," Malik said, "but I don't see the truck they used for the kidnapping."

In these hills the dark came on quickly. Yossi reached across Malik to take a flask from the glove compartment. "Liquid heroism," he said, taking a sip of the vodka and passing the flask to Malik.

Malik took a swig, then asked, "How's Sara?"

"Are you asking because of your interest in me or her?"

"She's much more interesting than you are."

"Many men have said so. The answer is she's angry with me because I won't leave this place. She pictures me as some kind of Parisian."

Malik laughed. Yossi pretended to be offended. "Do you think I am too much the brute to be French?"

"I don't think that country is ready for you."

"I told her much the same." He took another contemplative sip. "I don't know how many more times she's going to return to Israel. She's tasted life outside. I never really have, only as a tourist when my wife was alive. I must consider how I will be able to see Sara in the future. If she marries, it will not be to an Israeli, I'm sure of that. She's sick of the mentality. Of course, I want her to marry Jewish, live here, produce grandchildren for me, all the same things you imagine when you become old."

Evening was settling in and a light came on in the building. "There's somebody in there," Malik said, gesturing toward the garage. "I saw movement."

"We wait," said Yossi, passing the flask.

They sat for a while as the sky darkened. Then Yossi said, "If you are actually interested in Sara, you should let her know."

Malik was stunned. "Are you serious? Has she mentioned anything?"

"I sense something. I don't say that I approve."

Malik shook his head in disbelief. "If I thought she was at all interested in me . . ." He stopped himself, unable to connect the rest of the thought.

"Anyway, you'll have to wait. She has chosen to spend the last night of Sukkot camping in the desert. There's some festival. She said she wanted to remember the joy and beauty that she felt growing up here. It's the kind of thing she would say if she wasn't plan-ning to make a return trip anytime soon."

Malik was at a loss about what to do. He felt excited and timid. Unconsciously he traced the scar on his forehead. He could be dead soon, which he accepted up until now, but life suddenly unveiled the possibility of love. He silently prayed for more time.

"I've been wondering about what was so urgent that Weingar-ten would break off his meeting with you," Yossi said. "I still think Dina might have had something to do with it, because Weingarten was a sucker for girls. But Berger mentioned something else that was important to the chief—tickets to that Andrea Bocelli concert. The chief had all his albums. He has a picture of the two of them on the wall of his study. Maybe it was something as dumb as 'There's a guy with tickets to sell but you have to grab them, others are interested, so hurry.' "

"Using the tickets as bait. Interesting," said Malik. "The chief thought he could run off to buy the tickets and rearrange his meet-ing with me."

"Then when he arrives he's fucked."

A Palestinian police car approached and turned into the drive. Mohammed Faroud and another Palestinian cop got out of the car. Yossi hadn't seen them since they met in the cemetery after the chief was killed. The cops rapped on the door of the garage and presently it opened and they went in.

"This gets interesting," said Yossi.

"You know these clowns?" Malik asked.

Yossi nodded. "It's not a surprise to see the Palestinian cops and Hamas together. In Hebron they are the same, except for a few." Yossi paused. "But I thought Mohammed was straight."

"Flashlight in the yard," Malik observed. Someone was moving around behind the wrecked cars. Then there was the light of a door opening in the back, and quickly closing. "Whatever is happening is happening now."

They selected weapons from the trunk, Malik taking a shotgun and Yossi an assault rifle with an infrared scope and a laser sight; then they crept toward the low-slung stone structure and waited in the shadows.

Light from the windows illuminated the yuccas in front, a feeble attempt at landscaping. A man with an automatic weapon on his shoulder emerged from the front of the building and lit a cigarette. He idly kicked a rock in the drive.

"One of Zayyat's men," Malik said.

"That makes it official. No need to be nice about it."

As they were speaking, there was a staggered sound of ignition, then the Budget rental van drove through the open gate, passing within a few feet as Malik and Yossi crouched behind some bushes. They had a clear view of the driver. It was Itai.

"Son of a bitch!" Yossi muttered.

"Benny's shadow."

"How did I miss this?"

"We miss what we don't want to see," said Malik.

"Go around through the back," Yossi said. "I'll take care of the guy in front."

"Sure?"

"This is like old times."

Malik moved quietly around the building. Yossi waited until the guard went to close the gate. When the guard's back was turned, Yossi said, "Hey."

There was a look of recognition on the guard's face as Yossi drove a combat knife into his heart. Yossi caught him as he fell and let him down softly. The sensation of a man he had killed dying in his arms was not new.

Yossi moved to the front door. He tested it; it wasn't locked; he was inside before anyone noticed. Zayyat sat at a desk. Standing beside him was Mohammed Faroud.

"Yossi, what the fuck?" Zayyat finally said as he noticed the rifle pointed at him.

"Everybody be still," Yossi said.

There were two other men in the room. One was the other Palestinian cop. It took a second for Yossi to place the face of the man in the shadows. It was Khoury, the owner of the butcher shop where Jamal had worked.

So far no one had raised a weapon except for Yossi.

"You have no power anymore, Yossi," Mohammed said. "You're old news. Everyone knows this."

Yossi ignored him, eyeing instead the pile of cash on the desk in front of Zayyat. "Looks like you just had a big payday," he said.

Zayyat grinned, as if he were totally in command, despite the laser dot dancing across his forehead. A pistol was on the desk near at hand. Yossi recognized it as a Jericho 941, the same model as the murder weapon.

"That's right, Yossi. Our business partners just drove off with a hundred kilos of Lebanese smack."

"I noticed that."

"Then you understand that your friends are my friends. We can all be happy together. Plenty to go around."

"They're not my friends."

"Ah, too bad." Zayyat glanced meaningfully at the other men in the room, seeing that the odds were four to one. "You'd be wise to leave now, Yossi. A man without friends is a man in trouble."

"I didn't say I was without friends," said Yossi.

In the back of the room Malik pumped a shell into the chamber of the shotgun, a sound everyone instantly recognized. There was a dead silence.

Zayyat looked at his gun and then at Yossi.

"Help yourself," Yossi said.

"I will tell you a secret," Zayyat said. "Your death has already been arranged. If you kill me it will be no matter, I will have revenge. I will go to Paradise and soon you will taste the fires of hell."

"So what are you waiting for?" Yossi asked.

Zayyat turned and recognized Malik in the shadows. "You should have accepted my offer," he said.

Zayyat's hand darted for the pistol but he suddenly somersaulted over his chair, his body shredded by a shotgun blast, which sounded like a cannon inside the concrete walls of the garage. The room stunk of gunpowder and smoke. Malik instantly pumped another shell into the chamber and everyone stood very still.

"Your move, Mohammed," Yossi said.

Mohammed regarded Zayyat's messy corpse, then looked at his

men and shook his head. "Another martyr," he said as he swept the money off the desk into a valise. "We understand each other, correct?" he said to Yossi. Cooperation always came at a cost.

THE RAV'S COMPOUND was dark. The Budget van that had passed them at the Hamas hideout was parked in front of a disused stable with arched doorways, which backed up to a steep hillside. Across a swath of rocky ground was the old fortress that served as head-quarters for the movement. Several windows in the upper floors were lit. The night was quiet.

Yossi knelt and peered through the infrared sight on his rifle, then handed it to Malik. Through the scope he detected thermal images of a man stacking bricks of heroin in a cart. It was Itai.

"Your young cousin Omar is a quite a detective," Yossi said out of the blue.

"What makes you think so?"

"I never thought to find out Itai's birth name. Robert Friedman. So I looked him up. He and Aharon Berger were in a chapter of the Jewish Defense League in Boston. So they had a tie that goes way back."

As he spoke, another man emerged from the shadows and hoisted a stack of heroin bricks.

"Two of them, two of us," Malik said.

"Let's go."

When the cart was full Itai rolled it into the stable while the other man held the door. They appeared to be unarmed. As they entered a light came on and the room filled with a dim glow.

Yossi and Malik cautiously approached the door to the stables from either side, guns raised. At Yossi's signal they burst into the room.

No one was there.

Boxes of leather-bound books and old framed paintings lined the walls of stone and earth. Shelves contained canned vegetables and jams. Malik and Yossi exchanged a puzzled look. They heard the muffled sound of distant voices, but Itai and his companion had disappeared.

A flash of light through a crack in the shelves caught Malik's eye. The wall was lightly scarred behind the shelving, as if it had been repeatedly scraped. He pushed slightly and the shelving rolled away, exposing the entry to a cave.

Malik and Yossi crept into the rocky corridor, which was cool and moist. They could hear men talking in echoey voices. As they got closer the walls widened with cul-de-sacs carved out of the limestone and filled with skeletal remains, a vast catacomb.

"How many skeletons you think are here, Itai?" one of the men in the cave was asking.

"Many thousands," Itai said. "Even before the time of the prophets."

Yossi and Malik lurked in the gloomy corridor in view of the room where Itai and his confederate were unloading the heroin bricks. The room was large and roughly round, with a wall of neatly stacked bones. Generations of tomb keepers had followed the same pattern of arranging the bodies in an artistic array. In the center of the room, surrounded by the bones and near the mound of drugs, was a tomb of red marble inlaid with colorful stones.

As the two men unloaded the heroin, Yossi videoed them on his phone, and he continued to shoot when Itai finally noticed him. "Don't mind me," Yossi said. "Go ahead with what you're doing. The Shabak will want to see how hard you're working."

Yossi strolled around the catacomb, taking more video, as Malik covered him with the shotgun. "This is impressive," Yossi said. "I had no idea this was here."

"Nobody knows," Itai said cautiously. "You cannot reveal it. This is a sacred place."

"*Sacred*," Yossi repeated. "Sacred. And yet you use it as a dumping spot for your narcotics. I don't see how that's sacred. Lie down and put your hands behind your back."

As the men did so, Yossi bound their wrists with flex cuffs, then he casually sat on Itai and sent a text.

"Ask him about the tomb," said Malik.

"Yeah, that's interesting. Who's the guy in the fancy crypt?"

"One of the prophets," Itai said reluctantly.

"Which one? We've got so many around here."

"Cain."

Yossi shook his head in amazement. "You guys worship Cain?"

"We don't worship him, but we revere him. He is misunderstood."

"Don't discuss this," Itai's companion hissed in a low voice. "They are outside the faith."

"I think we got what we need," said Yossi. "Now you two come with us. Itai, if you say anything, make any noise, you're dead. This is not the police speaking. This is me, Yossi."

They walked back through the stone corridor, Yossi and Malik holding the two men at gunpoint. As they stepped outside Malik whispered, "Now what?"

"We put them in the truck and drive away."

Yossi heard a mechanical click and he wheeled in the direction of the sound, but before he was able to raise his gun a dozen security lights illuminated the men in a bright yellow glare. They shielded their eyes. Yossi and Malik still held their weapons but had no idea where to point them.

"Yossi, you idiot." It was Benny's voice.

"Benny, you're under arrest," Yossi said into the glare.

Benny laughed. "Bravo, Yossi. Chutzpah."

"I've already alerted Shabak. They're on their way."

"Tamar wouldn't take a call from you, even I know this. Put your weapons on the ground. Now."

Malik and Yossi did as they were commanded. Benny came forward in a shadow against the bright light. Other figures stood in the dim background. "Give me your knife," Benny said.

Yossi handed him the same knife that killed the guard at Zayyat's headquarters. Benny used it to cut the flex cuffs binding his men, who picked up the rifle and the shotgun and turned them on Yossi and Malik.

"So, American, I said you should be more careful in the future," Benny said. "Now you have no more future." He nodded and Itai clubbed Malik with the butt of the shotgun. Malik dropped to the ground.

"You are on our land," Benny said. "We have our own system of justice. Quicker. More efficient. Maybe a little primitive."

As Malik struggled to his feet, other figures emerged from the darkness—rabbinical students and acolytes of the Rav, not a one over nineteen. They were carrying stones. They formed a circle around Yossi and Malik.

The first stone hit Yossi in the shoulder. "Unbeliever!" the boy cried.

A torrent of stones followed. Yossi and Malik covered their heads with their hands but there was no escape. The faces of the acolytes contorted in excitement as the stones rained down, some of them weakly thrown, others striking like bullets. Yossi and Malik lurched awkwardly inside the mortal circle, seeking a place of safety that didn't exist as the stones came from every direction. Yossi sank to his knees, and then his hands fell to his side, too sapped to protect himself from the onslaught. A heavy rock struck the back of his head and he toppled into the dirt.

"What is going on here?" a voice thundered, but the stones continued to fly amidst the cries.

"Stop this!"

The acolytes recognized the voice of the Rav. He strode into the light, wearing a bathrobe.

"Grandfather!" said Benny. "We have the situation under control."

"You administer justice without me?" the old man cried.

"It wasn't worth disturbing your sleep."

Malik helped Yossi to his feet. The Rav looked at the two men, who were scarcely conscious. "Why do you come here once more?" he demanded.

"To enforce the law," Yossi said, his voice drained of strength. He leaned on Malik's support.

"You make such an accusation? We follow the law here. Not just Israeli law but the higher one."

"I'm no scholar, but I know the Torah would not permit you to finance the great temple with the profits from narcotics."

"We have nothing to do with drugs," the Rav replied indignantly. "Every shekel for the temple comes from donations."

"It's a good bet that there are no donations," Malik said. "This kid is keeping the money for himself."

Benny picked up a stone. "Why do we listen to this? We need to finish our business."

"Go into the cave, Rav," Yossi said, "you will find drugs beside the tomb of Cain. They came from Hamas."

The Rav stood in front of Benny and stared into his eyes. "Is he saying the truth? Did you violate the sanctity of the crypt?"

Benny turned away from his grandfather's accusation.

The acolytes looked confused but most of them dropped their stones.

"Maybe you thought Benny and Itai were selling drugs for God's purpose," Yossi told them, "but they were only doing it to make themselves rich."

"This is a lie!" Benny said. "We never put our hands on this money for ourselves. It was the only way to achieve our financial aims for the temple. Grandfather, I didn't tell you about it because I knew you would disapprove, but your ideas of fundraising were impractical. I was going to give you all the money when we made enough, but—"

Before Benny could finish his sentence the Rav slapped him with his bony hand. "You are a disgrace," he said. "I banish you forever from our community."

Benny looked at his grandfather with wild eyes, then shoved him to the ground, shocking the acolytes with his disrespect. "Don't listen to him!" he cried out to the others. "We will build the temple together! Without this old man, a new generation will—" But his speech was cut short by a stone that hit him just above the ear. He clapped his hand over the spot and looked lost. Another stone brought him to his knees. He looked up from the ground to see the Rav on his feet holding a large stone in his hands, about to bring it down on him.

"No, Rav!" Yossi said. "Let us administer the law here." Without another word, Yossi grabbed Benny's hands and cuffed them behind his back. The flashing lights of the Shabak vehicles coming up the hillside were just coming into view.

57

Final Things

Oct. 6, 2023

O mar was holding Dina's hand when Malik arrived at the police station. The boy stood and Malik embraced him. He was so thin, Malik thought. "Give us a moment," he whispered.

"You're alive," Dina said when Omar had left the room, her voice choking with emotion. "But you look terrible. You've got bruises."

"I'll be fine. Nothing broken, believe it or not. I'm going to have a terrible headache tomorrow."

"I was so worried."

"We've got much to talk about," he said. "Your visa has arrived so we'll have to go to Jerusalem to pick it up. Then we're free to leave. Are you okay?"

She nodded.

"I know it's a big change for you," Malik said, "but it's a good change. You'll be starting a new life. As for the university, the fall semester has already begun but you might enroll for the spring term. That'll give us time to look at colleges in the city and see what appeals to you. Your English is quite good but if you want a tutor we can arrange that. I see you're anxious, and I understand, but you'll find New York a remarkably easy place to live. People say it's hard but that's because it's a big city. Once you learn the subways and have a little money there's no place easier. Stores on every street, wonderful restaurants with cuisines from all over the world. I know I sound like the chamber-of-commerce spokesperson but it's all true.

So many New Yorkers are first-generation immigrants just like you. Within a month or two you'll be as native as anyone else. Anyway, I wanted to ease any anxiety you might have—"

She raised a hand to stop him. "Tony," she said, her voice quivering, "please don't talk."

"Sorry, I was blabbering on."

"When I woke this morning I suddenly understood so many things that I hadn't thought about before. You are a hero. Look at what you've done. And you have been so kind to me and my family. No one has ever been so good to me, not even Jamal. You are a very generous man. But my thinking is very clear. I can't leave my home."

Malik was moved but he also saw what a dangerous decision this was. "I wish you wouldn't throw away this chance."

Dina wept. "I'm so grateful. I always dreamed of leaving. But I belong to this place. There's a struggle here. It's my struggle. Our lives can't just be about conflict. Something has to change if we are going to survive. As long as I have life left, I must be a part of it."

Malik felt humbled by her courage, and tears flowed from his eyes as well. "Palestine needs heroes," he said.

"Can you do me a favor?" she asked. "I have no right to ask this."

"I will do whatever you ask."

"Take Omar. He's in danger and needs support that we can't provide. He admires you. At least get him out of this place for a little while. He needs to see there's a bigger world. It would mean so much to me."

SARA HAD DECIDED to spend her last night in Palestine at an all-night festival in the desert, near the kibbutz Re'im. She wanted to remember the joy that still tied her to this land. Yossi insisted he was fine and that she should enjoy her friends. She borrowed his car, along with a tent and bedroll, for the short drive into the Negev. The rave beckoned as a desperately needed antidote to the hatred and violence. She would be back the next morning and they'd have plenty of time to say goodbye before the evening flight. As she drove, she had a sudden impulse to call Malik.

"First you get him fired, then you nearly get him killed, I don't know why I should be talking to you," she teased.

"You're the one who called," he said, his heart jumping.

"I know. After our talk the other night it seemed like there was something unfinished."

"I felt the same way," he said. "Is there any way we can get together and hang out? I'm only here one more day."

"Me too. I'm flying back to Paris tomorrow night."

Malik felt the opportunity slipping away from him. He would never see her again if he didn't act. "Where are you now?"

She laughed. "I'm headed to a concert in the desert." She paused. "Maybe you could meet me there."

"I'll call an Uber."

TAMAR WATCHED the live drone footage from Gaza in the comms room in Shin Bet headquarters. She had ordered up the drone after seeing satellite imagery of apparent military activity near the Jabaliya camp. Hamas was drilling so frequently it had become normal. This wasn't unusual except in scale—well over two thousand Hamas terrorists were engaged in a nighttime exercise. She marveled at the precision of their movements, which reminded her of an elaborately choreographed opening ceremony for the Olympics.

If there is fault to be found in the culture of Shabak, it is that nobody wants to make the final decision. Tamar called in her long-time super, Herzl. He was a fixture in the organization, a wily bureaucrat with distinguished military experience, the very definition of what the job demanded. He was on the far side of middle age, potbellied, his face a mass of wrinkles, his clothes disheveled, his hair untamed and gray except for the black hairs spilling from his ears and nostrils. "Can't this wait?" he asked irritably.

"I'll need your approval for a strike."

"I'm in the middle of my grandson's birthday party."

"I wouldn't disturb you except that it appears to be a major action. I've never seen this many drilling at the same moment."

"When you say 'major' you mean an invasion of some sort?"

"I'm looking at thousands of terrorists."

"Have you talked to IDF?"

"They see the same thing we're seeing. But they haven't made a decision. I think they'd like for us to make the first move."

Herzl snorted. "Of course they would." He drove to headquarters after promising his wife he would be back at the table before the birthday cake.

"Okay, show me," he said irritably, jiggling the car keys he had not yet put back in his pocket.

Tamar moved her chair so that Herzl could take off his glasses and put his nose nearly on the screen. "A lot of fucking guys," he concluded. The figures looked like beetles moving in formation. "Let's play this out. The instant they rush the wall what happens? We have three layers of fences seven meters tall. We have watchtowers with remote-control machine guns every two kilometers. Sensors. Razor wire. Radar and infrared. There are only two crossing points operating and they are totally secure. Suppose a few such men succeed in getting to the wall. Can they go over it? No. We mow them down. All these dopes"—he gestured to the screen—"are dead men the moment we see them approach. Can they go under? We buried the wall to a depth of several meters and placed sensors in the ground so we know where and when they are digging tunnels. They have no navy, just wooden fishing boats. No air force. How then can they invade?"

"I don't know, sir, but it appears that they think they can." She handed him a copy of the Hamas scenario, "Jericho Wall," that Nir had referred her to. "I've read this and it describes a massive assault, using drones and motorcycles and even paragliders."

"We looked at this a year ago," Herzl said. "It's the Hamas wet dream. Purely aspirational. Their leaders are all corrupt. The Qataris have been doing us the favor of supporting them for years. Billions of dollars! Do you think the midgets of Hamas will walk away from that? No! They're addicted to the money. We control the flow and they know it." He handed the forty-page booklet back to her. "Don't bother to lose sleep over this."

"But their drills look exactly like what is described in here."

"Yes, well . . ." Herzl weighed his options. "It's the last night of Sukkot," he said. "Many of our soldiers are taking a holiday. If the terrorists try something desperate, we can summon them quickly. We have a base in Re'im that is practically on the fence line. Tell me, is there any possibility this attack could succeed? You make the decision. I'll approve it either way."

So typical of him to push the responsibility onto a subordinate. Tamar could envision the hearings, her televised testimony, one concerning an unprovoked strike on Gaza by the powerful Israeli military that kills dozens of people, some of them civilians, and always there are children. The condemnation of the liberal anti-Israel press around the world as well as the UN investigation inevitably follows. The other outcome: a surprise attack that wasn't really a surprise after all, but an intelligence failure of a war that didn't need to happen. One was likely, the other fantastical, surely doomed to fail.

"I suppose there's no need to take action at this time," Tamar said.

"Then I will return to the party and await your call if the situation merits it." In a low voice he emphasized, "Don't call me again unless you have a really good reason."

SARA WASN'T REALLY a fan of trance music, but there was something magical about the event, thousands of young people dancing, drinking, getting stoned, swaying in the warmth of soft autumnal breezes, the stars bright overhead. It was transcendent, a sensation of total freedom. *This is what I needed*, she told herself. Tomorrow night she would board a flight back to the pleasurable life she had chosen over the raw and vital Israeli existence, with its guilt and pride and many neuroses. She was experiencing the bitterness many exiles feel—that she had been emotionally expelled from her home and would never again be a native of anyplace. Paris was like living in someone else's house, that of a formerly fashionable socialite with quarrelsome children. France was riven by irreconcilable political differences, but it was someone else's culture, and besides, it was useful for an aspiring political scientist to take the measure of a society not her own. The rest of her life would be a tug-of-war between novelty and memory.

The music was an ocean, and she was bobbing on the surface.

There were no problems here, nothing difficult to decide, no moral arguments to be had. She drifted, judgment surrendered, arms upraised, waving goodbye.

"Sara."

The Ecstasy was perhaps too strong and laced with something. She felt a little loopy and when she looked at Malik he appeared taller than she remembered and maybe younger, although that could be the colored lights. It was a hilarious place to meet, in the middle of a sandy dance floor in the desert, under a canvas canopy shaped like a psychedelic flower. A giant Buddha statue seemed to float overhead, and a pair of blue skulls flashed on the giant screen. Without a word Sara reached out and pulled Malik deeper into the vibrating hive.

They danced looking into each other's face. It was a very powerful exchange. They didn't need to talk at this moment. They needed to assess, to discover each other in this mass mindlessness, utterly alone while surrounded by others who didn't notice or care about them, communicating by motion, synchronizing their movements, not touching because it wasn't that kind of music, but imagining touching. Then she walked out of the dance and into the desert, knowing he would follow.

58

October 7, 2023

Sara and Malik lay in her tent, the music from the rave still playing even as the dawn began to light the sky. What words there were came out in whispers. Malik's face was buried in Sara's hair, their exhausted bodies knotted together as if they could never be untangled.

"We're going to have to make some plans," he whispered, his lips brushing her ear.

"Umm," was Sara's quiet assent. "Paris?"

"I don't speak French."

"That's all right, I'm not sure I want to go back."

"But your studies."

"Four more months."

"I could study French while you finish up. Do they have someplace to eat in Paris?"

"If you like fast food and frozen dinners."

"That's what I thought. We'd be better off in Little Rock."

"Little Rock?"

"Much to be said for it."

"This is a real place?"

"I'd put it up against Paris any day of the week."

"Is it also holy, this little rock?"

"Thankfully no."

Sara yawned, then said, "The rockets again."

Malik heard them. He sat up and peeked outside the tent. It was near dawn, the darkest hour of the night. The rockets were fired in volleys, one after another, their bright tails like Roman candles. Some of the partygoers, dazed by hallucinogens, were gaping at the majestic display. The launch site in Gaza couldn't be more than a dozen kilometers away.

"Let's go," Malik said as he grabbed his jeans.

"It happens all the time." Sara opened the bedroll, inviting him back in. The sight of her body struck him even more powerfully than it had when they first touched; now he saw her entirely and he thought, *This is one memory I will never forget.*

"Seriously, get dressed," he said.

She put on her sleeveless black dress and sandals. When they came out of the tent another barrage of rockets raced into the sky, to be greeted by Iron Dome interceptors, dancing like boxers in the ring, darting and swooping and then chasing down the rockets and knocking them out with deadly explosions. Malik was awed by the technology but said, "We've got to get out of here."

HANI KHALIL ATE a light breakfast of yogurt and raisins, then exited the tunnel into the Gaza night, the waning moon about to dip into the Mediterranean. Dawn awaited. He walked down the streets, illuminated by the stars and the rockets, joining streams of other fighters in camouflage and carrying their weapons, each of them wearing the green Hamas headband, all moving silently toward their designated stations. Individual thinking ceased; they had become a single mental organism, resolute, assured that history would remember them.

He thought about his murdered family—his mother, Salma, his father, Abdul Wahhab, his younger siblings—now he was the last survivor. If he died today there would be no one to remember them. But because of his sacrifice they would all meet in Paradise. He read the plan one last time. The document began with a quote from the Quran: "Surprise them through the gate. If you do, you will certainly prevail."

Near the beach was a soccer field and beside it a former gymnasium serving as a storehouse for drones and paragliders. The operators had trained with these instruments for months, often at night, correctly believing that the Israelis weren't paying attention and that something as simple as working in darkness would disguise their capabilities. It was also possible that the gliders were too small to be picked up on radar or could be confused with migrating pelicans. The men made their ablutions in a sink and prayed, filled with the conviction that they were carrying out will of Allah and that the terrible action they were about to commit was the holiest moment in their lives.

After dawn prayer, each terrorist was given Captagon, an amphetamine laced with caffeine, meant to fill the fighters with energy and courage; in any case, it made them high. Within minutes, Hani's fears were washed away by a surge of exuberance coursing through his body. His life had always pointed to this moment; whether he lived or died had been decided before he was born. He was powerless to change divine will, and that knowledge filled him with peace.

He laid out the parachute wing on the soccer pitch. After combing the tangles out of the cords and making sure the rear edge of the boomerang-shaped wing curled forward to catch the wind, he connected it to a motorized trike. There were two seats, one for a gunman in front—his cousin Kareem—and the other for Hani, who was piloting. He pointed the apparatus toward the ocean to catch the sea breeze. Down the length of the pitch other pilots were preparing their fragile aircrafts, and behind the roar of the rockets they took off one by one, each waiting a turn until the next in line popped up off the turf. Hani eased open the throttle; the wing caught the breeze, forcing the trike to lurch backward, a tricky moment because it felt like a mistake, but it was that same motion that caused the wing to vault upward, and in the space of ten meters the paraglider leapt into the air.

Almost immediately the land fell away and the gliders organized themselves into formation over the Mediterranean, the sliver of sun catching their sails. For most of them, this was the first time in their lives they had been out of Gaza, and even though they were only just over the shoreline they could see shadowy ships in the distance moving about in the wider world. The pilots slowly pivoted and then they saw their homeland in the sunrise, brief and confined, and beyond that Israel, the West Bank, Egypt, and Jordan. Hebron, Bethlehem, and Jerusalem were close by, holy prizes so close at hand, soon to be won again for Islam. More rockets flew overhead, leaving clouds of black smoke that the paragliders flew through. Hani could hear the cheers of the residents of Gaza as the attack began.

The assault unfolded before him. The sky was his element now, and it was filled with drones attacking the watchtowers, the remote-controlled machine guns, and the omnipresent cameras. Simultaneous explosions erupted all along the fence line. From this height, the Iron Wall appeared insignificant. Munitions blasted holes through the once-invulnerable fence and bulldozers broke through in dozens of locations. Like a dam bursting, thousands of fighters poured through on motorcycles or in pickup trucks but mostly on foot. A fleet of fishing boats headed the short distance to the Israeli coast. They were eager to encounter the enemy, but the Israeli army was nowhere to be seen.

MANY OF THE THREE THOUSAND revelers at the rave were high on various psychedelics and unaware of the unfolding attack until the organizers were instructed by a security officer to shut off the music. "Code red! Code red!" the security officer cried. He ordered the partygoers to get down on the ground with their hands behind their head, a meaningless command that cost many lives.

The sound of machine guns was heard close by. Partygoers who were already in a surreal state of mind were too stunned to run. Those who did moved in slow motion, still living in a drugged illusion of safety. Maybe the Gazans were also having a party. A celebration? At worst it was a shootout between a handful of terrorists and the IDF. Some were live-streaming and providing excited commentary, as if they had all the time in the world. "Boom! Boom!" one of them said ecstatically as the rockets exploded. "Wow!" They knew that Gaza was only a few kilometers away, but it was inconceivable that Hamas had broken out of its cage and was on the rampage.

The sight of gliders gracefully dipping out of the sky toward the psychedelic tent like a covey of seabirds was confusingly nonreal, but then gunfire rained down on the revelers and shattered the hallucination. Every shot was an intended death for a Jew, a rebirth of the Holocaust. People ran in all directions or took cover where they thought they might be safe. They hid in the dumpster or behind the bar and the Coca-Cola coolers. They were easily killed. A terrorist walked down the line of yellow PortaPotties firing into each one. People who took to their cars ran into a Hamas roadblock. There was only one road in and out, Route 232, and cars backed up for as far as one could see. The killers took their time shooting the occupants or capturing as many as they could carry back to Gaza. They were slow and thorough, setting fire to the cars and shooting bodies already dead.

Hundreds of partygoers ran barefoot across the road into a broad open field, freshly plowed, with furrows deep enough to hide in, but gunmen stalked them, with clear sightlines down the rows in either direction. The footprints in the sandy soil were easy to follow.

Hani and Kareem had orders to "cleanse" Kibbutz Re'im—meaning to kill all the young men and kidnap anyone else—but the rave festival presented an unexpected opportunity, with thousands of Jews and nominal security. In addition to these orders, Kareem had his own mission. Hamas was offering a bounty for the capture of a Jew: an apartment and ten thousand dollars, enough to allow him to get married.

As the paragliders descended they invaded a world they had only fantasized: young people partying, drinking alcohol, taking drugs; women provocatively dressed, dancing, sex in the air, flesh on display, a world of sensuality despised and longed for but never experienced by any of the ecstatic young men who came to kill them. It was Paradise.

MALIK AND SARA RAN into the furrowed field where Hamas motorcycles couldn't go. Snipers shot at them, the bullets whistling as death passed them by. Malik was aware of people falling all around, but he held Sara's hand and they kept running, heads down, toward a patch of green on the far side of the field, a stand of sprawling tamarisk trees. They hid behind a narrow rise, panting for breath.

They saw terrorists capturing or killing anyone they found. Those who weren't shot were forced into the bed of pickup trucks or on the back of motorcycles to be taken to Gaza for ransom. Joining the Hamas shock troops were hundreds of emboldened spectators, some armed, many carrying only sticks or knives. One man came on horseback; some arrived in golf carts; another man hobbled into the killing field on crutches. Malik and Sara watched as a pair of teenage girls in party dresses were forced to strip. One of the civilians stabbed a girl while another raped her from the rear. Malik pulled Sara's face into his chest so she wouldn't witness what happened next.

Other partygoers had made it across the field and were also hiding behind the trees. There were too many of them, Malik figured. The killers were not likely to spend time tracking down one or two people, but a mass of them was an irresistible target. A phalanx of Hamas motorcycles filled the road nearby, a dozen of them turning off just past the plowed field. The Jews who were hiding under the tamarisk trees were surrounded with no place to flee. Some prayed and cried for their mothers, their breath coming in gasps. They would soon be discovered.

Through the field a single fighter was coming directly toward them, followed by a larger group, maybe thirty of them.

"Did you bring your father's car?" Malik asked Sara.

Sara nodded, unable to speak.

"Give me the keys."

"Don't leave me."

"Your dad has weapons in the trunk. We might have a chance if I can get a gun. You understand, right? The last thing I want is to leave you. If the situation were totally hopeless, I would wait here and die with you. But if we have a chance to fight back and escape, we have to take it."

The Hamas killer stopped and looked directly into the trees where they were huddled. No doubt he spotted a bit of color, a bit of fabric or a ribbon in a girl's hair. He raised his gun and then Malik stood up.

"Allahu akbar, brother!" Malik cried out.

Kareem grinned and returned the salutation.

Malik said he wanted to join the killing but he didn't have a weapon. Did the brother know where he could find one? Kareem assumed that Malik was one of the spectators joining the fray.

"I am looking for a person to capture," Kareem confided. "I prefer a woman, so I can sell her if I don't get my reward."

Malik asked about the reward and Kareem told him about the apartment and the money. "I saw many of them running in that direction," Malik said, pointing away from where Sara was hiding. "May Allah bless you with a prize."

Other terrorists observed the exchange and assumed that Malik was one of them. He hoped he would find a dead fighter so he could take the weapon and the Hamas headband; in that way he might be able to smuggle Sara out of the killing field as a hostage. But there were no dead Hamas fighters; there was no one to resist them.

He saw more killers coming toward him and he waved them toward Kareem, who was running east. Some of the fighters paused, then raced in that direction. Malik made sure not to look back at Sara, but he could tell that other terrorists were headed toward the tamarisk trees.

A REPORTER FROM HAARETZ had already called, asking for an interview about the arrest of the Kahanists and the killing of the Hamas bomb maker Ehsan Zayyat. Overnight, Yossi Ben-Gal had gone from scapegoat to hero. Now he had the pleasure of watching officials all the way to the top cover their asses by praising his courage. His body was covered with bruises from the stoning but no bones were broken. He was amazed to be alive. When the phone rang again he was surprised to see that it was Sara calling. He had been told to wait for a call from the prime minister.

"Abba," she whispered into the phone.

Immediately Yossi heard the fear in her voice. "Where are you?"

"I'm still at the festival. They're slaughtering us!"

"What? Who?"

"Terrorists! Hamas."

"Are you safe?"

"I don't know," she whispered. "I don't think they can see me."

"Are you alone?"

"Tony was with me. But he's trying to get to your car. You have weapons there, right?"

"No, I took them inside last night."

Sara choked back a sob as her last hope exploded. Malik was walking into the mob of terrorists completely exposed for no purpose at all.

"Tell me where you are exactly," Yossi said. "I'll come get you."

"No, please don't try, you'll only get killed. The roads are full of Hamas."

"Just send me your location. I'll find a way."

"Abba, where is the army?"

"They'll be there soon, I'm sure. How many terrorists?"

"Thousands of them!"

Yossi heard the deadly rattle of an AK-47. It had to be near Sara. "Play dead," he said. "Send me your location now. Don't move. The soldiers will come when you hear the helicopters. I'm on my way."

MONITORS FROM THE WATCHTOWERS suddenly went blank, all at once. Tamar assumed it was a power failure, but the backup generators failed to kick in. She might have called Herzl, but awakening him at dawn, given his mood, made her reconsider. There were still balloons—seven of them—tethered behind the wall, but only four were in service that morning. Tamar watched the footage coming from them and she saw grainy images, not a small group but an army of terrorists pushing into Israel. And then, one by one, the images from the balloons also went dark. Israel was blind.

Her IDF counterparts experienced the same visual shutdown. It all followed the Hamas plan outlined in "Jericho Wall." Military analysts had read the battle plan but even as it was unfolding a sense of disbelief clouded their understanding. These same analysts knew that Hamas was incapable of mounting a genuine attack on Israel, therefore what they were witnessing couldn't be happening. The idea that terrorists would block roads, storm kibbutz communities, and lay siege to an IDF command post, killing sleeping soldiers in their bunks, was a ludicrous fantasy. Everyone knew that Hamas had learned its lesson.

The Gaza Division of the IDF was based in Re'im, close by the festival, but the base was understaffed. Two commando companies stationed near the Gaza border had been moved recently to the West Bank to deal with settler violence. Half of the remaining fifteen hundred soldiers, along with senior officers, were away for the holiday and the Sabbath.

Tamar called the army chief of the Southern Command. He was at IDF headquarters in Tel Aviv. He had arrived when the first rockets were fired at dawn and immediately went into the bunker deep under the building, known as the Pit. He was surprised to get a call from Shabak.

"We think there's an attack in the south," Tamar told him.

"Rockets, we know. Why do you bother to call?"

"No, a real attack. But we can't see. All our imagery is shut down."

As she said this, the general noticed the head of the IDF intelligence group, Unit 8200, enter the room, pale and visibly shaking.

"Have you read their plan?" Tamar asked. "The first thing they will attack is the base in Re'im."

"That's impossible." The general looked at the intelligence officer. "Is Re'im base aware of a Hamas attack?"

"We don't know anything. We can't reach them."

As they were talking, the general got a text message on WhatsApp from a colonel at the IDF base in Re'im. "Save us," it said.

The general turned to his intelligence chief. "Where's our plan for an actual invasion by Hamas?"

"We don't have one."

The general looked at him in disbelief. "No plan at all?"

"Who plans for something that could never happen?"

MALIK WAS PLAYING a role, one he had been taught in the FBI when he was undercover. Confidence was key. You had to own the world you infiltrated, it was more yours than theirs. He was armed with the information that Kareem had given him, so that when he saw more

Hamas fighters, he didn't flee, he hailed them. "Brothers! If you are looking for women, they are in that direction!" he said. "Each of you will be given a reward!" He became the authority, bearing precious information.

He began to feel invulnerable, which was dangerous, but the longer he maintained his pose, the more he exaggerated his authority. "Hey!" he barked at one surprised fighter. There was a young woman on the back of his motorcycle. She looked at Malik with terror in her eyes. She was bleeding from a wound in her shoulder. "Is this all you have captured?"

"Yes, boss," the fighter said. "Only one fits."

"Leave her with me. I'll send her back to the base. Get another and bring her to me also. Understand? As many as possible."

The confused fighter nodded. Then Malik demanded, "Give me your name, you will receive the reward for each one you bring."

The fighter grinned, then rode away without his hostage.

Malik grabbed the woman by her hair and roughly marched her toward the parking lot. He knew how to play the role but he wasn't sure she would understand, so he told her nothing.

"Please don't hurt me," she pleaded in Hebrew.

"Shut up," Malik said in Arabic.

59

The Last of the Peacemakers

I srael was just awakening to the end of innocence.

A dingy Mercedes sewage truck made the rounds of the Old City of Hebron. Many of these buildings were on a septic system and toilets were often overflowing. Residents were furious when the truck passed them by and headed up the twisted gravel road to the police station. The war was nearly three hours old and most of Israel was still unaware.

Mrs. Telushkin was at the desk talking to Golda, who had the pleasure of revealing that her dachshund, Bruno, had been found. "He was at the animal shelter all this time."

"Was anyone apprehended?" Mrs. Telushkin asked.

"No, he was found by himself, searching for you, I'm sure."

Bruno looked away guiltily as Golda handed Mrs. Telushkin the leash.

As they talked, the sewage truck picked up speed.

The tank contained the final bomb that Ehsan Zayyat would ever fashion. He regarded it as his masterpiece. It was appropriate that the delivery should be made to the police station, where Zayyat expected that Yossi Ben-Gal would receive delivery, and perhaps his Arab friend, the traitor Malik. But neither man was present and Zayyat was dead.

Another dead man was driving—reported dead but not actually dead as he would be in a few seconds—Jamal Khalil, the last of the peacemakers. He had come to terms with the reality of his existence, which was that peace was impossible in this region. Nobody believed in it, few even wanted it. He had lived in a dream world until now. But that was over. Revenge was terrible, but also delicious. The missile that destroyed Salma Khalil and her family had awakened him from his dream. He was enlightened.

The guard at the gate saw what was happening. He fumbled with his automatic weapon, which he had never used in an official capacity and managed to fire just as the truck blew the gate off its track and Jamal called out his fateful praise of the name of the Lord.

The explosion could be seen for miles. It rippled red and orange, a massive bubble of flame. The guard was dismembered immediately.

The station was solidly built, but it was not made for this. Cinder blocks flew, gray smoke filled the rooms, and Sheetrock shattered like glass. The boom was followed by a loud *whoosh* as air was sucked into the vacuum the bomb left behind.

AVI'S LUNGS EMPTIED and he fought for breath. The young detective was flattened, as if he had lost a dimension and was just a stain on the floor. Nothing moved. His mouth tasted of metal. He was only conscious of trying to get air into his lungs but the air itself burned. His ears throbbed and rang with a single high note like a soprano screaming into his brain.

He became conscious of being able to move his fingers, the first evidence that he was still alive. He lay there, absorbing his survival, but unaware of what had happened. Morning sunlight streamed in, illuminating the dust in the air, which swirled like a blizzard. Avi slowly contracted, bringing his arms together and bending his knees. He rolled into a fetal position and lay there. Time was no longer an element in his existence. Alive or dead he was in eternity.

And then pain arrived, yanking him back to his life. He wasn't sure who he was other than the hurt person on the floor. As the throbbing in his ears relented and his breath returned he heard the tinkle of glass shards raining onto the tiles and then moans, punctuated by screams of pain, but they weren't his screams.

He started to crawl but the glass cut his palms so he paused and considered how to stand. It would require being intact and he wasn't sure he was. He used his desk to pull himself up. He could feel shards of metal in his neck and arms.

When he opened the door he saw that much of the building was destroyed. A small dog was dragging his mangled leg around in circles amid the rubble. Golda's body lay in pieces behind the desk, bits of blue hair dank with blood. He averted his gaze from the rest of her. *Why Golda?* he wondered—a meaningless question in a meaningless conflict. There was no reason why or why not.

A chilling scream came from someplace behind him, so Avi wasn't alone. He walked into the rear portion of the station, which was still standing but choked with smoke and dust, the air like sharp knives and filled with the bittersweet perfume of the explosive. The scream came from the jail. "Fire! Fire!" a voice called. "Help me!" Avi opened the door to the jail area, and flames leapt out. He dodged an electrical wire that thrashed about, randomly touching the cell bars, arcing and jumping wildly. The agonized figure of Aharon Berger danced in the flames in his cell as he burned alive. His body was black and within an instant he was no longer able to make a sound. Finally he fell to the floor and subsided into tiny movements.

The fire climbed the stairs to the storage room, searching for another victim. Dina was trapped. The door was locked, there was no window. Smoke crept through the cracks below the door and through the keyhole, but Dina couldn't see it, only a brightness that underlined the door. The heat was unbearable, and she prayed that death would find her before the flames arrived.

Avi heard the building groan, so he made his way back outside before it collapsed. Dozens of people had gathered to watch the station burn. The axles of the sewage truck remained with the tires still on them, nothing else. It was only then that Avi knew. This was always going to happen, the Arabs would revolt, and he would have to kill them. While this thought settled into his brain he remembered the Palestinian girl in the storage room on the second floor, which was now aflame. He would not bother to rescue her. She would be the first death of his endless revenge.

· · ·

IN THE FREEWHEELING CHAOS of the attack, Malik steered the captive Israeli woman through the terrorists toward the parking lot. Bodies were splayed out everywhere, some of them naked, some mutilated, but not a one of them alive. Many of the cars in the parking area were afire, filled with blackened bodies that were so recently young and dancing.

"Where are you taking me?" the woman asked in Hebrew and then in English.

Malik didn't answer. Nor did he have a plan for her. His goal was to find the car, take the weapons, and return to Sara before the terrorists got to her. What he would do then was unclear. Gunmen and hangers-on still roamed the rave site, occasionally squeezing off shots but mainly plundering any cash or jewelry they could find on the bodies. Some were stealing cars; they would take the keys from a corpse and locate the car by pushing the panic button on the key fob. Then they would drive back into Gaza with their prize. Malik used the same technique and heard a honk and saw the car flash its lights.

He let loose of the woman's hair and she just stood there. The wound in her shoulder would need attention. Malik allowed himself a glimpse at her face, which was slack from the trauma, her mouth partly open, her deep brown eyes unfocussed. She was perhaps the same age as Sara. Somebody probably loved her, maybe many people did, her family, a boyfriend, her companions. She wore a T-shirt that said LOVE IS ALL THERE IS.

Malik opened the trunk. Nothing there except a spare tire.

"Fuck!" he cried.

"You speak English," she concluded.

He looked into the trees as if there were an answer hiding there.

"My name is Iris," she said. "What's your name?" Then she repeated, "My name is Iris." She wanted him to know her name before he killed her. Somebody should know.

"I can't save you," he said. "There's someone else I have to take care of."

She looked at him, recognizing in that instant he was not her enemy but she would have to die anyway.

. . .

BY NOON the IDF had still not gotten organized to respond, dispatching only small commando units without sufficient firepower or cover. Helicopters were not authorized to fly because there was no imagery, although by now some television stations were sending reporters and the soldiers relied on WhatsApp videos to provide a narrative of what was happening and where. Even before the army arrived members of ZAKA, the burial society, were driving south in their refrigerated trucks to pick up the bodies.

In the absence of a plan, IDF soldiers were simply ordered to grab a weapon and "save people." For the first time in its history, all armed members of Shabak were also ordered into the field. Tamar had to stay because she was monitoring communications, but there was practically nothing to monitor, not even Hamas phones or radios, a practice that had been discontinued because it was seen as a waste of time.

The road south filled with freelance Israeli soldiers and veterans armed with whatever they had—pistols, shotguns, some still had service rifles. They were facing two thousand Hamas fighters with AK-47s, RPGs, land mines, and other explosives. The terrorists had pickup trucks mounted with .50-caliber machine guns and their motorcycles were fast and mobile. Each side yearned for confrontation so the encounters were fierce and head-on. Anything that moved was likely to die.

Yossi borrowed his neighbor's Land Cruiser so he was not confined to the highway. He drove through the fields heedlessly, knocking over fences and small trees. He could hear explosions and he saw fire arising from kibbutzim along the way. He drove through a farm and saw goats slaughtered in the field. When he came to Be'eri, a kibbutz just north of Re'im, he heard gunfire. He drove into a cornfield, then lay on the roof of the Land Cruiser with his assault rifle. The plants were just high enough to hide the truck. He waited only a few moments before spotting three Hamas fighters torching a house. He killed them before they knew where the shots were coming from. He wanted to kill more but he was in a hurry.

. . .

"YOU HAVE A CHOICE," Malik said to Iris. "You can get in the car or leave on your own. I don't know which direction to tell you to go. If you come with me you'll have to pretend to be my hostage. I've got to find my friend and this is the quickest way to do it."

"I don't want to die," she said.

"I don't either. But I have to go that way"—he pointed north— "where she is, and if I were you, I would head east, away from Gaza."

"I'm hurt," she said.

"I can see that. You'll need medical care, but that wound is not going to kill you."

She was frozen with anxiety.

"Iris," he said. "You have to decide now."

Iris got into the car.

SARA WAS ALONE. Three other people had been hiding near her but they bolted when they saw a group of killers heading across the furrowed field toward them. They were shot down. She prayed that the killers would assume that no one remained. But there was a terrorist headed her way.

She couldn't move, she couldn't look, but she heard his footsteps, and she silently begged for mercy, what she would call a prayer, which she hadn't done in a long time. At the same time she wondered what God would countenance so much killing in his name.

"Stand up," the voice said in English.

Sara remained frozen, playing dead.

"Stand up or I shoot."

Sara looked up. He was young, powerful-looking. He had the green headband that for her meant nothing but doom. His eyes surveyed the prize before him. "You will come with me," he said.

"You won't hurt me?"

"It's against Islam to injure women or children, so set aside your concerns, sister. You will be safe. You will be treated well."

As he was saying this a voice cried out, "Ya, Hani!"

Another Hamas fighter was headed toward them, leaping over the furrows in a gallop, waving his weapon overhead. "By Allah, you have a woman!" he said, staring at Sara in wonder.

"She is mine, Kareem," Hani said.

"Cousin, you don't have need of her. You have income from the death of your family, may Allah keep them. I have nothing! It is not right to deprive me of the prize. And look at her!" Kareem grabbed Sara's dress and ripped it open. "Allah be praised!" he cried, taking a step back to marvel at Sara's nakedness.

"Stop, Kareem, you are forbidden to harm this woman."

Kareem looked at his cousin, then back at Sara, who had gathered her torn dress together. Kareem hit her with the butt of his rifle and then turned to Hani. "I must have her, Cousin, I'm sorry." Then he shot Hani in the face.

Sara ran into the field as fast as she could, but she only got a few steps away before Kareem shot her. Then he wept for the loss of his prize.

SARA LAY ON the plowed ground. She was not in pain. The feeling was deeper than that. She had been alive for twenty-four years. In all that time she had lived facing forward, imagining her future, which until hours before had no certain destination. She had finally discovered what the rest of her life was going to be. As a little girl she had imagined love coming to her as a revelation, and that's exactly what had happened. She had never felt such certainty in a relationship. Everything was decided at once. She and Malik would be together.

But there was a debt she owed to her existence as a Jew and an Israeli, and that was her life. She had come so close to escaping the destiny that cursed the Holy Land. She had deluded herself that she could become someone other than who she was born to be.

She heard more gunfire but it didn't frighten her. She knew she was dead.

MALIK AND IRIS DROVE a short way down the road, weaving past abandoned vehicles. He came to the plowed field and parked, leaving the car running. "Iris," he said, "wait here. I'm going to find my friend and then we'll try to get out of here."

Iris nodded, but as soon as he was ten meters away he heard the car door close and the car careened back into the road. She wouldn't get far.

Two hours later, IDF helicopters were finally in the air and Israel went to war. It was evening before the Hamas attackers were turned back, but by then more than twelve hundred Israelis were dead and hundreds taken captive.

Yossi found Malik in the plowed field, holding the body of his daughter.

60

Shíva

Kfar Oren, Oct. 8, 2023

Sara was buried the next day, in accordance with Jewish custom to quickly dispose of the dead. Yossi placed her next to Leah. Many people came to the service but the truth for Yossi was that he was alone. The only person who grieved as much as he was Malik, but Yossi blamed him for leaving Sara to die. Malik blamed himself as well. He stood in the back of the crowd, wishing he had died at her side.

Yossi sat shiva in his home, receiving many guests. People were drawn in part because of his new renown, also because his tragedy was so profound. He had lost his daughter and most of his colleagues at the police station. Some of his old acquaintances from the army and his years in the police dropped by. Even Tamar appeared, broken and repentant. Yossi had no feelings for her, neither hate nor forgiveness. His loss was too big and Tamar was just a part of a larger failure.

In those early days after the assault, the country was in a coma. Words were uttered but unheard. The attack had been meant to terrify and it succeeded. Israelis knew that Hamas was counting on them to strike back, enacting their most vengeful thoughts, forcing the world to turn against them. But anger made them helpless to respond in any other way. At the highest levels, people spoke of expulsion and extermination, as if an entire population was responsible for the attacks and Israel had no hand in creating the conditions that caused Hamas to arise. The idea of peace became repulsive.

Malik kept his name out of the news. He wanted no credit for his actions, which wouldn't have done him any good anyway. He didn't intend to stay in the country a moment longer than he needed to. He mourned Dina's death. She could have made a difference in the future of Palestine. He mourned Sara. She would have made a difference in his own future.

He did need to finish with Yossi.

The door was open and about a dozen people were sitting in the living room or at the dining table eating apple cake. The aroma made Malik remember Sara's cooking. Yesterday she had been alive, he thought. Yesterday they had been lovers. Yesterday they had a future together. And today that was all gone.

He was noticed but not remarked as he entered. Most people didn't know him and those who did were unclear about his role. No one except Yossi knew about his relationship with Sara.

Yossi saw him and looked away. Malik found a seat near the window and sat by himself, quietly. People were speaking in Hebrew, telling stories he wished he could understand. He retreated into memories of Sara, her brilliant conversations, her smile, her laugh, all so distinctive but now erased from the universe.

"Come with me."

Yossi led him out on the patio and into the orange grove where they could have some privacy.

"I don't say I forgive you. You did what you thought would save her and it failed," Yossi said. "Maybe she never had a chance. That's what I think. It makes it easier. She never had a chance. But I'm still so angry. I want to kill them all, every fucking one of them."

"You know that won't happen."

Yossi thought about it. "I don't want to live with the feelings I have."

"You think killing would make you feel better?"

"I do. But I don't know where it would stop."

"If Sara were here, what would she advise?"

"Sara is not here."

"I know."

The grove was covered with fruit, weighing down the limbs. The citrus smell was like perfume, sharp and sweet, like Sara.

"I thought about killing you," Yossi confessed. "Not because you took my daughter away but because you're an Arab. I don't know if we can exist in the same world."

"If you did kill me, I wouldn't blame you."

"Sara would never forgive me."

Malik suppressed a sob in his throat. "I only had her in my life for a few days, but I allowed myself to believe we could have a future together. It might never have happened, but in those last hours together it seemed real to me—a happy life. I'll never have that again."

They both knew it was not possible to measure love. But their love for Sara was a bond, handcuffing them together. No one else could appreciate the feelings they had, so they were stuck with each other. Suddenly Yossi began to weep, helplessly crumbling in grief. Malik held him and they cried together. They were brave men but there was nothing to be done.

Epilogue

Before they went to the airport, Malik asked Yossi to stop at the Muslim cemetery in the Old City. He left Omar waiting in the car and walked into the space alone, carrying the box of his father's ashes. He passed the bench where Chief Weingarten's body had been found. Some of Benny's gang had confessed that he had staged the murder, although Benny himself refused to talk. Shabak was looking into the finances of the temple. Immanuel Cohen was under orders not to leave the country.

Malik went to the section of the cemetery where Jamal had shown him the resting places of his ancestors. The fresh grave belonged to Dina. Her charred body had been quickly buried. Malik knelt beside the mound of soil that awaited her headstone. He remembered his father and his struggle as an immigrant to provide a life of freedom for his child. They hadn't always got along; Tariq Abdul Malik had never become an American in the way that his son had. Now that son poured into his hands the ashes of what had been his father, then he stood and flung them into the air, one handful after another. "You're home," he said. Some of the ashes drifted back onto him.

"My father hoped I'd find something of value here, in the Holy Land," he explained to Yossi when he got back in the car.

"And did you?"

"Not what I expected." He looked at Yossi, feeling a closeness he had never felt with another man. "Here's the weird thing. I'm inheriting Sheikh Abdullah's land."

Yossi laughed. "You're coming back to the home country?"

"Not likely. If I really do inherit, I'll offer it to some school or something. My father did that. I'd like to extend the gift." They rode in silence for a bit, then Malik asked, "What about you? What are you going to do?"

"I've got to go to Paris and close up Sara's apartment. I've been in touch with some of her friends. I think I might stay awhile and try to understand it. Sara wanted me to go there, I think to become civilized."

"That'll never work."

As they rode Omar sat in back, staring out the window, imprinting the landscape in his mind so that it would never be forgotten.

Yossi pointed out a burnt-out tank on the side of the road. "See that?" he asked Malik. "From 1948. To remind us of what it cost, this land of ours."

"Maybe it's time to forget," Malik said.

"This is a problem. Here everyone remembers everything."

Yossi parked in front of the terminal of Ben Gurion Airport. Malik got Omar's duffel bag out of the trunk. Omar insisted on carrying it, even though he had to drag it. Yossi and Malik looked at each other.

"Thanks, 'Chief,'" Malik said.

Yossi smiled. "They haven't assigned me a station yet."

"Wherever it is, they're lucky to have you."

Yossi reached into his pocket and pulled out a small, crudely wrapped present. Malik opened it.

"It's a Jewish coin, from the Maccabees' time," Yossi explained.

"But this is from your collection!"

"So you will also remember, Jews were always here, and always will be."

They embraced. "Come visit sometime," Malik said.

"You too."

As Malik and Omar headed into the terminal, Yossi called out, "Tony!"

Malik turned.

"Pray for us."

Acknowledgments
and Notes on Sources

This novel was written with a mix of compassion and anger. I have spent much of my career living and working in the Middle East. The conflict between Israel and Palestine has colored that experience unceasingly. In my lifetime—which spans the entire existence of the State of Israel—I have witnessed seemingly unalterable obstacles to world peace and social progress rolled away. The Soviet Union dissolved. Apartheid ended in South Africa. America elected a Black man president. None of these historic changes seemed possible, but the longing for change, for justice, and for peace made them so. And yet this conflict endures.

Although this is a work of fiction, many of the conversations in this book have been harvested from interviews with sources or chats with friends, whether in Israel, Palestine, Gaza, or elsewhere in the region. This book is a product of that ongoing conversation. It certainly doesn't attempt to represent every perspective, but I've tried to present fairly those that are central to the conflict. Whether I agree with them or not, I have probed to find the truth upon which their argument rests. One cannot hope for an end to the strife without acknowledging the separate histories that each side claims.

Peace has always been possible. Difficult compromises are required, no doubt, but whenever a real opportunity for a breakthrough arises it is incinerated by the killers who cling to the fantasy that their enemies can be ethnically cleansed or exterminated. Peace is only obtainable through a diplomatic solution that ends the occupation. Until the extremists and ideologues are pushed out of power, the conversation about moving on from the conflict will always be stillborn.

I owe a deep debt to many sources who contributed to this book. Ali Soufan is a valued friend who schooled me on the FBI and operations in the Middle East. Andre Khoury, Ammar Barghouti, Sami al-Muti, and Christopher O'Leary all drew from their lifetime of investigative work in the region to inform the story. Khairieh Rassas was a charming guide to Palestinian life and history. Sufyam Tamimi explained the perils encountered by Palestinian farmers in defending their land.

I had a number of generous guides to the Old City. Jamil Sultan took me through the town and introduced me to Salah Khteeb, a Palestinian police officer. He and Radi Qazzaz, also a former Hebron cop, explained the restraints on their authority imposed by the Oslo accords. Yuval H., an Israeli intelligence officer, acquainted me with Hebron and the history of operations in the region. Noam Arnon, the longtime spokesperson for Kiryat Arba, introduced me to his community and spoke of his own clandestine exploration of the Cave of the Patriarchs.

I owe a special thanks to Issa Amro, a peace activist in Hebron who inspired much of my thinking about the character of Jamal Khalil. They are not the same person; Issa's commitment to nonviolence has proved to be more steadfast than Jamal's. Issa took me through the Old City and showed me his family's home, sealed shut by Israeli authorities for many years. We were accompanied by Barbara Debeuckelaere, an artist who was working on a photo essay about Tel Remeida, where Issa lived. Our tour was interrupted by a young IDF soldier who, unprompted, grabbed Issa by the neck and hurled him to the ground, his head missing a curb by little more than an inch. Then the soldier kicked Issa with all his force before other soldiers restrained him. I believe that if Barbara had not been filming the entire encounter, the soldier might have killed Issa, even with me as a witness. The hatred that entitles such actions is still confounding, as is the absence of a restraining hand on the part of government.

Daniel Lubetzky created Builders of the Middle East to foster a new generation of peacemakers. Through him, I met General Baruch Spiegel, Abdallah Hamarsheh, and Obada Shtaya, who share this vision. Amjad Abu Laban, head of the UN Relief and Works Agency, recalled the history of the refugee camps in the region. Edmund Fitton-Brown is a former British diplomat who has done important work in counterterrorism and the proliferation of narcotics in the Middle East. Edmund also did me the favor of reading the manuscript in advance, as did Nathan Thrall, Ami Pedahzur, Adam Rasgon, Stephen Harrigan, and Johanna Gruenhut. Their expertise captured many errors large and small. Thanks to them for their patience. The errors that remain are my responsibility.

Guy Clifton and Jeanne Ryan tutored me on medical issues. Victoria Heckenlaible was helpful about Syria and the refugee crisis. I also appreciate the insights provided by Cate Brown, Stephanie Saldaña, and James Zogby.

Behind all these names are so many others from previous trips.

In 2009 I performed a one-man show, also titled *The Human Scale,* directed by Oskar Eustis of New York's venerable Public Theater. Two years later we took the play to the Cameri Theatre of Tel Aviv. Many of the themes of that play, which was occasioned by the abduction of Gilad Shalit, are represented in this work. The play itself derived from reporting I did for *The New Yorker* in Gaza in 2009, following Operation Cast Lead. The seeds of this novel were planted in those experiences.

This is my first book with Peter Gethers at Knopf. In addition to Peter and his industrious assistant, Morgan Hamilton, our team includes Kevin Bourke, the production editor; Cassandra Pappas, the text designer; Patrick Dillon, the copy editor; Chip Kidd, the jacket designer; and Erin Hartmann, the publicist. I feel well taken care of, as I always have by in that wonderful institution.

A NOTE ON THE TYPE

The text of this book was set in Sabon, a typeface designed by Jan Tschichold (1902–1974), the well-known German typographer. Based loosely on the original designs by Claude Garamond (ca. 1480–1561), Sabon is unique in that it was explicitly designed for hot-metal composition on both the Monotype and Linotype machines as well as for filmsetting. Designed in 1966 in Frankfurt, Sabon was named for the famous Lyons punch cutter Jacques Sabon, who is thought to have brought some of Garamond's matrices to Frankfurt.

Typeset by Scribe,
Philadelphia, Pennsylvania

Designed by Cassandra J. Pappas